KICK START

THE SOUTHERN OAKS BOOK ONE

KALLYN JONES

Kick Start

Copyright 2021 by Kallyn Jones.

My Creative Jones Press

All rights reserved.

This book is a work of fiction. Names, characters, places, and incidents are the product of the author's imagination or are used fictitiously. Possible resemblances to actual events, places, or people, living or dead, is coincidental.

No part of this publication may be reproduced, distributed, or transmitted in any form or by any means, without prior written permission.

ISBN: 978-1-7377097-0-1 (ebook)

ISBN: 978-1-7377097-1-8 (paperback)

Editor: Taming the Ink

Proofread: D.A. Sarac/the Editing Pen

Cover Design: the Jones Design Studio

❀ Created with Vellum

Kick START

THE SOUTHERN OAKS BOOK ONE

KALLYN JONES

AUTHOR'S NOTE

Kick McKenna, the heroine in this story, is an autoimmune patient like me. Her experience neither represents the entirety of mine nor is it meant to represent anyone else's journey. As the saying goes, when you meet one autoimmune person, you've met one autoimmune person. Too often in this community, that which is one person's healing balm will cause another to flare, even when they share the same diagnosis. Our human bodies are fascinating, for sure.

The regimen that Kick uses to help her back to health is meant to be unique to her experience. The truth is, for the sake of the story, I went easy on her. If you are someone who shares similar health issues to her and manages them by different means, the story doesn't seek to judge or criticize in any way. Whatever gets you through the day is a blessing.

For the Autoimmune Warrior.
The one who works your buns off, even though it may not look like it.
The one who finds yourself flat on your back for days and/or weeks on end, through no fault of your own. You are seen. May your setbacks stay minor and every victory, no matter how small, be huge.

HARD OUT HERE

KICK

"**Y**ou've got to be fecking kidding," I muttered, staring at my doctor's sharp jawline on the video screen as she quietly spoke to her assistant.

Morning sun streaming through the window warmed my left shoulder, promising a perfect September day. With the oppressive humidity finally gone, my customers were more likely to sit outside on the patio than inside. It made the '80s girl in me want to belt out "Walking on Sunshine." I made a mental note to play an eighties mix later.

I wished I could be outside, enjoying an iced Americano and a quick break. Instead, I was stuck in my office, dealing with my body's shortcomings. Despite major victories in my decades-long battle with autoimmunity, this new flare was a doozie.

I absorbed the news from my test results as I waited for the doctor and eagerly let myself be distracted by a photo of me with my kids. We stood together, all smiles, at my coffeehouse's ribbon-cutting. I hadn't seen those proud smiles in months, and I missed them. These three were the reason I'd worked my butt off to get better. Bad news or not, I wouldn't give up on them now.

"Sorry for the interruption, Kick," Dr. Chaddha said, her face returning to the video chat window on my laptop.

"No worries," I answered, hoping a soft smile could hide my anxiety. We were running five minutes behind with about fifteen minutes of appointment left.

"So," she continued, "did you receive the new dietary guidelines we sent through the portal?"

I flipped through the pages I'd printed off. "Yup. You really think restricting stuff like artichokes is necessary? I thought prebiotics were important for my microbiome."

Dr. Chaddha lifted her copy of one of my many recent tests. "Given this lab panel, yes. A low-FODMAP plan will let your gut heal. Trust me." She dropped the papers. "After six weeks, we can address it again, depending on how closely you follow the regimen."

"What do you mean, how closely?" I sighed, tucking a wayward curl behind my ear.

"Well, did you see caffeine and chocolate on the list?" She pressed.

"Yes," I muttered. Or whined. A little.

"I meant to have my assistant put decaf on there too."

My brow creased. Was she kidding? "What? Why?" I'd prepared myself to stay engaged and positive through our tele-appointment. Truth be told, I expected some heavy-handed advice. Bringing an autoimmune condition into submission was ridiculously hard. I'd done it already. But the good doctor stepped on my pride with this directive.

"I sell only fair-trade, organic beans. And they're third-party tested for mold." I felt my face dropping into a stubborn frown. "The water is reverse-osmosis filtered. I don't see the problem here, other than the ones inherent in caffeine. Also, I've already been limiting it."

"Nice to hear." Dr. Chaddha scribbled on her tablet. "I want to make sure you're not reacting to the product itself."

"You understand my business is called the Perked Cup, right?" I said, hearing the sharp edge in my tone. How the hell does a barista abstain from her own product? How was I supposed to recommend a new flavor I couldn't test? I didn't think the good doctor would approve of the swish-and-spit routine either.

"This leads to my next point." A nervous smile crept across her face as if she were bracing herself.

Holy hell, now what? I couldn't imagine the news getting any worse. I gripped the edge of my chair, not sure I wanted to hear it.

"You've had a hard year with your dad passing. Plus your business responsibilities. And family."

As if I needed reminding. "Everyone has their issues, Dr. C. Everyone has bad years too."

"Not everyone has autoimmune diseases," Dr. Chaddha continued firmly. "If you want to avoid undoing all your past progress, I suggest you take three months off while you work my program."

If I had been drinking that Americano, I'd have done a spit take. As it was, the normal kaleidoscope of test-result butterflies in my stomach beat their wings into a frenzy. I was sure they were working up a tornado in there. I didn't lead a take-three-months-for-yourself kind of life.

I'd heard about other patients doing this, but the ones I knew of were either kidless or retired. Maybe I could do it in a year once my youngest graduated high school. But the kids weren't the only people who needed me. My employees did too. With the summer over and most part-timers off to college, we were already understaffed. Then there was Dad's cigar shop.

Dr. Chaddha's dark eyes narrowed. "Perspective is the key, Kick. Remember, you're lucky to be alive. You've been blessed to come this far. Don't stop now."

My belly laugh after her comment sounded a tad hysterical to my own ears. Staying alive had already cost me a fecking fortune. Dr. C's current set of recommendations had me staring down another path ending in a mountain of bills. Yet I should stop working for three months? Hire others to fill the gap? I bit my cheek to keep from snapping.

"Sorry to interrupt, Kick, but I need you in bathroom number one." My morning manager's strained voice over the intercom made me jump in my chair.

"What happened now?" I pressed the button and asked, ignoring my doctor's frown. Didn't she realize the interruption kept me from crossing full steam into Rudelandia and chewing her out? Was I solving world peace? No. I sold coffee to my neighbors. At best, it encouraged them and gave them a boost in their daily grind.

The tension in the discombobulated voice amped up. "Something big that it requires us both."

Right. Deana wouldn't bother me with a minor issue. Ever the eternal optimist, her anxious tone turned my internal tornado into an EF4. "Be right out," I told her.

I turned back to my webcam. "Listen, Dr. Chaddha, I need to fix whatever is happening here. I'll take your advice into consideration though."

"Mrs. McKenna, you haven't set up your IV schedule. Plus Audra needs to do your life coaching session. Give you her recipes."

JaysusMaryandJoseph. My arms phantom-ached at the thought

of new bruises and collapsed veins. Time off was one thing, but I swear I had PTSD from the last round of intravenous therapy. "I'll think on the IVs, and Audra can upload the files to my portal."

"Will you at least consider cutting back your hours? It's critical to relieve stress somewhere. And if you can't make our meditation sessions here, at least do it at home." Exasperation hovered in Dr. Chaddha's normally steady inflection.

A tightness settled in my chest while the tornado switched to full-blown nausea. I nodded at the monitor. "Thank you for your time, Doctor. I'll be in touch soon. Promise."

We cut the tele-session, and my shoulders slumped. How the hell had I ended up feeling back at square one? And there lay my doctor's point. Autoimmune patients sought management, not cures.

Even before this appointment, I monitored everything I ate, drank, how I worked out, slept, et cetera. It was all-consuming, though the real challenge lay in keeping it from being soul-consuming. Then there were years like this one when as soon as I thought my ducks were finally in a nice, neat row, life whacked me head-on and the little feckers waddled off again.

The rhythm of my footfalls in the hallway out to the dining room gave me some headspace to reflect. This flare was more evidence of my failure "to do health." Moreover, I feared my body would continue to betray me, no matter how many hoops I jumped through to keep it in line.

Kill the pity party and find Deana.

I took the last few feet of tile to mourn the progress I'd lost in my recovery. Inhaled deep and shook it off. I might struggle, but hell if I'd let my thyroid run me over. Taking a cleansing breath, I turned the corner toward the serving counter and remembered Dee had told me to meet her in the bathroom.

Deana Douglas, the source of the earlier voice, paced the

restroom hallway. An Out of Service sign stuck to the first door.

I groaned. "Did someone flood the toilet again? You could've just called the plu—"

Dee grabbed my arm and tugged. "Get in here."

I jumped, expecting to get wet feet, but the floor looked dry.

She pointed at the sink. "In there."

A large ziplock with smaller bags lay in the porcelain bowl. "Is that—"

Deana nodded vigorously. "We used to call them dime bags."

"I remember," I breathed, wondering if today's kids still called them that. "Did you look inside? Were they in the sink?"

"Yes. And no—they were taped to the side of the vanity. If I hadn't changed the garbage, I might've missed them." Deana fanned her face. "I think we need to call the police."

I bent over, sniffing, making sure they contained cannabis, but the little bags didn't give themselves up without opening them. Since I didn't have on gloves like Deana, I let it go. "Did you notice who used the bathroom this morning? Also, shouldn't we just throw this away?"

"Kick"—Deana heaved a motherly sigh—"someone tried to use our café… *your* café as a drug drop. We can't ignore it."

"Shit."

Dee was right. She was also late.

"Don't you have to get out of here too?" I asked.

Dee scrunched her button nose, reminding me of her doppel-gänger, Gladys Knight, bracing to hit a big note. When she had walked into my café, responding to my ad for a barista, I immediately thought of the megastar from our hometown, Detroit. Dee possessed the same class, sparkling smile, and hint of an edge. It's what initially bonded us—that and shared memories of growing up in Motown.

Deana untied her apron and folded it, tucking it under her arm. "You sounded off when I buzzed. I texted Genesis, and she's saving me a seat." Her granddaughter Geneva was about to play the *Hungry Caterpillar* in the first-grade fall play, and Dee was stepping out for an hour.

I waved her on. "Go ahead. Take pics of little Geneva for me please. I'll call this in."

"But—"

"Go before you get stuck answering questions and miss the whole play." To distract her, I added, "Maybe we can hang some of your recent work in the dining room again."

Dee chuckled. "I see what you're doing. Yeah, we can do that, especially with the senior portrait season underway." She turned for the door. "You're telling me about your appointment when I get back."

"Not going anywhere," I murmured. *Yet.*

AS A BOB MARLEY SONG LATER REMINDED ME THAT EVERYTHING would be all right, I swiped at a curl stuck to my sweaty cheek and pulled my elbows together to stretch my middle back. Then I donned a pair of gloves and looked around my café. Keeping it in order brought peace, especially during a crazy day like this one.

A senior officer from the Oakville PD had come and gone after questioning the staff and me forward and backward. There were only two other part-timers currently on the schedule. Officer Miller had shown me his sincere disapproval of my lack of security. Upgrading the system had been at the top of my list at the beginning of the year. He also complained about my letting Deana go to the play. I promised to have her give a statement at the station.

A quiet hum finally settled over the café as I swayed to "Three Little Birds." I opened the display case and moved the leftover breakfast pastries to make room for lunch items. Next was the bar top—a raw-edged hickory counter that looked more like a piece of art—the centerpiece of the space. It made me smile when it shone and was something I could quickly set to rights.

I let my hand rhythmically glide over its smooth surface while I lengthened shallow breaths, letting my thoughts go. Since giving my statement, I'd racked my brain to remember every customer we'd served.

Inhale for four. Hold for four. Exhale for five... Again.

As the streaks of cleaner evaporated, I caught the dark hint of my reflection in the glossy finish. The silhouette of my big curls shadowed the warm browns in the wood. They were extra exuberant on washdays like this one and reminded me of the Irish dancing competitions I'd been dragged to as a kid. For years I'd fought to tame the curls with dryers, irons, and goo. We'd called a truce when I embraced their wild nature and found better products. Presently I didn't have the heart to corral them in a scrunchie. Maybe later.

The distraction eased my mind and caused me to miss the woman sliding onto a stool at the end of the counter until she spoke, startling me.

"I heard you talked to your so-called doctor," my mother commented, setting my heart pounding.

She'd been in a good mood when she arrived with her neighbor. Perhaps she sincerely wanted to know about my appointment. I'd almost rather talk about that than who had tried to use my bathroom as a drug drop. The logic there escaped me, but maybe expecting a drug dealer to use logic was my first mistake. It ended up not being a large amount of cannabis anyway, thank goodness.

I stopped wiping and gave it a shot. "Dr. Chaddha confirmed the flare. She gave me a plan though." I scanned the dining room, hoping the subject would drop. I didn't see her friend. "Did Shirley leave?"

"Yes." My mother, Bobby Allen, lifted her cup to her lips, wearing a judgmental expression. One of her favorite forms of torture, it kept me always guessing, although it didn't necessarily equal an impending temper. "Did you lock your office door? My suitcases are in there, remember?"

"I don't lock it during business hours. But the back door is secure, and your cases are tucked under my desk. They'll be safe until Rachel's ready to drive you to the airport."

Bobby clucked her tongue. "We're already cutting it close."

"You'll be fine to go as soon as Deana gets back." My daughter, Rachel, currently manned the drive-through.

I reached for Bobby's cup. "Let me refresh this. It's probably cold." Still uncertain of her mood, I hoped a little kindness would allay her.

I handed her a new latte along with a nervous smile. She took a loud slurp and set the cup down.

"When will you see a real doctor and fix your nonsense once and for all?" She moved her forefinger up and down in my direction, further indicating I was the nonsense.

Annnd we're off.

"Dr. Chaddha *is* an actual doctor. She trained here at Lord University. Her methods are cutting-edge. Besides, regular doctors spent twenty years telling me nothing was wrong." I didn't dare say what they actually said since Bobby also thought my disease was in my head.

She shook her head, pushing button number one. "If you'd handled yourself like a bloody grown-up all those years ago, you'd still live your fancy NFL life, retired husband or no. You certainly wouldn't be working yourself to death in this backward town."

I rolled my head to stretch my neck. This was our game, our mother-daughter dance. In my head, I still waited for my dad to butt in with *"Now Bobby, let our Katie Girl be..."*

"You're the one who hates Oakville, Mother, not me. Moving to North Carolina and shortening the winters was the first step to feeling better." I sighed, shaking my head because an explanation was an exercise in futility. "Plus you know I hated the spotlight. What little still pops up on occasion drives me batty."

She tsked my first comment and ignored the second while rubbing her knee. "We all feel pain, Kick. Feeling pain means you're alive."

Tension traveled south back to my stomach, reminding me of what my doctor had said about stress. I spelled stress B-O-B-B-Y. "Definitely alive, Mother."

I spun on my heel to get away, looking out the window. It would be a welcomed relief to have her gone. Six blissful weeks of a seniors' cruise.

"Take care of her, Katie," my dad's weak voice sounded in my head. *"Maybe she'll finally find happiness."*

I begged the universe to let this trip do the trick. The universe had been stubbornly silent though.

Another deep breath kept my pulse in control. The café emitted the best aromas—blends of coffee beans, obviously. Once I completed the tapering-off period, I'd have to settle for only the smell for a while. I knew I'd survive. I had already learned to live with the smell of fresh pastries I couldn't eat anymore. For the first time that week, I reminded myself this was temporary pain for long-term gain.

I took a moment to gaze up at the mural of cats I'd painted near the ceiling, their colors done in the same warm latte-and-coffee-bean hues. Their playful curiosity represented the way I wanted to live life even when it seemed difficult. I waited for the peace of the dining room to fill me. Since opening the Perked Cup seven years earlier, I'd found my center within its walls. Relief came from the door chime, announcing a new customer.

A man strolled through the door. With the light streaming from behind him, the details were blurry from where I stood. Or Deana was probably right about needing stronger glasses. He was tall and lean with a familiar, immature swagger.

"Hey, beautiful."

As I stepped to the register to meet the new arrival, the blur became a recognizable face. A local kid the same age as my oldest, Dylan, named Garrett. I cringed at his words, hoping it wouldn't show, reminding myself to put the customer first.

The thing was, flirting would always be a part of my business. I knew this going in. I preferred friendly banter, but some men didn't understand the difference. I accepted it. Usually. However, when an attractive young man came in, my internal thoughts generally gravitated toward *who's your daddy?* never *want a sugar mama?* A twenty-nothing boy would always stay a boy for my intents and purposes.

With my body throwing its age in my face, it wasn't even slightly humorous. Perhaps he'd get the hint if I ignored it. "What can I get you?"

He flashed a cocky grin. "A large iced latte."

With an indifferent nod, I spun on my heel and filled his order. Remembering to upsell, I called over my shoulder, "Interested in a snack?"

"Other than you?"

I swear, the boy tried to make his pecs dance. It looked more like they spasmed. "Garrett—"

Rachel rescued me from making a serious mistake and rebuking him when she bounced around the corner from the drive-through. Without a word, she dipped her chin to me and stepped up to the glass case, her sapphire eyes showing the friendly patience I lacked. I gladly let my daughter take over for a moment.

Garrett pointed at a small case on top of the large food display. "Why are these separate from what's down here?"

"That's our gluten-free Blarney Scone," Rachel informed him, pointing to the sign on the upper corner. "It's lavender-almond flavored, which is great. You don't have to be gluten-free to choose it." She pointed to the larger case. "This one is our traditional blueberry recipe. We keep them separate to avoid cross-contamination." Rachel fitted her hands with a pair of disposable gloves.

"Guess I'll do the blueberry one. Thanks."

I handed Garrett his cup and scone, and he winked. "And thank *you*, gorgeous."

"It's Mrs. Mack, or Kick, please. You can skip the sham flirting too."

His shoulders stiffened. "Can't I cheer you up? You were frowning when I walked in. You just... you know, should smile more. Especially considering..."

Garrett piqued my curiosity. Bobby had needled under my skin, but I was sure he'd caught me squinting to figure out the mystery of his blurry form. "Considering what, exactly? And why can't women have all the facial expressions?"

He lifted a shoulder as if he'd never considered my question before. "You know, for your age. You should be proud you look good."

Boy, did I want to backhand the backhanded compliment right off his pretentious mug. I shook my head, wondering if he would ever get it, while dismissing it all the same. "Have a good day, Garrett." *Don't let the door hit you in the ass.*

He strutted out without another word.

I put my arm around Rachel and rested my head on her shoulder. "I thought your generation was supposed to be woke."

Having three inches on me, Rachel kissed the top of my head and rubbed my free arm. "Silly Mama. Even if some of us are woke, that one's still dreaming of the fifties."

"No kidding." I shook my head and grinned at Rachel, then grimaced when Bobby chimed in.

"You're such a chip off the old block. If you didn't flirt so hard, they wouldn't bother with you." She cackled from her perch at the counter. "You asked for it."

Annnd there went another button, possibly the biggest one. Did I ask for it? Sometimes my mother could twist her arguments, making me think up was down and I was a complete lunatic. Hell, she was the one who had drilled into me to smile no matter what.

I turned to Rachel, looking to grab a minute alone. "Can you cover for a few? My fat jeans were in the washer, and this pair squeezes so hard it's making me nauseated. I'm going to change into the backup pair in my office."

"Really, Kick? Fat pants?" Bobby scoffed.

"Yes." I bit back, saying no more because screw her. If I told her my current weight, she'd never let it go. Besides, every woman I knew had three sets of clothes. There were the ones you wore as a reward for working your ass off, the ones that fit on normal days, and the fat ones. Actual numbers didn't matter. After achieving the impossible and losing a hundred pounds several years prior, watching thirty reappear practically overnight was as off-putting as the return of the bone-deep fatigue.

"Sure, Mama." Rachel pity-laughed. "I'll be fine. Gran can help if we get a mini-rush."

I chuckled at my mother's sputtering and hustled to the back. Bobby had been one of my first employees, along with my father, and my son, Dylan. But Bobby and Dad made better customers. He'd pushed me to open an authentic Irish pub, but I didn't want my kids doing homework in the back of a bar. My body couldn't handle the late hours either. So, I'd designed the Perked Cup with the rich woods of a pub combined with bright windows, coffee, pastries, and a patio.

As soon as I could afford it, Deana came on board, saving my butt and my spirit. And I had to find more people immediately.

Five minutes later, after digging through my bottom desk drawer and only finding a spare pair of shorts, I sheepishly returned to the front, wearing them. I'd worn low-cut cowboy boots with my jeans. They were comfy and helped my feet last a long day. I caught my reflection in the mirror hanging over the office door. I looked like an extra in a country video, not a respectable forty-six-year-old entrepreneur. At least my bloated belly found peace. Unfortunately, my daughter had lost hers.

Rachel stood at the register, leaning back as far as her waist and neck would allow, while another neighborhood boy leaned over the counter, leering.

"Jonn, please, you know Cody and I are together." Rachel defended as I approached. She kept a polite smile on her face, though her fingers twitching at her thigh gave away nerves.

"Isn't it time you try out a real man? Dump him, babe," Jonn drawled. "Everyone around here knows Cody's a loser. I'll treat you right."

Whoa. "Thanks, but..."

My daughter the peacemaker was terrible at standing up for herself unless her brothers were the ones annoying her. Jonn stretched out his fingers and stroked Rachel's forearm. He tried to hold her hand, but she snapped it up to her chest, clasping her hands tightly together. The boy bled arrogance. The kind coming from money and too much spoiling, like he owned the town and everyone in it.

Perhaps the loss of his mother a few years prior contributed to his lack of manners. I decided it was a good day for me to educate the neighborhood boys after all.

It didn't matter that my favorite Prince song filled the dining room. It muted in my ears as my daughter's frantic gaze slashed to mine. All the stress, arguments, and annoyances of the morning scurried up my spine like steam ready to boil.

Screw with me, push my buttons, make me spend all my money on medicine and fancy grocery stores. *Fine.* Ask the impossible of me and poke me with needles. *Whatever.*

But don't. Mess. With. My. Kid. I tucked a stubborn curl behind my ear, ready for battle.

Okay, Jonn boy, class is in session.

2

WICKED GAME

THOMAS

*R*esistance coming from the locked door didn't register with Thomas Harrison's brain. He simply pulled the handle again, with vigor. He was on a mission, and a closed cigar shop didn't jibe with his schedule.

Then he saw the sign: PLEASE INQUIRE AT THE PERKED CUP FOR ASSISTANCE. SO SORRY FOR THE INCONVENIENCE. ~ THE STAFF AT MICK & HUGH'S.

Inconvenience?

That had to be a joke. Thomas tried the door a third time. Not a joke. He didn't have another thirty minutes to drive to a different shop and make it to the Durham Forest neighborhood on time.

He pivoted and found the Perked Cup's signage, taking off at a brisk pace. He fully expected to deal with a pimply teenager ignorant of cigars. No matter. When he found out his new boss liked an occasional smoke, he knew exactly what to bring to the Welcome Back social in the dean's garden.

Starting off on the right foot was paramount to making sure the man was an ally and as hands-off as the former dean had been. Thomas hoped a few thoughtful trinkets would help him build this rapport. Christ, the hoops he'd been jumping through to honor his contract with Lord University and keep his obligations to the other team in France wore on him. He could use a close friend at the university, and his initial conversation with the new boss suggested they shared some interests.

He reminded himself to nod and smile if someone brought up hurricanes at the party. It was September in North Carolina, what did they expect? They were lucky a quick shower was the only thing forecasted for the afternoon. He feared humanity might devolve, what with its reliance on small talk and the latest viral video. Then again, meaningless topics like the weather always irritated him.

Time spent locked away in his lab and at his property had an adverse effect on him. It affected his ability to "people," as his lab assistant called it. He feared it might be killing his soul too. Plus the mantle of professor still didn't feel comfortable on his shoulders. He wondered if it would ever fit.

As he opened the door to the coffeehouse, the blower nearly sent his fedora airborne. He grabbed at the hat to keep it in place. Thomas's gaze lifted, and he was dumbstruck.

A barista with shoulder-length curls was giving what-for to a customer. She told the boy what he would order and how he should behave in her establishment if he wanted to continue being served. Her head bobbed in a pointed rhythm to the Prince song playing in the background, turning her brunette curls into physical exclamation points to her arguments.

She stepped back, her curvy hip leaning into the back counter, her brow furled and focused.

She let a girl hand the boy his order. Keeping her tone low and rational, like a professor schooling a disrespectful student, she said, "Now, Jonn, thank Rachel for graciously making your iced mochaccino."

"Th-thank you, Rachel." The young man touched his credit card to the reader while stammering, his brow pulled into an angry V.

The barista folded her arms and nodded to the girl. "Thanks, Rachel. You can take the drive-through again." Her gaze shifted back to Jonn. "I'm going to tell you to have a nice day, and it's not BS. I really do wish you a better day, Mr. Graham. Then you'll return the kindness and go."

Was it wrong how her *don't fuck with me* air turned him on? Thomas considered doing something to piss her off—just to hear what she'd say to him—and ducked his head.

The boy took the cup and turned.

"Jonn—" she warned.

The kid grunted and murmured, "Have a nice day, Mrs. Mack."

"Thank you, son. I don't mean offense. But I won't tolerate any more of this behavior with my daughter, my employees, or another customer. We clear?"

Jonn nodded again and left, silently stepping around Thomas.

A smile woke inside him, and it might have reached his eyes. Thomas didn't smile much lately. The work didn't allow it. He sure appreciated the woman's lesson though. He liked the authority she held as she spoke, as much as her words.

She was fire.

Or was the spark igniting in him? Like glimpsing himself in a mirror, Thomas recognized his frustrations in her tight brow. A hint of sadness.

His attraction to her was instant, but he only had time for the occasional quick hookup. Something about this woman said she would consume him.

Like attracts like. Right. He saw his work in all areas of his life. *Guess the Law of the Instrument applies to scientists as much as it does to carpenters,* he thought.

"Look at Nathan Detroit," a voice snapped beside him. A brief look around, along with a fast flip through his mental memory bank to the *Guys and Dolls* reference, suggested the senior citizen at the bar spoke about him. Did she have a problem with a man wearing a suit? If he had to be in academics, he'd be damned if he went the patched-elbow blazer route.

The barista wore a friendly smile, reaching her eyes, as she turned from the back counter and greeted him. "Well, hey there, handsome. Is Maggie feeling better? Oh—" Her eyes flashed wide as she took Thomas in. "I'm sorry. You're not Hugh."

Another smirk caught him off guard. "Not according to my license."

The woman blushed, the light pink complementing her porcelain skin. "I'm sorry. My Uncle…" The lady at the counter hissed, and the woman adjusted her words. "My father's *friend*, Hugh, often wears a similar fedora. It's dumb… Not the hat. Your hat is very handsome." She gestured to her eyes. "I think I might need distance lenses. Anyway, what can I get you?" She raised her hands in a "stop" motion. "Wait, let me guess… A large Americano?"

"Good guess." He nodded. "But I'm here for cigars, actually." He pointed over his shoulder. "The sign said—"

"Oh right. One second." She held up a finger and leaned around the corner. "Rachel, I have a smoke-shop customer. Tina's due in five. You can cover for me again, eh?"

"Sure, Mama. Have Gran sit at the register. I'll get the rest."

The barista tucked a burnished curl behind her ear and took a long breath before addressing the scowling older woman. "Five minutes. I swear, I'll be right back."

Mother, daughter, and grandmother. Thomas took note. Neither looked too much like the other. The youngest wore her hair in long, raven curls, looser than her mother's coils, while the eldest woman kept hers in a straight, blond bob. He supposed both younger women favored their fathers. *Yeah, he spent way too much time contemplating genes and epigenetics.*

The barista approached with her hand extended. "Kick McKenna. Is this your first time visiting us?"

Thomas shook the offered hand, noting her confident grip and kind eyes, the hint of sadness still there. They were hazel—deep and earthy with splashes of bright gold. They reminded him of walking in the woods on his property. A subtle, pleasant warmth bloomed from his fingers to his elbow.

"Thomas Harrison. Nice to meet you... Kick? I've been loyal to the Durham lounge near campus, but it closed last month."

"Yup." She sighed. "Frank mentored my dad with his shop. The man earned his retirement." A somberness chased the smile away for a few beats. Kick shook herself and headed toward the door.

Thomas followed her across the parking lot, mesmerized by the sway in her purposeful stride. Out in the sun, Kick's chestnut hair came to life as a light breeze danced through it. A few strands of mahogany and gold wrapped around the deep brown. The colors reminded him of the cabinet he'd built for his office over summer break.

An edginess crept through him. *No time for this,* Thomas scolded himself again. The side of his right hand still tingled from her touch. He flexed his fingers and grazed it on his suit jacket, his other hand carrying his briefcase.

Kick opened the door and swept her arm inside. "Welcome to Mick & Hugh's. Again, I apologize for the staffing problem. It should be resolved soon. Are you interested in a particular brand?"

She looked up and frowned as if she were mad at the song that started when she tapped a row of switches. Tula's "Wicked Game" filled the store, but it was near the end, so whatever bothered her about it wouldn't last for long. "Fecking girl," Kick muttered under her breath.

"Pardon?"

Kick turned and lifted the corner of her mouth. "Nothing, I'm sorry. What kind were you looking for?"

"Padrons. I assume they're in the humidor?"

She nodded and pointed to the glassed-in space. "The line sits on the middle shelf. Help yourself."

Thomas took a joyful inhale when he stepped into the enclosure. The aroma from the leaves set him at ease while brightening his thoughts. If he didn't have to hustle to the luncheon, he'd consider chatting Kick up, welcoming a distraction from his stalled research.

He approached the register with an open box. "Mind if I take the whole thing?"

Her laugh bubbled, too husky for a giggle and... sexy. "Of Family Reserve? Anytime. A new shipment is due Wednesday anyway." She lifted the lid. "We've already sold two. Are you okay with that?"

"Fine."

"Is it safe to assume you have a humidor at home for these?"

Thomas patted his briefcase. "Most of them will be given away this afternoon, and there's a travel one in here for the rest."

"Perfect. Are you celebrating something then?" She glanced at him and added, "If you don't mind my asking."

Thomas liked her scrunched nose. He took it as a "hope I'm not offending" demeanor and liked it as much as her "take no bullshit" one from earlier, only this was cute. "I don't mind. I run a genetics research lab at the university and am taking over a biology class for someone on sick leave. There's a faculty social at the new dean's house this afternoon."

"Ooh, cigars are great for schmoozing. Nicely done. Are you at Raleigh State? My son—"

"No, no." Thomas interrupted. "I meant Lord University in Durham."

"I see." They completed the transaction, and Kick said, "Please come back again. I'm still sorry about the inconvenience. One of the owners died this summer, and the other partner's wife is dealing with a bad bout of pneumonia. I think Maggie's almost back to normal though."

Thomas furrowed his brow. Maybe he had a minute to spare. He tossed his thumb over his shoulder, toward Kick's café. "Is that the Maggie you referenced earlier?"

"Yup," she answered, blushing. "Sorry about that too."

Thomas snapped his fingers. "You called me Hugh, and this is—"

"Mick and Hugh's. Right." Kick turned toward a tablet sitting on the counter and scoffed.

"Everything all right?" Thomas asked.

Kick shook her head, then nodded as if she hadn't decided. "It's fine." She inhaled deep and lifted a corner of her mouth. "Thank you."

"No problem," Thomas answered, shoving his hands in his pockets. "I didn't mean to pry. It's none of my business."

Kick's straightened and laughed. "No worries. It's been a day already, but it'll turn around. It's early yet, right?"

"Sure." A flier caught Thomas's eye. It advertised an open-mic night at the Perked Cup. He lifted one. "This is tonight?"

"It is," she said, shifting her back before straightening again.

"I see." Thomas often relaxed by playing guitar, but it had been ages since he'd heard someone else live. He doubted he could make it back in time though. He turned back toward Kick. "Hey, do y'all ever—"

"Oh, *hell* no," she muttered. Her hand fisted at her hip. "Maybe Bobby was right about me."

Thomas tipped his head to the side, a crease in his brow. "Pardon?"

"Or there's something in the water." Her face contorted, looking a lot like anger. At what, he had no clue.

"Why do men think they're the answer to my problems?" Kick's eyes slowly surveyed every inch of him, leaving Thomas feeling like the scolded boy from earlier. He stood straighter, waiting for clarification.

"Let's get one thing clear." She tapped her finger on the counter for emphasis. "I. Am. Not. A. Cougar. I don't need to get my groove back. I don't *want* to be completed." She leaned in slightly, dropping her voice to a growl. "Sure, I roar. Sometimes I purr. But prowl? *Boy.* I. Do. Not. I've never auditioned for the role of MILF, and man-cubs like you need to quit assuming I have."

"MILF?" Thomas blinked.

"A mom I'd like to… Never mind."

He raised his hands in surrender. "I didn't mean to—"

Kick cut him off again, her voice growing louder. "Yeah, I know. You only wanted to compliment me. I'm not in the AARP yet, but I don't do young men in any fashion. No one's interested in your charity either."

He suddenly couldn't get away from the delusional woman fast enough.

With a quick shiver, her demeanor chilled. She strolled to the door, gestured for him to leave, then said, "Thank you for stopping by."

Thomas's tight grip on the steering wheel eased as his '69 Camaro made its way west. Driving was another form of meditation to him, and it lightened his indignation at Kick McKenna's rant. The engine's roar, the machine bending to his will, relaxed Thomas's clenched jaw, let him know he still had control. By the time he navigated the neighborhood on the edge of Durham Forest, he'd forgotten about the fiery woman and her wrong, knee-jerk assumptions.

Thomas's mind was back in the game, focused on his job and making a new friend. Hopefully, this boss wouldn't micromanage. He already had people doing that from France.

Roar, she'd said? Hot damn. His engine had revved at the sight of her flame. Well, too bad for Kick.

He found a perfect parking spot near the dean's sprawling colonial and stepped out of the car. An ominous cloud formation appeared right on time. He reached for his beloved briefcase, and his shoulders dropped with renewed frustration.

Of course.

In his haste to leave the cigar store, he'd left it behind. *Damn it all.*

3

SETTLE DOWN

KICK

"Great, you're back." I met Deana at the end of the display case, her warm smile the perfect prescription to help me jump into the lunch rush. After locking up Mick & Hugh's, I'd stormed back to my café and chilled a minute in my office, finding calm after another unwanted come-on. I was three for three in a weird day that was only half-done. This Thomas guy should've been old enough to know better. I mean, he was handsome, with soulful gray-blue eyes, a chiseled jaw, and a sexy chin cleft. But he probably still lived with his mom. Or roommates.

No. Just no.

I spent the time examining my interactions with Garrett and Thomas. Then came Jonn Graham. He'd had a crush on Rachel for years, but he'd never been so brazen before. I didn't know what had gotten into him. I hoped Jonn would take my scolding to heart and change his attitude.

If not for the stressful morning, I would've answered Thomas with a polite "no, thank you." Most days, that was all it took. No harm, no foul. Unfortunately, Professor Harrison had stumbled upon my last nerve and set me off. I saw my mistake and let the embarrassment wash over me. At least it beat guilt.

Deana laughed at my greeting as I retied my apron. She held the bus bucket of dirty dishes. "I've *been* back, Kick. Long enough to see you charge past me like Satan's hound had chomped on your heel." She took a long glance out the window. "Still, you beat the rain. It's about to open up."

Well, hell. There went my last hope for a perfect September day. And lunch on the patio. I bent to look out the window. I hadn't noticed anything looming earlier, but I'd been preoccupied. The dark cloud didn't look too big. Maybe my day would brighten once it passed.

Deana tapped me on the shoulder. "Want to tell me what's going on?"

I shook my hair and pulled it back, using the scrunchie I kept in my apron pocket. "Just men. All morning. Men."

"Another diehard fan find you?"

There was a frightening thought. Dee had found my silver lining. "Thankfully, no."

She chuckled harder, then lowered her voice, leaning in closer, getting serious. "Are you sure your mama had nothing to do with it?"

"Probably."

"I wasn't here, but I know you'd have been fine if Miss Bobby weren't hanging around. That woman has the passcode for pushing your grouch buttons."

I looked up to see my mother bringing her cup to the bussing box; then she sat back down at the bar.

"What are you up to?" I asked her, trying to sound cheery and not suspicious.

"I sat in the sunny corner after serving those two women gossiping about their grandchildren." She pointed to two locals who met here weekly. "It's cold here by the door." Her comment came out as an accusation, but I was tired of being baited.

"What I mean is, shouldn't you and Rachel have left for the airport by now?"

"My flight is delayed. Some storm in the Midwest made the plane late. You'd think they'd have a better system by now, considering there's always weather."

The little girl in me strangely welcomed Bobby's temporary animosity toward the airline. At nearly forty-seven, I still thought it was nice when someone else made it on her shit list. Except for when the attention turned to my youngest, her ultimate scapegoat.

Deana and I established ourselves at our stations, my part-time staff filling in where needed. I changed the topic and asked Dee, "How was your *Hungry Caterpillar?*"

Her face filled with pride and love. "Geneva's a natural. I told Genesis to put her in an after-school theater class."

I was about to recommend the camps Rachel attended when she continued, "But I want to hear about this doctor's appointment. Is it as bad as we thought?"

We leaned against the counter, monitoring the house, but forgetting the conveniently silent lady sitting at the bar. The chill in the stainless steel of the work area moved through my braced arms. It cooled the last of my hot temper, helping me gather my thoughts. I raised my hands, my thumb and forefinger a smidge apart. "There are things to figure out, but I'll get through it."

"Don't play coy, Kick," Deana scolded, crossing her arms. "Some weeks I see more of you than my husband."

I leaned into her for privacy. "You were right about stress. Dr. Chaddha said the loss of Dad, coupled with a hot summer and Liam's last year in school, et cetera. It put me over the edge." I shrugged. "It's a decent-sized road bump."

"I hadn't thought about your impending empty nest," Deana added. "I remember that year. It was terrifying and exciting. Gordon and I spent Maceo's senior year planning the trip to London we took in September. But I was afraid of the quiet house when we returned."

"Hey," I said, tapping her arm, "don't remind me."

"Sorry. What's the doctor want you to do about it?"

"Added therapies and food changes to stop inflammation. I can't have any caffeine until the New Year. I'm still processing it up here and here." I touched my head and my heart, knowing from experience these change-ups required their own version of the stages of grief. I had to let past progress go and accept this new starting point. It would be the Zen thing to do. I wanted to scream and punch a wall, which might have helped for a minute. I wouldn't recommend making coffee with a broken hand though.

"We have great decaf."

"Oh, that's out too, for at least six weeks. And I have to meld something called a low-FODMAP food plan with my autoimmune Paleo one. I think it leaves chicken, green beans, and blueberries."

A chuckle burst from Deana before she caught herself. "Tell me you're joking."

I grabbed a rag and wiped the counter. "I am. Mostly."

"Cute." She bumped my hip. "You've got this though."

My nails tapped a rhythm on the stainless steel. "The doctor wants me to take three months off. Can you believe it? I can't possibly, not when Hugh needs help too. But maybe I should cut back hours here?"

"Am I *not* here for you?" Deana spread her arms. "Let me hire some folks. *Use* me, boss lady."

"You have enough going on yourself," I countered. "I don't want to dump my issues on you. Not when you watch the grands in the afternoon and your photography business is gaining traction."

Dee's hands moved over each other in a circular motion. "Spread it around. Give me some. Give Dylan some. You know."

I shook my head. My oldest, Dylan, worked the counter at the cigar store. He'd done it primarily to spend time with his grand-dad. Now he worked to fill in the gap. But he was finishing up grad school and getting ready for big things in the tech world. "Dylan's thesis project is ramping up. He should cut back at the smoke shop, not add more hours." I tapped my chin. "What would you think about Jake taking over for me as night manager?"

Jake Quick was a young veteran who worked evening hours at the café while he finished his business degree. He'd already bumped up to full-time hours and did many of the things I'd require of a manager.

"There you go." Dee nodded her head.

"You wouldn't mind sharing the second office?"

"Not at all. I'm mornings; he'd be nights. Delegating would do you some good."

"Thanks." I wanted to hug and kiss Dee. I crossed my fingers Jake would be up for the promotion. I wasn't certain what his postgraduation plans were.

Deana's eyes warmed, the mother in her coming out full force. "This isn't the end of your healing. You've come too far already. The staff and I'll do what we can to help."

A loud scoff broke our private bubble. "Isn't your drama queen act exhausting? It sure tires me," Bobby butt in. My shoulders fell. We should've waited until she left. Then again, she was already supposed to be gone. "No wonder you keep complaining about low energy."

"Now, Miss Bobby," Deana said, "Kick's worked hard to get this—"

"The help's defending you now?"

Deana walked off toward the drive-through, muttering, "One Mississippi, two Mississippi…"

I bit my cheek and let her go. She'd be back in a heartbeat anyway.

I whipped around and glared. "You will never speak to her like that again."

Bobby waved me off with a flick of her wrist and a smirk. "Just admit defeat and convince Hugh to sell Mickey's bloody smoke lounge. You know you're looking for an excuse to get rid of all this. Quitting is what you do. Ever since you quit dancing, you've flitted from one thing to another like a drunken butterfly." She cackled at her own joke, the master gaslighter on a roll. "Maybe then you'll feel better and have time for a man again. You know if you hadn't been so focused on yourself, you wouldn't be in this shit now, right?"

"Hang on." I threw my rag down. "Are you saying—?"

"If you had stopped whining about not feeling good, you wouldn't be alone," Bobby snapped. "It's past time someone pointed out the obvious. Your father used to shut me up on this, but he's not here anymore, is he?"

Ah, the mother of all buttons, right there. The source of my nightmares for eight years. Life's biggest guilty verdict. I'd collected a lifetime of them. "There would've been an accident either way, Mother," I protested.

"I wasn't there, Miss Bobby, but even I know one thing isn't the other. Nobody gets out of life without struggles. I don't think you have." Deana's bravery knew no end.

I hustled over to the drive-through, my cheeks so hot I was

certain they looked sunburned. "Tina, you have Rach's spot now." I pulled Rachel toward the back. "Take my AmEx card from my wallet and get your grandmother out of here. If her plane is still delayed, go to the airport and buy her lunch. Hell, shop for all I care, just *git her awa*. Please, sweetheart." Though raised in the Midwest, my father's Irish lilt found me when agitated. A memory flashed of him asking teenaged-me to take Bobby anywhere and give him peace.

Rachel gave me a quick hug. "Sorry, Mama. I heard some of that, but the drive-through was too lit to leave."

FORTUNATELY, THE LUNCH RUSH KEPT US BUSIER THAN A TWO-BIT hooker on BOGO night. Putting smiles on customers' faces soothed Bobby's cruelty. Deana switched the music to my alt-rock playlist to kill my temper and keep me bouncing, even though it wasn't her taste. By midafternoon, we had a break and took our lunch together. We shared a table in the sunny corner. Dee ate a Santa Fé chicken wrap and chips. I had a Cobb salad and apples with a dip from home. I noted how the lunch didn't fit the new low-FODMAP plan. *Well, hell.*

I wore my reading glasses as I tinkered with the upcoming schedule, figuring out where I could take time off for appointments. I decided to give acupuncture a try, hoping it could work in lieu of IV therapy.

"Feeling better?" Deana asked between bites of her wrap.

"The *momster's* gone, so... yeah."

"Kick, your mama has more issues than *People Magazine*. I mean, where are you with all this?" Deana asked, waving her free hand toward my laptop screen.

"Still absorbing."

"But you've done it before."

"There's the thing." I sighed. "When my stomach went haywire and the pain amped up, I thought going back to the original regimen would fix it. It's also why I joined the HIIT group. When I asked Dr. Chaddha why it didn't work, she said it was courtesy of the dreaded P-word."

"Which P we discussing?" Deana asked.

"Perimenopause," I moaned. "Apparently the rules are different now. Doesn't matter that it's only been five years since the last big protocol and the weight loss. Something about estrogen and my metabolism being more stubborn now than before. Here I thought it was almost impossible *then*."

"Oh, shug." She patted my hand. "That'll settle down."

"I don't know, Dee," I said, a hitch catching my voice.

"What are you really afraid of?"

I set my pen down, along with the reading glasses. "Worst case?"

Dee's eyes managed to show sympathy and say "duh?" at the same time.

"I've worked hard so my best years can be ahead of me. But what if this is as good as it gets? What if I spent my best years being sick and there's nothing left? You know how the Psalm I like reminds me of the good stuff?"

She nodded. "Psalm Sixteen?"

"Yup. Right now I'm trying to believe 'the boundary lines have fallen in pleasant places,' but I can't. The boundaries are choking me. I want more."

Dee squeezed my hand. "There's your stress talking. Have you tried meditating?"

I felt my own eyes flash with annoyance. "I've looked at some apps, but none seem right. I don't know. It's adding more stress when I think about it, like I can't cut it there either."

"I'd be happy to show you the app I use." I didn't know Deana had tried mindfulness. She piqued my curiosity. "Either way, everyone meets their fears now and then. Did you know my Maceo and his wife are having issues? It's not his health, but he's terrified his vision of the future is about to go bust."

I shook my head. Poor guy. Dee had great kids.

"I'll tell you what I told him: don't cross bridges before you get to them. Let me help. Leave the hiring to me. Have Jake do scheduling. Shoot, he can help with staffing too. He's a smart boy. He's a wonderful choice, Kick." She stretched her arms to their sides and began shaking her hands and flapping her arms. "Now, do like me and shake this off."

I complied while laughing. "You do this with your grandkids?"

"Better believe it." We took a deep breath and giggled some more. The action had a remarkable effect, and I honestly felt better.

"You got this. Plus we'll be here to keep you in line and on track. Before you know it, this will be a memory and something else will bother you."

If we'd lived in Ancient Greece, the woman would've been an oracle.

4

SIMPLE MAN

KICK

"*A* peace offering, Kicky," my best friend's smoky voice said to my back. A plastic container squeaked across the counter as I turned around. It had to be yummy. She was a fantastic baker. I had watched Cyndi Sendaydiego walk in from the parking lot, and she'd accurately assessed my level of peeve. She had promised to help me set up for the open-mic night, and fatigue was setting in thanks to the crazy morning. I took a moment before greeting her.

I lifted the corner of the container and sniffed. "Lumpia," I whispered in awe. Okay, this was a good apology. She'd been experimenting with gluten-free flours, claiming they made her tummy feel better too.

"Papa's recipe, modified of course," Cyndi confirmed. "These are the best so far."

I didn't have the heart to tell her the rolls were probably off the menu for the foreseeable future. Besides, how much worse could a few goodies make me feel? I'd pop some activated charcoal and cross my fingers afterward.

I lifted my eyes and caught true repentance in hers. "Thank you, chica." I grabbed two forks and two knives, handing her a set. We had time to catch up before the show.

Since she'd arrived late, I expected her to come in ragged or at least frazzled. Instead, Cyndi looked like a million bucks, from her silky black, chin-length wedged bob to her wedged flip-flops. Being tiny, she was into wedges.

Her tan skin glowed, and her beautiful gray eyes (one of the traits courtesy of her mother's European ancestry) glowed.

A low-cut, V-neck tee couldn't hide a tiny hickey. I instantly knew why she'd stood me up.

She lowered her sunglasses to the tip of her nose and flashed a smile. "Anytime. Sorry I missed helping. It looks great in here though." She twisted uncomfortably in her seat as I studied her. "I accepted an offer I couldn't refuse."

"You got some." I crossed my arms. "What's his name?" Cyn didn't cancel often, and between us, it was usually me asking for a hand. She'd been through a lot and fought her way back too. She worked hard and played harder, as they say. And possessed a metabolism I'd sell a kid for. If I were in her shoes, I'd also take a detour when given the opportunity.

A grin started at the right side of her mouth and slowly spread to the left. "Manu."

"Seriously? You skipped out on me for tanned and exotic?"

Cyndi had the nerve to close her eyes, lick her top lip, tilt her head back, and squeal. The students studying on the far side of the dining room looked up from their books. "Make sure you add tall to the visual." She smirked, picking off the lumpia wrapper.

I laughed at her antics while my stomach growled, and I dug into my plate. We had each other's backs when it counted. We became close while rooming together at Michigan State University. Like any successful lengthy relationship, we'd learned which battles to pick and which to let go.

"You're forgiven if you tell me about him," I offered with a smile, cutting my rolls into pieces. "You know I live vicariously through you." I swallowed my bite. "Oh, Cyn, these are heaven. Thanks, sweets."

"You're most welcome, Kicky." Cyndi went full finger food with hers, speaking between bites. "Manu runs a food truck. I'm helping him with his books so he can get a permanent space next year. Anyway, I took him to lunch, as I do with all new clients. We started talking, and..."

"You liked his menu."

She nodded her head and licked her upper lip again.

"Think this one will be serious?" I asked lightly, ever hopeful she'd take the plunge again.

"*Pfft.* Did I say relationship? It's sex. We're too busy for more."

"Hey, fam." My youngest, Liam, flew through the front door, eyed our food, and reached for one of my rolls.

Cyndi tapped his hand away. "Get your own food. These are Mama's." *Yeah, we had each other's back.* Liam kissed his godmother on the cheek. "Fam?" she asked. "This is new. Do I count as a fam?"

"You're Aunt Cyn," Liam countered. "Of course you're fam."

"It's not new," I added. "Between your business and his after-school activities, you haven't seen each other in a while."

"Yeah, thanks for coming out tonight," Liam said, rounding the counter to fix a drink and a snack. He lifted a cup toward Cyndi, asking if she wanted one. I'd been so caught up in myself

I'd forgotten the first rule of running a coffeehouse—the blasted coffee.

"Yes, please, dimples. Are you nervous?" Cyndi used her pet name for him, but my kids were used to multiple nicknames. It was how my family showed both approval and disappointment.

"Naw," he said with a sassy grin you find in a high school senior. Liam ruled his world. "This is my practice crowd." He leaned down and kissed my head since he'd already grown nine inches taller than me. I liked how he'd never fully entered the "moms are idiots" stage. Then he flashed us his killer dimples, the reason for Cyn's nickname. It was a habit the girls in his orbit encouraged. My baby was growing into a beautiful man regardless of my readiness for it.

Liam turned his attention to me. "Can I take this stuff to your office? Gonna bust on some homework before the show."

"Definitely, weeman." I nodded and shooed him away. "Want me to send the band members back as they arrive or keep them out here?"

"Send them back, please." With the backpack still over his shoulder, a plate and cup in his hands, he shuffled to the office. I swore I heard a table of girls sigh.

It was our first open-mic night of the fall. My newly promoted night manager, Jake Quick, helped me set up the sizable pieces, then I gave him the night off to celebrate. The minute I'd offered, I regretted it. I still waded in denial regarding how much my health had backtracked.

A few minutes before the start time, my father's business partner, Hugh Reynolds, entered and slid onto the stool next to Cyndi.

"Hugh!" She threw her arms wide and leaned into a hug.

"I should come in here more often if this is the greeting I get," he answered with a smile in his eyes.

"You could come in more often, period," I said, leaning across the bar, receiving and returning a kiss to the cheek. "Great to see you. Is Maggie well?" He nodded, eyes bright. We'd both been so distracted since Dad's funeral, it felt like I'd lost both men over the summer.

"She gone?" he asked.

"Honestly, have you been staying away because of Bobby?"

Hugh raised his hands. "She's been a bear since the funeral, plus taking care of Maggie… I'm sorry, Katie, but I didn't want the missus around Queen Bobby's temper."

"Tell me about it," I answered. "You'd think she might've liked Dad or something." Hugh had been my father's best friend since moving to North Carolina. Unfortunately, their wives didn't feel the same. "It's great to see you. Can I get you anything before I start this shindig?"

"Did I see a piece of the quiche I like?"

"We still have a couple, yes."

"Add a decaf the way I like it, please."

"Got it." I set about making Hugh's belly happy and fixed a cup of decaf for myself, following the dietary sheet's recommendation to ease into the coffee abstinence.

As the after-school crowd headed home, the dining room buzzed with warmth and excitement. Customers settled in for a few hours of the unexpected. The sign-up sheet always held its share of singers and bands, but the number of poetry performances and even stand-up acts had been growing. I hoped the teens who performed saw the Perked Cup as a safe place to develop their talent.

Waning light from the sunset brought my focus to the amber illumination in the space. The coffeehouse was ready for the day's third act.

I filled a small glass of water and popped an anti-inflammatory supplement, coaxing my body to hang in there, letting the smell of the roasted beans and hiss of the machines sustain me. This might have been my plan B, but the Perked Cup was intended to serve the community along with a fine cup of java.

Whether people stopped by for a quick cup of "get you going" and a smile in the early hours, a story hour and social time for moms and their littles midmorning, a quick boost and to-go lunch, a safe place to study after school, or an evening gathering spot, I enjoyed putting smiles on people's faces. I was still living the dream and hoped I could hang on to it.

WHILE WALKING OFF THE STAGE, HAVING INTRODUCED LIAM'S band, Metaphorical Chemistry, I noticed Professor Harrison lingering near the door. I knew he'd come for the attaché. A cardigan had replaced his suit jacket, and the fedora had disappeared.

I planned to approach him directly but ended up tossing him a shy wave from the safety of the service area. I didn't know what to make of him now that I'd calmed down. Perhaps I'd read more into the formality of his suit and arrogant demeanor. Now he stared at my son's band as if taken by them. He seemed more casual and yet—I don't know—isolated. It was like he was unfamiliar with being in public. It seemed strange for a professor, even a young one.

My waving caught his eye, and Thomas moved to the counter. He leaned in to hear me as I asked, "You're here for your briefcase, aren't you?"

Relief flooded his face as his shoulders visibly relaxed. "Is it here?"

"In my office. I'll go get it." I gestured to an open spot next to Cyndi. "Have a seat."

"Mind if I get a coffee too?"

I laughed at the question, tempted to shoot him my typical sarcastic response, but I didn't know how he'd take it, given the way I'd yelled earlier. "Not at all." I tapped the shoulder of one of the part-timers. "Madison can take your order, and I'll be right back."

Walking out with the heavy briefcase in hand, Liam's words stopped me from the stage.

"Most of y'all know my mom runs the café. She's worked her ass off"—I shot him a glare, which got me a dimpled smirk in return—"to make the coffeehouse something we could be proud of." He looked over his shoulder and back to the small audience. "The band and I thank you, Mom, for letting us play."

As far as I knew, no one had told him about my day, the diagnosis... any of it. His words were a reminder that while some people knew which buttons to push to bring you to your knees, others knew which ones could make you soar, make the bad days worth it.

My nose tingled as he settled his guitar and quickly added, "This is for you." They proceeded to play Lynyrd Skynyrd's "Simple Man." He'd tinkered with the song on his own for years, but I didn't know his band had earnestly practiced it. When Liam was little, he took to the idea of a song about a mother and son. He'd belt it out from his car seat while we ran errands.

He changed the opening lyrics from "only son" to "youngest son." I bit my lip to keep my emotions tight. The gleam in Liam's eye said he knew he'd gotten to me. My memory flashed to the day he pranced into preschool without a second look back. That's a funny thing about parenting teenagers; their toddler selves tended to hide in their growing bodies. They wait within shadowed memories, quickly jumping out when you didn't expect it. The reminder he was the last of my children occasionally sucker-punched me too. It was easy to go about my daily routine, forgetting how the raising part of my job as a mother was ending. I was crazy about this kid with a heart bigger than the planet, and I didn't know what I'd do after he left.

I returned to the service area and almost teared up again when I caught the emotion on Cyndi's face. Family by choice could be better than blood. Then I saw the spread in front of the professor and laughed. It didn't occur to me he'd settle in, though my reaction probably came more from a release of emotion.

I raised the briefcase. "Here you go. If you're staying, I could keep it back here. It's kind of heavy for the undermount hooks." I gestured to an open space on a shelf at the end of the bar. "I promise it's dry and safe down there."

"If you wouldn't mind, thank you." He smiled and finished eating his... sandwich wrap, the last slice of quiche, and a piece of shortbread.

I GATHERED THOMAS'S PLATES AND WIPED THE COUNTER WHEN HE finished. It was an excuse to take a big breath and humble myself. The band had finished, and the overall volume of the room had lowered for a poetry reading, so I didn't have to yell. "I want to apologize for earlier. I'm sure you didn't mean any offense in asking me out. I mean, of course you didn't. And I don't usually take offense when it happens."

Nice going, Kick. How far down your throat will this foot go? "Anyway, you were kind of my last straw in a morning with tough diagnoses and rude customers, not to mention some eejit left weed in our bathroom. I think my pushed buttons were looking for a target and I overreacted... So yeah."

His eyebrow popped up in question. "I didn't... I meant to ask if there were other open-mic nights. Specifically on the weekends. I'm often busy at night."

Cyndi and Uncle Hugh had watched our entire exchange, and they burst out laughing at my expense.

"Oh shi-it," I stuttered. I didn't have a stutter, but my brain had shorted out.

Please God, let me become invisible. Grant me this one little thing. Pleeaase. I looked down at my arm. Super pale. *Still visible.*

"Can we start over?" I extended my hand in greeting as I felt the blush rush up my chest to my hairline. "Kick McKenna. Chief coffee brewer. Also self-absorbed foot eater. Sorry, open-mic nights are always on Mondays. Weekends are for themed nights or single-act bookings."

A sweet smile reached the corners of his eyes, making them crinkle without pulling at his lips. He took my offered hand and shook it once with purpose. "Thomas Harrison. I'm familiar with the foot-eating habit. Bad for digestion."

"Great sweater, my dude," Liam told Thomas before he asked me if the band could hang out in my office again. They wanted to review their set without groupie interference. Plus Liam's best friend since first grade, Jacklyn Moore, was new to the band. That they had stayed friends through awkward years and ridicule from classmates made me proud.

"He's not a dude, Lee. Dr. Harrison is a professor," Cyndi said.

Thomas tipped his chin. "Thanks, pal. Thomas is fine though, unless you're my student. I liked your music. Has the band played together long?"

Uncle Hugh added his compliments, and the three males put their heads together, talking about music and future school plans.

Cyndi pulled me in to whisper in my ear. "Is this the guy with the zoot suit you told me about?"

"Shh," I scolded. "I never said zoot suit. Those are from the roaring twenties. See his pants? They're more…"

"*Mad Men.*"

"Precisely."

She nudged my shoulder. "What do you think though? He has potential."

I laughed, caught the men looking, and bit my lip. I turned back to her. "The whole Mr. Rogers thing is a bit weird, don't you think?"

Cyndi's eyes shifted toward the fellas without turning her head. She studied Thomas for a moment, and I hoped she wouldn't crack a joke at his expense. For some reason, I felt protective of him.

"Remember the semester you made me watch the classic movies with you for a class?"

I wrinkled my nose, wondering where Cyndi's thoughts had turned. "Sure."

"I had a mad crush on young Cary Grant. He was *fiiine*." She drew out the word and sighed. Her eyes flashed to the side again. "Professor-man has the same vibe. And face."

I ducked my head to look at Thomas without him noticing. Raven hair, cleft chin. The eyes were lighter, but she had a point. I nodded slightly.

Cyndi added, "I bet his female students swoon when he walks into a lecture hall."

"Bringing back memories?" I teased her, then bit my lip, regretting the comment. "Sorry."

"No worries." She smiled as if remembering something. "Even if it was wrong, some of those memories are awesome." Cyndi tucked some hair behind her ear, and her eyes dimmed. "It ended up being only half as bad of a bad habit as Joel was."

I tried not to flinch at the mention of her ex-husband. I'd introduced them and felt the sting of his infidelities personally, but this day had been hard enough. I didn't want to add more spilled milk to my guilty feelings. I stepped away from the counter. "Gotta introduce the next act."

After a few minutes of clapping and talking, I was back across from my bestie while the men still conversed. The current topic involved the merits of Stevie Ray Vaughn. Liam excused himself, and Hugh and Thomas switched to cigar talk. There was only one more singer scheduled, and the crowd had thinned. I couldn't wait for the performances to end so I could leave too. My pillow called to me.

I quickly tipped my head toward them to silently ask Cyndi if she'd noticed Hugh and Thomas still chatting away.

She scooted a stool away and leaned over so no one could hear. "Get in there and flirt with him." She even swatted my hand.

"What? No." I croaked, still embarrassed about my earlier behavior. The men glanced at us, then turned back to their tête-à-tête. I stage-whispered, "I meant... isn't it weird how they're getting along?"

"It's cute," Cyndi answered. Then she added, "So he's a little odd with the clothes, and maybe there's an air of a superiority complex. Come on, Kick, maybe the universe is sending you a message."

"Funny," I started, "I thought the universe gave me the silent treatment."

"That's because you keep declining its calls." She squeezed my hand. "Life doesn't wait around for you to feel like it."

Fatigue influenced my snapped response. "So I should, what? Wrap my hand in his collar, drag him to the back, kick the kids out of my office, and bang his brains out?"

She sighed with her own pent-up frustration with me. "It would be a start. Come on, Kicky, there's nothing wrong with a little fun." She leaned in and kissed my cheek. "Whatever. Night, chica." She pulled her purse strap over her shoulder and mouthed, "Think about it."

I bobbed my head to agree while Hugh swallowed Cyndi in a goodbye hug. Then she shook Thomas's hand and gave him a wink. They both watched her strut out the door, then turned to me.

"Well, Katie, time for me to get back to Maggie," Hugh declared.

After giving him two carrot cakes in to-go boxes and receiving the same bear hug Cyndi had, I introduced the last performance. I'd left my reading glasses at the counter and had to do the trombone-arm stretch to read the scratch on the clipboard. Then the boy didn't show. I gleefully wrapped up the evening while the dining room cleared out as if someone had yelled "fire!" I couldn't wait to leave the clean-up to Madison and Liam. He was finally responsible enough to lock up for me.

They approached at the same time.

"There's an aura in my vision, fam," Liam said, his eyebrows knitted tightly together with the sign of an early migraine.

"Did you take your spray?" I asked, reaching up to brush his curls off his face. Of my three kids, Liam's hair was most like mine.

"I forgot to put it in my backpack."

"Lee," I scolded, shaking my head. Jax offered to take him home, and I waved them on.

I turned to Madison, who looked a little peaked.

"You know how I'm supposed to close, Mrs. Mack?" she asked.

"There's a rumor going around to that effect," I responded.

"I have a sore throat." Her eyes popped when she swallowed.

Annnd my pillow would have to wait a bit longer. I sent her home, rang up two more to-go cups, then noticed Thomas rising to leave. I walked to the end of the bar and held up his briefcase.

"Don't want to forget this twice," I said with what I hoped was a friendly smile and not a tired grimace on my face. It was an idiot move to let Jake have the night off and not arrange for another part-timer to close.

"Today was the first time I'd ever forgotten it," Thomas said, looking down at the attaché. He gave me a shy smile. "You have a nice place."

"I apologize again for earlier. And please come back."

"I'll try." The smile grew as he dipped his chin good night. Cyndi's voice in my head urged me to do more, be playful, be… hell, *not me*. But my body didn't care. It took everything I had to follow out the last of the customers and lock the door. It was ten minutes before closing, and the day demanded it end.

I flipped over the chairs and swept the floor. Stevie Wonder encouraged me not to "worry 'bout a thing" while I danced a slow cha-cha with the broom, hoping it would give me enough of an energy burst to leave the café clean. The day's earlier tension settled in my hip, making me limp. I had a cane in the office, though using it while straightening the dining room was impossible.

My mind distracted itself from the pain with can-do thoughts of recipes to experiment with when a vigorous knock at the door startled me.

Thomas Harrison stood on the other side.

5

CROSSROADS

THOMAS

*H*e wanted to laugh at the misunderstanding between himself and Kick, but her assumption offended him. She received the benefit of the doubt because of the way she'd comported herself in the evening. Thanks to the people around her, including her customers, he figured their first encounter was a one-off.

Didn't mean he held an interest in a friendship, though he did like talking to Hugh. The man had convinced him to visit Mick & Hugh's over the weekend. He'd mentioned watching college football, and Lord University was playing an away game. As far as the

Perked Cup went, Thomas could stop in now and then. Kick made a damn fine espresso, and the food beat the hell out of the small plates from the faculty party. He could push down any attraction and keep it to an eye-candy-only situation. He was friends with plenty of attractive people, and it never bothered him.

Thomas's first mistake occurred when he looked up after placing his briefcase in the Camaro. If he'd kept his head down, he would've driven home perfectly ignorant and fine. On autopilot, he checked his surroundings, glimpsing the graffiti on the brick wall next to the Perked Cup. He did a double-take, hoping the foul words on the brick wall were an aberration due to being lost in his thoughts. But no.

Something told him to remove his gun from underneath the front seat, tuck it into his waistband, and walk the perimeter of the café, especially the back alley. If the so-called graffiti artist lingered, he'd hold the idiot until the police arrived. One lonely camera guarded the back alley, and who knew if it worked. No indicator light showed. Someone had damaged the back door lock. It held but would need replacing immediately. Kick had to get a security upgrade. Wasn't it handy Thomas knew a guy?

Thomas froze when he turned toward the café's door. Silhouetted by low lights, Kick danced with a broom. His heartbeat picked up as he observed her swaying with her pretend partner. She knew what she was doing. Despite favoring her right side, she moved with fluid and grace. Kick threw her head back and smiled at a private joke, loose curls falling into her face when they tipped forward. He wished he knew what was so funny.

She was stunning like this. Even in the shadow of her hair, her porcelain skin glowed. The delicate tone suited her. Thomas shook himself from his stupor and resumed walking. *Give her the information and go home. No distractions.*

Her startled smile upon unlocking the door surprised him. Their interactions had been awkward at best all evening.

"I know I handed you the briefcase this time," she said.

He shook his head. "The case is fine, thanks. It's…" He turned and pointed. "You should see this."

"Oh hell. What now?" she asked around a yawn.

Thomas waited for her to lock the door, then stepped aside. A cane had leaned against the table with her purse. She used it as she traveled the sidewalk. He wondered where the limp came from. They both shined their phone lights on the wall in the unusually dark space. A streetlamp, which should've lit the area, sported a rock-sized hole he bet was new. The two sentences were still visible, thanks to neon yellow paint.

Your a drug sellin hoe

and

Jesus is cuming.

"JaysusMaryandJoseph." Kick sighed, her disappointment and defeat settled into her features, pulling at his heart. Her fingers hovered over the letters in the second line.

"Don't touch it. You could leave fingerprints if it's still wet," Thomas warned. "Not sure if it matters, but just in case."

The hurt on her face broke his resolve, and a wave of anger washed over him. A few minutes earlier, and he might've been able to beat the little asshole for this. He couldn't leave her to deal with the vandalism by herself. What if said asshole was watching and waiting? Something about the act seemed more violent than the words suggested. It had Thomas's hackles raised.

On that thought, he scanned the parking lot one more time.

Kick kept staring at the paint and said, "I'm too tired to laugh about the grammar, but seriously? Is this a *U*?"

He gestured toward the wall as the humor in the words hit him too. "Maybe the overspray suggests closing the *O*?"

"Nope," Kick answered and pointed again. "There's a down-stroke with a terminal, here. It's almost a serif. I think the overspray is chalked up to lack of paint skills. This genius thinks 'coming' is spelled with a *U*. That's like a second-grade spelling word."

She took a breath and yelled, her body shaking with each word, "I hope Jesus enjoys it!" Then she muttered, "I am too *through* with today."

A chuckle sputtered from Thomas. He bit his lip to hold it in. "I didn't realize y'all had a garden tool display either." He cringed at the dumb pun. Why did this woman have him on edge?

As she turned the key in the door, her hands shook and she grumbled, "I know, right? I should've guessed this shitty day would end weird—vandalized by the Chick-fil-A cow."

Another snicker escaped from Thomas as he nearly lost his composure. Fortunately, Kick didn't notice his puff, like that of a kid hitting their first note on a trumpet.

THOMAS COULD'VE KICKED HIMSELF FOR STICKING AROUND WHILE she gave a statement to the police and arranged to have the paint cleaned. It didn't take long for him to do his part, but he felt bad about leaving her alone. Her features were a mix of anger and exhaustion—utterly spent. Thomas hoped Kick didn't play poker. From what he'd read of her pretty visage, she'd lose big.

He did not understand what was wrong with him unless the late hour affected him too. It wasn't like his current situation was new. He'd been laser-focused for a while. Women stayed low on his priority list since he'd moved to North Carolina. When one occasionally landed in a slot on the list, she learned the deal up front: no attachments, no commitments, and an expiration date was imminent.

He sat in a chair in the corner where the stage had been and found his thoughts mulling over the song her son, Liam, played earlier. The lyrics of "Simple Man" running on a loop in his head became an indictment of the way he lived.

When had it happened? The problem was, he remembered each

time his life had taken a turn toward more complication. Hell, he couldn't remember the last time he'd followed his heart for the sheer joy of it. He'd locked it up tight in a box, keeping emotions at bay and helping him stay the course. But the song reminded him of other things. Things that used to be important. Life shouldn't be so complicated for one man; then again, maybe it should. From another angle, he carried enough baggage to fill a cargo plane.

The song looped through his head another time, and he found a speck of encouragement in the words. Maybe it would help to have more people in his life. Yeah, he could stop back here once in a while, remember what it was like to be normal.

"You don't have to wait with me for the... the guy... Steve? Seth? You know, with the key thing."

"You mean the locksmith?" Thomas asked.

Kick offered him a bottled water, which he gladly took.

"Yes," she gasped, falling into the chair next to him. Her cane dropped to the floor. "Brain fog is the most annoying part." She rubbed her eyes and continued, "What's with the broken lock though? The officer thinks whoever did it used the music as cover."

"I'm not leaving you here with a bum lock. What if they come back?"

They sat in a shy silence, sipping their water. Kick hummed to Don McLean's "Crossroads" playing over the speakers. It gripped him in the chest more than anything she'd done so far. To say this woman differed from most of the women in his life would've been a gross understatement.

"Did you know your logo makes a double helix?" Thomas blurted, uncomfortable with his thoughts.

Kick smiled. Despite the exhaustion showing all over her face, the smile lit her up. "I do know, yes. Few people notice because I meant it to be subtle. Good eye."

Thomas shrugged his shoulders. "I'm a geneticist. What's it mean?"

She took a pull from the water bottle. "I go out of my way to provide a different cup of coffee. Sure, we have syrups and such, but most of our customers appreciate our effort to make the base product as healthy as possible." Kick clicked her tongue. "Not that it's helping me now."

"Can I ask you something?" The double helix reminded Thomas of an earlier conversation. He suppressed the voice in his head, telling him to mind his own damn business.

"Stephon," she answered, leaning back into the perfectly worn leather chair, her eyes closed. Between the dark circles there and the slight tremor in her hands, he assessed Kick to be at her breaking point physically, if not emotionally.

"Pardon?"

"Stephon's my locksmith. Sorry. Go ahead and ask."

"No need to apologize." Thomas sat in silence while he gathered his words. "I'm having trouble reconciling who you've been this evening and—"

"The card-carrying member of the bitchy cliterotti who chewed your ass up this morning? Yeah, me too."

Thomas burst out laughing. It started as a quiet snort and grew into a hardcore belly laugh. His hands and core warmed and hummed with an old sensation. He concentrated on it, certain it had nothing to do with attraction. Then he spotted the confusion on Kick's face and quickly pulled himself together.

"It wasn't a joke," she deadpanned.

And the laughing fit resumed. Lord, he couldn't remember the last time he'd laughed, let alone split a gut. Her words tricked his self-control into dissolving, but it had been looking for a release. His day was stressful too. Maybe not equally, but close.

He sat up and found Kick staring, nonplussed, her arms crossed at her chest. The pink Perked Cup T-shirt she wore complemented her ivory skin. The neckline scooped without being too tight or too low. Now, what her arms were doing to her cleavage? He looked away to keep from ogling. It was rude. Plus he'd be damned if he'd let a great rack bend his focus. Or his will.

Thomas pulled himself together. "Bitchy what?" He raised his hands. "Never mind. Anyway, I wouldn't say that... All right, maybe you were... a bit." One last deep sigh and he was back to his proper self. "Earlier, you mentioned a diagnosis and weed?"

"You don't want to chalk my behavior up to an irrational, female, Irish-American temper?"

"Should I?" Thomas looked around the open area. Large, rustic tables anchored one corner. This comfortable leather lounge area offered a different experience, as did the industrial bistro sets scattered throughout. Kick had thought hard about appealing to each type of customer. You didn't get this kind of insight by being a selfish hothead. No, it wasn't a foul temperament he'd run into earlier. Something had her off her game.

Kick sighed, sat upright, toed off her boots, and pulled a heel onto the seat, resting her elbow on her knee. "It's nothing that won't work itself out. I've seen some dumb shit in my café, but I've never had a customer tape a bag of weed to the bathroom vanity before."

"Is that what the graffiti was about?"

She lifted a shoulder. "Maybe? Except how would a vandal with bad grammar know about it?"

"Unless both criminals are the same person. Maybe he's mad you took it from him," Thomas added, rubbing his chin.

Kick yawned, making her jaw pop. "Ooh, good idea. When I check in with the OPD tomorrow, I'll see if they've thought of it."

"And the diagnosis?" Thomas asked.

Flicking her wrist, Kick answered, "Just a setback."

Thomas raised a hand. "I didn't mean to pry. Really. It's my research. My brain's always thinking about genetics. The way it contributes to illnesses fascinates me."

"Okay." She studied him intensely, then muttered, "You asked

KICK START | 53

for it." Kick straightened her back and began. "I have two autoimmune issues: Hashimoto's thyroiditis and celiac disease. I was close to remission, but it's been a rough summer." Thomas's bouncing foot filled the silence until she continued. "My dad was Hugh's business partner. He's the one who died in June."

"My deepest condolences. How awful."

Thomas wondered why Kick did a double take. Then her spine appeared to collapse over her knee. "Thank you. My son and I are trying to help Hugh keep things going until he's back full time, but he never liked working the front of the store. He needs time to figure out what to do next." Kick sat up, lifting her hair off her neck. "Anyway, big surprise, I hadn't been feeling well. This morning my doctor confirmed the flare and a possible third autoimmune attack, blaming all the stress."

"I see."

"Can't begin to explain the mountain of garbage between my mother and me. With Dad gone..."

"It's worse?"

"I'm getting buried by it."

Thomas thought back to the morning. "The lady sitting at the counter this morning."

"Yup." Kick removed her hairband and redid her ponytail while Thomas's gaze rested on the pointed tip of her ears. Something about them made him soften to her plight even more. They held a correlation to an old spirit—and suffering.

"My mother says I'm a hypochondriac, seeking attention by pretending to be sick. At least she's out of my hair for now."

Thomas lifted an eyebrow and smirked. "Tell me you didn't hire out an assassin."

The question brought a sly, delightful smile to her face. "You did get the correct first impression. No, she's on an extended cruise. I hope doing something for herself will soften her somehow." Kick put her foot back down and sat straight. "Now you know. And again, I apologize for earlier."

Thomas didn't want to be moved. He couldn't care less about the plight of sick working mothers who didn't understand the concept of balance. Yet he found himself probing. "Is there a plan? For your flare."

Kick collapsed back into the chair, and Thomas watched the weight of her world grow heavier. "Yup. There are temporary dietary changes. It's like a detox thing." She let out a low sarcastic laugh. "And I have to change the way I work out." Her hands flew to her head in a brief, upset burst. "Shoot, I forgot to tell Cyn I can't do boot camp anymore. She's going to kill me since I talked her into joining the class."

Thomas rubbed the bridge of his nose, feeling the effects of his long day. She didn't make any sense, and his own tiredness tested his patience. "I thought exercise is paramount to improving your health. What are you supposed to do?"

"This part I remember without notes. Since my workouts have been wearing me out more than they should, for the foreseeable future, an hour-long moderate walk is better than squeezing in a hard workout for a short amount of time. It's been stressing my adrenals, causing cortisol levels to rise." Kick turned her head and gave him a small smile. "My dog will like the slower pace anyway. Still, the group was fun and supportive."

"Will Cyndi be your walking partner then?"

Kick shook her head. "She prefers machines to nature and must have bodies to ogle. My dog is my little nature buddy."

Thomas's brows pulled together. "How little are we talking?"

"Research, huh?" She shrugged and lowered her hand to knee height. "Koosh is tougher than she looks if that's what you're asking. Anyway, I'll be fine once I process everything." Kick tucked a stray curl behind her ear. "Lately it seems like every few months everything I know to be true flips on its head... *annnd* now I'm whining." She turned her gaze to Thomas. "Sorry. Life truly is good. 'The boundary lines have fallen for me in pleasant places.'" She bobbed her head as she recited the words.

He turned to her, surprised by their familiarity. "Psalms?"

"Yes. You know it?" Kick's face perked up.

"Certain things in life imprint themselves so deep they never leave."

She nodded.

Thomas settled uneasily into the club chair. He didn't like to think of Kick walking alone, even though he knew women managed fine on their own every day. Still, he'd bet money the dog wouldn't matter if trouble came their way. He quietly sipped his water, keeping his thoughts to himself. He didn't want to risk stumbling into another argument with her. Besides, since she meant nothing to him, it didn't matter.

Wasn't there an uptick in attacks on women on local greenways though? The news reports made it sound like the victims were at fault for running alone. Hell, one of the reasons he ran at all was for the peace to get away and sort through his thoughts. It would suck to have to stay constantly on guard.

THE LOCKSMITH CAME AND WENT, LEAVING THE PERKED CUP secure again. Not to Thomas's standards, but it would do for now. Thomas couldn't get over how much their security lacked. He turned to Kick as she relocked the front door, pulling a business card out of his pocket. "First thing tomorrow morning, call this guy. Please."

She dropped the key in her purse and took the card. "Excuse me?"

He tipped his head toward her hand. "This man is like a brother to me. He's also a security expert. Promise me you'll call him and bring your business into the twenty-first century. I promise he'll take care of y'all and won't overcharge."

She looked up toward the streetlight, the broken one. "Jaysus, more money. Some days I'd swear if you cut me, I'd bleed Benjamins."

Thomas placed his hand on her foreman. The contact buzzed, and she quickly withdrew. He mirrored her action, though more from the shock of the feeling than the sensation itself. If he'd slowed his thoughts, he'd admit he liked it.

"Promise me you'll listen to his advice. There's too much invested in here to risk a successful break-in."

Kick admitted, "It's been on my list for a while."

Thomas fought a relieved grin. "Now you know who to call. Banger's the best."

"Banger?" Kick shook her head. "Never mind. It's too late to consider where he got the name." She hooked the cane over her arm before placing the card in the same pocket as the keys. "Thanks for this. For keeping me company too." A huge yawn shook her body. "I probably would've slept through the knocking when Stephon finally arrived."

"You did," Thomas said, keeping his smile shaded. He took a step backward and nodded his head. "Have a good night then."

"You too. Thanks again."

Kick leaned against the wall and began scrolling through her phone.

Why wasn't she walking toward a car?

He planned to wait and make sure she pulled away safely. Isolation didn't trump being a gentleman after all. He unlocked his door, opened it, and froze. *She's capable, asshole. Just slide in.*

Thomas turned around. "Why aren't you moving?"

Kick looked up from her phone. "I'm too tired and in too much pain to bike home."

He tipped his head. "Bike?"

Her eyes had returned to the screen. "Yeah, car's in the shop." She gave her phone a waggle. "I ordered a ride."

"I should go."

"Yes, you should."

It was a challenge more than agreement. Yet he couldn't leave her there. She'd given him an out, letting loose her problems earlier. And she'd set them straight. Eventually.

She'll be fine. Slide in and go. Damnit. He set his chin and called out, "Get in."

She waved him off. "Seriously, Thomas, you've done enough. I owe you a month's worth of free coffee at least. Go."

Thomas shook his head with purpose. "I'm taking you home. You're not riding with a stranger."

She approached the car, her eyes narrowed and lips pressed into a similar thin line. "Like I know much about you?"

"Have I hurt you? I'm here. It's no problem. Get in." He nearly growled, his last ounce of patience slipping away. He reached across the front seat and unlocked the passenger door. Thomas watched her notice the classic Camaro.

Despite her weary gait, her eyes brightened, and she gasped the way most women fawned over babies. "It's mint," she stated, not questioned.

Thomas nodded his head, and her smile placed another crack in his dried-up soul. *Simply a fellow muscle-car lover.* But this felt different from the occasional gear-head chatter. It *meant* something to have Kick notice the car, like appreciating the vehicle meant she appreciated him.

As she passed the hood, her hand slid over it, first the tops of her fingers, then her hand flipped, and she glided her whole hand over the surface—a genuine caress. Thomas lost his breath. His eyes tracked each finger's exploration, nearly at eye level from his vantage in the driver's seat, swearing he felt them on his body, on his— He cleared his throat and swallowed.

"Beautiful," she whispered.

Agreed, he thought.

Kick opened the door. "Well done, professor. I have a newer Camaro. I love it to bits." She slid in, shut the door, and buckled the belt. The corner of her mouth ticked up. "I bet the rideshare driver wouldn't be so grumpy." Had their shared taste in rides energized her some?

Through his foggy head, he wanted to bite back that he should be in bed. But it would've been cruel, considering how thoroughly exhaustion showed in the way she carried herself despite her car enthusiasm.

To confirm, she collapsed into the leather seat and declared, "Jayz, even my hair feels tired." She was right. It didn't have the same wild bounce it showed off in the morning.

Thomas stole glances at Kick as he drove. Her eyes closed, so he relaxed the leash he kept on his desires, watching her almost continuously thanks to empty streets. She looked perfect in his car. The leather seemed to embrace her like it didn't want her to leave, like the seat was made specifically for her.

"One thing I don't understand."

"Shoot," Kick answered without opening her eyes.

"You thought I was asking you out, but you wear a wedding ring."

From the corner of his eye, Thomas observed Kick's thumb turning said ring on her third finger. "It's a mother's ring. My daughter's birthstone is a diamond, so a jeweler friend repurposed my grandmother's wedding ring and added the boys' stones to either side."

"So you're not married."

"What?" Her brows furrowed into a deep V.

He cringed. Of course she was single. She would've called her husband instead of letting Thomas wait around and help her otherwise. "I'm sorry. Dumb question."

Kick chuckled, her eyes still closed, her voice gravelly when she answered. "No worries. I'm too spent to judge. And no. I *was* married." She raised her left hand. "My hand felt bare after, so…"

"I see." Thomas shut his mouth to keep from further embarrassment. He couldn't shake how much he hated the idea of this woman being alone. He didn't know why he cared.

GPS did its job, and he pulled into Kick's driveway. Thomas touched her hand to wake her and caught the peaked flush on her face. Hoping he wasn't overstepping, he lightly placed the backs of his fingers on her forehead and damned if she wasn't warm.

"Shit, Kick, I think you're sick."

She started, patting around her face. "Oh. It's nothing." She gave him a shy smile. "Par for the course for pushing so hard today. No worries."

He stared at her for a beat before saying, "Want me to see you to the door?"

Kick silently waved off the question. Well, fine. She was a grown woman.

She opened the door, stepped her right leg out, then turned back with a sweet smile. "Thank you for going way above and beyond. I hope you stop in again sometime. I'm serious about the free coffee too."

Thomas's eyes tracked Kick limping around the car, and the pull grew. In the headlights, the sheen on her face was more pronounced. He saw the graying of her pale skin, the slowness of her steps. Seeing this side of her really did anger him. Not at her, but for her. She shouldn't have to put up with it.

Christ, one minute you're fighting lust, the next you want to protect her from the world. But he couldn't protect her from her own body, could he? There wasn't anything Thomas could do for that. *Put it in reverse and drive. Let it go, man.*

He rolled his window down. "Hey, Kick?" She turned back to him without approaching the window. "When are y'all planning to go walking?"

She tapped her temple and whispered. "Argh. Stop making me use my brain." Her eyes tipped up to the sky, tongue rolling in her cheek like she was scanning a mental calendar. "Wednesday, Friday, and at least once over the weekend. Why?"

"What time on Wednesday?"

"Seven thirty. After Liam leaves for school."

He had a faculty meeting not long after. "I'll come with you."

"It's fine, Thomas. I don't need a—"

"I'll be there," he declared, using the tone he used with an obstinate student.

She narrowed her eyes and parked her hand on her hip. He suddenly felt like the student waiting for a correction. Thomas popped his head back into the car to add some distance. She wasn't a young girl to be handled. Kick was an experienced mother—a fascinating woman—but he wouldn't admit it.

"Fine. Do what you'd like, *professor*. Meet me here, but I'll only wait ten minutes. I have a lot to take care of before I settle into the new schedule." Kick turned toward the house and wobbled, then stopped and looked back. "I promise I won't be mad if something comes up."

He thought he heard Kick say, "I'm used to it," but she'd already resumed her stagger to the house.

Thomas put the car in gear and cranked up his Blues station.

No big deal, he thought. He liked to exercise anyway.

What harm could it do?

6

IT'S EASY TO FALL IN LOVE (WITH A GUY LIKE YOU)

KICK

*F*riday morning, around eight o'clock, I kept wondering what the hell I was doing walking with Thomas Harrison on my local greenway, my dog's leash firmly in hand. As expected, he'd canceled Wednesday morning, but I didn't mind. Unloading my problems in one blurp to a relative stranger had the unexpected result of clearing my head. In the past, honest sharing had made close friends run for hills, so I had expected Thomas would do the same.

That first slow walk on Wednesday nearly drove me bananas though. I kept catching myself trying to power through. Then

Liam gave me an idea to try. So far, so good. Except every time I paused, Thomas would walk ahead of my dog and me.

When he did it initially, I had my head in my phone or had let the dog sniff out an interesting find. And when I looked up? Whoa, the view made my eyes pop.

It was a warm, cloudless morning, so I wore a pair of hiking shorts and a tunic-length tank over my sports bra in case tummy bloat showed up. Thomas, however? Who knew a b-o-d-y was under the suit? The archaic rule of walking five steps behind a man didn't seem so bad if it meant following an ass like his. Add in muscled shoulders and biceps, I worried about getting the vapors if he overheated and took off his tank.

"Mind if I ask where your nickname came from? Is it short for Catherine?" he asked.

My dog, a hound-mix rescue named Macushla, found a communal pee spot right as an Eevee appeared in the app. I was already close to evolving my first one, and the silly excitement of it made me hum. "What'd you say?"

He turned and came back to us. "I asked about the origin of your nickname." He looked at my phone screen. "What're y'all doing? You're going to trip over something with your face in the phone."

"Sorry, Professor Grumpypants." I showed him the Android. "Liam suggested *Pokémon Go* might help me slow down without getting frustrated. I tried it out for a short loop yesterday. Koosh liked it too. You should play." I batted my lashes with vigor. When his scowl didn't dissipate, it occurred to me my sunglasses obscured the joke. "Sorry, we're slowing you down." I shrugged. Embarrassed and disheartened, I confessed, "I didn't know what else to do. It goes against my nature to dawdle."

Thomas took his phone out of a pocket and downloaded the app, his appeasement lifting my spirit. It wasn't long before we were catching critters and easing our way down the path, my dog enjoying her fill of smells thanks to our meandering pace.

"The nickname, huh?" I said after catching a Squirtle with high combat points.

"Just conversation. And curiosity. You don't have to—"

"It's fine." I chuckled. "After Monday, you had to notice I'm an open book. Anyway, it's short for Kathleen. I didn't like it for a long time. It was my introduction to a lifetime of tug-of-war between my parents."

"How so?" Thomas's dour expression morphed into one of interest and empathy. I couldn't help but notice how he gave his attention fully, once he decided to. It didn't take long for the floodgate, known as my mouth, to open.

"Dad always called me Katie, my mother took to Kick. She got the name from her obsession with the Kennedys, who had a sister with it. Typical to Bobby's side of the family, it was more of an insult. The more I objected, the more they used it. I begged teachers to call me Katie, or even Kathleen, at school, but only one ever overrode Bobby. Since it was the seventies, the adults stuck together."

"Sure."

"It's water under the bridge. At the time, classmates used it to tease. You know, *Kick me, Kickball.* It took a while to realize they only did it to those who let them. My dad's mom helped me own the name and turn it back on the playground bullies, as well as the ones in the family."

Figuring I'd said enough, I walked on in silence, working with Macushla to walk on my right.

"Aren't you going to tell me what happened?"

"Seriously?" I didn't think even Deana knew the full story of my name, beyond the Kennedy sister connection. No one ever really cared.

Thomas shrugged. "I have a feeling it'll be a good story."

What the hell. I continued, "While waiting on the bell one morning, this monster of a girl targeted me. She started in on the typical teasing, so I said, 'How about I *kick* your arse?' Then we threw down."

Thomas stopped walking and leaned in, a mischievous grin on his face. "Kathleen McKenna, were you a fighter?"

"Only in defense. Or if someone picked on my friends or my little brother." A light breeze diffused the blush threatening to overheat my already warm face. "She threw the first punch. The principal called home anyway."

"As they do."

"Yeah. Granny Allen was staying with us, and she came to the office since both my parents worked." I laughed at the memory. "The principal told Granny I'd been suspended for three days for swearing and fighting."

"Yikes."

I nodded. "When I insisted the other girl threw the first punch and I'd said 'arse' and not 'ass,' Granny did her five-foot-one best to get in the man's face. She was adamant European swear words didn't count in America and defending oneself wasn't fighting, so he had no case against me. She negotiated it down to taking the afternoon off. Then we stopped in a Sander's ice cream shop and ate hot fudge sundaes. It ended up being worth the cuts to my knuckles."

"Cuts?" Thomas's eyebrows knotted in confusion.

"The girl had braces." I laughed. "I miss Granny. She scared my mom." I held up a finger. "Wait. Not true. Bobby was afraid of *her* mother, but Grandma Sullivan was mean. Bobby respected Granny Allen. I could breathe when she visited." As if it was a suggestion instead of a statement, I took a long inhale and slowly released it. "I took her stance on European swear words as far as I could as a kid. Still use some of them when I'm upset."

My gaze had fixed on Macushla inhaling some scent in a stand of weeds as I shared my story. Opening up to Thomas felt both uncomfortable and natural. I didn't consciously want to but kept finding myself compelled. After stopping, I looked up at him, waiting for the next question, and felt his gaze piercing not only through my sunglasses but through me. I took a deep breath to fight the tightness in my chest, wondering what the outcome of his assessment would be.

The gentle roll of the nearby creek soothed the fluster. Two other women with dogs and a couple ran by us, getting in exercise while the temperature was still enjoyable and—I assumed—before taking off for work. But we weren't a couple, and I didn't want to be a part of a couple. What I *wanted* was the confidence boost of a successful run, not the head-muck that came from a body forced to putter.

He quietly said, "You seem comfortable with the name now."

I laughed at the memory he evoked. *Three generations from my mother's family had gathered around a kitchen table—the first holiday meal after my playground fight. My aunt had used my nickname with her particular bite. "This one thinks she's a kick, doesn't she?"*

"If you mean I kick arse and take names, then yes," I'd answered. It was the first time I didn't let their use of the sneer shut me down.

The spanking had been worth it. And Daddy had given me an extra dessert to apologize for the women's behavior.

"Yeah. Embracing it had the opposite effect on Bobby," I told him. "She's the one who hates it now. But it reminds me to fight for myself. Sometimes literally."

My phone vibrated in my hand. "Ooh, a Jiggly Puff popped up." *A Jiggly Puff should look like a middle-aged mother.* We slid our fingers across our screens to catch the Pokémon. "You're going to get ahead of me in no time. My kids say campuses are loaded with Pokéstops and gyms."

"I'm not playing this on campus," Thomas countered with a sardonic chuckle. His brow knitted back together like it was the default position.

"Suit yourself. It's getting fun." We spun a Pokéstop, and I received a gift package to give to a friend . I heard his phone notification ping. "There. I sent your first gift."

"This is ridiculous," he groaned.

"Come on, Gramps." I chuckled, giving Macushla a wiggle of her leash. "We're almost to our halfway point."

Thomas surprised me with more thoughtful questions, showing me he was honestly interested in my life. He shared what he could about his research but clarified it was considered top secret. Then he received a call, reknitting his brow and returning his face to a state of grumpiness.

"Excuse me. I have to take this privately." He stepped off the path, disappearing into the woods. "*Oui, Grand-père.* What can I do for you?"

"No worries," I called after him. "I'll take Koosh down to the creek." I wasn't sure if Thomas heard, but I made sure he could find us when he finished. Was he French on his mother's side? I liked that he still had at least one grandparent after sharing about mine. They had all died. I wondered if the man lived in France or here in the States.

I waited while the dog splashed in the creek, delighted to see water Pokémon show up on my screen. Between catching them and mulling over our talk, I didn't notice Macushla cut from my right side to my left after spotting a squirrel. Moreover, I paid no attention to the leash. She charged after the thing, taking me out with the efficiency of an NFL safety tackling a running back. One second my feet were firmly planted on a leaf-covered, shady foot path, the next they'd swapped positions with my head. In the process, my ankle twisted, and I might or might not have heard a *pop*.

I lay on the ground, wondering why the stars were out at the same time as the diffused sun rays that dotted my face. An intense pain shot up my leg from my shoe to my thigh. Macushla apologized with whimpers and kisses.

"Shit. What happened?" Thomas crouched down and helped me sit up. As he fixed my Michigan State ball cap, his worried expression threw me. I didn't know what to do with his concern, even though any friend would have done the same. It had to be this new-old idea of friendship with a *boy*. After becoming a single mom, Cyndi took on the role of my plus one on the rare occasion I needed it. Or my dad did. Befriending a man had become a foreign concept after years spent in the divided world of husbands and wives.

He brushed debris from my calf, revealing a shallow gash from a piece of broken glass. My screaming ankle had me reaching for the laces to loosen them.

I remembered the Pokémon game and called out, "My phone—"

"Here," Thomas answered, placing it in my hands. "Nice job picking a case. There's not a scratch on it. Unlike you." He stood and grabbed my hands, pulling me up onto my good leg. "Is there a clinic nearby?"

I pushed away his advancing hands, embarrassed enough. "Sorry, pal. None within walking distance. It's only a sprain anyway. An ice pack and Ace bandage will be fine."

He lifted my wrist and draped it across his shoulder, his other hand at my waist. "Lean on me at least." He took Koosh's leash in his free hand.

We step-hopped for a couple hundred feet at a snail's pace before the ache in my leg became a roar. I was determined to make it back home with whatever pride I had left. Besides, what was the alternative? Sit on the ground and cry? It had been stupid to take my attention from Macushla. She could never resist a good chase.

We came to the steps leading up to my neighborhood, and I almost did cry. Only four blocks to home and an ice pack, but the cement flight might as well have been a hike up Mount Mitchell.

"Shit," I said. "I forgot about the stairs." I tried to hold on to the railing and one-foot hop. My good ankle rolled, making me land on my butt again. The zing to my sacrum manifested in a guttural groan.

"Enough." Thomas scooped me up in his capable hands. He managed the steps and kept the dog out of his stride like he practiced the maneuver regularly. I opened my mouth when we reached the top step, but he warned, "Not a word about putting you down. We're going to your house and then to a doctor."

"No, Thomas. It's okay. Really. I'm too heavy for this. I'll—"

"I said enough, Kick. Your ankle looks rough. We should make sure you don't have a hairline fracture."

"This is embarrassing," I growled with frustration. But hey, now I really knew Thomas would scram, right?

"You have a hard time taking help, don't you?" he bit back. We had to make a ridiculous sight—he and I arguing as he carried me. Only Macushla acted happy to be in our little trio.

After a couple of beats of silence, I answered, "It's not what you think. It was a hard lesson learned many times over."

Thomas's gaze snapped to mine as I interrupted his thoughts. "Pardon?"

"I used to ask for help. Despite what people offer, I've learned the quickest way to lose a friend is to share about a struggle. As soon as the words were out of my mouth"—I snapped my fingers on my free hand—"Poof. They disappeared."

He inhaled deeply and adjusted his hold on me. "What about your current friends? Cyndi or Hugh or others?"

"They have their own issues," I answered with a sigh. "When I first got sick, my mother's response to the devastating news was 'Nobody wants to hear your sob story.' It was a cruel and cold thing to say. But she turned out to be right. So, I muddle through tough times. They eventually pass."

"On your own." The way he said it told me Thomas understood.

"If I can afford to hire help, I do. Otherwise, yes. Obstacles usually resolve given enough time." My foot began a throb so strong it had its own heartbeat. "*Jaysus*, it hurts."

I tucked my head into Thomas's neck to focus on my breathing, hoping to slow the pounding. Something about being in his arms, inhaling his scent, relaxed me, if only a little. He had a point. It was nice to let him carry me. A girl could have gotten used to it. One day.

Yet my scarred past cautioned me against getting too comfortable. It was my God's-honest truth—a shoe always perched at the ready, waiting to drop. But boy, it would be so nice if the shoe stayed put for once.

Thomas smelled amazing, even with a little sweat, more from the growing heat than our pathetic exercise. I inhaled deeply, recognizing sandalwood and lavender, two of my favorite oils to diffuse in the house. An underlying essence that was uniquely Thomas and equally relaxing. My body gave in to his hold.

"Did you just smell me?" he asked with a rattled edge.

Hell yeah. "No." I deflected. "I'm trying to adjust my breathing and slow my heart rate to see if it'll slow the rate of swelling. Sorry." His heartbeat pounded against my side, almost as fast as mine.

"Don't apologize." We came to an intersection. "Which way?"

I pointed straight ahead. "Are you sure you don't want to put me down? I won't mind."

"Kick, stop. I'm fine." He adjusted me as we made our way across the street.

"At least you're finally getting a decent workout."

The corner of Thomas's mouth lifted, and his eyes formed the kindest crinkles. "I lift more than you in the gym."

Okaaay then. "Really?"

The crinkles deepened as his smile transitioned to a chuckle. "Why do you sound excited?"

If a person could slump while being carried, I did. "I've gained weight with this setback. I'm not supposed to care, but it's the easiest thing to measure when it comes to health." I took a long sigh. "It's embarrassing."

Thomas assessed me from head to toe. "You're embarrassed?

About your appearance?" He shook his head. "I understand not feeling well, but you look—"

I set my fingers over his lips, not sure I could handle a joke. Thomas didn't know how raw the topic was thanks to Bobby. And I'd had enough of oversharing for the day.

"Fine," he said through my fingers. "You look perfect…ly fine."

"Really?" I asked again, like a desperate teen.

"Yes. I was going to say more, but I was afraid you'd wallop me with your free hand."

"I'd never."

Thomas's sarcastic laugh had me thinking of the morning we met, when I'd yelled at him. A step around a tricycle in the sidewalk sent a zing up my leg and shut me up. I welcomed the distraction since I already regretted telling him too much.

I focused on my up-close view of his shoulders and arms, which testified to his workouts. The emotions he stirred in me were ancient. I'd forgotten how to recognize them, let alone know what to do with them if I did. So, I chalked them up to gratitude and settled into the ride.

Besides, there was no way I'd allow a spark of interest for a man so young. I'd made a vow that ran deep and long, straight to my core beliefs. He might not be as young as my son, but he was off-limits in my book. And I offered him nothing.

I tried to lighten the mood with a joke. "I think I understand the retro clothes now."

"What're you talking about?" Thomas passed me a look of incredulity. I feared I'd insulted him.

"If your female students knew this"—I patted his hardworking chest and almost died—"was under your suits, they'd be all up in your business."

A shy smile returned to the corner of his mouth. Hell, it was sexy too. Then guilt tried to stir, as it always did if I considered moving on.

"Are you… complimenting my body?"

"Stating facts, Professor. Isn't that what scientists do?"

"Nothing's wrong with my clothes. It's rude when people show up to class like they've just rolled out of bed. Professional dress shows I care about my classes. Besides, my students think I'm a fine teacher, thank you. Seems to work."

"We haven't hung out much, but you kind of seem a bit hermit-ish. Frankly, it surprised me you picked teaching for a profession." Thomas's Adam's apple bobbed as he stared straight ahead, his eyes forming irritated slits under his brow.

Argh. I'd gone bitch-clit again.

I immediately regretted my words. Why did I seem to turn into the Wicked Witch of the Southeast around this poor guy? Since our times together had been on bad days for me, what did I really know about him? Once again, open mouth and insert purple-swollen foot.

"Can I take my words back? They're unfair since I still hardly know you. I'm sorry."

Macushla tried to stop and smell who-knows-what, and Thomas efficiently kept her on track with a slight correction. "Apology accepted." We continued for a few steps in silence before he gracefully explained, "I spend most of my days in the lab. But lecturing has been a surprise. I took the class as a favor, but it's reminding me there's more to life than research. The lab tends to follow me wherever I go if I'm not careful."

We stepped off a curb, and I hissed at the jolt of impact. "Hanging in there?" he asked.

I nodded, unable to speak for once, and turned my head back into Thomas's shoulder, blowing quick breaths to get above the throb.

"Stop smelling me, please," he clipped. "It's creeping me out."

"I'm trying to meditate," I snapped back. "My doctor wants me to learn it to help with stress, but I haven't had a chance yet. I figured Lamaze breathing might help with the pain.

"Keep it up and you'll hyperventilate. You're breathing into your chest."

He did his best to inhale into his belly and had me follow him. It surprised me how much it helped. I mumbled into his neck, "Left at the next corner. You'll recognize the stone facade from there. Maybe you're right about the doctor. I should call Dylan and have him take me to the Urgent Care. Where did you put my phone? I could call him now."

His adjustment was more of a jostle, like a physical repri-mand. "For Christ's sake, let me take you. I can have my TA cover today's lecture. Then I'm not due at the lab for hours."

I returned to my breathing, trying to close out the neighbor-hood noises and escape the pain. The sound of landscapers mowing lawns aggravated the throbs in my foot.

Thomas lightly tapped my arm. "Don't fall asleep on me. I didn't see you go down, but it looked like you might have blacked out when I found you. You should be checked for a concussion too."

"Leave it to me to get a TBI from tripping. I wasn't sleeping though. I was trying to meditate again."

"It's a good idea. It may be more important than your workouts."

"Not you too," I groaned.

I knew the moment Thomas recognized the stone porch of my house. His strong shoulders relaxed, and I worried again about how much work I'd put him through. At least I wasn't bloated since bloating could lead to gas. And just... *nope.* If that had happened, I'd have run home, sprained ankle or not.

Then he said, "I use a meditation app. I can show you how it works if you'd like."

I rolled my eyes like a teenager. "The blasted universe won't leave me alone, will it?"

Thomas's chuckle rumbled through his chest, making me want to purr. *What the hell?* The pain had to be fritzing my brain.

I'd even forgotten to ask him about the phone call from his grandfather.

SUNLIGHT SPILLED THROUGH THE BATHROOM WINDOW, A WARM AND golden dawn. A shadowed man crouched in front of me as I sat on the edge of my tub. He pushed a curl behind my ear. I didn't recognize him, but somehow I knew I loved him. His hair was shoulder-length and queued, with a gorgeous peppering of silver at the sides. I couldn't see much of his face, aside from a chiseled jaw.

This man's love was so deep it brought tears to my eyes. Despite the yellow light coming in the window, there was a cool essence around him. It's what diffused my view of his face, his body, and his clothes.

Then he spoke. "You own my heart and soul. Open your eyes and find me."

I sprang up, sitting in a cold sweat. Though dizzy, it wasn't from the pain meds in my system. The dream was so vivid every second of it clung to my thoughts like a sticky irritant. It swirled in and out of my head to keep me from falling back to sleep.

Replaying the vision created a deep lament. I'd had the dream so many times in the past five years my longing for an unknown man built to this unbearable level. I was desperate for clues about him, but the dream rarely changed.

I hated the foolishness even if no one else knew about it. Who fell in love with a fantasy? But my heart hurt for him. I scanned my memory again for evidence the man was *him*—the other love who haunted my dreams—but *he* was bigger, broader. His hair receded with waves. Then there were the dimples no one could ever forget. No, this was a different man, and the guilt I felt was almost too much.

The first time I had the dream, I thought I'd met an angel and glimpsed an afterlife. As time wore on, I became more attracted to his presence, silly as it sounded. His voice softened the hardest nights. The days following a dream drove me insane as I'd ruminate on who he could be, if he were real, if I'd ever find out. Granny Allen had told me plenty of stories of the Fae as a child, but none of them involved handsome dream-men like this. Since they'd become their own version of torture, I either wanted an answer or to be left alone forever.

I wondered if dating in the real world would make him go away. But my health, the kids, the business, and then my dad's passing had left no room for it. I thought about Cyndi's comment again, about the universe sending me messages. But the universe could also wait until my ducks aligned again.

I grabbed the crutches nearby and maneuvered into standing with a wince. I refused opioids, and standard pain meds were wearing off. I prepped a mug of ginger tea and a snack to go with the next round of drugs once I'd made my way into the kitchen. I turned on music to clear my mind and help me sleep some more, hoping the mystery man stayed the hell away this time.

Maybe I'd try the meditation app Thomas installed on my phone. Professor Thomas Harrison—he was an enigma shrouded in mystery. Why didn't he want to speak to his French grandfather? Every time I visited the memory of our walk, Thomas's face grimaced after his phone rang. And the mad dash for privacy, like he couldn't get away from Koosh and me fast enough. I didn't know whether to sympathize or fear what it could have been about.

Why were the answers I craved all so elusive?

7

COLD LITTLE HEART

THOMAS

*T*homas sat at his desk, studying the marks in the quarter-sawn oak—anything to delay checking in with *Grand-père*. He shifted his shoulders to remove his blazer, only to catch sight of it already resting on the coatrack in the corner. He triple-checked the lock on his office door. Ran a hand through his hair. His laptop booted up, glaring at him with its bright light, mocking him. *Coward.*

Images of new acquaintances shuffled through his mind, including the students who'd taken the time to stop by during office hours, revealing an interest in biology beyond a checked box for graduation. Two showed promise as future undergrad assistants in the lab. Agreeing to teach a section of biology had its pluses. So did doing a favor for the dean.

Thoughts drifted to Kick McKenna making quick work of the rude kid when Thomas had stepped into her coffeehouse. Too many students had the same air as that boy, as if Thomas received them not quite ready to adult. He secretly wanted to turn a few lectures into what he termed "applied biology" and teach basic life concepts, like Kick had done.

Kick's face continued flashing through his mind. Thomas hadn't responded to a woman in such a primal way in a long time. Her vanilla-and-tropical scent surrounding him while he carried her, or the few times his fingers brushed the side of her breast. He'd awakened, forced himself to not stiffen like a preteen boy. She would've jumped out of his arms and hobbled home for sure. He chuckled at the proverbial picture, then felt remorse. He hated her pain.

Thomas couldn't shake the notion Kick could help keep him from losing himself. Favor or not, he'd taken on the extra work of teaching out of fear. He hoped exposure to more students, and people like those at the Perked Cup, would keep him sane. His isolated life wasn't only making him "grumpy," as Kick called it. Thomas feared he'd become a sentient statue, outwardly representing the man he used to be, but inside was nothing but cold stone.

Reliving these new moments beat the hell out of his usual ruminations. Had it really been ten years since the last ascension ceremony? It was when he'd developed his plan to go into research. Paul's ascension had been as beautiful as the others Thomas had witnessed in his time with the secretive *Felidae*. He wondered where the kindhearted man was presently. Could Paul help their cause from the other side as much as he'd hoped? Lately, Thomas recognized the same weary gaze the man had carried when looking in the mirror at his own visage. But he planned to make his contribution here, on this side, and then he'd ascend. Some days the idea thrilled him so much he swore he'd do a dance during the ceremony. The days Thomas dreaded most were the numb ones, where he no longer cared either way. Those days, he was certain he'd become that statue.

With the laptop ready, he took a cleansing breath and entered the login information. Unlike his teaching computer, this was a tiny machine with one job. Using an encrypted network, his friend and colleague, Banger, had set up, Thomas logged onto the website for the Felidae Society. The eyes of a graceful black jaguar stared out from the landing page. Obsessed with security and deflection, the Felidae presented itself as a conservatory for protecting endangered cats. They'd raised millions for the effort since the front end of the site went live.

This backdoor kept up the ruse in case the wrong person found it. It protected the closed world in which Thomas lived. The group purposely chose the mysterious big cat as the fake face of the Felidae who also lived in the shadows, walking and sleeping near people without anyone knowing.

Anxiety flowed through his fingers as he typed in his information. Too much hung on his latest round of experiments, and they had failed. He entered the update as if it were any other report, hoping no one would notice. His fingers moved as quickly as possible so he could get in and get out while those in Bordeaux, France, slept soundly at the Felidae headquarters.

Thoughts drifted to Kick again and her stubborn attempt to limp home with a sprain. Her nose scrunched when she insisted CBD cream and ice would suffice. But he had to be sure there wasn't a hairline fracture. He kept returning to the memory of her wrinkled-up nose and the way she fidgeted in his arms until she'd surrendered, relaxing, giving him her trust. The victory in their moment together outshone any progress in the lab. It was the kind of emotional success he looked for in his work. It was the kind of victory that made him feel something again.

Or he needed to get laid.

His phone rang fifteen minutes after Thomas began correcting quizzes. "*Grand-père*. How are you, sir?" The cheerful greeting sounded forced to his ears.

"Good to catch you, young man," Alaric Kraus, *Grand-père* to those in the Felidae, responded. The predicted urgency transmitted over the phone, a crisp contrast with his usual tone of warmth and encouragement. "I will cut to the chase," he continued. Thomas smiled into the phone. Modern idioms didn't come naturally to the unique leader of the Felidae, but *Grand-père* practiced them. Thomas was also pleased to hear Alaric's more ancient, Northern European accent stayed firm. It was the first thing to draw him in all those years ago. "What happened?"

Thomas sighed, owning the disappointment. "What can I say? I hit a wall. You saw the evidence of Toni's transition? I'm confident about her. It's the why and the how that still hide from me."

"Perhaps it means she's not worthy to be Felidae. Have you thought of that?" The old man's voice boomed before Thomas could answer. The remark stunned him; of course Toni was worthy. "She should move in with you. I keep telling you this. Fresh samples would help your work, and a change would be good for her. A new start."

A shadow passed by the frosted glass window in the door. Thomas willed the person to knock so he could end the call. Unfortunately, the shadow made a sharp turn and moved in the opposite direction. The lab associates usually texted if they had an emergency anyway. He reluctantly returned to the call, determined to end it as soon as possible. He had an unending loyalty to the Alaric and the Felidae, but family came first. The superior attitude of the Felidae leadership grew tiresome.

"Toni's overwhelmed and not only by the Felidae," Thomas countered. "She's staying with Joe in Virginia for her health. He's taking the lead in her transition, per my direction. I'll visit them before I see you." He paused, then added quickly, "That is, if there's still a reason for me to present in October."

"What do you mean, if there's still a reason?" Alaric snapped. "I want you here. You'll come. You have a month to fix this, no?" *Grand-père*'s confidence was a breath of fresh air in the beginning. Lately it had morphed into obstinance.

"Fine." Thomas considered defying the order to attend the fall meeting. Others did, but he'd given his word. "Anyway, the first goodbyes are the worst, and as long as Toni's husband is living in the memory care center, she's staying near him. If we push too hard, she'll leave us. Then where would we be?"

"True, true," Alaric conceded. "The husband. You Harrisons are a strong stock."

"Technically, Toni's a Paci."

"Are you saying she hasn't changed her name yet?"

"No." Thomas backpedaled. "Her identity is squared away, but we're still new to her. She relates more to the Italian side of her family. Hell, the memories she holds of Joe are from photos and stories from when she was a girl. It's a lot to navigate, *Grand-père*."

"Yes. I see."

Finally. It could be nearly impossible to make the old ones understand the difficulties of life in the Felidae, not that Toni was a member yet. Locating a relative midtransition was the lightning strike Thomas had almost given up hope of finding. Alaric, and the few his age, gladly separated themselves from the modern world. They had created the Felidae to be a refuge from it.

"You're not discouraged, are you? You sound different," Alaric said.

"An idea is floating around in my head regarding the research. Should we also study regular people? One of my other relatives or even a friend, perhaps?"

"Friend? Surely you're not wasting your time on laymen."

The idea was so reprehensible to *Grand-père* he said it as a statement. To him, Felidae Society members who worked in the outside world were equal to zookeepers. Thomas grew most frustrated with the prejudice, though he understood the motivation for it. The Felidae lived in fear of being found out.

"How's *Grand-mère's* team doing?" Thomas changed the subject to avoid answering.

He envisioned the old man's hands animating his *pfft* as it came through the phone. "Ellie's people are holing up in Oxford. They're keeping everything close until October."

This was new. Thomas and the Oxford crew had a great working relationship, but he had needed no cross-team input lately. "How odd," he said, "my new first assistant came from them. She's been a great help and hadn't mentioned anything off. I've been planning to call Nigel and thank him for the recommendation."

"If you must. Don't expect a long chat."

"I can look into it though."

Again, Alaric made a decidedly French sound of doubt. It reminded Thomas why the man felt like family when they first met. He'd missed having elders in his life.

He finished the call with promises to press on while fielding more feeble attempts at encouragement from *Grand-père*. He'd bought himself some time by telling the old man it would take at least the month to get fresh results.

Thomas's eyes blurred as he finished the quizzes. He didn't know why he'd taken them from his TA, other than a desire to get something accomplished. He removed his guitar from its stand, settled onto the love seat tucked in a corner, and played to clear his head.

Thoughts shuffled again, from concern for Toni and how hard it was to transition, to how long he'd have to be absent in the middle of the semester. He resented the insistence on in-person meetings now, with videoconferencing so easy. He hoped his students excused his absence.

Through it all, he kept wondering how Kick was healing. Carrying her home had been like handling a firework shell and hoping the fuse wasn't lit. He cringed at memories of adjusting her and causing more pain. Thomas relived the shame of letting her think his struggle was because of her weight and not the situation in his shorts. Kick had no reason to be ashamed. He hated accidentally putting that on her but still believed the truth would've been worse. She made no qualms about his attractiveness, which he appreciated. She had also made it clear she'd do nothing about it, thank goodness. Kick wanting more—hell, anything—from him was unacceptable. He'd get himself sorted and work their new relationship into an easy friendship, something suitable for both their schedules.

He unconsciously played the Prince song he'd heard when he entered the Perked Cup. It wasn't his usual genre, but the connection between the song and her warm, forest eyes created an earworm he couldn't shake.

Noxious gas filled the cramped space where Thomas crouched. He ached everywhere, especially in his heart, as the shock from Uncle Theo's death set in. Joe hadn't returned either, leaving Thomas utterly alone. Again.

This terror gripped him like no other. His helmet had been knocked away with the blast, and he tore off his mask, desperate for the gas to take him. He begged for the peaceful finality of death. He was on the edge of consciousness when light rays broke through the fog. A female figure reached for him and stroked his face, pushing back his hair. The yellow light surrounding her shadowed frame quieted him, giving him hope.

Her full lips smiled brightly, but he couldn't see much else. The smell of air after a spring rain at home replaced the repulsive stench of the surrounding gas.

"Believe in us." She spoke in a low purr.

Shaking his head, he cried out in anguish, "It's been so long. I don't know if I can anymore. Are you even real?"

The woman he loved without reason squeezed his hand and answered, "Find me." He crawled after her as she faded away. A loud crash woke him as his head hit the hard floor. Thomas had rolled off the love seat in his office.

A pounding knock at his office door threw off the effects of the dream. They had tortured him for too damn long. Thomas used to fight waking up so he could linger with his dream angel. Now he resented her and his unending need for her. He despised himself for craving an illusion.

What were dreams anyway but the brain stem processing energy while the prefrontal cortex rested? The keyword there being *energy*. They occurred mostly during times of stress, and the failure in the lab had him on edge. After the stressful phone call to *Grand-père*, that had to be the answer.

"Professor Harrison? Is everything okay in there? I thought I heard your voice," his associate, Presley, asked through the door. She knocked twice again.

Thomas swung his door open midpound. "What?" Her startled jump clued him to the rough nature of his greeting, and he paused, remembering Kick's comments about surliness.

"Sorry to disturb you, Professor. I texted and called, but you didn't answer." Her eyes scanned him, and Thomas wondered how bad he looked. "I-it couldn't wait," she stammered.

He forced a smile. "Don't worry about it, Presley. Come in, please." He gestured toward a visitor's chair. "I could use the distraction." Lowering himself into his oak chair, Thomas asked, "Please tell me it's good news?" Light from the streetlamp outside his window made a delicate shadow pattern on the wall over his shoulder. Thomas checked his phone and noted the time. He'd slept for over an hour.

"Look at this." Presley slid a folder across his desk.

Thomas sifted through the report. "We determined it was junk a while ago."

His assistant stood. "If I may?" She separated the papers into three piles. "I don't think it's *all* junk. Look." Presley leaned across the desk, pointing. "The variants here and here are the same, but the control samples show no sign of them." She gave Thomas a bright smile, stirring his pride. Breakthroughs in the lab were fulfilling, but the discoveries of a promising protégé were golden.

"Do you think we're looking in the wrong place?"

"No, Professor." She sat back down, staying at the edge of her chair. "What if what we're looking for isn't in the same place for every person? I think we should expand the reach."

Thomas thought about who had provided his study material and the number of possibilities even this tiny genetic pool offered. "Like a recipe? You think there may be multiple ways to, say, make a cookie?"

If it were possible, Presley brightened more. "Oh, there are endless numbers of cookie recipes, Professor. One of my house-mates eats Paleo, and she came home with a package of them last weekend. They looked normal, but their ingredients were totally different." Presley's energy flowed from her as Thomas considered her point.

"Do we have enough samples to expand upon?"

Presley rubbed her knees as she stared at the wall behind him. Thomas could practically see her mind running through the catalog of tubes back in the lab. "I think so."

"Then do it. Write up a plan we can go over before our staff meeting in the morning. Will tonight be enough time for it? You can fill in the details later." Thomas could already think of ways to implement Presley's idea, but it was her baby. A good mentor should allow the student room to bloom.

"I'll make sure it's enough time. I'll go over a few more things in the lab if it's okay." She collected the papers and set them back in the folder.

"Works for me. Remind me to send Nigel a care package of North Carolina goodies. I owe him for recommending you to my team." He meant it as a sincere compliment, but a deep blush rushed up Presley's face and neck. He waited for her to say anything, but the young woman stared at the floor. Thomas stood and turned his back to give her a second. "I have to get to the lab myself. I'll escort you back."

As he slipped into his jacket, Presley gravitated to a table by the small sofa. She bent to study a photo on it. "Wow," she gasped with awe. "This picture is amazing."

Thomas knew it well. Nearly a hundred years old, he kept it nearby as a reminder of why he worked so hard.

Presley pointed at it. "This guy in the middle looks exactly like you." She stood and smiled again. "I see why you're into genetics. There's some strong DNA running in your family."

His promising assistant was one of his brightest so far, and she did not understand how right she was.

8

NO SCRUBS

KICK

*D*eana had an appointment Monday morning, so I opened the Perked Cup, welcoming the morning flow while keeping my crutches nearby. A weekend of rest, ice, massage, plus all the allopathic and naturopathic anti-inflammatories I'd thrown at my ankle had it on the way to healing. The hardest part of serving customers so early had been convincing myself that smelling the coffee while drinking a glass of lemon water would wake me up. The caffeine moratorium was underway.

Another of my favorite scents floated to my nose after the

door chime rang. For a split second I thought my father had come in before opening the cigar store, like he used to do. A tsunami of emotions washed over me when reality caught up with my primal brain. The amount of life that could fit itself into a single moment overwhelmed my senses. I grabbed the back counter, my knuckles blanching with the effort to stay upright. No wonder my energy constantly dragged. Seeing Hugh's face chased away the minute of sadness. I'd forgotten my father and his close buddy often wore the same cologne. He hadn't used it when he visited last week.

He situated his wife, Maggie, on a stool, took her jacket and purse, and hung them on the undermount hooks. Then he settled on his own stool. Watching how Hugh still courted Mrs. Reynolds, after nearly fifty years married, gave me hope *even if my shot had failed*. Maybe my kids could break the cycle with their own happy endings. I wondered if my parents ever even tried.

"Look at you two honoring me with your presence this morning." I leaned across the counter and hugged them. "What can I get you?"

Maggie coughed, the remnants of the pneumonia hanging on. Hugh spoke for them. "Our usuals, please. We've missed breakfasts here."

"Let's cross our fingers the cruise will snap Bobby out of her funk."

"Unless they're doing lobotomies aboard the ship, I wouldn't hold my breath, honey," Maggie said. Hugh corrected his wife's criticism with a touch to her arm, but with a smile, I let him know it was fine. I didn't believe my words either. I carefully moved through the service area, filling their orders while Rachel worked the drive-through. She'd bailed me out when a virus traveled through our skeleton crew.

Hugh took a sip of his latte before stretching his neck to look over the counter. "You're limping, Katie. What happened?"

"And here I thought I'd perfected the air cast waddle." I leaned on the counter for a beat, giving my foot a rest. "It's sprained." I relayed the crazy story of tripping over Macushla's leash on the greenway and my mortification over Thomas having to carry me home. Thankfully, they stayed quiet about the Thomas part. No one else had. Hell, Deana had us practically married off already. Thomas had stopped in one other morning last week, wearing a similar suit and fedora as he wore when we met. Dee had remembered the description and immediately hit it off with him. She'd given her approval, *as if there were anything to approve.*

My real problem consisted of how often I'd thought about him carrying me. It felt nice to be in his arms for our long walk home, despite the humiliation. His smell and the squeeze of his arms came back to me at random times, shaking me.

"Shouldn't you be off of it?" Maggie tsked.

"I've been resting it, but duty called. We're short-staffed at the moment."

Hugh's eyes filled with a pang of unnecessary guilt. "I'm leaning too heavily on you too. I'm sorry."

I patted his hand. It wasn't all that bad. Most of my duties included covering deliveries, letting Hugh know what products to restock, and counter sales when I wasn't at the café. Okay, maybe I was working too much. "It's temporary. Everything will be fine." Eventually.

Maggie leaned in. "I'll work the floor today. Liz is scheduled for the afternoon, so you can rest."

I gave Maggie a kiss to the cheek. To be honest, guilt ate me up too. The business and camaraderie my father and Hugh had built up had virtually disappeared over the summer. "It's good to see you're feeling better."

Right then, Jake Quick entered the café and greeted us. He'd been with me since leaving the military three years prior, so he knew the extended family. Becoming my night manager strengthened his position as an honorary McKenna. "There's one of my brilliant fixes now."

The Reynoldses pivoted between Jake and me, confused.

"You're looking at the Perked Cup's new night manager."

Hugh shook Jake's hand. "Congratulations, young man. Guess you finally have that degree?"

"Thanks, sir. Two classes this semester and one next, then I'll be in the clear." We chatted a bit more before Jake headed into the back to do paperwork.

Hugh looked at his watch. "You said night manager. It's still morning, Katie."

"Yeah, well, thanks to my ankle situation and Deana being out today, he's here early. Jake and Dee are in charge of our hiring search."

They both finished their breakfasts while I helped another customer.

"I do have a specific to ask," Hugh said as I worked near them. "I don't mean to pile on—"

"Not at all." I cut in. We both needed to stop tripping over our guilt. "Ask away. You know the smoke shop is important to me too."

He blushed and said, "Well, I'd like to run the gift-card poker games again. Dylan is pulling together a group one Saturday a month. But what would you think about a seniors' game again? If I organized it, would you mind hosting? It could bring the regulars back in, you know?"

I couldn't keep a huge grin from spreading across my face. Hugh's idea suggested he was back and crawling out of his funk. Maybe I could do it too. "I'd love to. It's a wonderful plan."

Hugh added, "A couple of people have shown an interest in working the counter too." He winked at me. "You should be off the hook with the other duties soon."

Music to my ears. Checking another box off my to-do list almost made my ankle stop throbbing. Most of the ducks still wandered in the wild, but a few were lining back up.

I said goodbye to the Reynoldses right before Big John

Graham surprised me with his appearance. We knew each other from the local Chamber of Commerce meetings, but our worlds didn't overlap anywhere else. Aside from the aggressive, workaholic personality he showed everyone, I'd often wondered if I'd offended him somehow. I couldn't figure out where the offensive mistake happened though. The café provided coffee for the meetings, even when I couldn't attend. But he'd always kept a national competitor's to-go cup glued to his hand. I wondered if Young Jonn had told his father about our encounter.

"Well, hello, Mr. Graham. This is a surprise."

"Call me Big Jonn, Katie." He perused every inch of the dining room as he glided to the ordering area.

"Katie?" My father's friends were the only people to still use the name, and it didn't settle right in my ears. Perhaps the name itself didn't fit anymore.

"Don't the men in your life call you Katie?"

The men in my life? Thomas's face flashed before me, throwing me off. Big Jonn threw me a cocky flash of teeth that might have been a grin. It reminded me of the playful yet immature way Liam tended to use his smile to get his way, common for a teenaged boy. But for a middle-aged man?

I was still unpacking the odd comment when Big Jonn waved his hand. "No matter, Mrs. McKenna." This time he drew my surname out like it was heavy in his mouth, as if I were claimed property. But he'd always come across as an old-school "man's man." In Chamber meetings, he reminded me of some sports agents I'd met in my former life. I chalked up the bravado to a misguided sense of the importance of appearances.

"Gimme one of y'all's coffees with cream. I thought I should take a few minutes out of my day and check on you."

"Really? Oh, okay." My neck suddenly heated. I took a scrunchie out of my apron pocket and pulled my curls back. Then I washed my hands and made Big Jonn's order. I passed the mug over.

"I haven't seen you at the Chamber meetings since earlier this year. Then I heard about the attempted break-in and vandalism. Is everything okay, Mrs. McKenna?" His tone gentled with a concern I had never experienced from Big Jonn. Then again, we'd only ever spoken professionally.

"It's Kick, please. Yes, there were some setbacks this summer, but I plan to be back soon. As for the other, the town has nothing to worry about. The store's security is being upgraded."

"Kick... cute." He smiled in a teeth-flashing way. Women in the area tended to throw themselves at Big Jonn's muscles. And money. Active in the way he led his family's third-generation construction firm, he had plenty of both. *He went through women the way a pub patron went through free peanuts.* It made any appeal disappear from where I stood.

He pressed his hands together. "Let me get to the point. I heard about the bag of goodies found in your bathroom. From one entrepreneur and single parent to another: Do y'all need help?" He lowered his voice to a whisper. "If y'all're selling drugs to make ends meet—"

I raised my hands in defense. "Hang on, the police know the stash wasn't mine. Why would I call them if the cannabis belonged to me? And why would I leave it in a bathroom?"

He turned to look around, then met my gaze again. "This place is adorable. Even if I didn't do y'all's interior, you made the best of it."

"Um—" Is this the root of my transgression in his eyes?

"Anyway, would a loan work for you? I'd like to help quell the rumors." He tapped the counter. "Your little café has become important around here."

Rumors? My brows rose. This was quite the jump. "I'm fine financially, thank you. We think it was a nitwit kid who thought they could hide the bag and pick it up later. Probably after school. On the other hand, what rumors have you heard?"

He set his cup down. "People are concerned about you being a single mother and all."

"I'm not the only one in Oakville, let alone the Triangle. Or the world."

"It doesn't look good, Mrs. McKenna. They think you're selling drugs to kids out the back door and said your manager actually found them in your office to cover for you. They're calling you…" He whispered again, "Immoral. Like the graffiti said."

"Immoral?" I squeaked. Was he serious? Cyndi loved to call me a nun. "The café's a safe place for kids after school. I'd bounce anyone caught selling drugs here."

Big Jonn touched my hand. Let it rest on top of mine as if it had been invited. The gesture reminded me of his son with my daughter, only not as aggressive. "Good to hear. *I'm* not doing any accusing, mind. These are just things people say. Terrible things… You're sure no one on staff's selling it?"

I laughed. "You're kidding, right? The police interviewed each employee. No one fussed over it. They know I'd fire them in a hot minute too."

He took a pull from his coffee and shrugged. "Of course they do."

"Who are these 'talking people,' Big Jonn?" I wanted to confront them head-on.

"No one to worry about, Mrs. McKenna. Just some posts on the city's Facebook page. I thought y'all should know." He stretched his hands toward me, then back. "Like I said, your little business is important." Big Jonn sheepishly tilted his head and gave a light chuckle. "I was prepared to buy you out and keep you on as manager, if it would help. Figured you could help me in return."

JaysusMaryandJoseph, I couldn't believe my ears. "Thank you for this enlightening information, Mr. Graham. I assure you, the café's fine. I also spoke with Detective Ross over the weekend. The OPD isn't worried about the incident, and neither am I."

There was something small he could do for me though. Just because we didn't click, it didn't mean we couldn't be friendly. I made a point to never turn away a potential business ally. I added, "If you want to pass that information back to where it came from, I'd happily give you free coffee."

"Big Jonn," he insisted. He took another pull from the mug, set it down, and walked away, leaving half the drink. "I'll see what I can do. If anything else comes up, give me a jingle." He chuckled from his belly this time. "My number's on the billboard on the corner."

"GOT A MINUTE, MAMA?" RACHEL ASKED. SHE CLEARED HER throat several times as she made her way into my office. Instead of casually dropping into the club chair as I expected, she remained standing, her gaze settling on the clerestory window above my printer stand. Storm clouds were usually the only things visible from her angle, and it was a clear day.

I removed the reading glasses I wore to see Rachel better and discovered she stayed blurry. Scheduling an eye appointment went to the top of my to-do list. I gestured to the chair. "There's always time for you, sweetie. Whatever it is, spill."

"It's probably nothing." A nervous giggle escaped her lips, giving my heart a small stab. Why the hell was my girl nervous around me?

I inhaled the essential oils diffusing in the corner closest to me—lavender and sandalwood with a drop of rose. I'd chosen it to relax so I could focus on paperwork instead of my ankle. I flipped the ice pack on my propped-up ankle, put a smile on my face, and caught her expression in the light. Something was off. "Are you sleeping okay, Snow? You look pale. Are you eating?"

Rachel sank into the chair with dramatic flair. "My stomach's been bothering me, but it's just school. Everywhere I turn, there's a fork in the road, and I don't want to screw it up by taking the wrong one."

I thought about Six Forks Road—a major road in Raleigh, the city we edged—and its initial origin as a six-way crossroads. The intersection, and the original community, were long absorbed by the capital city. Problems had a way of doing the same.

"Is this really about school or your personal life?"

"Yes?" Rachel said, biting her lip, her lower lids shiny. "I think I should drop my education major. Or maybe come back to it later."

Crud. I wondered if her double theater-education major would pull her in two directions. I wasn't thrilled when Rachel showed signs of bite marks from the acting bug. In her years at Pierce University, she'd been molding herself into the proverbial triple threat while I'd secretly hoped she'd work with me. But I'd never press the issue. Truth be told, the girl began singing, dancing, and acting before she formed proper sentences.

"Why?"

"The senior production is intense. The more time I put into it, the more I want it to be spectacular. It's become overwhelming." She shifted in her seat. "You think the teaching thing can wait?" Rachel's eyes brightened as she moved to the edge of the chair, explaining the details of the original musical, the agents and producers who planned to attend the performance.

She slumped back down. "What if I regret going for it?"

I leaned on my desk, resting my chin on my folded fingers. "Regrets come more from doing nothing. If you're pulled in this direction, there's no reason you shouldn't test the waters. Besides, teaching shouldn't be a consolation."

I remembered the years she used to line up her dolls and stuffed critters to play teacher. It reminded us of the Disney princess she favored, with her dark hair, sapphire eyes, and ruby lips, surrounded by pretend animals and Little People. She didn't simply look like *Snow White*; she acted like her too. It became her identity.

"You know, Snow, forks aren't necessarily about right and wrong. They can be a choice between two amazing things."

Her lips twisted with confusion. "I don't understand."

"You're loaded with so much talent you can *choose* what you want to do. Relax and see where it goes. When the road turns, follow it with open curiosity. You don't have to have all the answers right now. Hell, look at how I've had to reinvent myself."

"What if I'm afraid?" She dipped her chin, and a tear fell. My drama princess.

"Life is scary, sweet girl. Living is facing your fears, and the easy path often has a way of ending up the most painful."

A dark cloud seemed to park over her head as her shoulders pulled farther down. My girl might've loved her drama, but I didn't take to this shift at all. "You mentioned multiple forks. Is something else going on?"

Rachel chewed on her lip as her eyes traveled to the window again. Had all this been the warmup to the actual issue? She hemmed and hawed, then spilled. "This is really, *really* hard. But I don't know who else will give me an honest answer. You know? It's not like I can ask the boys or anything."

"What would you ask your brothers?" Where was she going with—

"*IsAnOrgasmTheSameWithSomeoneElseAsItIsWithYourself? OrIsItSupposedToBeDifferent?*" She blurted out the words in her rush to get them said.

JaysusMaryandJoseph. I jumped in my seat and banged my ankle on the side of my desk. "Fecking hell!" The pain made my eyes roll.

"I'm so sorry. I'm so sorry," Rachel chanted as I tried my best to wave her off. Talk about forks in the road. We'd driven off into a ditch. We had to get back on track, or I feared she'd never ask me anything of consequence again.

Buck the hell up and give your best grown-up advice.

Deep down, I floated, knowing she'd trusted me enough to ask me something so sensitive and not rely on her equally inexperienced besties for answers. Or, *God forbid,* her older brother.

"It's fine, sweetheart. I should've kept the brace on." To gain a moment, I searched my desk for topical pain cream and rubbed it in before setting the ice pack back on my black-and-purple cankle.

With the time it took to resettle, I time-traveled to Rachel and me in our minivan, listening to TLC. "Waz a sckwub, Mama?" Her squeaky voice imprinted in my memory as I'd simplified the story of "No Scrubs," for her preschool mind. Had I known then what I knew presently, I would have told her a scrub was a boy named Cody Dalton, and she should abide by the wisdom in the lyrics.

"Tell me this: has Cody ever learned to drive your Accord?"

Rachel swung her foot as she answered. "No. But mostly we Netflix and chill when we get time together."

I shook my head. "The boy refuses to learn a manual transmission, and it's a *surprise* he can't find his way around what makes you hum?"

"*Mom,*" she scolded.

I raised my hands. "Seriously, the boy's about as useful as a football bat." Cody wasn't a trust fund baby per se, but he lived like one. From where I sat, their relationship had run its course a while ago.

"Then being with him should be better than with my b-o-b?"

Are you kidding me? "Absolutely. And it doesn't do him any favors to fake it."

"Please stop." Rachel mumbled, "Maybe this was a mistake." She stared at the floor a beat, then rolled her wrist. "So you're saying I need to teach him how to...?"

"First ask him if he wants to learn." The boy was *terminally* lazy.

"True." Her defeated tone broke my heart. I wanted better for her but didn't like how the journey to better would have to begin with the pain of a breakup.

I wanted to give her hope, but I also knew Rachel asked more than a mechanical question. This wasn't about navigating parts. It was a talk about navigating the heart—a heart at a crossroads.

I shifted my foot off its perch under my desk and strapped on the air cast. "I hear kids talk about their sex lives in the café. Don't look so shocked. They're loud little buggers." I leaned toward her, wiggling my fingers to get Rachel to grab them. "Anyway, it's like they're trying to understand it by wandering around a dark forest with a flashlight. They find a piece—say an orgasm—and declare 'I found sex.' But it's not the *whole*. Then they shine it somewhere else and see hookups and say 'Oh, here it is.' But it's only horizontal exercise. So they still aren't putting it all together."

I squeezed her hand. "Ask yourself if you've found pieces of it or all of it. The bits satisfy some people, but I think you're saying you want more. Understand?"

"I'm not sure. How will I know I've found what I want?" Her brilliant blue eyes met mine with hope.

"You'll know in the connection. When the pieces are in place, it feels like the best worship service and Christmas morning rolled into one. Not because of the how, the what, or the why, but because of the *who*."

Rachel's nod told me she'd heard. I hoped it helped, not only with her lazy boyfriend but with the choices she faced. Like any mother, I wanted her to be fearless.

I tapped her hand. "One more thing, though I'll probably regret this more than anyone else. Please, Snow, break your give-a-shit meter. Smash it to pieces right now."

"My what?" She giggled, looking at me like a marble had sprung loose.

"Most women take until they're thirty to trust themselves;

until they're forty to stop giving a shit about what other people think; and until they're fifty to realize no one was thinking about them in the first place. I believe it's why so many ladies in their sixties and on are carefree. They live by the meme 'Dance as if no one's watching,' because they figured out everyone's so busy navel-gazing that no one ever was watching. Save yourself the self-induced pain and criticism."

Rachel bit her lip, glanced up, and smiled, contemplating what I said. "What if I end up pissing you off?"

I wrinkled my nose and grinned. "If it comes to it, I'll do my best to eat my words. Promise." My heart lightened at her trust and the new turn our relationship had taken. The continuous background aching of my ankle lessened. I chalked it up to endorphins coming from helping my daughter. I treasured the revelation that my girl was becoming something I'd never had growing up. Rachel was my friend.

"And here I thought you'd tell me to get a better rabbit or dump Cody's ass." She laughed.

"Oops. Too much?" I cringed, then chuckled. "You could do those too."

The warmth returned to her eyes. "No, Mama. But it's time to get back out front. As soon as my shift finishes, I'll schedule time with my adviser. *And* I'll talk to Cody."

"There's my brave girl."

Rachel's gentle waves bounced in her ponytail as she turned the corner to the hallway and stopped short. "Oh hi, Professor," I heard her say. Knowing there was only one professor who visited the café lately, I dropped my head into my hands.

9

IT'S MY LIFE

KICK

*T*homas cleared his throat. He stepped into my doorway with his head down and hands in the pockets of his black, pleated slacks. A black dress shirt and silver tie topped them off. The missing suit coat allowed for rolled-up shirt-sleeves. Why did my eyes linger on his forearms?

He lifted a hand, pivoted, and pointed his thumb over his shoulder. From this angle, his ass nearly melted my eyes. The material fell over said backside like a waterfall flowing gently down a mountain, as if the field of flax that grew this linen had been planted especially for him.

Perhaps I was looking for distraction from my embarrassment.

"I could head back out if you're busy," he said.

"How much did you hear?" I scrunched up my nose. Thomas came across as old-fashioned to me. Maybe it was the suits, but this might be the moment he'd had enough of me.

A slow grin spread across his face as he crossed his arms, then his ankles, and leaned against the doorjamb. "I should schedule you as a guest lecturer for my class while I'm gone next month. It is Biology after all." He took a step toward my desk. "May I?"

Flustered, I straightened my spine, ready to defend myself, unsure how to read him. "Be my guest."

He took the club chair Rachel had used. He lifted his gaze to meet mine with eyes as bright as his tie and smirked. "A football bat?"

My hands flew to my hair and ended up tucking back stray pieces. "Oh Jaysus. The thing is... see, their relationship should've ended already, but I don't want to interfere." I stared at him for a beat. "Why didn't you say something?"

"Y'all caught me off guard, and I froze. It was... an unusual conversation for me."

I'll bet. "My kids and I are unconventional on purpose. I knew a long time ago I didn't want my daughter relying on a boy to teach her what her body liked. So when she started menstruating, I..." My hand flew to my mouth. In my embarrassment, I almost overshared about Rachel. I felt my skin heat and almost cried.

"What's wrong?" Thomas asked, suddenly rising out of his chair.

I shook my head and waved for him to sit back down. "I almost told you something private between my daughter and me." I kept shaking my head, willing it to go away.

Thomas leaned in. "Hey, you didn't though."

"It's something Bobby would do, has done many times. I can't believe I defaulted to it."

"But you checked yourself. It says a lot in my book. I'm not judging. Not this or your advice… shit… I stopped in for coffee and wondered how your ankle is healing."

I leaned my head on my hands, the tension flowing out my fingertips. "It's what you'd expect."

"Do you need pain meds?"

I woke my phone, checking the time. "In an hour." I reached under my desk and set the bag of melted ice on my desk. "This didn't last long."

"How about a refill?"

"No, I'll…" I didn't know why Thomas kept wanting to do things for me. He'd even checked in with texts over the weekend. Somewhere in the back of my brain, a voice reminded me that friends helped each other. If Cyndi had asked, I wouldn't second-guess her. I handed him the bag. "Thanks, and thank you for thinking of me."

"Does it feel weird?" He smiled and stood.

He did *not* throw our talk about asking for help in my face. "Why did you?"

Thomas shrugged. "I honestly don't know. Most people don't get my attention. But you… Your smile is a treasure. I hated to see pain take it away."

"Are you telling me to smile more?" I asked, tiny bristles shivering down my neck. "Because I'll have you know, I might prefer my men friends to be pretty and silent."

He shook his head and laughed, turning for the door. "Wouldn't dream of it, Kick." His hand tapped the jam twice before he added, "A man who demands a smile from a woman doesn't know what makes a woman smile in the first place."

"And you do?"

"No, Kick. *You* do. It's just fun to be around to see the light shine when it happens."

I wiped the perspiration off the back of my neck when he left me alone. Did the man have any idea how he kept blowing me away with the simplest words or gestures? And I'd nearly bitched him out again. I hated the boxes my family threw me into and never let me escape. For all intents and purposes, I'd almost done the same thing to Thomas.

"CALLED BANGER YET?" THOMAS ASKED, SITTING ACROSS FROM ME in the dining room. When my stomach grumbled, I walked out front with him and grabbed lunch.

I swallowed my bite of salad and answered, "Your security guy? It's on the to-do list."

"Do y'all want me to arrange it? This upgrade should happen now; don't let your ankle put it off."

"Oh my God!" Rachel cried out from across the room.

We turned toward her, along with everyone else. Several sets of customers filled the dining area, including Mr. MILF, Garrett. He sat with a group of friends and acknowledged me with an ambivalent chin tip. I chalked it up as a victory for me and growth for him.

I waved Rachel over since I shouldn't go to her. She showed us her phone, her forehead quivering with hurt and fury. A picture of a naked woman in a shower, her leg up on the tub edge, stared at us. The caption said it was Rachel and called her Oakville's favorite slut.

I brushed a small tear off her cheek. "This isn't you."

"I know. But everyone thinks it is. Look at the comments. It's going viral."

My stomach flipped as I read the misogynistic filth written about my daughter. As a general rule, in dance classes since she could walk, Rachel defaulted to proper spine and shoulder alignment. It broke my heart to see her curl into herself next to me.

At a loss, I turned to Thomas. "Is there anything I can do about this? Should I call the police again?"

"I could call Banger," he offered.

"Can he handle something like this?"

He leaned in, eyes narrowed. "Definitely."

My phone pinged with a text from Dylan. When I swiped it, my stomach turned again. "What the hell is going on?" I showed the phone to Rachel and Thomas. "Someone threw a brick through the window at Mick & Hugh's." I clicked on the photo Dylan took of the attached message: WE WON'T STAND FOR IMMORALITY IN OAKVILLE.

The shopping center maintenance company had the minimum requirement for surveillance. I doubted there would be decent footage of the person who threw the brick. I guessed this was related to the earlier vandalism and the horrible gossip Big Jonn had mentioned, but why did it turn on Hugh too? Did it have to do with my helping out somehow?

"Okay, Thomas. I'll call him after I speak to the police. Again." I hugged Rachel. "Don't worry about the photo, Snow." I pulled back to wipe her tears and catch her gaze. "Go about your semester on campus. You don't have to take any more shifts here. Deana, Jake, and I will handle the café, okay? Focus on classes, and I'll get this sorted."

"But what about the…" Her voice hitched, and mine followed suit. My hands itched to choke the monsters who so stirred the vitriol in the comments. Vandalizing my store was one thing. Someone had attacked one of my babies—"the things people said?"

"It's wrong and cruel, and those vile people pile on to make themselves feel superior, sweetheart. I'll find a way to fix it." I took her chin between my thumb and fingers. "Hold it up. You hear me?"

She gave me a tearful nod.

THOMAS CHECKED THE TIME ON HIS PHONE. "I HATE TO DITCH Y'ALL like this, but I have to get to the lab."

A police cruiser parked by the smoke shop as I was hobbling out the door. I waved a casual hand in front of my face. "It's all good, Thomas. Thanks for coming by." I pivoted toward Mick & Hugh's. "I'm sorry I can't walk again this week, but maybe next week?" Thomas's hand wrapped around my bicep, making me turn back.

"Kick?" He bent his knees slightly as an aggravated navy gaze met mine. It struck me how Thomas's eyes could change with the light from silver to navy. Or maybe it was his mood. "I didn't stop by to schedule a walk. I like your shop and the crew. Why don't you want my help?"

"Want your help? Can't you see what's going on here? I've got enough to balance without trying to meet the needs of your hero complex." I'd snapped, not only my words but my emotions. A shock ran down my arm from where he touched me.

"Hero complex? Come on…" Thomas drew in a long breath, his face shifting. Like a magic trick, the irritation I'd kindled died, and his eyes softened to tiny crinkles. "Talk to me."

I released the breath I'd been holding, but my chest hitched. My tears had long dried up, being replaced with this annoying, reflex. I chalked it up to having cried myself into a deficit eight years before.

"It's…" I tipped my head up to the sky, collecting the stampede of thoughts. "Someone told me about rumors going around that I'm selling drugs to kids. This cigar shop incident feels connected. I want to know who's doing it and make it stop. And now they're messing with Rachel?" I sighed, returning my gaze to Thomas. "I wish my dad were here, but I'm glad he's missing it too."

His grip on my arm loosened and became a friendly caress. I'd have paid for a hug at the moment, but we weren't those people. Yet his expression and the tenderness in those strokes, reaching around my shoulder and to my back, communicated we might be able to be better friends. Then again, upset women had a way of wringing out the emotions in the most locked up of men.

With a grave tone, he responded, "I'll call Banger from the road and see if he can come by in the next twenty-four hours. Text me after you're done with the police, all right?"

I nodded my head in agreement and appreciation. We said our goodbyes, Thomas moving to his car and me to the police cruiser across the parking lot.

HOURS LATER, MY DUCKS WERE BACK IN ORDER—THE POLICE report filed, the broken window boarded up, Rachel tucked safely away in her apartment. Her roommate, Isabella, had called their posse over for pizza and a cheer-up session. Liam was at band practice and planned to stay late to do homework. A fresh dose of pain meds worked their way through my system as I sat in the quiet of my living room. Too keyed up to watch the latest binge-able cable show, I sat in a corner of my leather sectional sofa and gave the meditation thing a try.

I was beat from the day and the pain, and Thomas, if I was honest. My thoughts short-circuited whenever they turned to him. An unwanted attraction mixed with guilt I didn't want to admit, let alone visit. I couldn't remember a man having flum-moxed me before. Thomas's quiet persistence drew me in, and it had to stop. I could deal with friendship at arm's length, but no more.

I stretched my legs out, placed my hands in my lap, closed my eyes, and focused on breathing.

Inhale, two, three, four. Hold two, three, four, five. Exhale, two, three, four.

I should order dandelion tea. Local honey too. Liam wanted frozen dinners, and I refused to buy those hot pockets...

After ten minutes, I'd mentally planned out the next three

days, had a list of groceries, and remembered it was time for Macushla's check-up.

Typical for me, whenever I quieted my mind, it took off like the latest SpaceX rocket.

Shit.

Perhaps I needed to give the app thing a try. If Deana swore by it, it had to be something. The app loaded, and I shifted my body into the directed seated position. So the problem was with my posture? Huh.

I followed the instructions for the twenty-minute session. It was calming while also invigorating. I felt fantastic. My ankle no longer throbbed, my chest opened with deep breaths, and the tightness in my spine eased.

The session ended with me thinking this could be a good thing. Dr. Chaddha, Deana, and Thomas were right. Meditation could be the key to turning my flare around, and I wouldn't have to do the IV treatments.

Having veins both small and deep, my body protested the treatments as much as it benefited from them. My last foray into my doctor's treatment room ended up with repeated blown veins and subsequent track marks scarring my hand. *Om*-ing my way back to health held a definite appeal. It was a hell of a lot cheaper too.

I became aware of a change in light while my eyes were closed and relaxed. I opened them to find a soft, barely blue glow surrounding my skin and stealing my breath. I leaped off the sofa, hoping to escape it, remembering to land on my good foot at the last minute.

"What the hell?" I shook my head, hoping my eyesight was playing a new trick on me. But the light, the glow—whatever—stayed with me. I limped around the living area, attempting to shake it off, yelling every swear word I knew.

It undulated an inch or two above my skin, the movement growing around my wrists, ankles, knees, chest, and lady bits, like it was swaying to a rhythm. The color in those areas shifted to a darker hue. I swore I heard a low hum and spun toward the shelves surrounding my fireplace, my eyes catching on the sound system, making sure everything was off.

Should I call an ambulance? Nope.

I'd probably end up having a psych evaluation. I crossed the space to the kitchen sink, letting a hard stream of cold water splash over my hands.

The icy chill shocked some sense into me, letting me know: (1) I was awake. A thought I might be lucid dreaming initially flitted through my mind; (2) If I calmed enough, the light died down; and (3) I needed to recheck the labels on *everything* I'd recently put in my body.

I'd had some oddball symptoms over the years, but this one rivaled the weirdest. Hell, it beat out my recurrent mystery-man dreams. I spent some time researching the side effects of my pain medicine and the CBD tincture I'd taken in the morning, though I was sure if a hallucination were a possibility, it would've happened right away, not twelve hours later.

At the end of it all, I logged onto my doctor's patient portal and scheduled the IV treatment. Meditation definitely was not my thing. Dr. Chaddha, Deana, and Thomas could all go jump in a lake. I only hoped my veins would hang in there this time. And that this glowing incident was a one-off.

10

THESE DREAMS

KICK

I awoke the next morning with a wet face and pressed my palms to my cheeks. The Dream Man had visited me again.

Some nights the visions were like nightmares, because I wanted him to leave me alone. Other times they left me hopeful, and I tried to sleep as long as I could, enjoying our time. This dream crushed my spirit. I couldn't shake how real he seemed, though I didn't know how to find him. It wasn't like someone could Google "hot, middle-aged, silver fox." Okay, you could, but it didn't help. Thankfully, the filters on my modem kept the creepy stuff away. Besides, I'd bet money the object of my dream time wasn't a porn star. My brain never worked that way.

Unsure how to solve this mystery, I rose and put one healing purple foot in front of a well pink one. Liam left early for school, allowing me time for a light workout. Focusing solely on bicep curls and floor work gave me enough mindfulness, thank you very much.

Thomas's friend, Banger, had scheduled a meeting for ten at the Perked Cup. Anticipating the expert's input, I pondered my daughter's safety. Her building had security cameras, but college kids often propped open exterior doors. While it would bring comfort to have a solid system at the café, the mother in me sweated most over the viral photo.

BANGER MCHENRY PULLED UP TO THE CAFÉ ON A HARLEY AT precisely ten o'clock. I heard the bike before I saw the man. He was shorter than Thomas yet as wide as my son, Dylan, a former linebacker.

His bright blond hair, cut military close, gave off a special-ops vibe. Warranted, I suppose, for the head of a security firm. Banger's nose carried the telltale jag of a previous break. The center of his blue irises were so pale they almost appeared white, but with a wide navy outline. I started when my gaze met his, grateful for the counter separating us, though I doubted it would deter a guy like him.

His eyes scanned the dining room, a grimace telling me he didn't approve. My first impression second-guessed Thomas's judgment.

"Kathleen McKenna?" He scowled.

I slowly slid my hand out to him in greeting. "Kick, please. You must be Banger?"

"Gotcha."

"Thanks for meeting me so quickly."

We moved to a table in the office where Banger produced a check sheet covering every detail of a business's security requirements. In as few words as possible, he grilled me on the current alarm system and walked through his ideas for an upgrade. With all the blood, sweat, and tears I'd put into the café, it was difficult to view my surroundings with the same skeptical eye. I became equal parts grateful, panicked, and resentful of the need to upgrade.

I tucked a curl behind my ear. "This looks like an overkill response to some pranks."

Banger didn't coddle or patronize me. He pulled the morning paper from his satchel, opened it to the Opinion Page, and laid it on the table. The headline stared at me, mocking: DRUG DEALER MASQUERADES AS INSPIRING ENTREPRENEUR.

I sank into my chair. "I know. I read it earlier." The rumors Jonn Graham warned me about had surfaced, the article mostly half-truths and innuendo.

"This isn't a prank, Kick." He jerked his thumb over his shoulder toward the front of the store. "Sales are down. Correct?"

I nodded my affirmation. Customer traffic had come to a stop. I hoped the pull of a caffeine addiction would override the smear campaign quickly.

"My company will help."

I took a deep breath and capitulated. "I guess you're right. Can you show me the camera placement again?" My hatred for being treated like a victim equal to how much I hated being treated like a perpetual patient, I decided to appreciate his straight talk.

After another twenty minutes of schematics, it was a relief to let him examine the café by himself. I gave up any ideas of inroads to a future friendship with the man. I finally empathized with those who gave me a hard time about resting bitch face. Banger possessed a resting asshole face. Or maybe it was a resting psycho face?

Though Thomas and I had moved past our initial prickliness

with each other, I could see where the two men found common ground. They both walked with airs of otherness, like they might not completely fit in with us regular folk.

An hour later, I jumped again when Banger cleared his throat. I'd been composing an ad for baristas. I cursed an annoyed, *shit* under my breath.

Banger strode over and placed his adjusted schematic on my desk. His suggestions made sense, even as he explained them via drawings and grunts. A sense of renewed security had already taken hold in my gut, though the changes were only on paper.

We sat for a quiet minute as I reviewed his plan once more, envisioning how the monitoring would work. Banger cleared his throat, interrupting my thoughts. "Your logo has a double-helix in it."

"Yes," I answered. "Not many people pay attention to it, but it was intentional."

"It's weird," he grunted.

"Thomas liked it." I wasn't sure why I was defensive. I found it interesting they both picked up on the design. I thought the lines representing the hydrogen bonds—as I remembered it—were subtle and doubled fine for steam.

Banger shrugged. "He *would* like it. No offense."

I considered explaining the concept but decided a quick "none taken" sufficed.

He shook his head as if shivering and said, "I still can't believe you've gone this long without decent security."

You'd think I'd done it as a personal affront. "We don't have anything worth stealing here. Most of the transactions are electronic. Hell the students even have credit cards these days. I don't want it to feel like a fishbowl, especially since the café is a refuge for more than me."

"Someone already tried to break in. You'll appreciate thorough coverage. If you'd had these cameras"—Banger pointed to spots on the schematic—"you'd know who left your surprise package in the bathroom."

True. "I-I just…" I'd been so tired the night of the graffiti, and honestly, the weed and mangled lock both felt like pranks. Why did anyone care?

Banger tapped on his tablet and laid it down, showing me a satellite picture of the shopping center. The image was clear enough to see Liam taking out the trash.

"Welcome to the fishbowl, Kick." His voice was eerily gentle, like he was teaching me a new law of the universe. In hindsight, he was. The dose of reality scared me more than a slanderous newspaper article. Banger continued, "My crew will make sure you're safe." His eyes narrowed and he added, "I Googled you. You used to live much… bigger."

Ah yes. Here we go. Too many people—men in particular—assumed I spent my money on designer labels and hair appointments because of how life *used* to be. "Which is why things purposefully changed when we came here." I took a breath to keep myself in check. "I've built my life *my way*, Banger. For good or bad."

I left my desk and stood by the clerestory window, watching clouds pass. I hated people making assumptions about me and money. "Between my medical bills, our family foundation, and other responsibilities, the discretionary account isn't what most might assume it to be. Given the complexities I can't control, I like to keep life as simple as possible."

"Family Foundation? *You're* the McKenna Family Foundation?"

"Yes. I… We are." A manager ran my nonprofit assisting autoimmune patients who couldn't afford the out-of-pocket costs of their treatment. I preferred to stay behind the scenes. Website photography even focused on staff and patients. In place of my time and energy, a sizable percentage of an inheritance and settlement I'd received went to keeping the foundation running, especially when fundraising efforts ran light.

He made a gruff "Umph" noise, then asked, "You set for the install tomorrow, same time?"

"Yup. I'll be here. I have a medical appointment in the afternoon though. My manager, Jake Quick, will be available then."

11

ANYTHING GOES

THOMAS

*S*tepping into the Perked Cup, Thomas knew Kick was at the helm before he saw her. A Prince song filled his ears. She used music to create atmosphere. If the eighties and nineties classics played, Kick and her crew buzzed behind the counter in a happy mood. Classical music meant calm, for the after-school study crowd.

He heard an edge in Kick's voice as she conversed with a customer. An annoyed sigh preceded her answer. The polite yet adamant "go away" vibe was clear to everyone in the shop, except the bozo pestering her.

"Looking like the yards gained record might break this year," Bozo said.

She handed him a to-go cup. Good, he'd leave soon. Hairs on the back of Thomas's neck prickled. Kick gave him a blank smile. "Records get broken, as they should. New players need something to shoot for."

"Won't you be sad?"

"Not at all."

Thomas swore Kick hadn't inhaled since he first glimpsed her.

"When are you finally gonna take me up on watching a game together? I'll buy the beer. Maybe we could catch the one tonight at Finnegan's Wake?"

As much as he acted like it, Bozo didn't know her. She couldn't drink beer. It wasn't gluten-free.

Kick sighed and shook her head. "No, sorry. I'm… swamped right now." She squeaked a fake laugh. "I even forgot about tonight's game. I'll read up on it tomorrow."

"Maybe the next one. Or we could—"

Thomas's hackles rose fully. The guy wouldn't take the hint. Thomas made his way around the line and behind the counter. He wouldn't have made it that far unnoticed under normal circumstances. This man had Kick off her game in more ways than one. Thomas slid an arm around her waist and dropped a kiss on her jaw, just below her ear. A buzzing sensation spread across his lips, a physical manifestation of a hum. Like being able to touch your favorite song.

Kick froze as her eyes shot wide open, but he couldn't tell if it affected her the same way.

"Good afternoon, darlin'." Ringlets fell into her face as Thomas grinned at her. The lavender-and-vanilla scent from when he'd carried her filled his nose again. He inhaled deeply. A third exotic fragrance mixed with the two today, making his heart race.

Given how he acted on impulse, Thomas expected Kick to either go along with the ruse or fly off the handle and wallop him. She shocked him when she stayed still as if someone had shocked her with ice water.

Bozo turned to Thomas. "Y'all are together?"

"Ah—" she began.

Thomas offered his right hand. "Thomas Harrison. Kick's significant other." Christ, he'd gone off the deep end, his desire to protect Kick growing. He simply offered an easy solution to make her problem go away. No harm, no foul. *He hoped.*

"Jim Porter." He turned back to Kick. "Why didn't you *say* you were taken?"

Kick did a double take between the men—at least she moved again. "It's not—"

"We're new." Thomas interrupted her, perhaps a little foul.

Her brows rose as her jaw gaped, but she didn't set anyone straight.

Jim dipped his chin and grinned like he was in on a secret. "Gotcha." He raised his cup and stepped away from the counter. "Thanks for the pick-me-up, honey. Let's hope the pass reception record stands, yeah?" Sketching a wave, he sauntered out the door.

Kick answered with a slow nod as a red flush spread up from her chest.

Thomas smiled wide. "You're welcome. Can I have a large Americano please? For here."

"*I'm* welcome?" Kick's cool demeanor finally melted as she leaned in and grumbled, "You *kissed* me, and"—she pointed to her chest—"I had it handled."

"It was an innocent greeting to the cheek." He heard a low growl from her throat. "Oh, come on. Everyone here knew that idiot was bothering you. Except for him. What was with the football talk anyway?"

She turned to the espresso machine, muttering, "Jim talks

smack to get attention. A harmless hazard of the job. So what if he pressed a little harder this time?" Thomas darted out from behind the serving area and sat on a barstool in time for Kick to hand him the finished mug. "You don't think you overreacted?"

He took a quick sip and vocalized his approval. "Do *you* think he'd have left if I hadn't stepped in? If nothing else, I expedited his exit."

"Argh." She spun on her heel, stopped, and turned back, defeat in her voice. "Anything else I can get you?"

Thomas leaned back and glanced at the display. "The chicken wrap."

"Chips?"

He pointed at plates in a rotating display. "What are those?"

"Gluten-free brownies. Everything in this case is gluten-free."

"Are they any good?"

"Better than regular."

"Can I have one instead of chips?"

She shared an exasperated laugh and shook her head. "Of course."

It sounded like bells ringing.

The music had switched to the Staple Singers, which he preferred to pop. She let a new employee finish the last customer and leaned onto her elbows in front of Thomas, her eyes narrowed.

"The thing is, why can't *my* no be sufficient? I understand it's bad business to piss off customers, but you walk in, snap your fingers, and Jim's in line." Kick rolled her eyes. "It bothered me as a young woman, but it's *beyond* frustrating now. I see now why some of my friends embrace the invisibility of menopause."

Thomas winced at her comment. An invisible Kick McKenna was an oxymoron. He imagined her well on in years, still commanding a room. "Men are taught to press on and keep their eye on the prize. That kind of shit. It's a poor answer, but it's the game, Kick. You have to know it too."

"Games change, people change. Hell, laws change. Women aren't property anymore. Why can't the other half of the population accept it?"

"Give it time."

"I'm afraid Starfleet uniforms will be the fashion when *the time* finally comes." Kick sighed, dipping below the counter to retrieve a sleeve of napkins. She filled three nearby dispensers.

Thomas took a few bites, enjoying the food almost as much as the company. For some odd reason, a fired-up Kick kept lighting something in him. He also heard what she had to say. Without looking up, he muttered, "I'm sorry, Kick. I shouldn't have butted in. My hackles went up when I sensed your discomfort."

Kick stayed near, wiping down the counters and checking the monitor every few seconds. "It's okay." She sighed. "Unfortunately, it's not illegal to be an asshole. I mean Jim... not you."

Thomas couldn't help his smirk.

They stayed silent for a beat as they went about their business until Thomas couldn't take it. Despite his tiredness, he wanted to talk to nonacademics, forget about the research for a bit.

"New glasses?" he asked.

Kick paused her wiping, blew at a curl. "Yeah. These are progressive lenses. Another reminder I'm getting old. Cyndi said I look like Lisa Loeb. If I can't live in the nineties anymore, at least I can look like I do."

"They're ho—"

She folded her arms and glared. "Don't you say it."

"Why?" The glasses gave Kick a sexy librarian vibe. She had to know she was hot.

"What's with the antics? Why aren't you surly?" Kick pressed.

"Is it a requirement?"

"I might prefer it." She twisted her lips, studying him. "I'm not sure what to do with cheerful, encouraging Thomas."

Ah yes, there was a reason he'd stopped in for a meal despite working all night and testing through lunch. A dose of Kick's spirit was like a shot of B12— Hell, it became the whole alphabet of vitamins. He wanted it more than the caffeine boost. The esprit de corps in the café had been lifting his moods whether or not she worked a shift. But it, too, was Kick's doing. She possessed a superpower for bringing people together.

He usually only found this lifting energy with his family or Banger. Lately his family had become a source of worry, while Banger had a darkness growing behind his eyes.

The man occasionally disappeared on secret, freelance missions, making use of his security skills. Thomas suspected his friend had become involved in something especially grim.

"Sorry to disappoint," he smirked and took a bite of the brownie. "What's wrong with being nice?"

"Too much like flirting." Kick took an awkward step back and scanned the new security monitors. "We don't do that, Thomas."

The morsel stuck in his throat. Was he flirting? Definitely. Would it be so bad though? Being here made his blood feel like it flowed right again. A deeper part of him, the quiet place holding his locked box, didn't want to admit that flirting with this woman meant more than it usually did.

Thomas gladly focused on Kick's obsession with the monitor Banger's team had installed. He figured her eyes were traveling to it for the same reason a tongue fusses with a sore tooth. They both could use another subject change too. "What's going on with the monitor?"

Kick's exhale of relief almost insulted Thomas's ego, but he ignored it.

"Jake's in the back, finishing up with a new hire he's taken on by himself."

"Oh?"

"It's a big deal for me… the delegation." She blew out a breath. "It feels like I'm giving my kids the keys to the car."

Thomas paused in midraise of his coffee cup and set it back down. "I bet y'all had a hard time there."

"I threw up the first time Dylan drove off by himself." Kick nodded ruefully.

Thomas barked a laugh, getting a few head turns from it. He didn't like the image in his mind, but it didn't surprise him either. "Jake's a smart guy. He won't hire a chump. I can tell he thinks the world of this place. Of you."

Kick laughed. Though Thomas hadn't meant to make a joke, he'd take it. "Thanks." Her brow furrowed as she watched someone walk by the corner windows. "And thanks for shaking off Jim earlier. Right or wrong, he'll give me a few months' peace now."

Thomas didn't like to think of that bozo loitering and picking up where he left off. He didn't like Kick being under surveillance either. He also buzzed with annoyance that *he* might not be enough to send the guy away for good. Where did that come from?

The significant-other comment was a joke, not wishful thinking. One friend helping another. Right? His normally noisy brain, constantly running new formulas in the background, went silent.

The person Kick had been watching entered the shop. Her creased brow slid into a neutral mask after a determined sigh. He recognized it from his own dealings with overprivileged students.

"Afternoon, Jonn, what can I get you today? A mochaccino?"

"Word around here is you're short-staffed."

"Oh. Nope. We're okay. Thank you."

Thomas's hackles awakened again. He was near certain that was a lie even if Jake hired whomever he had in the back.

The kid tapped the counter like an old-time salesman going for the close. "Dad said you could use someone from an influential family. I can be that person. Part-time's fine with me too."

"He said what?" Kick's eyes flashed in surprise. "I'm sorry, he's wrong. We're fine. Doesn't your dad have anything you can do?"

"I don't like his business."

"I understand. My kids aren't interested in mine either. They're their own persons."

Jonn brightened. "Yes. That's why I'm going to work with *you*. You get me, Mrs. Mack."

Kick laughed. "You might be right but not in the way you think. I'm sorry, son." She leaned into the counter. Right then Thomas recognized the kid as the one she had set to rights the first time he'd walked in. She continued, "Go to school. Find your calling, like my kids have. You won't do it here though. I'm sorry."

Jonn balled his fists as he pivoted on his foot and stalked toward the door.

"Anything I can get you to-go?" she called after him. "On the house."

"No!" His bellow caused some customers to look up from their laptops and a few to take out their earbuds.

Kick blew out a slow breath and rolled her shoulders as she moved back toward Thomas.

"Wow," he muttered.

"Kid doesn't understand the word *no*."

"Yep. You're wise to steer clear. You finished hiring?"

She scrunched her nose and dropped to her elbows, keeping her voice low. "I fibbed to get Jonn to back off. Do you know his father offered to buy me out the other day? Think he wanted it for Jonn?" She shrugged, wiping at an invisible spot.

Another man had pressed his will on Kick? Thomas caught a growl stirring in his chest and held it back. She seemed to have the situation handled. "You know this guy already?"

"Jonn's dad? We're professional acquaintances. He played it like he was being charitable. He's cuckoo if he thinks I'll sell though." A wide yawn made her jaw pop. She fanned her face with her hand. "Woo. Excuse me."

The internal battle over concern for her well-being and his commitment to minding his own business resumed. But what the hell, he'd already erred on the side of butting in. Why not finish it? "Aren't you supposed to lighten your workload?"

"Trust me, I am. I'll clock out in about thirty minutes, after the five-o'clock dance-off."

"Do I want to know what a dance-off is?" He winked at her. "Need a partner?"

Kick's blush and laugh made his day. "It's unnecessary. Stick around and see for yourself. The afternoon homework time ends at five. The kids pick the song and shake off their studying stiffness." She tapped her fingers on the solid wood countertop. "In fact, Liam and his friend Jacklyn signed up to lead tonight's. They should be here by now. If they don't show, I'll teach you the cha-cha slide."

"What makes you think I don't know it?"

"You do? Then you can help me lead it," she said with a wink. "I'll be glad to get home and relax, though I still have to put in some time with my laptop. I'm almost finished with a marketing plan to repair the damage done by that newspaper editorial."

"What're you doing?"

"So far... I have an interview scheduled with the same paper, more advertising for the open-mic nights, and two Halloween parties next month. Oh, and a coupon too."

Kick's phone buzzed. "Excuse me. I have to take this." She stepped against the back counter. "What's up, Uncle Hugh?"

Thankful for the break, Thomas reminded himself he had enough to worry about with his own family. He added Joe and Toni to his list of follow-up phone calls. Dammit, he'd stopped into the shop to take his mind off his problems, not to take on more. The hum from kissing Kick did more than buzz his skin. It clouded his judgment. Yet Kick had no problem maintaining their established boundaries.

"You're kidding? What a bummer." The disappointment in Kick's voice grabbed Thomas's attention. "No, I see why you want to play poker with a full house. Ha. I was looking forward to Friday though."

Pay no attention. It's not your problem.

She swept some curls behind her ear. "It's fine, Hugh. We'll make it happen when everyone's feeling better."

Dammit. She sucked him back in. Thomas snapped his fingers and shifted to catch Kick's eye. "How many players do you need?"

"Hang on, Hugh." She put the phone to her chest and whispered, "He's out three, but Hugh's only found one new player. Friday's kind of late notice."

"Count Banger and me in for sure. It'll be fun."

"But you haven't asked him."

Thomas waved his hand. "He'll come." He'd fuss, but Banger would do it. The guy enjoyed hanging around older men as much as Thomas did.

Kick's face lit up like a sunny morning after a tropical storm, making the involvement worth it. There was the missing smile that made him jump into action earlier. Thomas meant it when he'd said Kick's smile was a treasure.

She went back to her call. "I think I found your two players." Her giggle tickled his ears and warmed his chest. "No, not my boys. You remember Thomas Harrison from Liam's open mic?"

Kick went over her list of loose ends for the evening, then ended the call. Her tongue peeked over her top lip and stalled in her cheek as she wrote a new item on a piece of paper. Christ, he was losing it, and he'd probably like it.

"Yo, fam." Liam entered the Perked Cup with a girl Thomas guessed was the Jacklyn that Kick had mentioned.

"Jax and Liam! Where've you two been? I thought your group planned to work here on AP Psych vocab this afternoon."

"We did, just not here. One of the girls told us her parents banned her from the café. I've heard other kids say the same thing. Don't worry about it though. They're just assholes."

"Lee," Jacklyn scolded.

Kick scrunched her nose. "Crap. Sorry guys. I'm fixing it."

Thomas dug his nails into his hand. He would not get involved in this. Playing poker with Hugh and his pals was enough.

"*StillWantUsToPickASongForTonight?*" Liam asked his mother in the way teens did. When a student did it to him, Thomas wondered if it was a trick to mess with his mind.

"*DoYouHaveASongPickedOut?*" Kick returned, her words a similar blur.

"Wha?"

"Ha. Gotcha." She laughed at her tease while the kids stayed nonplussed. "What d'you pick?"

"Oh." Jacklyn perked up. "'Cake by the Ocean.' We made up a dance."

"Sure you did," Kick muttered. Her energy appeared to have spiked with the arrival of both kids. "On the stage?" Both kids nodded vigorously. "Uh, Jax, what about the lyrics? I mean, your parents don't like certain—"

"You won't tell them, right?"

Kick shook her head. "Only double-checking. I swear they have spies or superpowers."

"True," Liam answered, rolling his eyes.

Kick turned toward the back. "I'll cue it." She pivoted back to the kids. "Oh, can you two come up with a dance for old-school song on Monday?"

"Like Matchbox20 or something?" Jacklyn asked.

Kick sighed as if her feelings were hurt. "I was thinking Motown or, hell, even Prince. But sure. Why not?" Kick raised her hands as she walked away, muttering, "That's what I get for asking *teens* about old-school stuff."

Kick stood at the food case, her chin propped in her hand, a somber expression on her face as she watched the pair perform on the tiny stage.

"Y'all right?" Thomas asked after scooching over a few stools.

She sighed. "They grow so fast. Sometimes it just hits me that my days with him are limited."

A distant memory popped into his head of a raven-haired sprite coaxing a horse to lower her nose by dropping oats on the ground. The girl was tiny enough to run under the animal's belly. And the mare treated her like an adopted filly. It became a ritual. Mabel, the horse, ate the treat while the girl hugged her neck, threw her tiny leg over, and slid down to her withers when Mabel lifted her head. Thomas remembered the bittersweet pain of how quickly life changed and shared a knowing smile with Kick.

She stealthily wiped an eye. "Rachel and her friends started this five-o'clock business. She's staying away thanks to the viral photo nightmare. But I miss her."

"Maybe you should go see her."

"I'm supposed to be resting, not driving across Wake County."

"Just sounds like stress talking. How's the meditation going?"

Kick turned her head and growled.

Message received.

12

DREAM ON

KICK

*M*ick & Hugh's buzzed with a familiar party atmosphere on Friday evening. It helped to have my body showing signs of improvement. Hugh arrived with Butch and Elliott, two of the old regulars. Each man greeted me with a bear hug and a cheek smooch. I sensed Dad's spirit settling into a corner of the room, waiting to check in on us.

I floated around the lounge, taking unofficial drink orders—everyone brought something to share—while Hugh and Butch divided up poker chips. I sensed a soft brush on my shoulder and a barely there whiff of my father's cologne. Hugh was across the room, so the scent wasn't his. I smiled toward my father's favorite chair and whispered, "Thanks, Dad."

The world quieted in a way it hadn't for months. My chest loosened with the comfort of being surrounded by surrogate fathers. Thoughts flitted to my last talk with him. "I never made your Ma happy. Help her find her peace, Katie Girl." *I hope the cruise is what she needs, Dad. I'm trying.*

"Where are the newbies?" Hugh asked.

Before I could answer, the doorbell chimed, interrupting the Herb Alpert album playing over the speakers. Thomas and Banger walked in, each wearing a scowl.

"Two of the newbies are here," I answered, turning toward them. "Evening, fellas. Everything okay?"

Thomas bent to kiss my cheek and handed me a six-pack of a local India Pale Ale. My hand rose to my cheek to feel the delicious hum. Were we officially greeting like this now? Again, it took me by surprise, more by how much I liked it than any question of boundaries. I didn't know why the simple gesture bewildered me. My earlier guests had squeezed me like a roll of Charmin, and I thought nothing of it. Thomas's simple, respectful hello had me contemplating the vapors. Not over his body but because it was him. Moreover, he took me in like *I* was a sight for *his* sore eyes.

Thank the heavens he answered my question before I could talk myself into a freak-out.

"Someone's grumpy because he didn't win our sparring match." I caught the humor in his soft accent and grinned like a silly schoolgirl.

As a child of an immigrant in a city with few natural-borns, I'd grown up around differing lilts and had an ear for them. Until Thomas, I'd thought I'd become immune to the charms of a soft accent. It was time to get a grip and focus. The future of Mick & Hugh's depended on it.

"Umph. Said someone's *you*," Banger answered with a grunt while handing me a fifth of a rare highland Scotch. Thomas made a point of rolling his eyes. "Thanks for the invite, Kick."

"Did you almost smile, Mr. McHenry?"

He shrugged and reset his face to its normal grimace.

I looked back at Thomas. "Were you two boxing?"

"Sort of. We belong to an MMA studio in North Raleigh. The sour face over there claims I cheated. He's just mad he didn't think of the move first."

"True," Banger conceded, rubbing his midsection, followed by a round of laughs from the rest of the room.

Thomas pulled me to the side after the introductions. "Y'all right? Don't mean to pry, but it looks like you've been crying?"

"Seriously?" I couldn't think of any reason for it. I entered the office and peeked in the mirror on the wall. "Oh hell." I looked like the love child of a raccoon and a Kewpie doll.

"What happened?"

"I can't wear my glasses while I apply mascara, but I can't see without glasses. Something *might* have smudged when I put the frames back on." It was a mess. I removed my glasses and swiped a finger under my eyes, smearing it more. "Lovely."

"Here." Thomas pulled a tissue from the box on the desk and stepped toward me, his wrapped finger leading the way.

I leaned back as far as I could.

"I won't poke you," he said, his brows furled.

"It's hard to tell without glasses."

He dropped the Kleenex into my hand. My memories rewound the past half hour, embarrassed by how I must have looked. "I need a magnifying mirror. No one tells you this happens when you get old."

"You're not old, Kick," he said over my shoulder, watching me. "It's fine, really."

I fixed my eyes by dabbing while holding my glasses at angles to help me see. "I'm glad you did, Thomas. It's what friends do." I turned around and smiled. "Thank you."

He gave me an awkward smile back and opened his mouth to respond when the doorbell chimed again.

"Hold the thought please. Hugh's guest has arrived." My hopes for the night took a turn when I saw the man walking through the front door. It was Big Jonn Graham. Maybe he'd at least buy a box of cigars. Or a case.

The man shook Hugh's hand. "Y'all's place looks great even if you used a competitor. But I forgive y'all." He leaned in and laughed heartily. "This time."

Then Big Jonn greeted me with an unusually friendly bear hug. "You look lovely, Katie." I didn't want to slug him in front of the guests. I figured Hugh had his reasons for inviting the man.

THE MEN TOOK A BREAK AN HOUR INTO PLAY. I'D SLIPPED AWAY TO properly finish my face clean-up, figuring a minimal look beat a demented anime one. I also checked in on Jake at the café a few times. For the first time, I left someone else in charge of the fall teen party and mentally patted myself on the back.

I laughed when he said, "Not to complain, but we know you're monitoring the camera feeds."

"I've peeked," I admitted and waited for Jake to finish chuckling. He had me. Banger's Angel Security system allowed me to monitor the café from my phone. It was my favorite feature so far. "The cameras don't tell me what you're thinking, so I figured I'd check-in."

No surprise, Jake made a great host. My confidence in the decision to give him more responsibilities increased. My grand scheme might work after all—eventually.

The men stretched their legs, refilling their plates and plastic highball cups. Jackets hung from the backs of chairs. I made a note on my phone to shop for a proper coatrack when I had time.

It wouldn't be long until temperatures required heavier outerwear. My eyes traveled to Thomas's Mr. Rogers sweater. He had removed the fedora he wore coming in, and some hair fell onto his forehead.

Thomas and Banger shared an easy rapport with Hugh, Butch, and Elliott. Big Jonn did his best to command the room. My father had filled the role before, and Big Jonn slipped into the opening with acumen.

After Big Jonn's greeting, Thomas had played hot and cold for the next hour. As he made his way toward me at the makeshift bar, his brow lowered like Atlas's weight hung on his shoulders. Still, he made a handsome, albeit quirky, sight. He wore a short-sleeved, button-down, with black, silver, and cream vertical stripes. It looked like an homage to midcentury bowling shirts—high-end ones, but still.

"Another IPA?" I asked.

He handed me the empty. Our fingers brushed in the exchange. The same sensation passed through my hand that had thrummed my cheek when he kissed it. He didn't acknowledge the interaction, so I ignored it too. *Hell, it probably came from one of my latest medicines, while he felt nothing at all.* "I'll take two fingers of Defiant neat this time."

"Snacks?" I tipped my head toward the half dozen bowls of junk food at the other end of the table.

"Big Jonn's an old friend, I take it?" he blurted.

I poured his Defiant and whispered, "Not at all. I almost walloped him for the Katie comment."

He looked confused. "But the other men call you that."

"Dad's *friends* call me Katie. That's all. He's the guy I told you about who asked about buying me out."

"The spoiled kid's father? Of course." Thomas nodded his head, looking like he'd matched the names and faces.

"Right."

"And he's single?"

The statement surprised me, and I answered with a chuckle. "I guess so. Why?"

He lifted a shoulder as I resisted the urge to snark. There was no way Thomas would give off jealous vibes. I had to be reading him wrong, which frustrated me. I wanted to be friends with the relaxed and attentive Thomas, but that man was hit or miss.

"He keeps tracking you. He's interested, Kick."

"Absolutely not." I squeaked a quick laugh. "He's strictly an acquaintance."

Thomas took a bite of a pot-sticker-looking thing, still frowning.

I thought about Big Jonn turning his ego *and libido* on me and shook my head. "I guarantee I'm too much trouble for a guy like him."

"A lot of men seem interested, Kick." He tipped his head toward the table. "Even Hugh and his buddies."

"What? No, no. They're happy to be together again. It's my job to be hospitable and accommodating, but I'm only your humble server." I scanned my outfit from my dark jeans to my lightweight green tunic sweater. Fun, but absolutely nothing suggestive. "They think of me as a niece."

The return of Thomas's frown said he didn't buy it. Was he jealous? Then why did he act like he was trying to push me toward Big Jonn too? Why was I explaining myself?

Thank goodness the rest of the men came over to refill plates and resume play.

"You two look deep in conversation," Big Jonn said with a goofy smirk.

Before I could answer, Thomas's phone rang. His brow lowered more. He showed the phone to Banger, who also frowned. He turned to Hugh and asked, "I have to take this. May I?" He pointed to the office.

"Be my guest," Hugh said, sending me a questioning glance. I shrugged a "no clue" in return.

He hustled to the room, answering the call on the go. "*Allo, Grand-père. ... Oui. Un moment.*" Banger followed closely behind.

Big Jonn leaned in and whispered, "Grandfather?"

"Beats Godfather," I said, jokingly, worrying my tongue in my cheek. "This has happened before. I think he's helping him with a project." I hoped. The amount of secrecy around the man sometimes woke my stomach butterflies. I hadn't known Banger was in on it though.

"I saw the newspaper article," Big Jonn said, his hand moving to my bicep. "Are y'all okay? Sure you don't need a loan?"

What was with him trying to give me money? I stepped back, not sure why. Big Jonn was friendly and caring, but I wanted to be off his radar for some reason. Maybe it was the last two encounters with his son. "The article is a nuisance, but we're fine, thank you."

He leaned into the table and lowered his voice. "Isn't business down?"

I supposed it was an obvious conclusion to bad publicity. "It's temporary." As long as the medical bills behaved.

"Good, good." Big Jonn raised his glass in my direction. "Like I said before, we entrepreneurs look out for each other."

Big Jonn was a third-generation contractor. I didn't think of him as an entrepreneur, but I wasn't going to call him out on Hugh's turf. I gave him a half grin for an answer and reached for a seltzer water for myself.

"So." Big Jonn bent his head toward the office. "I didn't know y'all were dating," he said in a soft voice.

Was Thomas right? Something was in the night air. I clarified. "We're friends."

Big Jonn slowly nodded as he stared toward the office. "Good. Good." His attention turned back to me. "You've been alone, how long now? Plus Leo's leaving soon, isn't he?"

"It's Liam, and yes, he's a senior."

"I can see how attention from a young guy like him might be flattering, but I'd be wary if I were y'all."

My nose scrunched as I tried to figure out why Big Jonn cared. "There's no need to worry. I'm a big girl, and I'll be fine there too."

"Maybe you're working too hard." He swayed his head lightly. "When's the last time y'all… had a little fun for yourself?"

"No offense, Big Jonn, but I don't see where it's your business. I'll consider dating when I'm ready. Frankly, life's swamped right now."

"You should tell the professor over there, because he won't take his eyes off you. But if you're not into him and want some company sometime, give me a call."

I knew about the way this man ran through women. We might have the love of our small town in common, but that was it. I put a fake smile on my face to psyche myself up for turning yet another Graham down, but Hugh saved me.

He touched both our shoulders. "Are we playing or gossiping? I want my chips back from that hustler in the office."

Banger and Thomas returned to the lounge as if on cue.

"Whining about losing, ye ole codger?" Banger asked, a surprisingly warm grin on his face.

"Sit down and deal, ya thief," Hugh called back.

I let out a big sigh, grateful to be out of the hot seat, and quietly laughed at the idea of jumping into the dating scene. I wandered into the office for some peace and to turn up the air filtration in the lounge. It had been a while since it had seen so many lit cigars at the same time.

I sat at the desk, counting the days until my doctor-imposed prohibition would end. I wanted to slam back two fingers of that Defiant like no one's business. The men weren't *trashed* per se, but the volume had grown loud enough to hear through the closed door, and it focused on Thomas. Elliot and Hugh were at the heart of it, but everyone joined in the rib over his wardrobe choices and subsequent nicknames. It compelled me to head back out there to be an ally.

"...wore one just like it in '63."

"...should have an old bowling team logo on the back."

I strolled in with a tray of water bottles and began handing them out. "For the love of Pete, gentlemen, stop the yapping and play. Shouldn't someone have won by now?" I set a bottle near Thomas's place.

"Got somewhere to be, Katie?"

"No, Hugh, but you're wearing me out and an excellent host never falls asleep on her guests."

"Big plans for tomorrow?" he asked.

"Some quick shopping and working from home." The first thing on the list was a magnifying mirror. "But I have strict orders regarding my sleep schedule." While I wasn't lying—I thought they'd have finished already—my goal was to take the heat off my friend. Only Hugh didn't take the bait.

He pointed to Thomas. "You should bring this one shopping with you. He could use a woman's eye."

"Quit picking on him, Uncle Hugh." I placed a bottle down by Butch. "A man has a little retro style, and you bunch go nuts."

"Retro?" Thomas asked, an eyebrow lifted in confusion.

"Nothing wrong with bringing him into the twenty-first century."

"Do I really need a new wardrobe?"

Oh crap, I had to backpedal quickly. I wasn't a mall-goer. An entire day spent buying a new wardrobe was my idea of time spent in purgatory.

"Liam says Thomas's stuff is—and I quote—vibin', fam. He says the thrift store look is in. That part's not a quote. He'd said something about it being spicy though."

"Thrift store look?" Thomas pulled his shirt away from his chest and looked down. "Maybe I should get a few things."

Like a sucker at the animal shelter, my heart cracked. "As long as we don't spend all day at the mall, I'd be happy to help."

Banger dropped his cards with a gruff. "I'm out."

Big Jonn ran his hand through his hair. "I'm out too."

Thomas's spirit perked up while Hugh beamed like a proud father.

What the hell?

ALMOST LIKE BEING IN LOVE

KICK

*W*here the hell are the makeup mirrors? I wandered the aisles of Target for an hour with plans to meet Thomas at the inside coffee bar in fifteen minutes. I wanted to finish my shopping so he wouldn't suffer the torture of a typical Target list. The experience was scary enough for those of us who wrote them.

The place was a zoo, due to it being a Saturday morning. Happily, most of the items on my list were already in the cart. If I could only find—

"Can't believe y'all started without me."

"Jaysus, Thomas." No surprise, I jumped. I shot eye daggers his way while his sparked an amused silver. At least his mood had lifted from the night before. He didn't seem permanently damaged by the men's teasing either. The sight of him relieved my tension even if his methods could have put me in a cardiac care unit. "You're early."

"I am. You passed by, looking frazzled, albeit determined."

I scrunched my nose in frustration. "I can't find any high-powered makeup mirrors. You know, the kind that could reflect light into space?" I tapped the frame of my glasses. "To keep last night's fiasco from happening again."

"But you were beautiful once you took it off. You're lovely without makeup now."

Holy cow. Mr. Sweet was in the house, taking it to new heights.

"Thanks," I exhaled. "But even natural beauty is an illusion. A girl likes having the option to spruce up on occasion too. Turns out, a blurry mascara wand coming toward your pupil is as terrifying as a finger in a tissue."

A hint of a blush dotted his cheeks.

I raised my hands in frustration. "Anyway, they appear to be hiding."

We turned down the last aisle in the makeup area. "Ooh, there are some." I steered the cart toward one, with Thomas following. "Here's what I want." I bent to look in the first one. It reflected the normal side, so I flipped it over.

"Sonofabitch." I wheezed while jumping back. "What's the magnification of this thing... a thousand?" I turned my head to the side. I looked like an old hag, certain a tiny creature was mountain-climbing one of my pores.

"It thinks I'm Dorian Gray." I turned to Thomas, terrified. "Is my face really this bad?" I wasn't compliment fishing. This was an awakening. I'd caught a good glimpse of future Kick.

His eyes flashed with the universal male expression of *keep me out of this.* Smart man.

There was no helping it. Another check in the mirror and the unibrow shredded my last threads of dignity. "Why hasn't anyone told me my brows are a hot mess?" I squeaked. This mirror purchase was so overdue.

Thomas reached over and flipped the thing back. "Here. See? Gorgeous."

"On this side," I argued. I kept trying to calculate how long I'd walked around deluding myself that I looked okay. "I don't want any delusions when reality is a flip away. You can't fix what you can't see." I rotated the mirror back and winced. *Was that sun damage?* But I wore hats.

A wiry hair grew out of my neck. *Hell.* I tried to discreetly pull it out.

He sighed and shooed me out of the way. He stepped over and put his face in the view. The pores on his nose looked like tire-eating potholes too. "See? Everyone's frightening up close."

"Ha!" I pointed at him. "You *do* think I'm scary." I knew he'd been placating me.

"Christ," Thomas muttered, "walked right into it." He righted himself and turned to me. "No. I'm saying you're as human as me. I'm a scientist. You can take my word for it." He smiled and whispered in my ear, "Accept your beauty as reality. Age doesn't matter."

"You don't understand," I countered. "I'm not afraid of reality. Not being able to trust my eyesight is what's scaring me. I might as well walk around with the hem of my skirt tucked into my underwear."

He raised an eyebrow in response.

"Bet no one would say anything either."

With no tolerance for patronizing, I had to know if he listened. I turned my head to catch Thomas's gaze. My nose brushed his jaw and caught his scent. Sandalwood and lavender thrilled my senses. I closed my eyes and touched his hand. Lost in the moment, my mind checked out, leaving my foolish heart in charge.

I opened my eyes to find his closed jaw flexed, breath shallow. He turned toward me as he inhaled, his eyes squeezing as if in pain. I cracked. For a beat, I could picture more. But was it fair? Or proper? I'd captured lightning in a bottle once. No one did it twice. Besides, it ended up leaving me with a world of regret.

"Kick," Thomas pleaded, my name a rasp. The sound snapped me out of our what-could-be bubble and back to the real world of a crowded store. No matter how much I tried to fight it, reality kept biting me in the ass.

"What're you playing at?" Thomas asked, practically gasping as he looked at me again.

I searched his eyes gone dark—lust mixed with annoyance, maybe?

"Right. Sorry. Shit. I didn't mean to." I shook my rattled head, my breath hitching. Fortunately, his attitude lightened, telling me he wasn't angry. Perhaps he was as confused as I was. I touched the handle of the cart, and the thing zapped my hand.

To make matters worse, the mirror wasn't for sale. The Target people had attached it to the shelf for sampling products.

"What the hell?" I looked around and caught the flash of a red shirt and khaki pants from the corner of my eye. We chased down the saleswoman, an older lady with a sweet face. I pointed at the mirrors. "I'm looking for one of those to purchase."

"Sure, honey," she soothed. My exasperation must have shown. "Follow me."

Thomas and I fell into step like obedient children, past four aisles and around a corner to the hair-care area. *Huh. Who knew?*

Five different models sat on the bottom of the case, one exactly like the evil portal of truth from the makeup department among them. I should've known it would be the most expensive, but it also had the highest magnification. I scooped it up. *Mirror, mirror in the box... please be nice.*

"What's left?" Thomas peeked over my shoulder at the list on my phone.

"Dog food and treats for Macushla. One section over, I think. Then I'm all yours."

"Wonderful." Thomas carried a basket with a card in it.

"Aw. Who's the card for? If you don't mind me being nosy."

He looked at the basket and lifted a corner of his mouth. The partial smile was sweet and sad. "Someone in my family is going through a hard time. Her husband has Alzheimer's."

So that's what the calls were about. My suspicions suddenly cleared, I declared, "Your *Grand-père*."

"What? No."

Another dead end with no explanation. Why was Thomas always so vague? Holy Hades, this nut was impossible to crack. I didn't know why it was so important to me, but the truth suddenly became essential. I gave it another shot. If it were for an aunt, he'd have told me his *uncle* was sick. "An older sister?"

Thomas's jaw flexed. He turned to me with a clear stare and said, "Yes."

"It must be hard to be away from her." Both my hands wrapped around his bicep, seeking some way to comfort. My brother was younger than me and back in Michigan. I couldn't imagine how hard it would be to support a sibling in her situation.

It also struck me how Professor Grumpy Pants had a heart of gold. Few siblings clung close to each other through their trials. People usually relied on parents for that.

"It's sweet of you to let her know you're thinking of her. I check in with my brother on the phone or with stupid texts, but we don't even do holiday cards anymore."

"Toni's not much into technology." A sad smile spread across his face. "I think she'd prefer corded phones with rotary dials."

"Then it's extrathoughtful on your part. I'm sure your act of kindness will brighten her day."

We kept our conversation easy as we shopped the men's department. I wasn't sure I wanted Thomas to change much about his look. Sure, the pleated, flowing pants might be out of style, but he rocked midcentury fashion. We'd planned to head down to the Village District after, where the real hunt would begin.

I figured we'd start small and casual. I parked him in front of a display of graphic T-shirts while I sorted through a clearance rack of button-downs.

"Why should I pay Coca-Cola to advertise for them?" His prickliness reared its head as he lifted a long-sleeved pullover.

"It's tribal identity," I called over my shoulder, shuffling through a few cute plaid shirts in a similar cut to the previous night's. I figured it would be easier to win him over if the general style were familiar.

"It's my go-to soda, but I don't feel compelled to yay team about it." The softly accented words were said by my ear, making me jump and sending a shirt flying. Thomas wrapped me against him with one hand and grabbed the rogue button-down with the other.

"Are you determined to resprain your ankle? You're like a spooked filly today."

The man had no clue. Our earlier interactions played on a loop in the background noise in my mind. He'd called me "gorgeous," "beautiful," and I think "lovely." What was with his thoughtfulness and attentiveness? I hadn't suffered through any horror show experiences with men, but I still knew it was a rare quality. Did he really notice as much as it seemed, or was I projecting? I'd watched the women I knew misread an interest plenty of times. I wanted no part of it.

"What are you doing?" I asked, breathless from the adrenaline rush.

"Keeping you from falling?"

"We're friends, right? We decided we'd be friends?"

"Believe so. Why?"

Surrounded by racks of clearance shirts, I let it out. "Friends don't call each other gorgeous or handsome, Thomas."

"They do if it's true." He smiled and added, "All right, I don't write sonnets about Banger's eyes, but he couldn't care less about his pores or eyebrows. If he asked me, I'd tell him straight."

Thomas set the shirt in the basket. "Nice call." He dropped his carryall in the cart and placed both hands on my shoulders. "I'm saying this as a friend because it should be said. I can already tell you're ingenious as hell, caring to a fault, stunning inside... and out... fun, and you need to ask for help a helluva lot more."

Whoa, the man was trying to break me wide open in the middle of the men's department.

For no good reason I could think of, I dropped the pretension and the guilt. I let him see what his words did to me. I peered into Thomas's eyes and found his longing, his loneliness, and his desire to help others in an attempt to fix the first two. I glimpsed at how a soul mate might look. It scared the ever-loving shit out of me.

"Did you mean the things you said to Rachel the other day? About the magic coming from the connection?"

"It's in the who," I recalled. "You know I did. Why?"

"I can't remember the last time I had... the magic." Thomas grabbed the front of the cart and headed toward the checkout. "This is enough for today."

He'd gotten to me, but I'd gotten to him too. I saw it. He'd accidentally let me in.

And thought it a mistake.

"T-Thomas?" I sniffed, trying to keep the rude sound away from the phone, but my nose wouldn't stop running as I tried to hold off an ugly cry. The medicine swimming through my veins played with my emotions.

"Kick? Are you crying?"

"S-sorry. I shouldn't have called."

"What's wrong?"

I heard someone say, "Professor Harrison," before the sound muffled. I knew he'd be at work, but I'd hoped he might be in his office doing whatever academics do between lectures. "Shit. I'm bugging you. Never mind."

"Kick, tell me what's wrong or I'll call Banger, have him track you down, and come there anyway."

"Can Banger really do that?"

Thomas ignored my deflection. "Where are you?"

"Near campus." I let out a deep shudder. "I finished the first IV and my car won't start, and I'm exhausted from the medicine in the cocktail, and I can't think clearly 'cause I'm so sleepy and—"

"I'm on my way."

Guilt and humiliation flooded me. I should've been able to keep it together to call a tow and rideshare. "No, don't. I... I'll figure it out."

He inhaled deeply, reminding me of myself with my last thread of patience. "Already left the office. I'm glad you called. Let me help. Text me the address and I'll be there in twenty."

Text. *I should've texted him instead of crying like a damsel in distress.* "Oh. Okay. Thank you." The last came out in a whisper.

Forty minutes later, we were on I-85, heading to my house. Thomas had secured a tow for my Camaro while my brain floated around in the fog of the medicinal cocktail. As much as I hated to admit it, he'd been a white knight when I needed one.

He came alive in the helping. A soothing jazz playlist serenaded us as I held on to consciousness out of a sense of obligation and gratitude. Thomas tapped his fingers on the wheel to Chet Baker's sexy version of "Almost Like Being in Love." It hit a bit too close to home. I quietly scoffed at the way the trumpet seemed to tease my stubbornness, my vow, my survivor's guilt.

"What's wrong?"

I shifted to my left side so I could see him with half-opened eyes. "The chocolate and caffeine cravings have kicked in. I'd give a kid if I could have a frozen cola and a candy bar."

"There's a Sheetz at the next exit. We can stop and get them."

"No," I said through a jaw-cracking yawn. "I said *if* I could, as in, they're not allowed."

"Oh. Sorry, Kick. Must be hard."

"I'm getting used to it. My body's making steps in the right direction. I thought the cravings would've resolved by now though. Instead, they continue to call to me."

"Oh?" Thomas kept his eyes on the road while chuckling.

"Yes. And they speak with an accent, though not buttery like yours. Well, I guess so, but it's not Southern, it's Spanish... like Antonio Banderas." A blush formed on my cheeks, and I tucked my hands under them, hoping the chill in my fingers would stop the flush. "They whisper, '*Shjust* a *leettle* bite will be fine, *Keek*. One *leettle* square won't make you *seek*.'"

Thomas muttered, "She thinks I sound buttery?" missing my joke. "What about Antonio?"

I groaned. "He's a lying rat bastard. Lately all forms and any amount of chocolate make me regret it. It took an embarrassingly long time to admit, but chocolate is a bonafide dietary issue. Except... why wouldn't my body be *happy* it's out of my system if it doesn't like it? Anyway, anyone who says food cravings aren't real is *another* lying rat bastard."

He reached over and rubbed my shoulder. "How about I pick up a water instead?"

I couldn't help the audible yawn. "That'd... be... wonder...ful." Then the peace of sleep overtook me.

Thomas woke me after he parked and helped me into the house, grumbling at the lack of an alarm system.

As if trying to defend my honor, Macushla greeted us, circling my feet until she filled up on our scents and barking extra loud at Thomas until he crouched and petted her ears. The little traitor took thirty seconds to offer her belly.

"Tell me y'all have personal protection."

I glared at him through my half-mast eyelids. "You mean a gun, don't you?"

"Of course."

"This is a safe neighborhood, Thomas."

"For the love of—"

"A can of wasp spray stays on my nightstand with a baseball bat next to it." Another jaw-cracking yawn and a wince from aching muscles halted my steps. They had locked in my curled-up position in the Camaro's passenger seat. "Twenty-seven-foot straight spray and no holes in any bodies. Plus Liam leaves his shit lying around everywhere. I can't even walk through the house at night without risking bruises. If someone breaks in, they'll break their neck before getting to a bedroom."

"Christ, you're stubborn."

"I don't trust myself with a gun, Thomas. I know my limits." I'd made it to the kitchen counter, straining to lift the kettle.

"What do you mean?" he asked.

I lifted my gaze and stared him down before saying, "It's not easy living with autoimmunity, especially when it takes decades for a doctor to believe you."

He mouthed the word *Oh* and walked toward me. "Let me do this." Thomas finished filling the kettle and turned it on. "What're we making?"

"The ginger-green tea. The second shelf on the left." I pointed to the cabinet behind him.

Koosh began barking, taking two steps toward the door, whining, and then repeating.

"Oh hell, she didn't get her walk. My house manager, Carmen, is home sick." I carefully lowered to pet her. "And Mama forgot about your exercise."

"I'll take her."

I looked up at Thomas. "Do you remember where the greenway is?"

The corner of his mouth lifted in a secret smirk. "How could I forget?"

I flinched again, this time from the memory of him carrying me home.

"If it's not too much trouble, I'd be indebted."

Thomas laughed. "That's what it'll take?"

"Don't remind me, pal." It seemed my mortification knew no bounds. I stood and groaned from the aches. *Note to self: pound the water on IV days.* "Anyway, Koosh doesn't have to go far. A few pee squats will suffice."

He held his hands out to me. "Come here."

I obediently followed directions as he spun me around. To my surprise, he began kneading my sore shoulders until I practically purred. One particular hard knot brought on a blissful moan followed by Thomas's audible gasp.

He cleared his throat. "Can I ask you something?"

"Sure."

"How were you planning to drive home?" His fingers found a lump on my other shoulder. My head fell forward, breathing into the bliss.

"I wasn't originally. My friend Cyndi had planned to take me, but her own emergency came up. With no time to rearrange things, I decided to nap in my car, then drive home after rush hour. A rideshare was my next option if you weren't available, but it's an expensive trip."

"Doesn't your foundation provide rides to patients?"

I shook my head. "Not for me. I'd only take funds away from a client."

Thomas's fingers had found enough trigger points to make my shoulders relax.

"You're an excellent masseur."

He paused and cleared his throat again. "The next time your ride cancels, call me immediately. I get the feeling more water and a nap wouldn't have cut it."

"That's because it's the beginning. It'll get better with more treatments as long as my veins hold up."

"This is miserable, isn't it?"

I shrugged and let my head fall to the side. If the professor gig didn't work out, the man had options. "Depends on where you focus. It was worse when doctors didn't take my symptoms seriously... like there was no hope."

Thomas patted my back, indicating he'd finished. "Can you make it to the sectional?"

I looked over my shoulder. "If I couldn't?"

"I'd carry you."

"I'm fine."

"Go sit while I finish."

I followed his orders and sat on the sofa, focusing on my breathing, hoping to ease the last of the discomfort with a few minutes of meditation. My doctor's staff had shamed me, once again, for not taking the recommendation seriously. I counted on the muscle-relaxing effect of the medicine to keep me from "glowing" again, but I wouldn't have attempted it if I'd been in my right mind.

In the end, I didn't even see a spark. I woke up several hours later when Liam came home. The velvety comforter I kept on the back of our recliner had been wrapped tightly around me. Macushla had tucked herself into my legs. A large glass of water sat on a coaster on the coffee table.

I guzzled the water and made a trip to the bathroom. Koosh's food storage box had a note taped to it: I ate dinner (One scoop?). I found my phone and sent Thomas a text.

Me: I fell asleep.

Thomas: Oh good. Thought you were ignoring me.

Me: Ha! Thanks for taking care of me and my dog. One scoop was perfect.

Thomas: My pleasure, darlin'.

Me: I forgot to ask... Are you free Sunday evenin

14

SUDDENLY I SEE

KICK

I watched Hugh and Maggie Reynolds navigate the high-top tables in the bar area of Finnegan's Wake, my neighborhood pub. Hugh and Maggie had eaten dinner early and spent a few minutes with my gang before leaving for an event at the senior center. I hoped to give them enough positive experiences to keep them coming around after my *momster's* imminent return.

Then Thomas and Banger arrived. The four of them greeted each other and shared a few words by the host stand before the Reynoldses pointed our way. The bar's owner, Finnegan

O'Dowd, was taking our orders, giving me cover when I accidentally sighed at the sight of Thomas. I indulged the secret pleasure of watching him weave the same path Hugh and Maggie had. Thomas wore the crisp, navy button-down we'd picked up in the Village District in Raleigh. It made his eyes glimmer as much as I'd thought it would. He also wore the jeans I'd found at the same men's shop.

Cyndi, sitting to my right, did a double take and whispered, "I heard that. I knew you were into him."

"Shush. You heard relief. I wasn't sure if he'd come. The man should get out more." It was why I'd also invited Banger.

"Get out more, eh? Sounds like someone else I know."

"Behave." Cyndi never missed an opportunity to nudge me back into the dating world.

The men joined our group, and Cyn piped up before I could make formal introductions. "Hey Professor." She sashayed in her seat until she noticed Banger and her back stiffened.

"Miss... Sendaydiego," Banger said.

I didn't know they knew each other.

"Ra—" A swift slice of Banger's chin interrupted her. "Mr.... McHenry. You may call me Cyndi."

"Are you two acquainted?"

"We've met," she answered vaguely.

Cyndi's tone told me to drop the subject. Banger's vibes reinforced the idea, and I didn't mind. I was happy to have so many friends and loved ones together. If Bobby had been in town, I wouldn't have done anything to celebrate, thanks to her way of making celebrations more trouble than they were worth.

"Gentlemen, you already know Cyndi, I guess." I moved to her right. "This is my Rachel and her roommate, Isabella."

"Bella's fine, Mrs. Mack." She waved and shifted back for the server to set a platter of wings on the table. The men dipped their chins in acknowledgment.

"Then we have Liz, who works with Hugh, and Jake, who you

know from my team." I finished the other side of the table. "My oldest, Dylan, his roommate, Hen—" I cleared my throat. "I mean Dummy."

He flashed an impish grin. "You can call me Dum."

I shook my head and continued, "You know Liam and Deana. And last, we have Dee's handsome other half, Gordon."

"Hear that, sweetness? Kick thinks I'm handsome," Gordon said, joking, his deep voice resonating like an old-school disc jockey's.

Deana laughed as her hand brushed his shoulder. "The entire room knows you're handsome, G."

With plenty of space on the bench to my left, I extended my hand. "Have a seat. Grab some wings, and we'll add your orders ASAP." The enormous table Finn had reserved for us had bench seating on the long sides and room for two chairs on the ends. Thomas took the open space to my left, but Banger surprised me by scooching Cyn and me down and sitting on the other end.

Thomas reached his arm around my shoulder and gently squeezed. "Happy birthday. Quite the clan y'all have here."

"We don't do parties often and took advantage."

"Why don't y'all have parties?"

I raised a shoulder and answered, "Bobby," hoping it would be enough.

"Ah."

Finn's chef made sure our orders arrived at the same time, and we ate a jovial dinner. Finnegan's Wake was a rare kitchen that had my back when it came to my food issues. His chef, Randy, had recently been diagnosed with Celiac disease. Over the past year, I'd helped him tweak the menu to make life easier for folks like us, without being obvious for everyone else.

More importantly, the conversation at the table was a dream. Everyone joked, shared, and gave. I couldn't have asked for a better birthday. When the afternoon football game ended, leaving all the big screens playing the postgame analysis, Finn started a playlist Liam had passed to him with my favorite songs. Besides our easy mix of assorted conversation, we sang and danced in our seats.

Now and then, I'd notice a sadness in Dylan's or Rachel's expression. It was the only downer in our fun night.

After dinner, Banger, Dylan, Liam, and Dum left the table to shoot some pool. The friendly competition seemed to lift my oldest son's mood, but I knew what bothered him. His girlfriend, Suzy, had been a no-show for any family function since the funeral.

A similar thing irritated Rachel, so I reached across the table for her hand. "No Cody, huh?"

My daughter's look turned deadly. "He said he's studying."

I honestly didn't mind. "Isn't he? Dyl said Suzy is off with a study partner or something too."

She lifted a shoulder. "Homework didn't bother Cody when he went drinking with the guys last night or watched football this afternoon."

I turned away to keep from adding my two cents. I didn't care if either showed, but my disappointment for my kids could make me say something I'd regret. Thomas gave me a supportive smile, reminding me he'd overheard the talk Rachel and I had regarding her relationship. A blush crept over me, and I turned back to my daughter.

"Maybe he was hungover earlier?" Rachel growled in response. "It's not like he'd want to hang out with a bunch of old people, honey."

"Bella's here. So is Dum."

"Bella's a good friend, and Henry thinks I'm his second mama."

"You know Dummy doesn't let people call him Henry. Right?"

"It hurts my motherly sensibilities to call him that." I tapped my finger on the table. Another item for my to-do list. "A man about to finish his MBA shouldn't go by *Dummy*."

Cyndi placed her hand on my arm. "You can't fix everyone's issue, chica. Sometimes you have to let them figure it out."

Thomas leaned in and whispered, "She's right, you know."

Deana and Gordon nodded along. A nagging to the fourth power.

"I'm trying," I quietly answered. It was wearisome to see my babies sad. Their technical status as grown-ups didn't make it any easier.

A small roar rose from the pool table. Our group turned as one to see Dylan and Dummy giving high fives. Thomas bumped my shoulder. "I'm sure it'll be all right."

The opening bars of Luther Vandross's "Never Too Much" played, and Gordon stood, holding his hand out to Deana. "Let's dance to our song like normal people." He led his wife over to the corner where musicians played on weekend nights, enfolded her into his large frame, and lost himself to the song and their love.

Thomas, Jake, and Liz talked about school and the military while Cyndi chatted with the girls about her side business making jewelry. I barely heard a word as the Douglasses captivated me with their moves on the small dance floor. I wondered what it would be like to do that too. I knew it would feel as good as my friends made it look. But I couldn't think of a future when the past kept holding me back. Tears crept up to the bottom of my eyes as my secret birthday wish made itself known. To keep them at bay, I turned my head to one of the silenced television screens on the wall. Cyn tapped me on the shoulder and arched an eyebrow.

When the song wrapped, she stood and announced, "Come on, gang. Gordon was right. We should dance."

Stevie Wonder's "My Eyes Don't Cry" began as we approached. Deana raised her arms, declaring, "Let's Hustle, y'all."

I pointed at her. "If you yell 'Change steps' this time, I'm swatting you."

Deana laughed while making room for us. "You're bossy on your birthday."

"I'm bossy every day." Getting up had already changed my mood.

"True."

"Nice job, Professor," Deana encouraged, watching his smooth steps.

"Thanks." Thomas easily kept up with us like a pro.

In the meantime, I lost myself in the steps and rhythm. It was one thing I missed about my cut hours at the Perked Cup. My staff and I practically danced through our shifts. It was why Jake and Rachel knew the steps as well as we old folks.

When the festive opening of KT Tunstall's "Suddenly I See" came on, I was swaying toward the middle of the group. Thomas seemed to magically appear in front of me, raising my arms as he led me in a familiar forward lockstep, then paused.

He tilted his chin and asked, "How's the ankle?"

"Doing well." It was wrapped, safe in a moto boot and healing fast, actually.

He arched an eyebrow. "Trust me?"

I surprised myself as shock turned into a grin. I did trust Thomas, *darn him*. I liked this brazen side of him. He looked rakish, like he had a special secret only for me. I smiled my affirmation, daring him to go for it.

He held me both gently and firmly, carving out space for us to do a proper quickstep right there in the bar. The rest of the gang helped us by stepping back to the wall, giving us more floor space. The basic steps came back to me as if I'd never stopped practicing. It had been years since I'd thought of a progressive chasse, let alone *done* one. Thomas made it easy to follow his lead. He moved me with the precision of a seasoned dancer and the protectiveness of a lover.

And I wanted all his dances. I wished his hips were doing more than directing my moves in space. I wanted him to take possession of my will. I remembered him carrying me in my neighborhood and admitted my secret truth. I'd loved every second. I was starting to crave his arms around my body, no matter the circumstance, his scent filling the air I breathed.

Our bodies felt right, pressed together, shoulder to foot. Our hearts beat together, into each other, for each other. His hip shifted, and mine responded. His thigh flexed, and mine allowed him into my space. Each muscle told me what it would be like to be with him. He wouldn't push or pull me. We'd move together as a unit.

A part of me I'd thought dead reawakened on the dance floor before my friends and family. I couldn't stop laughing as I let this old life fill me. Like the singer, I knew exactly what I needed. My heart longed to start again. No, I craved it. As long as it beat with Thomas's.

This was joy, the purpose of dance and love and life. I would have stayed in his arms the rest of the evening, lived right there. But the song ended, though the gift would stay forever.

We stood together, breathing heavily, wishing we could be alone and take it to higher levels, and the bar broke out into applause. I caught the surprise on Thomas's face when I jumped up and threw my arms around his neck.

"I haven't danced the quickstep in *ages*. Thank you for giving it back to me." I kissed his cheek since it was an established practice in our tenuous friendship. "Best present of the night."

I slowly slid down his body, barely cognizant of the rest of the room, feeling how our dance affected Thomas as much as it did me.

"Oh hell. I'm sorry." I blushed and tried to hop back.

He refused to let me go and grunted, "Stop. Apologizing." He shook his head and continued, "What are you doing to me?" He took a step away and turned back. "Have dinner with me. Any night this week. Just us."

I couldn't answer him. Not yet. My head still spun with

emotions. This was more than attraction, more than us. I'd caught a peek at who I could be. I wanted privacy to sort it out. At the same time, I wanted to shout my revelation from the parking lot.

I turned to my friends. Cyndi and Deana stared at me with smug grins. The action had also stopped at the pool table. My boys stared, their heads tilted like curious puppies. I laughed again at their confusion since the same emotion buzzed through me. For once, I didn't care. It was amazing to roll with the moment.

Banger glared. No surprise there. *Well, to hell with him.*

Thomas must have seen his friend's look as well because he headed straight for the foursome. The intense body language between the two told me someone wasn't in our corner, but I decided nothing would burst my glee bubble. It was my birthday, during a rough year. Grabbing Cyndi and Deana's hands, we brought the rest of the girls on the floor and shook our stuff, doing a mean Jerk to the song "Mercy," already half-done. Pink's "Raise Your Glass" followed—Rachel's signature song. She made her mama proud when she took it over like a pseudo-Karaoke, letting her stress go for a few minutes.

Gordon and Deana were the first to leave since the next day was an early workday for both of them. It didn't take long until it was just me, Cyndi, Banger, and Thomas.

"Go ahead to the car, man. I'll be there in a minute," Thomas urged his friend.

Banger said his goodbyes with a simple, "Kick." He gave Cyndi the manly chin tip and casually strolled out the door.

Thomas pulled an envelope out of his jacket pocket. "This is for you."

I slid a card out of the loose flap and laughed. "Who *doesn't* want a kitten shooting rainbows out of its eyes on their birthday?" Without thinking about it, my arms slid around his waist.

My ear against his chest heard his heart tapping a rhythm as rapid as mine. "Thank you. Yet again."

Thomas's hand slid over my curls. I'd worn my hair down and hadn't been to the restroom since leaving the table. Heaven only knew how wild it looked. I stepped away, tucking a coil behind my ear, gathering my wits again.

"You still haven't answered my offer for dinner," he said. "I meant it when I asked."

How could I deny our pull? The least I could do was spend some more casual time getting to know him. "Sure. It would be lovely. I usually eat dinner alone on Thursdays. Would that work? I could cook or—"

"Thursday's perfect, and it's my treat. Let me take you to my favorite place."

The usual panic over a newly suggested restaurant sparked. "I don't know, Thomas. I'm hard to feed."

"Hey." He lifted my chin. "Solving problems is one of my favorite pastimes."

Afraid to be a pain in the ass, I nodded my head. "Okay. Let's do it."

Finn approached, giving Thomas a receipt. "Thanks, man."

"Can I settle the bill, Finn? I have to get Cyndi home." She'd drunk both our allotments of alcohol in exchange for my taxi services since I couldn't imbibe.

"It's settled." Finn's eyes flicked to Thomas.

"You're kidding?"

Thomas shrugged his shoulders. "It's nothing. Happy birthday."

The hell it was *nothing*. My boys alone ate enough for six people. But I wasn't about to make a fuss at Finnegan in his place. He received a flash of stink eye though.

Finn handed me a certificate.

"What's this?"

"Two free birthday drinks and a piece of flourless chocolate torte. When your moratorium, or whatever you called it, ends. I feel bad you didn't get to celebrate properly."

"Thanks, buddy." I gave him a quick hug. A few years older than Dylan, Finn had taken over the pub two years prior when his father had a heart attack. From what I could tell, he'd grown the business, like it was in his DNA.

"Hey, we entrepreneurs stick together, right? I mean, you bailed me out when you talked Randy off the 'my career is over' ledge after the Celiac news."

"Bless his heart. I remember the feeling."

Thomas shook his head, smiling. "Of course you did." He said his last goodbyes and left.

After giving Finn one more thank-you hug, I spun Cyndi toward the door too, refusing to look her way. I could *hear* the thoughts in her head the entire time I'd been talking to Thomas and Finnegan.

"Zip it, Sendaydiego. Not. One. Word."

15

SO NICE

KICK

Thomas slowed his Camaro in front of an award-winning Italian restaurant in downtown Oakville. His eyes lit up as he turned to me, telling me this was the place for our first date. The butterflies awakened in my stomach, as alarm bells clanged there. I didn't want to discourage him though.

I quickly opened the gluten-free restaurant finder app I used when eating at new places. The community rated it one star—not Celiac friendly. The autoimmune part of me warned this was a bad idea, but the part of me that craved normalcy told it to shut up and enjoy Thomas's company. Instead of politely asking if he had a second choice of cuisine, I let my insecurities over being out with a significantly younger, handsome man take center stage in my thoughts. Embarrassed and out of my league, I followed him down the sidewalk and into the foyer of Stefano's, second-guessing every decision I'd made so far.

Pulling my hair back in combs suddenly seemed outdated and didn't cover my pointy ears. The vicuna sweater dress I'd chosen to show off curves morphed into a frumpy sack in my mind. It also washed out my skin, the summer's kiss of color long gone. And surely he'd have preferred spiky pumps to my comfortable wedge-heeled boots.

Thomas, on the other hand, worked his light gray fisherman's sweater and black slacks like a film star. The color contrasted with his olive skin and raven hair while brightening his silver eyes.

The smell of garlic bread, sauce, and cheese represented trouble, but insecurity distracted me too much to pay attention. Thomas squeezed my hand. "The owner's a friend of mine. Stefano assured me he expanded the menu for gluten-free diners."

"It's sweet you thought of me." I sent a quick prayer to the universe for it to work out. I didn't want to burst his bubble, but low-FODMAP foods did not go with Italian cuisine. It was hard enough to eat on the autoimmune Paleo plan in this place. For me, eating had become about so much more than gluten. Finding an Italian place with both gluten-free and low-FODMAP knowledge would be a huge ask.

Thomas tensed and set his lips as he opened the door, his knuckles white on the handle. "Try it please."

I steeled my spine. Is this what dating would be like from here on? Hell, the last time I dated, we ate in a campus cafeteria. Fancy meals equaled a sub shop. It was time I grew up and figured it out. "Lead the way, Professor."

Stefano greeted us and escorted us to a reserved table. The

two men shared about how they met when Thomas first moved to the area from Manhattan. The authentic food reminded him of his favorite place near Soho, so he ate here often. I smiled along, having had no clue Thomas had lived in New York. There was still so much to learn about the man.

"*Professore*, you don't visit me lately. At least you make up for it by bringing the beautiful Kick McKenna here." Stefano sent me a flirtatious wink.

With a polite laugh to hide my embarrassment, I answered, "It's good to see you, Stefano. I've missed the Chamber of Commerce group."

He lifted my hand to kiss it. "Those meetings are a bore without you." He pulled out my chair and asked Thomas, "Shall I bring a carafe of Sangria?"

Thomas placed his hand on his heart and said, "You know how I love it, but not tonight, my friend." He eyed me for a beat. "How about two club sodas with lime instead?"

Stefano didn't hide his shock. I feared we'd insulted him. "Certainly. I'll have Anita bring them."

"Thanks."

We spent some time with the menus. For me, it was infinitely torturous, trying to piece together a way for something to work. My thoughts raced through the list of approved foods. It was a shorter list than the restricted ones. *I should leave.* Maybe get an appetizer and go. I couldn't even order a simple caprese salad.

I wanted to flee but also wanted to hear more about Thomas's past in Manhattan and his current research. Every time his gaze lifted to mine, the relaxed excitement I found there kept me from saying anything. I bit my lip and scanned the menu some more until it blurred.

Finally the dreaded time to order arrived.

"I'll have the chef's special with a house salad and dressing," Thomas said.

"Garlic-mushroom risotto," the waitress, Angela, said as she wrote. "Any wine?"

I tapped his hand. "Please. Go ahead."

Thomas sighed and answered, "Sure. Your Nebbiolo, please."

"Yes, sir. And for you, ma'am?"

I took a minute to inhale deeply and dove in. "Any chance you can do the risotto without garlic?" I'd known for a while garlic bothered me, but until my last appointment, I didn't understand it had to do with being a FODMAP food.

Anita laughed in response. "It's already made."

Shit, shit, shit. My eyes flew over the offerings again, my tongue worrying my cheek. "Okay, I think I have it. I'll take a house salad. Hold the tomatoes, cheese, and bell peppers. Double the avocado, keep the olives, and add grilled chicken please. But no garlic or onion on the chicken. Salt and pepper will be sufficient. Oh, and absolutely no croutons. And I'd like the marinara side dish with the gluten-free noodles." My stomach could forgive a little sauce splurge for one night, right? At least authentic Italian cuisine didn't put garlic in a marinara sauce, and this place was the real deal.

Thomas rolled his eyes and arched an eyebrow.

Angela nodded. "O...kaaay." She took a moment to write everything out. "Any wine tonight?"

"The club soda's fine. Thank you."

"We don't want the bread basket either," Thomas added with a tense smile. I feared our night out might be over before it began.

Angela twisted her mouth. "As you wish."

And then we were alone again, staring at each other with so much to say, but no words would come.

"I'm sorry, Thomas. I embarrassed you in front of your friend."

His eyes narrowed for a moment before answering. "No, and stop apologizing. It's just... I don't understand. You weren't like this at the birthday dinner."

"Finn's staff knows me. You remember what he said about his chef?"

"But the risotto is gluten-free. I ordered it to show support, aside from it being the best I've ever had."

The sentiment gutted me. I reached for his hand. If I could have cried, I would have. "Garlic is a huge item on my *no* list. I don't want to risk the wine right now either, though it might have been okay since alcohol burns off in the cooking."

"I see." Thomas tipped his head back and blew out a long breath.

"I hear you." I scrunched my nose and added, "Maybe this is a good thing. This is my life, Thomas. It's intense now, but I'll always be high-maintenance. Aside from food, there are also rules for cleaning supplies, skin care, hair care, makeup. It's a never-ending life of rules." He could use a fat dose of honesty if he were having a tough time eating out. It also gave Thomas an out before our friendship went any further.

His gaze held mine for an uncomfortably long time. Finally. he said, "It's easy to forget. You don't look sick."

"My mother loves to hit me over my head with those same four words. And I don't know how to respond anymore. Should I feel guilty about it? Or grateful? You didn't know me before the diagnosis."

"What were you like?"

"Like I'd been drugged most hours of the day, only I couldn't sleep when I lay down. Lost hair at a frightening rate. My skin..." I shook my head. "And inflated. I told you about the weight and the boundary lines."

"The psalm."

I nodded. "It helps. The rules can be a blessing. You won't hear me apologize for the way I eat. And not because I'm in a more acceptable size but because I *feel* better. It lets me live again."

"Hey, we all have shit, you know?"

"Do I ever. You ever hear the quote 'Nothing tastes as good as skinny feels?'"

"Didn't a model say that?"

"Yeah. She got hell for it too. But I get it. Working in an industry where an added pound could lose her millions? Learning to hate fattening foods is a fantastic coping strategy, from where I sit."

"Like with the chocolate."

The memory made me smile. "Boy I hope it's temporary, but yeah." I took a long sip of my soda water and reminded myself why sugar was on hiatus. *This is healing, not a punishment.*

"I'm curious though. Can't they do anything for a cure?"

Laughing, I said, "Only if my genes change." Then I added, "Hey, maybe you can help with it."

Thomas coughed as his soda went down the wrong way.

When his throat settled, I asked, "Can we talk about something else? Your research, maybe? How's it going?" Unfortunately, he had to cough some more.

The restaurant interior ended up larger than it appeared from the outside. We sat in a solarium with sprawling chandeliers set to low light. Off of it were two additional dining rooms, characterized by dark wood, with burgundy tablecloths and candles on top. Against the window in the middle room was a stage occupied by a jazz trio composed of a pianist, a bassist, and a guitarist. Thomas leaned toward me and said, "I have a better idea. Let's dance."

"Well." I hesitated. "Where?" Taking over Finnegan's on a Sunday night was one thing, but I wasn't sure about it becoming a habit.

Thomas gestured toward the piano with his head. "You can't see it from our vantage point, but there's a dance floor in front of the musicians. Trust me, it's all right." He came around to my chair and pulled it out for me.

I took a deep breath and smiled, taking his offered hand.

There was something about him challenging my trust. "They're not exactly playing a quickstep."

With his hand at the small of my back, he tipped his head toward my ear. "We can handle a little jazz."

"True." He led me by the hand to a tiny parquet floor. Three senior couples were already on it. Their cuteness put me at ease, as did being back in Thomas's hold. He kept us to the basics this time, with no attempt to clear the floor as the trio played "So Nice."

Miss Virginia, a regular from the café, was on the floor. My smile wouldn't contain itself as I watched her with her husband. Obviously together for decades, their bodies communicated with the slightest hip or shoulder gesture, anticipating each other's moves. They let me know Thomas and I had much to learn, though I enjoyed how well we already moved.

"Good to see you tonight, Miss Virginia," I said to her as Thomas floated me toward them.

"You too, dear," she responded with the warmest smile. "You're beautiful in your pretty dress. And such a handsome partner too." I giggled as she batted her eyelashes at Thomas.

Stefano's head shifting left and right broke my focus on our bubble, and I moved my hand to Thomas's chest. "Do you think he's looking for us?"

He caught my sightline and the restaurateur's gaze, then nodded. "Our plates are ready." Weaving our way back to our table, he leaned into my ear and said, "You know that couple?"

Nodding, I answered, "Her. From the Perked Cup."

"Sorry, Kick," he murmured.

"For what?" I looked up, confused.

"Everyone but me has commented on how beautiful you look tonight."

I blushed. "Thanks. I didn't tell you how devilishly handsome you are in your gray and black either. We're out of practice."

"Yes, we are," he answered with a sigh.

. . .

"Can I interest you in dessert?" Stefano asked us as he stacked our finished plates. "Our crème brûlée is marvelous and gluten-free."

"Perhaps another time. Thank you," I said with an apologetic scrunch of my nose.

As he walked away, Thomas leaned into me. "The dairy?"

"Yes. Nice deduction," I responded with a slight smile. "I have an idea. There's a dairy-free flan in my fridge. Let's dig into it. It's not Italian, but we can overlook that."

"I'd love to. Let's go."

The first flutter gurgled in my stomach halfway home. Sometimes I'd only experience a bit of bloating, so I ignored it.

The second grumble whacked me from the inside as we turned in to my sub. It felt like a bad science experiment bubbling in there. I grimaced, leaning forward and digging my fists into my stomach, hoping Thomas's attention to the road kept it off me. Activated charcoal could do the trick. There wouldn't be any dessert for me, but I could plate one for him.

As we walked up the path to my house, a monster cramp stopped me in my tracks. It took my whole will to keep from falling onto all fours. "Oh hell." No sense dodging the truth now; a long night was ahead.

"Y'all right?"

"No, Thomas. I'm sorry, but I have to give you a rain check." I sat on my front stoop when another cramp and growl twisted in my stomach. He frowned, looking confused. So I continued, "Something went wrong with dinner."

"But you grilled Angela on the ingredients." He sighed like he had doubts.

"It happens. I'm always at a chef's mercy. If the staff doesn't have the proper training..." I winced as another gripe rolled through me, trying to keep the groan on the down-low. "There are ample opportunities for contamination."

"But how?" There was an edge to his voice as another pain

166 | KALLYN JONES

grabbed me on the right side.

"If I had to guess? The chicken shared the grill with something breaded. Or the salad prep person put the required croutons on the plate, realized there weren't supposed to be any, and flicked them out instead of making a new one. Or the noodles had buckwheat. I should've asked about it. Even though it's considered gluten-free, I react to it. I don't know, but... ahh!" Another cramp hit the left side, taking my breath.

"Can I do anything? Make tea?" His hand gently brushed my cheek. "You're flushed."

I nodded, too upset to answer, and handed him my house key. He eased me up and through the door before I took off running. I barely made it to the master bathroom, too embarrassed to use the guest one and risk Thomas hearing. I spent at least twenty minutes in the bathroom, fuming at myself for letting this happen. My stupid, stupid wishful thinking. Would this ever get any better?

When my body gave me a breather, I checked the mirror. My makeup was so smeared from sweat I had to take another minute and wash it off. By the time I'd changed into yoga pants and an MSU Spartans football T-shirt, my resolve had cracked. I sat on the sofa, my head in my hands, afraid to look for Thomas.

"Kick?" I jumped, not realizing he was so close. Thomas set the teacup on the coffee table. "It's mint."

"Thanks. Great choice."

He sat and touched my knee. "When we arrived at Stefano's, you wanted to leave, didn't you?"

"Yeah." The word stuck in my throat.

"Did I say something to make you think we had to stay?"

My head hung. I didn't know how to be a couple anymore. Hell, because of me, we were barely friends. Every time we'd try to start, something happened to me to shorten our time together. "He's your friend, Thomas. You were excited, and you *tried*." I turned to him so he could see my sincerity. "I wanted you to have this victory. I still appreciate what you did for me. Sometimes it's just not enough."

"I'm so sorry." He cradled my clammy hands in his, warm and tender. But his apology was also my last straw. None of this was fair. In my head, I knew no one promised me a fair life, but I didn't give a shit anymore, the brave face and fake strength vanishing.

Before I realized it, I recited the psalm as I rocked. "The boundary lines have fallen for me in pleasant places; the boundary lines have fallen for me in pleasant places; the boundary li—"

Thomas shifted on the sofa, closer to me. His hand gentled my back as he cooed, "It's all right, Kick."

"No, it's *not*, Thomas. We should be laughing and eating flan. I want to know more about you. I'm so high-maintenance I drive myself nuts!" I wasn't crying, but the waves of pain kept sweat running down my face.

"Are you giving up? Because I see it as a lesson learned for both of us. I defaulted to my *fixer* impulses and didn't ask your opinion. And you should feel comfortable enough with me to call me on it. It's a speed bump, but we'll get past it."

Molten lava raged. Every time I'd given him a way out, Thomas stayed, adding joy and lending a hand. It was like he was being punished for it as much as I was. I glanced at him and grunted, "The boundary lines have *not* fallen for me in pleasant places. There. I said it. You can tell him I said it too!" It would have come out as a screech if my voice could have stopped catching.

"Tell who?"

"God, that's who. I don't care if he knows I'm pissed. I'm tired of the three steps forward, two steps back cha-cha-cha that's my life. I'm tired of making plans and my body laughing at them."

I ran my hand through my hair, not caring if it frizzed. "The

Psalm doesn't comfort. It judges. The words are a goddamn boot to the back of my neck, keeping me stuck to the ground, keeping me from taking care of my kids the way they deserve. My business. My friends. My body gets my best energy. They get what's left. And it's never enough."

On a roll, the anger continued, mocking. "You know what I've really given up, Thomas?" He raised a sympathetic eyebrow but didn't speak. "Spontaneity. I used to find a truce with my mother when I took her for drives to explore new towns. But she *insisted* we eat at local diners, which I can't do because I can't guarantee" —I pointed at my stomach—"this. She won't allow me to pack us a lunch either. It's her way or the highway, so we lost our last connection. I don't know how to help her be happy like my dad asked. When will my efforts ever be enough?"

As quickly as I vomited the words, they stopped. Gasping again, I put my hands to my face, hot from sweating, eyes wide and shimmering, but I didn't cry. I hadn't truly cried in years. My family trained it out of me as a girl, more so in the past eight years. Instead, my breath hitched. Annoying as hell, but it wouldn't stop. The tornado inside me had become a volcano and blown up.

Mortified, I whispered, "I'm so sorry. You didn't need to hear my crap. *Shit.*"

Thomas kept his gaze down and shook his head, his voice hoarse. He gently covered my hand with his. "Don't apologize. It sounds like this was overdue. Did it help?"

My throat locked as I lifted my head. Where was the silence a minute ago when it was imperative to shut the feck up? All I could do was croak and shrug.

He squinted at me and touched my forehead. "Hey now, darlin', you're warm."

16

JUST WHAT I NEED

KICK

I settled into the tub the following afternoon, moving the detox process along. With headphones on, an audiobook playing, the chromotherapy lights cycling, and jets circulating sea salt and oils, I set my head against the bath pillow and blissed out. Salt water eased the rashes still burning in unmentionable places. It also renewed my perspective.

I loved my home, worshipped my bathtub, had the best friends and family (mostly) a girl could ask for, an engaging career, and I'd come a long way in the health journey. Nothing overpowered a gluten reaction like good news. Earlier in the day,

I'd checked in with my contacts at the McKenna Family Foundation and discovered we could take on a new family. Despite my hurdles, I couldn't imagine navigating autoimmunity without decent finances.

Suddenly Deana burst into my bathroom, causing me to jack-knife into a ball to cover up. My phone flew end-over-end, but I caught it at the last minute, saving it from a watery grave.

"What the hell are you doing?" I screeched, reaching for something to cover up with and only finding a washcloth.

"Let it go, shug. It's not like you have something I don't," Deana responded, sneaking a peek. "You could use some of mine anyway."

"Really? From where I sit, you still have your privacy and your dignity," I retorted.

"I rang the bell. You didn't answer. Can't a friend check on a friend?" She sat on the tub-surround. "What are you doing anyway, listening to that romance everyone's talking about?"

"Why are you here?" I asked, rubbing my eyes and jerking. Even my lids were raw.

"Why are you in the tub in the middle of the day?" Deana countered, not backing down from her perceived right to barge in.

I swept my hand over my body, hoping the washcloth would stay put. "Trying to relieve this lovely rash."

She bent down and studied my face. "Your chin's bright red."

I was tempted to show her my ass.

She stood, tsking, but softened her tone. "I brought you soup. It's the coconut thai you like, plus their nasty green juice. Liam said you had no food when he ate twice his weight at lunch. I thought you might be hungry."

I took a deep breath, willing my heartbeat to return to normal. "We have plenty to eat. My boy's too lazy to cook. Lee once told me there's a difference between *food* and *ingredients*. The soup sounds amazing though. Thank you, sweets."

Deana held a towel up as if I should let her wrap it around me like one of her grandbabies. I shooed her away instead. "You still complaining about me seeing your birthday suit? I don't see why you're stressing so much over a few extra pounds. The curves are cute."

"You're adorably petite and curvy and work them like a CEO, right?" I asked.

"You know it."

I knew from her tongue clicks and comments she viewed my anxiety over the recent weight gain as ridiculous. It took a second to come up with the words to explain.

"Remember back when you went on the big diet and you said you felt trapped in the wrong body? You were glad to add a few pounds back on."

"I do. It taught me about gratitude for what the good Lord gave me."

"The opposite has been true for me. When I look in a mirror, I see an inflated skinny girl wondering what the hell happened—and before you call me ungrateful again, Dr. Chaddha doesn't approve of my BMI either. But the swelling, the aches, and the fatigue get to me." A glance at my pruney fingers told me it was time to get out. "At least the bloating stopped and I don't look pregnant anymore."

"Yeah, it's weird when you do that."

Deana dropped the subject as quickly as she picked it up. We'd talked weight so many times over the years. We both agreed there was more to health than numbers on a scale. It was nice to have a friend who'd been through most of my original recovery and didn't criticize me for the relapse. We each supported the other, and I loved her for it. I dropped my forehead to my knees. "Can I meet you at the dinner table?"

"Are you asking me to stay?"

"If you have time, I'd love it." While fundamentally different, Deana's schedule was as packed as mine. Between Gordon, her two children, and three grandchildren, she barely had time for her photography passion. The fact she made space in her afternoon for me didn't go unnoticed. She dropped the towel on the surround.

"I'll get the bowls."

"Thank you," I called out as the door shut, then quickly dressed in yoga pants and a THEATER MOM T-shirt Rachel gave me for my birthday. I made a quick readjustment to my hair from its high bun to a low one.

Dee saw me enter the dining area and said, "Are you wearing a bra?"

"Why?" I asked, looking around. "Are the boob police here?"

"No," she answered as if I were a petulant toddler. "I was going to ask how you're still so perky, but never mind."

"Oh." I sat in my chair and lifted a spoon. "Benign breast cysts. I'm full of Mother Nature's middle-aged implants."

"You don't say?" Deana looked at me like she was trying to figure out how to score some cysts for herself. "Gives new meaning to the Perked Cup, doesn't it?" She dissolved into laughter at her wisecrack.

"Have you *not* heard my boys make this joke? I almost changed the name in the beginning when Dylan wouldn't stop. He says I kept it out of spite." I took a bit of soup and set the spoon down. "Okay, what's going on? First the curves comment and now the boobs. You're up to something."

The perky joke hadn't fully fizzled, and she giggled again.

I sent her my best glare.

"Fine. I know how discouraged you get when"—she waved her hands toward my stomach—"you get sick. I thought you might like a reminder that it isn't *all* bad."

She was right. I did. "Aw. Thanks, Dee. Bobby's criticisms have been playing on a loop in my head. Wish you would live in here instead." I tapped my temple.

She patted my hand. "One of these days, we'll do an exorcism."

We spent an hour eating, drinking, and catching up on our staff and families. I poured Deana a glass of iced tea since nothing could get her to try the green juice.

Deana's visit lifted my spirits until she brought up Thomas. She snuck it in while she trounced me in two-player spades. "You going to see Thomas again?"

"I don't know. It might be too much. I mean, why would he want to put up with this? You know what Bobby says. How men don't put up with troublesome women." She took another trick while I laughed. "Are you going to wipe the floor with my yoga pants?"

"What would my family say if I let you win? Besides, your mama is a difficult woman, to put it nicely. Let me make this clear: you *are* going to see Thomas again." Deana bit her lip, holding firm, narrowed eyes staring me down.

I sighed. "You won't let the Thomas topic go."

"Um, nope. I knew you were sitting in this house, talking yourself out of a good thing before it even started. Let him make it up to you." She clapped the table with each word. She gave me another glare, the one which made unruly children behave on the spot. And me too, apparently.

"How small is this blasted town? Or is my house bugged?" I looked under the table for signs of a listening device but wouldn't know one if someone stuck it to my shirt. I'd only texted the team about being glutened and taking a day to recover. Technically, I wouldn't be better until Monday but was only on the schedule for Friday.

"He stopped in for a snack before my shift ended."

"Did you talk about me?" I didn't know what I thought about them gossiping, not as if it would matter.

"Aren't tomatoes on your forbidden list now?"

I hung my head, busted. "Yeah."

"Sugar, you had no business being in an Italian restaurant. Self-advocacy isn't only for you. It helps the rest of us too."

I dropped my head to my hands. "I know. You're right. How much did Thomas tell you?"

"You worried him. I think his waters run as deep as yours, if not deeper."

"How do you know? What did he say?" I'd suspected the same.

"You don't work in a coffeehouse without learning how to observe."

"You sound like a bartender."

She moved her hands up and down, as if weighing the two professions, telling me there wasn't much difference.

"I'll think about it. You mind if we call it a night? I'm already tired."

"Sure."

I walked Deana to the door and helped her into her sweater. "Thanks for giving up your photo-retouching time to set me straight." I had the feeling her talk with Thomas motivated her more than Liam's whining had.

"I couldn't let another day go by without setting you straight."

"Dang. How bad was your talk with the professor?"

She opened the door and stood in the space to keep the dog from dashing out between her legs. "Don't blow this, Kick. It could be good, for *both* of you."

17

LOVE FOR SALE

THOMAS

*S*omber clouds shifted, allowing sunrays to filter through the trees on the campus paths, giving them a cathedral-like appearance. Thomas considered this appropriate as he slogged through the spongy trails to go sit in the chapel and disconnect during the pipe organist's practice session.

A panicked call from his assistant, Presley, had him rushing to the lab to work on Toni's latest tests. Fortunately, the grave error she thought she'd made was easy to fix. The panel he reported to at the university never pressured him as long as he showed consistent effort, but *Grand-père* and the Felidae Society members were a different story. They wanted results yesterday. As did Thomas.

After spending most of the night in the lab, he'd meant to get a few hours' sleep in his office. But a predawn storm kept him awake by blowing a tree branch against the window. Plus every time he closed his eyes, another pair like a spring forest appeared in the darkness. He couldn't stand the defeat he saw in them and the belief he'd put it there. For a reason he didn't understand, Thomas wanted to show Kick he was different, someone she could trust. But he'd tried to serve her in the way *he* wanted to, not in the manner she'd needed. He'd inadvertently forced her to pretend everything was fine. Until it wasn't.

So Thomas sought the peace of the chapel before his lecture. The organist was working on a César Franck chorale, which helped pacify his restless spirit any time it touched his ears.

Thomas stepped from the dark gray of the vestibule into the magnificent light of man's vision of a holy space. Stained-glass windows lined the nave's clerestory, projecting the welcomed arrival of sunrays as if Christ Himself rode on them.

The rainbow flood of colored and clear light lifted Thomas's mood to almost enjoyable levels. He hummed "Here Comes the Sun" to himself as he made his way to the middle, taking in the surroundings while quietly respecting those around him. His chosen spot in sight, Thomas turned the corner to his row, mindful of his case so it wouldn't make noise against the pew.

He stopped midstep. He couldn't believe his eyes. *There she sat.*

Four rows ahead, drenched in sunlight, her head bent in a book, Thomas knew her.

His case dropped on the pew before his knees gave out, his ass landing on the leather attaché.

After all these years, could she be real? How could she simply be sitting in a church?

Heads turned to glare at him for making noise, but not his angel. Her hair glowed in the sun the way it did in his dreams.

Presently, it looked lighter, nearly platinum when touched by rays floating through clear panes. He chalked it up to the nearness and brightness of reality versus the haze of dreams.

Where had she been all this damn time? He thought of Kick and almost didn't want his angel to be real. The revelation took him by surprise. No. After waiting for so long, he had to see it through.

Thomas watched slim hands periodically turn a page. The rest of her remained doused in a vibrant mix of colored and clear light. She wore casual clothes. He hoped like hell she wasn't a grad student. No way would fate toy with his heart and make a relationship with his angel unethical once he'd found her.

He sat for a moment, preparing a greeting. Given the time he'd dreamed of this woman, why hadn't he ever practiced one? Did she dream of him too? What if the dreams were only one way? There was only one way to know for sure.

Thomas slumped in the pew. Should this be like the time he'd turned down meeting his blues guitar idol so he didn't have to risk disappointment? No. This was different, dammit. How could he dream of her for years—*years!* —and not say something when the chance presented itself?

He rose from his seat and took the fated first step, practicing his opening as he made his way to the side aisle. Thomas reached her pew, placed his hand on the endcap, and turned, "Excuse me..."

The woman adjusted her position and looked up. Only it wasn't his angel looking up. It was a young man. *On the effeminate side, but definitely male.*

Heat raced across his features, obliterating his thoughts. New words scrambled for purchase. Mortification had Thomas tongue-tied until... *Ted.* Ted was the name of the organist. "Have you seen Ted yet? Looks like he's running late. Do you know if he canceled?"

"I'm not sure. I don't come in here much. Just waiting on my girl."

Shock dried Thomas's throat as he croaked out a few words in reply. "Sorry to disturb you. Guess he's not practicing today."

"No worries, Professor. Have a good day." The young man's eyes returned to his book.

Thomas shuffled back to his pew in a whirl of anger, embarrassment, frustration, and despair. He fled the chapel as if someone had pulled a fire alarm, yelling at himself the entire way to the lecture hall.

Somewhere in his subconscious, he'd known it had been a fool's fantasy all along. She was nothing more than his mind wrestling with loss and loneliness, a result of his isolation. His "dream angel" was a delusion his mind made up to keep him moving forward when his psyche begged to give up.

In hindsight, the student looked wrong, even from behind. He was too light, too delicate, too sloppy.

By the time he set up his materials on the lectern, Thomas had a plan. No more relying on a goddamn dream. No more living like a hermit. He'd find the drive to expand his world or risk losing his faculties. Though music and the gym were essential, neither were enough to fill the void. He'd been ignoring the signs, believing personal entanglements were a hassle.

He remembered Kick's words to her daughter. *The magic's found in the connection. Not because of the how, the what or the why, but because of the who.*

Did she know then that she'd hit the nail on the head for Thomas? He'd find a way to reengage and keep his vows to the Felidae. Even if it killed him.

TAKE ON ME

KICK

*M*y mystery man visited me in my sleep again. Covered in a sunlit haze, I recognized him by the way he made my heart flutter. I reached for him, but my hand filled with light.

"Where've you been?"

"Waiting for you," he answered.

Longish tresses floated through my fingers, though I couldn't see them. He turned his cheek into my hand, and the familiar gray strands at his temples caught the light. I closed my eyes, allowing the warmth and brightness to fill me. I inhaled the still-ness he offered and exhaled my melancholy.

We floated down winding stairs to a secret sanctuary and walked a gardenia-filled path. When light beams occasionally broke around us, I saw his boots, pants, and a coat from a different time, but I couldn't identify when. My lack of interest in any history class not involving artwork, biting me in the ass, even in my dreams.

My dream lover touched my stomach where it still ached. The pain dissipated in an instant. He touched my jaw, and the rash there vanished too, leaving porcelain skin.

I placed my hand over his heart, sensing its slow beat beneath my palm. He sighed at the sensation. I'd never considered I could fill a need in this mystery man from out of time. But he craved my touch as much as I did his. As fast as he appeared, I knew he was leaving again.

"Please stay," I begged. "I'm better when you're around."

A rugged hand moved around the space, directing my atten-tion to the porch we now stood on. The same gardenia bushes defined the outside edge, a gentle breeze making their fragrance surround us.

"This is all you, lady. I walked with you down here, but this place and everything in it is your doing."

I thought he was referring to meditation, and I remembered recent attempts and the subsequent glow they caused. My hands tucked against my chest for fear of discovery. "I'm not so sure."

My body lightened, and my feet felt like they could break free of gravity. But my dream man worked my hands apart, lacing our fingers. "Don't fear the light. It's you too." Then my body felt the welcomed pressure and presence of a hug without the sensation on my skin.

He added, "Come back here anytime you need to." Next came the sensation of lips gently pressed to mine. "Thank you for showing me around. If you don't mind, I'd like to stay awhile."

"But I want to stay too."

"No, angel. See who's at your door. Hurry."

19

YOU DO SOMETHING TO ME

THOMAS

"*H*ey stranger. Sorry it took a while to answer."

After three rounds of knocks and bell-ringing, Kick opened her door. Her wild hair and adorable squint gave away her just-woken status. An instant grin spread across Thomas's face. Then his thoughts turned to what it would be like to wake with her. He knew his sleep would be deep and restorative with Kick in his arms, the opposite of his solitary nights.

In his mind's eye, he wrapped a chestnut coil of her hair around his finger and kissed her perfect bow lips. He wondered if she ever smiled in her sleep.

But he didn't come to Kick's house to scratch an itch. Embarrassment chased his smile away. He wasn't used to losing control over his thoughts, or his heart, like he did around her.

"Everything okay?"

Thomas held up the bags he carried. "You're asking my question for you."

Kick stepped aside and swept her arm, permitting him to enter. She yawned and said, "Sorry, I was napping. Are you...?" She leaned around a corner and checked a clock. "Yeah, you're early."

"My turn to apologize. I finished quickly and had spent too much time in my office this week. I was hoping you might be up for a walk and your Pokey-Go game."

When he said the word *walk*, Kick's dog barked and ran in circles.

"Shhh! *Chhtt.*" Kick snapped her fingers, but Macushla had keyed herself up and couldn't stop wiggling. "Crap. Settle down. He didn't know."

"Didn't know what?"

"The *W* word has *Harry Potter*-type magical powers over Koosh. When someone says it, she practically apparates to the person with expectations for an immediate... you know."

"Then how do y'all talk about going outside?" The dog resumed her vigorous barking.

"*Stop.*" Kick laughed. "She knows the *O* word too. We use ambulate, but Liam swears she's catching on to it. Anyway, it was nice of you to come by." Kick leaned in and sniffed the bags of food in Thomas's hands. "This smells wonderful. You said their kitchen is dedicated gluten-free?"

His smile returned, knowing he'd found a way to right his wrongs. He'd called earlier and offered to stop at the new café in Durham. "Thanks for taking another chance on my dining-out skills." Kick received the takeout bags so Thomas could hang up his leather jacket. He followed her into the kitchen.

"Thomas, don't be silly. You did nothing wrong. Not everyone is as sensitive as me. Plenty of people will appreciate the effort Stefano made with his food." She set the bags on the counter and placed her hand on his arm. "Please don't blame yourself."

He wished he could do more to fix things—use his connections to recommend a new doctor or a new study—to make life easier. But when he looked into it, he found Kick was doing exactly what she should. "How about I'm glad to have this do-over?"

She dipped her chin, smiling. "Do-overs are amazing. Do you mind if I take a minute to freshen up? My head's still cloudy from sleep."

"Not at all. I'll set our places."

"Fantastic. Be right back." She padded off to the back of the house, muttering, "Bet I look a hot mess."

She had the "hot" part down, though Thomas was keeping his head in the friend zone. He might have given up on an isolated life, but he didn't have to get sucked into the whole shebang *even if Kick's feistiness captivated him.*

While plating their food, he laughed when her complaint reached his ears. "You've got to be kidding! What a fright."

With the food ready, Thomas explored the rest of the first floor of Kick's house. A bright, open space, the blue ceiling caught his eye first. It matched the sunny midafternoon sky, complementing large windows on three sides of the great room. The kitchen opened onto the dining area, with a rustic table in the center.

Opposite the window in this area was a wall of art, comprising three small pen-and-ink drawings of her children as babies. Kick's signature graced the corner of each one. Two large illustrations hung on the same wall. One illustration was a Cole Phillips piece he recognized from an old magazine cover. He liked the use of negative space, causing a young flapper to blend into the background. Or perhaps she emerged from it?

The last piece was modern, a Malika Favre, playing with the same theme.

She returned and pointed at the Phillips work. "I can never decide if the girl is fading or emerging from the background."

"My thoughts too. What do you think's the difference?" Thomas asked.

"My mood," Kick answered. "For me, it's my mood."

She wore gray yoga pants with striped socks, a Hurricane's T-shirt, and a red cardigan. Slightly wild, the relaxed look fit her personality. The sweater ended above her hips, and he liked her form in the stretchy material. Her ass was another work of art. She'd clipped her hair loose at the neck, adding to her sexy, casual appearance.

"I still have the dairy-free flan. How about dessert?"

Anything for added time in this bubble he was seeing as a refuge. "Sounds perfect."

They settled on barstools and ate for a few minutes in silence. Bryan Ferry sang "You Do Something to Me" quietly in the background, competing with muffled dream barks from her sleeping dog.

Kick stared at Thomas, setting off his insecurity, suddenly aware there was more on the line for him than there had been when he'd made their plans. He raised both his eyebrows inquisitively, and she ducked her head with a shy smile.

Maybe they both felt a shift.

"Thanks again for the do-over." She swayed to the song as she ate. If music played in a room, Kick almost always found a way to dance to it. He guessed listening to it healed her, similar to the way it restored him to play it.

"Trust me, darlin', it's my pleasure."

They spent the rest of dinner listening to Cole Porter tunes, talking genres, favorite movies, and books. Their opinions overlapped in music—minus Kick's love for eighties alt-rock—and musicals. Kick sang along with some Broadway songs while

Thomas joined in. His voice had never matched his ability to play an instrument. Kick called "uncle" when he tried adding his off-key voice to "Not While I'm Around" from *Sweeney Todd*.

She threw her fingers over his mouth, laughing and nearly falling off the stool into him. Kick's free hand landed on his thigh to catch herself. Caught up in her giggles, she didn't notice his muscle twitch or jaw clench. He didn't mind. Her company, her old soul mixed with youthful enthusiasm, meant more to him than any attraction. Hell, it *led* to the attraction. It was his motivation for keeping a smile on her face. He considered it a victory anytime he made Kick laugh, and thought himself a king for it.

"Please stop. I don't want to ruin my favorite Broadway tune. Rachel and I watch *Sweeney* at the end of every school year to blow off steam." Kick gasped through her laughter.

Thomas didn't hear a word as his attention focused on her fingers on his lips. Who was he kidding? Somewhere between her chewing his ass out and their first dance, he'd begun wishing for her mouth on his until it became a craving. He feared he'd lose his mind if he never knew how she tasted. He allowed a shiver to travel up his spine, hoping it would snap him out of his impending madness.

The music changed. Louis Armstrong's version of "La Vie En Rose" filled the space as the mood in the room also took a quick turn.

Kick closed her eyes and let out a deep breath. "We need to talk about something." She waved her hands around as if she didn't know where to begin. "This song... It's, well, it's all good, you know? Hell. Let me start over. The other night... my life... Things get hard, but I don't want you to think I'm not grateful for what I have. My break was only for a minute. It's not me."

Thomas rose from his stool and paced. The disturbance that sent him to the chapel in the morning seeking peace raced through his system again. His heart demanded he comfort her, but he didn't have the right, not the way he wanted. Something cracked in Thomas despite his plan to hold back. He slowly walked to Kick, pulled her off her stool, and wrapped his arms around her. She remained rigid at first, then like an ice cube on a hot sidewalk, she dissolved into him. And he glimpsed the part of himself he was missing.

Her lack of tears surprised him. Perhaps she'd cried enough in private. Her breaths hitched at first, so he held her until their breathing synced. He could have held Kick forever. There was a familiarity in her pain, allowing her to give back to Thomas as much as he gave her.

"Emotions aren't right or wrong, Kick. I don't judge you for them," he soothed, looking down at her. "We feel how we feel. I knew it wouldn't take long for you to find your brave face again, and here you are."

Kick stayed in his embrace for a long time without speaking.

"It's been a while since a man held you, hasn't it?"

She laughed out loud while she nodded against his shoulder. "Pretty pathetic."

"Not at all. I haven't truly held a woman in a long time. It's wonderful." Thomas let his cheek fall against her head, soaking up the emotion as his lashes drifted shut. "It's not weakness to show vulnerability. In fact, it can point to our greatest strength."

Thomas opened his eyes again, watching Kick study him from under her lashes until her mouth ticked up. "Why does it feel like I could tell you the same thing?"

He cleared his throat and returned her smile. "It's easy to recognize our desires in others when our souls share the same aches."

The dog broke their tension. She trotted into the kitchen, barked for dinner, and pointed at the cabinet containing her food. "Like clockwork, you are. Hold on." Kick eased out of Thomas's arms and filled Macushla's bowl, setting it in the mudroom.

She returned to the kitchen and filled two glasses with iced tea, herbal for her, and peach black for him.

"Can I ask y'all something?"

"Anything." She returned to her stool and gave him her full attention.

"Promise me you'll ask for more help." He raised a hand to hold off a response. "I know you've done it in the past, and folks bailed. I'm not running. Let me be a better friend. Let me in, Kick."

She shook her head with passion. "You don't know what you're asking. I mean, I know my friends love my kids and me. But some things are too much." A tear began a slow descent down her porcelain cheek. "Have you seen any other women in my life? Mothers in particular? I used to have a boatload of acquaintances through the kids and such. Each setback saw more fall away until there were none.

"Hell, Liam's best friend, Jacklyn's mother, and I used to be close. She has a different autoimmune disease, but we bonded over doctor's appointments and body aches. We supported each other in our illnesses. I thought we did anyway. Until my weight loss and I showed signs of remission. It was a shocker to get judged for doing too well, but there it was. When I suddenly became single, she dumped me altogether. Can you believe she acted jealous, like I might steal her man? Not that I blame her. Not really."

"Why the hell not?"

Kick rubbed her arms as she put together her answer. "Every illness is different. What heals one person makes another worse. One thing they have in common is they mess with our heads. I'd forgotten about the loneliness. The recent appointments make me miss so much of my life and my crew."

Thomas leaned in, resting his hand against her cheek, brushing another tear with his thumb. "There are. If nothing else, let the persona go when I'm around. Put the mask away." He wanted to pound on every person who'd let her down.

"What makes you say I wear a persona?"

"I remember the story you told me about your name. Kick. It's a shield. I get it, but I hope you can get comfortable enough to drop it around me." Thomas didn't miss the irony that his own life was a charade, but peeking at the man he used to be when he was with her gave him hope. He could let his mask drop in her presence even if she didn't know he did. "Kick can take care of the world and everyone in it. I'd like to see more of Kathleen."

She quietly laughed and fell into Thomas's shoulder. "You want me to fill up your hero complex quota."

Thomas adjusted Kick to meet her eyes. "Your strengths can lift my weaknesses too." Even if she wasn't fully informed.

"You're talking of more than friendship, Professor."

"Perhaps. Can't we test the waters and see Kathleen? Maybe there could be an *us*." Christ, who opened the door and let his heart run wild? He meant every word slipping from his mouth though.

"An *us*, huh?" she asked with a teasing grin.

He nodded. "Got to admit, it's nice having you to myself. We can go slow. Hell, we both have a boatload of responsibilities. We've no choice but to go slow."

"So what? Dinners? Workouts? Weekends?"

"We both eat. We exercise. I was serious about rides from your doctor."

"What exactly do you want from me, Thomas?" She sounded irritated and impatient, but her face darkened with sadness and doubt.

He answered the question by standing between her legs, bending down, and kissing her.

Hard. Desperate.

Thomas's mouth demanded she kiss him back, acknowledge his desire, and validate it. The longing to taste her shook him, creating a new vulnerability, begging her to be in the same place as him.

Kick responded by deepening their kiss. She moaned as she folded into him. Her desire announced itself as she wrapped her arms around his neck and stood, pressing her body into his.

Thomas whispered in Kick's ear, "Was that enough of an answer? What do you have to say now?"

A smart smirk lifted one corner of her sweet mouth. "The flan tastes better on you." She brushed a thumb over his mouth to wipe off her gloss, and Thomas gasped at the gesture. He didn't dare wish for a time where they could be a complete couple, taking care of small wishes along with the big ones. The thought made a pretty picture though.

"Who are you, Thomas Harrison?"

"Too many things. With you, I'm a man again. I'm me." He was swept up in a wave and riding the crest. He'd taken a chance, ready to backpedal if he'd gone too far. Kick's response made him want to celebrate each moment with her as the gifts they were.

"Um, what just happened to our friendship?"

Thomas's eyes creased as his mouth slowly formed a broad grin. "Let's say it's evolving."

"Do that again...," she said, her breath catching. "Now."

He eagerly obeyed. There might have been magic in their connection. More than magic if they'd been other people.

His lips kept smiling as they softly brushed hers, a blessed refuge from everything stirring his restlessness. This kiss was slow, warm, and delicious. She was right too. The flan tasted better shared between them. He took his time exploring her mouth and her lips, occasionally pulling on her lower one. He turned his back to lean against the counter while keeping her against him, content to stay right there. Their mouths opened, and their tongues learned how to dance together. They possessed as much rhythm in their kiss as they did on a dance floor.

Focused fully on each other, they didn't hear the engine of the car as he peppered kisses along her jaw. Or hear the dog trot expectantly to the mudroom when his lips traveled down her throat, curving her back slightly over his left arm. They didn't hear the door open or close. Thomas's senses focused solely on Kick's giggle and moan as he found a ticklish spot.

"The hell, fam?"

20

SECRET

THOMAS

"Then we sprang apart like we'd had a fire hose turned on us," Thomas told Banger.

"Have to say, brother, I'm with Team Kid. What the hell were you thinking?" Banger sat in a chair in the third-floor office at Thomas's house. His friend had come by to use Thomas's shooting range at the back of his property, then run the forest trails.

"It shocked Liam to see his mom kissing me, especially in their house. I'd expect it of a typical teen. He's a good kid though. Helping him with a physics assignment this week and then jamming on a couple of guitars was fun. I hope to find time to get to know Kick's other two better as well."

He stared at Banger a moment. "You, on the other hand, act personally affronted, and I'm not sure why."

Thomas set a box of folders and notebooks on a portable table and opened the top file. For a split second, he'd forgotten what he wanted with the box. His brain refused to focus on anything substantial, and it drove him nuts. When he looked out the window toward the trees, hazel eyes smiled at him. Leaves on the shrub near his kitchen door had already turned a dark brown with reddish edges and an overall burnished gleam, like her hair.

He'd had a hellish week. Still, he couldn't shake the possibilities whispering in his ear whenever his thoughts drifted to her. They'd only managed a coffee break and ride home from her latest IV treatment since their dinner do-over. Their conversations and quick kisses fueled a desire for more. Kick dazzled Thomas, and he had to tamp it the hell down.

What had him discombobulated all evening was the goodbye kiss after he'd settled her on the sofa with an ice water. He'd cradled her jaw in his hands, his thumb stroking her delicate neck before finding the pulse at the base. Then their beats synced up, as if their cells had declared them simpatico. When the kiss ended, Kick's lips turned a cherry red and stayed puckered for a second. He wondered if she was aware of it. Or maybe she missed his lips when it ended. He sure as shit missed hers.

And the buzz when he touched her? It became sweeter with each caress—like smooth jazz. It seemed Kick noticed it too. An idea bloomed that their meeting might be more than coincidence.

Dammit all, his thoughts had drifted again while Banger was speaking.

"Fuck all, you're not listening," Banger protested, running a hand over his buzzed cut. "The woman is fine, sure, but hanging out with her—and her kid—is trouble. Would your wiser, older friend steer you wrong? I see the 'maybe it could be different with this one' look on your face right now. I'll spare you the anguish and tell you it's not. Kick sticks her nose in *everyone's* business. You think she won't pick up on your secrets? On us? The Felidae will always be a problem."

Thomas opened his mouth to protest and swallowed it back. Banger was right. Plus the man loved a good pontification. Who was he to hold Banger back?

"I get you're lonely, but stick to the plan. Find another *bic*. You remember those—*disposable women*? They're a no muss, no fuss release. You haven't given it a real shot since you moved here." Banger walked to a credenza at the far end of the space. Thomas kept a small bar there, and his friend poured two fingers of Scotch into a tumbler.

Thomas spoke while he made two stacks of papers from the folders he skimmed. "I'm done with throwaway girls. Hookups work for you, but it's become a dreadful bore. And I've honestly never known a *bic* to be no fuss. They promise to be at first, then they beg for more. Next thing you know, they've gone psycho."

"You're talking about the blonde from Manhattan."

"She followed me here and showed up at my lab in nothing but a trench coat and heels."

Banger swallowed his drink and chuckled.

"She *took the coat off*, man. In front of my associates."

Banger continued laughing until he snorted, wiping his eyes. "Because *you* couldn't cut her loose."

"The hell I couldn't. She wouldn't take the cutting. She thought I was playing hard to get and almost got me fired."

Banger poured more whiskey but said nothing. Thomas took it as confirmation that maybe the games wore on Banger too.

"Kick's frankness is refreshing. She's sticky as you say, but she'd never pulled a bait and switch. We can be friends, even excellent friends, and still have our own shit since her schedule is as loaded as mine. Because, you know, she's actually grown.

Hell, we had planned to hang out tonight, but I have to finish this stuff." Thomas raised the folder, then stopped to chuckle. "She acted *grateful* I canceled. Said she wouldn't feel so bad about the times her health or her schedule made her ditch plans too."

Banger returned to his seat and took a sip from his glass. "Naw, brother. Kick may understand moving slow, and I believe she won't play games, but she's a swan. She mates for life, and she's looking at you. Think about it. Why is her dating now such a surprise to her son? You had to have rocked her world to get her this far."

Thomas shook his head. "Kick's had a shitload on her plate. There's something I relate to. Stop worrying, man."

Banger raised his glass. "What about Vivienne? *There* was the perfect woman for men like us. You set her up so she could run her life while you went about yours. *Jings Crivvens*, I'd give anything for a find like her."

Thomas shook his head. "We lived that way before I met y'all. It was before my commitment ceremony to the Society. I was in a different headspace back then. The world was bigger too. There are similarities though. Kick has work, family, and her recovery to focus on. I have all this. It's probably what drew me to her, to be honest."

"If you say so. Don't forget I warned you." Banger walked toward Thomas and the box. "What are you doing anyway?"

Thomas ran a hand through his hair. "Trying to fix a crisis at the lab. Remember my first assistant, Presley?"

"Nigel's recommendation from Oxford?"

Thomas nodded. "That's her. Or it was. She died Monday. A hit-and-run while she was walking to her boyfriend's apartment. Police are still looking for the driver."

"Fuck, brother. I'm sorry. Did you tell Nigel?"

"Briefly. He's hard to get ahold of these days." *Grand-père's* cryptic warning came back to him, but he had more pressing issues to deal with. He'd do some digging when at the conference in Bordeaux.

Thomas continued, "I spent Wednesday with Presley's parents." It had been the hardest damn day he'd had in ages. It brought back memories he'd long buried—would've preferred they stayed so too. "Going through her locker contents now and sorting out what the lab needs from what could be shipped back home. The university has already lined up candidates to interview tomorrow. They're getting as pushy about my work as *Grand-père* is."

It helped to have Banger nearby while Thomas sorted through his assistant's things. The young scientist had shown so much promise, and Thomas had been fond of her. It would've been harder to go through Pres's desk contents alone.

Banger sat at Thomas's computer. "You good for me to update your machine now?" Thomas wondered if his friend sensed his need for companionship.

He answered while shuffling through another notebook. "That'd be great. Thanks."

Banger cracked his knuckles. "Since I'm here."

They worked in silence for thirty minutes before Thomas lifted a folder and a thumb drive dropped to the floor. A piece of tape with PROF. H on it piqued his curiosity. "What's this?"

Banger held his hand open and received the drive. "Perfect timing. Let me restart."

Thomas turned back to the box. The pile for Presley's family was half the size of the notes for the lab. Mostly, they amounted to duplicates of his own, but they were university property. The neatness and thoroughness of the work were indicative of his former assistant. He would miss having her in the lab.

"Uh, brother? You better come here."

"What's wrong?" Thomas moved around the desk to read the monitor. "Holy Christ."

His hands shook against his thigh as Banger clicked through a series of files and photos. The pictures were of Thomas in a World War I uniform. There was another of him in a double-breasted brown tweed suit with Vivienne at her dress shop's opening. Then came Thomas at Vivienne's funeral. A thick mustache with muttonchops didn't hide his bone structure. Neither could the gray hair or the soft wrinkles around his eyes. Thomas couldn't deny the similarities between him and the pictures, but he thought he had buried them from the public. The Felidae should have destroyed them. They had people in governments around the globe.

Presley had made notations, speculating the photos were of the same man and not a set of descendants. He thought back to her comment about his strong family genes. A note commenting on how he appeared younger ended with a circle and underlined the word *mitochondria*. *Good guess*, he thought. He also thought the key to his situation lay with the ancient bacteria powering every cell. As freaked as Thomas was, he still admired her research. Yeah, she would've been a huge asset.

Thomas grabbed the back of his neck. Somehow he'd let his guard down.

Banger broke the shocked silence. "There's a folder in here on Nigel too."

Photos and notes on their European counterpart, dating back to his participation in the Boer War, popped up on the screen.

"It's a good thing she never saw the paintings and photos you have around here," Banger said.

Thomas ran his hands through his hair. "This isn't funny, man. She practically figured us out." He pointed to a text document. "This mentions the Felidae Society. How was she able to get this far?" Thomas felt himself grow angry with Banger. As the head of Felidae security, he kept the members hidden.

Banger focused too deeply on the computer screen to answer Thomas. Knowing him, the man was already chewing his own

198 | KALLYN JONES

ass out. Banger clicked another file, opening a letter. He let out a low, "Fuck me," as he read.

"She planned to blackmail me?" Thomas croaked. So much for missing her. The letter was an ultimatum—make Presley a test subject, or she'd go public with her findings, starting with the dean.

"There's a folder in here with Toni's name on it too."

Toni's children didn't know she still lived. Releasing this information would've hurt them. Ruined lives. Blackmailing Thomas was bad enough, but screwing with Toni's life? He grew furious. "Dammit all to hell."

"You would've been. We dodged an armor-piercing bullet here."

"But did she tell anyone? Pres was a brilliant assistant. Capable and reliable. Do you think she would've blurted this out to a friend? Her boyfriend? I have a hard time believing she would, but—"

"You'll be leaving that to me now," Banger assured him.

With impeccable timing, Thomas's phone rang. "Shit. It's the old man. Did you send out vibes?" he said jokingly, looking for anything to ease the squeeze in his chest.

"Say nothing. Let me look into it." At some point, Thomas had to get to the bottom of Banger's recent pullback from the Felidae. He thought Banger and Alaric had resolved their bad blood.

"You sure?" Thomas answered the call. "*Oui, Grand-père.*"

Banger nodded his head while mouthing, "Not a thing."

21

HOLD ON LOOSELY

KICK

I sat on the imaginary porch in my mind, surrounded by the comforting scent of gardenias. My meditation practice had been taking me back here since I'd first dreamed about it. Unfortunately, my companion hadn't shown up again, but like he'd said, the place was mine. I learned to sit there anytime I wanted to refresh. Positivity and hope lived on the porch, filling me up with reinforcement. Boy was it a requirement presently. My mother had returned from her cruise the previous night.

Bobby wasn't allowed on my porch. The annoying voice she'd

weasled into my mind stayed at the top of the stairway leading
down to my precious space. It was a relief to maintain some
headroom free of her. I didn't even mind seeing the cool glow
around my skin when I traveled back up the steps and opened
my eyes. Instead, I embraced the humming tingle accompanying
the light, certain the glow would quickly fade.

My phone beeped a text alert. It took a minute to reorient and
remember where I'd put it. I fished the thing out of a cargo
pocket in my pants and swiped.

**Thomas: Will you be available in thirty minutes? It won't
take long.**

Me: I'm at the Perked Cup all day.

Thomas: I'd like to speak in person if it's all right.

**Me: If you don't mind coming here. I'm decorating for
Halloween and meeting with a sales rep.** Someone had broken
my drive-through speaker the night before. The poor thing
looked like they demolished it with a baseball bat.

Thomas: You're not wearing yourself out, are you?

**Me: No worries. Just finished meditating or whatever.
Feeling good.**

**Thomas: Wonderful! Great job. I'll see you soon. Finishing
up notes for my new assistant.**

Me: Sounds good.

I replaced my phone and walked out to the front of the café
with a stupid grin on my face.

Cyndi stood at the counter, ordering from Deana's new hire,
Crystal. Jake and Deana had both done a fantastic job filling our
staffing holes. I hadn't been able to see our newest girl work on
her own, so I stood back and observed.

"A flat white. Sub the steamed milk for half-heavy whipping
cream and half water," Cyndi ordered. She gravitated toward the
persnickety when it came to coffee. I think she enjoyed giving
specific directions.

"Amazing. Any flavor?" Crystal prompted.

"Sure. Sugar-free lavender."

"Ah, perfect," she enthused. I'd heard Crystal's way of receiving an order was as unique as Cyndi's way of placing one.

I chuckled at the confused V on Cyn's brow.

"Hot or cold?"

"Hot please," Cyndi said.

"Definitely. Anything else?"

"Yes. The pumpkin scone."

"Absolutely. Fantastic." Crystal's encouragement bordered on orgasmic.

My hand jumped to my mouth to contain a snicker. From what I could tell, Crystal's zealous style came naturally. I shuffled to the drive-through.

Deana was working it without the squawk box but had a break in traffic. "I love your new girl."

Dee smiled at the comment.

"You didn't tell her to be more..."

"Exuberant?"

I nodded, trying my best not to giggle.

Deana shook her head and released her warm chuckle. "Naw. It's all her."

"I love it. She brightens the place with her coffee evangelism."

"What about you?" Dee asked. "You happen to sneak some caffeine in your office?"

"No. I'm being good. Why?"

"Oh, I see now. You have a Thomas gleam in your eye."

"Excuse me?"

"I saw you walk out here all smarmy. The professor looks good on you."

"Stop. And behave. He's coming by in a bit."

"This will be fun." Her laugh followed me as I finally reached the counter.

"How's the morning going, Crystal?"

"Wonderful, Mrs. Mack. What brings you back out here?"

My job? Then again, so much time spent away made it feel less like mine lately. Maybe I wasn't the only one. I hoped I'd be able to go back to normal and not have to make a new normal. I changed the subject. "This here is my bestie, Cyndi. She's part of the Perked Cup family. Thank you for taking great care of her."

Crystal's eyes opened wide as she shook her head. "It's fabulous to meet you, Mrs.…?"

"Cyndi's fine, honey."

"Wonderful." Crystal turned back to me. "I try to give everyone their deserved service."

"I noticed. Thank you. Deana found a gem in you."

"She's chill."

"Yes she is," I answered, assuming she meant *awesome*. After giving Crystal instructions to refill the napkin dispensers and do the bathroom check, I made myself a cup of herbal tea and set it down opposite my friend's.

"Is she on drugs?" Cyndi whispered.

I laughed and the tea almost went down the wrong pipe. "I wouldn't ask that too loudly." We were still dealing with the fallout from the newspaper article. I shrugged anyway. "It seems to be all her though. Mmm. This is good."

"You mean fabulous?" Cyndi asked, imitating Crystal's enthusiasm.

"Sure. Who knew cardamom and cinnamon would be a wonderful midmorning pick-me-up?"

She leaned across the counter and sniffed the rim. "Smells delicious."

"I know. Deana hooked me up." I bent to my elbows, leaning on the counter. "What brings you in this morning?"

"Checking in. How did it go with the dragon lady yesterday?"

"Fine." My mother seemed happy to be back. For her anyway. She filled the ride home with anecdotes from her trip, telling me about the beautiful places she'd seen and how they contrasted with "those poor people's lives" who live near the excursion sites.

Cyndi wiggled in her seat. "How did she take the news of Thomas?"

The door chime rang, followed by my son, Dylan, rushing in, saving me from having to answer. I hadn't said a word to Bobby. To me, there was no news to report. We definitely weren't the kind of close that required sharing with my mother. I didn't know if we'd ever be. I still didn't think I'd want to risk my heart again.

I turned to my boy, his chest puffed, linebacker shoulders wider than normal, a peculiar strut in his step. "Morning, lad. Would you like an Americano before work?" He was about fifteen minutes early for opening Mick & Hugh's.

"Sure. A double. Thanks, Mom. I have a question too." He bent down and kissed Cyndi on the cheek. "Morning, Aunt Cyn. Good to see you. This is more for you anyway."

"What is, honey?" Cyndi asked.

"Can I get a loan from my trust fund?"

I situated the porta-filter and turned around. "For the business launch? Your final project's far from finished." Not that I would know anymore. My kid's lips were locked tight regarding his thesis. "Isn't it early to be pulling money to finance it?"

He slid onto the stool next to Cyndi. "It is. I want the money for an engagement ring."

Hell-to-the-fecking-no. My hand shook so I nearly dumped the boiling water in the cup. Times like this made me want to curl myself into a ball and disappear. Or scream at the men who'd left us. Dylan benefited from men galore when he was a cocky little boy, and the stakes were *PBS Kids* programming versus *Nickelodeon*. Now when he really could use a man's ear and wisdom? He had me. *Thanks, guys.*

My boy needed a wife like he needed a hole in his head. Most *definitely* not a self-possessed-workaholic-med-student-with-her-own-family-dysfunction-issues wife. No way would I let him lay a finger on that money for a ring.

"Sweetheart," I started cautiously. "If you can't afford a ring from your bank account, take it as a sign to wait. Suzy has at least two more years of medical school."

Dylan turned from a twenty-four-year-old man to a toddler with puppy eyes in a heartbeat. He fixed his face on Cyndi, looking for help.

She raised her hands in defense. "Don't look at me, kiddo. I put the sing in single. I'm in your mama's camp."

My bestie. Loved her. We were definitely getting neighboring rooms at the old-folks' home. "You already live together, Dyl, and both your lives are intense this year. Why now?"

"Maybe *I* need it," he muttered.

I handed him his drink in a to-go cup. "Fine. What about asking one of your grandmothers? They both have multiple wedding sets, and they're gorgeous. The one Grandpa bought Bobby for their thirtieth anniversary is stunning. She doesn't wear it anymore."

"She has four grandsons. Don't forget Uncle Bert's boys."

"I haven't. You're her favorite by far." I held no delusions about Bobby's sense of fairness.

"Doesn't she still want it? Grandpa's death is so recent."

She all but threw it in the coffin with Dad. "I think she'd love a chance to be a part of your moment. Grandpa had amazing taste too." It had pissed me off when he'd given her the two karat ring as a peace offering. Another pointless effort to make her happy. After Bobby's icy response of "How nice. Isn't it odd how diamonds have no color?" I'd begged him to divorce her and finally seek his own happiness.

"I'll think about it. Thanks, Mom." Dylan kissed Cyndi and me on our cheeks and headed off to work. I swore he stood a little taller when he left. No small feat for my ginormous son who'd wanted a plan to feel secure. Perhaps I helped him after all.

. . .

"THE FIRST LINE OF BUSINESS." THOMAS OPENED HIS ARMS WIDE for me to enter when we were safely in the privacy of my office. I stepped in, clinging to his waist, tucking my head against his chest, breathing in the sandalwood he probably used to wash or shave with or both. Thomas did more or less the same, burying his face in my mass of curls. I'd removed the scrunchie earlier to relieve a low-level headache.

Being together chased my doubts away. Since the first embrace in my kitchen, these stolen minutes filled me with hope and steeled my backbone as much as they turned me into a lust-crazed woman. We stayed like this until our heartbeats fell into sync. I was equal parts excited and terrified to admit I wanted more. Sometimes I wanted him every day. But we didn't have daily. So I pushed down the signs of clinginess and took what I could get.

Thomas peppered my jaw and neck with slow kisses. I flicked back my hair, giving him better access. His attention at the spot where my neck and shoulder met made me giggle, drawing a burly purr from him. "Discovering your spots is my new favorite hobby."

My hands trailed under his T-shirt and up across the tight muscles of his back. "I enjoy discovering you too." A desire to see him, to be with him fully washed over me until confusion set in. It was too soon, especially with Liam at home. I didn't even know if we'd *ever* become overnight people. The real problem was not knowing precisely what we were doing, what our goals were. If there *were* any. If I could ever get past the past.

Enjoy the now, eejit. You never know when it'll be gone.

Thomas scooted us to the edge of my desk and placed me between his legs. His lean made our heights match, so I took advantage. A flirty, teasing bite to his lower lip turned into a pleasant surprise when Thomas dove in, devouring me with an open mouth and his hungry tongue. His hand traveled from the back of my neck, down my arm, to my stomach. Jaysus. This. I'd missed it.

We both gasped and hummed like bees finding a favored flower when he pulled me closer until I brushed against his erection. Could he be ready for more? Or did he have the same apprehensions as me? We were moving a lot faster than I'd ever done, but I knew if Cyndi were in my shoes, she'd already know whether Thomas had any birthmarks and all that.

Without thinking, I took more, subtly giving Thomas's cock a grind until his movements froze. "I'm sorry darlin'. We need to stop."

"Wha—?" I breathed, the pull back to responsible Kick McKenna almost painful. My eyes swept him from head to toe when it hit me what was off when he'd walked in. "Hang on, why are you in a T-shirt and jeans in the middle of the day? Is everything okay?"

Thomas's cleft chin quivered with what could've been laughter at my undoing or unshed tears. I know I wanted to cry from the loss of his lips.

He tucked a curl behind my ear. "Time to talk."

In an instant, he masked up again; part of me was jealous of the ability. This hot-and-cold aspect of Thomas's personality wore on me too. From what I'd overheard in the café, it was the current way of dating. I figured I had to get used to it. Deep in my gut, a voice told me there was more, that he held back something big. But the truth wasn't always a friend. More than once, I'd considered it an enemy and would have gladly embraced self-delusion in hindsight. I wanted to be an easy place to fall, trusting it to be enough.

We each sat in a club chair before Thomas stated, "I'm leaving earlier than I'd planned for Bordeaux. Tomorrow, in fact."

"Oh." We'd made plans for... "The Raleigh State football game with Dylan and Suzy?"

"Yeah." He sighed, rubbing the back of his neck. "I have to cancel. It's about work."

I searched his eyes for signs of remorse, but as a person with plenty of experience canceling plans, I also knew the self-preserving value in distancing yourself from disappointment and moving ahead with the alternate course.

"Well"—I reminded myself to *be* the safe place—"we both knew things like this would happen." I leaned across the open space and grabbed his hand, lacing our fingers. I let the gentle hum roll through me even though it still startled me. His heavy calluses remained a mystery to me. It wasn't what I'd expect from the average professor and was another reminder we still had a lot to learn about each other. "It's about the research?"

Part of the mask lowered when he answered, "Yep."

"Can you get time for yourself while you're gone? I heard it's lovely there."

Thomas's hand moved up my arm to my neck, and he pulled my forehead to his lips for a gentle kiss. "It is lovely." He let his head fall to mine on an exhale. "Your sweetness... I thought you'd be upset. This makes it harder."

I moved back to meet his gaze. "Thomas, we both have responsibilities. It's why we agreed to slow and casual."

"Yes, but..."

His work was a genuine passion, I wondered if he had any room in his head, let alone his schedule, for more. "Do you not want to go?"

He shook his head, found my hand again, and kissed my knuckles. "I hoped we could..."

I giggled. "Tell me about it. But I'll be here when you get back." If he only knew how many times I'd done this before. In my old life, I used to wait for weeks at a time before my husband would return. I often showed up alone for the kids' events. Hell, the last time I'd let myself think about dating again, I vowed never to get involved with a man who traveled for a living. Then again, I'd also vowed never to date a younger man. My breath grew shallow as my chest tightened. Here was my sign. We should let go and get out before we went too far.

"Thomas—"

"These past few weeks... you've been so good for me. I wish I could explain it better. Seeing you, talking to you, texting you. Hell, when you send me silly Pokémon notifications in the middle of my day and it's instantly better. Something in me is shifting." He lifted his head. I don't know what he found in my gaze, but his own suddenly filled with terror. "Damn, I've said too much."

But he hadn't. He'd said the words I needed to hear. "No, sweets. I feel the same. Please finish."

"Some crazy things have happened at work."

"Your assistant," I said, stroking his palm with my thumb. I couldn't imagine losing a protégé so tragically. My heart hurt for him.

"Yes, and more after. I'll get a lock on it. On me. I've been second-guessing myself at every turn. But you..."

"Me?" I waited and saw the words he couldn't say in his eyes. I wanted to keep him too. In whatever form we could find to work. Whatever it was we were doing, it helped. I kissed his palm. "Me too."

"You're making me want to whisk you away to someplace private."

His near pout made me smile. "Not very patient, are you?"

I received a sexy grin in return. "Normally, yes. Nothing steers me from my decided path. That's why I'm out of sorts over you."

"Ooh, flattery. Go on." I batted my lashes.

"I'm serious, Kick. Not upset, just confused. I don't know how to veer off my course, but it's all I can think about."

His words threw me. I wanted to help Thomas meet his goals, not interfere with them. "Maybe you should get a new compass?"

"Perhaps." Thomas tipped his chin like he took my words to heart. The words "let me be your compass" sat on my lips, itching to come out. I couldn't release them. While Cyndi's voice in the back of my mind egged me on, daring me to seduce and coax more from him, another one told me to be at peace with the present. That voice sounded a lot like Deana.

"How long will you be gone?"

"Ten days now. Since I'm going early, if I can leave the scheduled end, I will."

"Will you have time for calls? It's okay if you won't. I know how all-consuming business travel can be."

He stood and pulled me into his arms again. "I'll make time." He kissed my temple and said, "Can we get away when I come back? It doesn't have to be far. Maybe a simple overnight at my house?"

"I'd love to," I answered, unable to hide a grin, thinking of the things I'd like to do with him with an entire night's time and seeing the same thoughts reflected on his face. "But we already have plans for dinner with my kids next weekend."

"Right."

Based on the way he bit his lip, sexiness notwithstanding, I figured he'd forgotten. "Is it still on or should I—"

"No, no. I'll aim to get back for it. We can talk through the rest of our schedules while I'm gone."

"I'd like that too."

We sealed our plans with another thorough kiss, taking my breath away and almost making me beg to tag along on his trip to France.

"Y'all mind feeding me something to-go? I have to meet my neighbor soon." He held out the hem of his T-shirt. "The reason for casual clothes. My TA is teaching today."

I tsked and rolled my eyes in a sarcastic joke. "Make food for you? I suppose." I laughed and remembered something. "Do you have a ride to the airport? If you have an early flight, I could drop you off on the way to my IV appointment."

Thomas's shoulders dropped as he remembered what he'd promised me. "Dammit. I'm supposed to give you a ride."

My hand moved up his arm and stroked his back to ease his mind. "It's fine. Work has obviously demanded your attention."

"It would be great to see you again." He squeezed me tight and said, "Can you be at my place at seven thirty? I'll make breakfast."

"For me? Are you daft?" I laughed. Thomas had proven he took my food allergies seriously, but breakfast was a different animal.

"Only for you." He turned us away from my desk and whispered in my ear. "Don't worry, darlin'. I've paid attention."

What the hell. If I couldn't let Thomas fix a little breakfast, we didn't deserve to move forward. "Sure. Why not? I'll see Liam off to school and head over. You want me to bring anything?"

He kissed the top of my head and opened the door. "Just you. Thanks for trusting me."

My smile stayed broad as we walked out to the dining area, our fingers laced as Thomas followed me down the short hallway. Then we turned the corner, and my steps halted. My mother sat on a stool at the counter, staring straight at us. More accurately, she lasered in on our clasped hands, a shit-eating grin on her face.

22

TAINTED LOVE

KICK

I dropped our hands and bolted for the counter, all business and service-oriented. Thomas didn't embarrass me, but until I knew for certain how to define us, we would be Bobby's new ammo of choice. Like a gun collector eager to fire a new weapon on a range, she would hungrily absorb this intelligence and shoot it off when it could do the most damage.

I quickly filled Thomas's order and sent him off with the friendly smile nearly every customer received, knowing exactly how cold I came off. I saw the confusion on his face as he pressed a quick kiss to my cheek, making it pinch with a sharp shock.

Deana watched it go down, taking a break from her inventory check to make sure I knew she saw me flinch. She told me how much I'd disappointed her without a word exchanged. Hell, I'd disappointed myself. I hated how my resolve crumbled when things didn't go as planned.

"I heard about... *him*." Bobby tipped her head in the door's direction.

"Good afternoon, Mother," I said as brightly as I could, ignoring shot number one while calculating which child had to die for blabbing. Probably Rachel.

"Regardless how much you deny it, you'll always be a bloody chip off the old block."

If I had a dollar for every time she'd said those words, or any other cliché for that matter. I deflected. "Aw, you missed the café when you left, didn't you? You should know, Hugh and Maggie have been stopping in again. They're doing well."

"*Pfft*," she answered, and I cherished the small win. I got her to answer my dig before responding to hers. Yes, it was petty. We were in danger of slipping straight back into our diseased habits.

"It's a wonder Hugh's chicken-shit wife goes anywhere other than the house and the senior center. Since he has a secret thing for me, it'll be fun to run into them now that I'm free."

Eww. Her words inspired an eye roll so thorough it was a wonder I still used glasses. There was no way I'd honor her ridiculous comment with one of my own, so I shifted back. "What brings you in? I thought you'd still be unpacking."

She jabbed her thumb over her shoulder, toward outside. "I have to get groceries. *Someone* left my refrigerator empty. I thought I'd see what your little group is up to before I go to the store. You sure you can afford the extra help? It's not like your father's around to make you more money." As if she honestly cared.

While working on the assembly line at General Motors, my father developed a side interest in stocks. He turned out to have a talent for it and grew his hobby into a side hustle. When I came into money, he turned it into enough to enable me to bolster the foundation and support trust funds for each child. Overall, I didn't hurt for funds but was aware of how quickly a café and an out-of-pocket doctor could soak up my bank account when not closely monitored.

"Kyle's keeping an eye on the money, and Cyndi keeps the books balanced. There's nothing to worry about." Before Dad passed, he'd taken Hugh's nephew, Kyle, under his wing. Kyle grew it into his own business.

Bobby checked her watch. "I don't like to shop when there's still a chance of a screaming toddler wandering the aisles. Get me a decaf cappuccino."

One decaf latte coming up. Bobby always ordered a cappuccino despite her hatred of foam. I figured she simply found the word cool to say. She wouldn't let me correct her anyway.

"I offered to have Carmen stock your kitchen before you came home, but you told me no."

"No, you didn't. You probably *thought* you offered but forgot to say something. You do that, you know. You should tell your fancy doctor about your poor memory. With what you pay her, the *least* she could do is fix it."

Did I imagine it? I searched my memory bank and remembered our last phone call. I'd offered. If only she'd agree to email or text, I'd have written proof. Bobby proudly proclaimed an aversion to technology.

As I finished making her latte, three customers came in, giving me an opportunity for distance from Bobby, though her glare persisted. Crystal and I worked through another late-lunch group while Deana finished up in the back. The whole time, Bobby regaled tales from her cruise. When I could, I laid out the photos on the counter—actual photos. I admit, it was cute— admiring the gorgeous views from the Caribbean and South America. Every picture was filled with faces we'd never know, but the customer line and my crew learned their names, where they lived, where their grandchildren went to school, and whether their children were treating them right. Oh, and if said male children were married or single. Insert another eye roll.

At one point, Bobby leaned toward me, gossip-style, her favorite posture. She tipped her chin toward Crystal. "That one's the village idiot."

"The fu— Hell she is," I whisper-yelled back. "She's wonderful and you'll leave her alone."

"As long as she keeps away from me, we'll be fine. Since you are here, get me another cappuccino. You've finally figured out how to make it right." Bobby shivered and made a face. "No bloody foam. They never got it right on the ship."

"Fine. I'm making it to-go. Then you can pop in on Dylan and ask him about his thesis project. It's coming along."

She waved me off. "I don't understand computer stuff."

"He'd explain it. Plus I think he has a question for you."

"Yeah? Is the shop still filled with smoke?"

Mick & Hugh's never filled with smoke. They invested heavily in air filtration, but she swore the store made her wheeze. "You'll be fine. It's slow this time of day."

She nodded her perfectly straight, limp, honey-blond bob thoughtfully. It highlighted her still crisp jawline and pert nose. A stunning woman, despite her consistent scowl, she was the opposite of me in virtually every way. "I'll do that. Thank you, dear."

"Have a nice afternoon, Mother." Happy to know we'd pulled it back from our usual cliff, my thoughts kept rerunning whether I'd offered to stock her kitchen.

Deana returned to the front, her purse over her shoulder, to make her usual end-of-the-shift to-go cup.

"Hey, Dee, did I offer to fill Bobby's fridge and pantry?"

She turned to me, her lips pursed. "I heard her, Kick. And yes. You offered to have Carmen do it though."

"Well, yeah. She's my house manager. She grocery shops for

me." Lord knew I'd have no time or energy for it. Plus Carmen rocked. She'd saved my bottom many times.

"First, your mama thinks you eat weird food. Second, *if* she agreed, it would only be when a family member did it. Let it go, Kick. She's never gonna change. I heard her describing the local people in her pictures. That woman's a stone-chiseled—"

"So I didn't imagine it?"

She shook her head and laughed. "You're straight. You won't be in tomorrow, right?"

"Nope." We gave each other one-arm squeezes. "See you next week."

Liam passed Deana at the doorway. He beelined for me, a worried line running through his knitted brow.

"Something wrong, weeman?"

"Have you heard from Snow?" he asked.

"No." As far as I knew, Rachel was safe and sound on campus. Thank goodness. I'd had my fill of family problems, but he gave me the feeling my plate was about to overflow.

Liam handed me his phone. "More viral shit about her went around school today."

23

SAY IT RIGHT

THOMAS

*K*ick jumped when Thomas whipped open his kitchen door; her fist stayed frozen midair, ready to knock one more time. He was still damp from a shower, jeans only half-buttoned, barefoot.

"Hey," he said, catching his breath.

"Hiya," she answered, worrying her tongue against her cheek. He was almost too distracted to remember he thought it a cute tell of Kick's anxiety. Almost.

"You're early. I just got out of the shower."

"So I see." Her hand opened and gently touched the nasty scar on his left bicep. "What happened here?" She'd seen him with a tank on when they exercised. And it was a large, ugly thing. How was she now noticing it? He didn't have the time, or the will, to tell the story of the scar. Neither the false one most people heard or the real one, not that he could tell her the truth.

He deflected. "It's chilly out there. Come on in." Thomas stepped back and watched her pass.

"Thank you." She stopped at the bench in the mudroom and laid her sweater down. Stepping into the bright kitchen, she spun in a circle, taking in the sunny space he'd updated first. He had done most of the renovations himself. "Oh, Thomas, this is beautiful. You did it?"

How did she conclude that without clarifying? He was beginning to think Kick could read him easily. Too easily.

Thomas covered her hand as it came to rest on the island counter, getting her attention. "I have to finish getting ready, darlin'."

"Darlin' still? So I'm not in the doghouse?"

"Pardon?"

"The last time we saw each other, I treated you like gum stuck to my shoe. Yet you still call me darlin'. Does this mean we're okay?"

Though he'd lived all over, he'd remained a Southern man first, calling any woman with friendship status darlin'. "Are you apologizing?"

Kick's shoulders dropped with her head, her shame screaming in her body language. "I am."

He sat in a stool at the counter, giving her his full attention. "Are you embarrassed by me?" He could relate to being hot and cold with an interest, though this was the first time he'd been the receiver.

"How do I explain this...?" Kick's head tipped back. She scratched at her temple before tucking a curl behind her ear. "It's best if Bobby hears as little as possible for now. I wanted time before she knew about us. If we… if we go our separate ways, she'll use it against me forever."

Thomas studied Kick's profile as the sun caught the curls at her crown, turning some a bright copper against the field of brown. He reached over and pulled back the one on her cheek. She'd given him a boatload of dysfunction to parse. One thing stood out though. "We'll be friends no matter what, Kick. We won't be going our separate ways."

She laughed and gave him her full gaze, a doubtful arrow or two shooting from it. "Really? Friends who kiss and grope each other into oblivion? Come on, Thomas. We're supposed to be planning a weekend away. I don't think it's for private cappuccino-making lessons."

Thomas shivered. "Good. I hate foam." For some reason, the comment made her belly-laugh. He was glad to lift the vibe in the room even if he didn't know why. "You know what I mean. We're friends with…"

Two of Kick's fingers suddenly covered his lips. "Don't say benefits. The phrase makes my stomach turn. Besides, I get we're going slow, but FWB is a total lose-lose."

Thomas turned his chin to kiss her palm. He knew slow. He did slow blindfolded with his wrists cuffed behind his back. He'd figure out the rest later. Hardened to the guilt that came from holding back, he said, "Don't worry about yesterday. You lost the ability to control what and how much a troublesome person knows. I've been there too."

Kick shook her head. "I can't believe my ears. Thank you."

"Still need to get ready. Mind waiting down here?"

"How about I make breakfast?"

Thomas glanced at the clock on the stove. Their delay made him run late. "Fantastic." He pointed to the fridge. "How do you feel about smoothies?"

"You kidding? It's the nectar of the immunocompromised. Your smoothie's in a master's hands. Now shoo." She waved him off with a smile. Thomas thought about her smile as he bounded up the stairs to his bedroom, his body humming with pleasure.

THOMAS HEARD KICK SINGING FROM THE UPSTAIRS LANDING. He couldn't help grinning as she danced at the kitchen sink, cleaning the blender. He stayed in the shaded area at the edge of the archway, watching her. Curls were bouncing, her pert ass swaying to Nelly Furtado's "Say it Right" while she sang along. She wore yoga pants and a T-shirt that fell to her hips. He'd learned she chose them for comfort and easy vein access—her IV day uniform. They did wonders to highlight her hourglass figure. She was a forest nymph, seducing him with her movements and sweet voice. Lost in the song and her work, he watched her lush lips move and eyes occasionally close from emotion in the reflection in the window. The need to adjust himself surprised Thomas. He wasn't a boy who worried about control. He was a man who defined himself by the word.

The words.

The words flowing from her mouth were the ones tapping on his soul for attention. They resembled the ones he kept locked away with his other impossibilities.

Seeing her in his space burned his heart more than the desire for a woman's touch. Outside of a cleaning service, Kick was the first woman to spend time here, and she didn't know the significance. Banger was the only other person who regularly visited Thomas's house, his sanctuary.

The room itself, gray cabinetry, black granite counters, and sage walls fulfilled his wish for a masculine, functional, and bright kitchen with modern conveniences. He designed it for himself; only Kick made the space look like a home.

He should have rushed breakfast and scooted them out, never to let it happen again, but he liked the view. He wanted more of it, feared it could become an addiction. As he glimpsed how life like this might work, the desire grew. Yet responsibilities to the Felidae pulled on him more than the weight of the luggage he balanced in his hand.

So he watched, frozen between his *musts* and his *wants*, knowing they wouldn't mix. *Screw it*. He left his suitcase and laptop bag in the hall, entered the kitchen, and encouraged Kick to finish the final bars of the song while he danced her around the airy space. The whole time, he contemplated the possibility of "what if."

SLIDING INTO THE PASSENGER SEAT OF KICK'S CAMARO, IT STRUCK Thomas how they'd gravitated to the same model vehicle—his almost fifty years old, hers about two. Like attracts like. For the first time since he'd received *Grand-père's* call, he was glad to get out of town. His mind and his libido kept wandering to places it had no business traveling. Trapped in her muscle car, reciting baseball stats in his head wouldn't help take his mind off the woman sitting next to him. He finished the smoothie she'd made. It tasted better than any he'd ever blended. *Damn her*.

Kick draped her left wrist at twelve o'clock on the steering wheel while her right hand caressed the shifter. It was another way she reminded Thomas of himself, driving like a champion rider bonded to a prized horse. He savored the feeling when he was alone in his own machine.

"For feck's sake."

"Wha-?" Her sharp tone jolted Thomas's thoughts.

She pointed to the SUV in front. "If this idiot's Rover can't handle the one-inch lip in the intersection's repave, he should take it to the sidewalk with the other Big Wheels. I mean, really? There's no reason he can't... oh, I don't know... drive over the tiny bump in his premium SUV."

He eyed her curiously. "I suppose." Fortunately, they maneuvered through town traffic quickly and eased into the twists and turns of a flowing country road again.

"Now look at this charmer," she complained about an oncoming car crossing the double line multiple times. "This one thinks her half of the road runs down the middle." She honked, and the driver's eyes lifted from her lap, then corrected the heavy sedan. Kick grunted. "Like I want to go another round with a texting bitch."

Thomas looked at her and laughed. Her eyes shifted to the side. "What tickles your funny bone?"

"I didn't peg you as a road rager."

Kick glanced over again. This time her jaw dropped, her posture defensive. "It's not road rage. Road rage is holding it in until you explode. I, on the other hand, say what's on my mind before it turns into a temper. So here I am, traveling happy as a bird because the bad juju flew away." She turned her head, a crazy, wide grin in place for emphasis.

Her eyes turned back to the road as she sped up. He needed this. Focus on her flaws and get back to reality. She wasn't a mystical forest goddess. Kick was a typical, moody human.

She chanced another glance, and they erupted in laughter, Thomas shaking his head.

"Okay," she said, lifting her palm off the wheel in surrender. "I promise to be a lady for the rest of the ride." Her profile beamed. "But you know, Southern women can be nasty behind the wheel. Heaven forbid you meet one in a carpool line. Can't tell you how glad I am that those days are done."

"Banger told me something new went down with your daughter's harassment situation."

"Yeah." Kick brow creased. "The cyberbully attacked again. Unfortunately, Rachel has to keep the social media accounts for networking. Her boyfriend isn't supportive either. She should... Well, never mind."

"Why didn't you tell me?"

Kick glanced over. "I called the detective to make sure the harassment gets recorded. Since no one's threatened her per se… Well, Banger said he'd see what he could do."

"Y'all can tell me about these things, you know."

She shrugged a shoulder. "I wasn't sure you'd want to hear from me after the way I acted in the café, let alone hear me go on about my daughter's troubles."

Was his head really so far up his ass? He knew she'd screwed up in the coffee shop, but he'd been so focused on his own shit he'd barely given it a thought.

They fell into a comfortable silence, listening to music. Thomas resumed studying Kick's body as it handled the car. His eyes locked on her right hand. She was oblivious to the careful caressing of the grip as she harmonized with the singer on the radio. He could almost feel her hand doing the same thing to him. From the way she'd perked up, Thomas figured the song was a favorite. Soon she was equal parts driving and dancing. Thomas's breaths quickened, and he squeezed his eyes shut as he counted to slow his heart rate. The arousal became a given, but he didn't want to sport wood running through the airport or for the duration of the drive.

"You can nap until we arrive."

"Nap?"

"Your eyes keep closing."

"Oh. I was enjoying… the song."

She smiled brightly. "Yeah, 'Everlong' is great."

Thomas studied her profile, still swaying as she watched the surrounding vehicles. "You dance all the time, even here in the car. Did you ever take lessons?"

The morning sun through the trees edging the road striped her face in light and shadow like a strobe light. Her neck snapped to him. "What?"

"You're a natural dancer. You follow me like a proper partner. Even here, you've kinda figured out how to make a car dance."

He opened his hands. "So I wondered if you've had formal training."

Kick nodded and chuckled, but not from happiness. Her stare traveled far into the past, the noise sarcastic. "I was Bobby's prized student at her dance studio growing up. Taught classes as a teen. She expected me to become a pro and do what she never had a chance to. Make her look good. She didn't take it well when I stopped."

"What happened?"

Kick bit her lip and focused on traffic instead of answering. When she finally did, the words came slow and deliberate. "No one alive knows the entire story. In short, there was a betrayal, and it killed my dancing dreams. I'd rather not say any more if you don't mind."

Thomas tapped her hand as it gripped to the shifter. "All right. I'm glad you got it back."

A corner of her mouth lifted as her head tilted toward him. "No one's ever taking it from me again. And you make it fun."

The radio lit up with a jazzy song, sending Kick wild. He thought he heard Pee Wee Marquette speaking and shook his head. She cranked up the volume. "Come on, Thomas. You can't sit still for this one." She swayed and shimmied to the song. Her hands circled and crossed each other as she rapped along with the singer.

Thomas laughed and did his best car dancing to "Cantaloop (Flip Fantasia)" until g-forces pressed him into the seat belt. At the same time, her hand flew to the stick, and she down-shifted to merge into a traffic snare.

Instinct made Thomas throw his arms out. One braced the dash for him, the other went to the side for her. And grabbed a handful of tit. He'd brushed fingers along the side of their softness already. But damn… the weight, the fullness in his hand… perfect.

Embarrassment swept through him, freezing him in place.

Except his fingers twitched. Kick looked down, her previously panicked face melting into lust. Or embarrassment.

A guy in the car next to them flashed Thomas a thumbs-up. Then her nipple peaked between his fingers. They both gasped.

"I'm so sorry."

"Are you okay?" Kick breathed, sounding like Marilyn Monroe.

Thomas swallowed and almost choked on his cottonmouth. His hand flew to his lap. "Fine."

As they inched through the bottleneck, Kick quietly worked the car, biting her lower lip. When she chanced a glance in his direction, guilt, and possibly lust, filled her sweet face. "I let myself get distracted."

Adorable, feisty, vulnerable. The attraction he swam through wasn't just from holding the best thing his hand had felt in a long time. Her openness drew him in like steel to a magnet. Even when she kept information to herself, she was upfront about it. The word he couldn't shake, the one he was afraid to admit? *Sexy.* Christ, Kathleen McKenna was sexy as hell.

He couldn't take it anymore. "Spend the night with me when I get back. I'll have dinner with y'all. Then you can come back to my house."

The air between them stilled. Her posture slumped. "No, Thomas."

Why did he open his big mouth so soon? Oh yeah, he wasn't used to traditional relationships. They promised to go slow, and he'd pushed. "Right. Sure."

She reached across the console and squeezed his hand. "I want to spend time with you, and I want to have dinner with the kids." Kick bit her lip and glanced Thomas's way. "It would feel weird to eat and take off."

"Weird how?"

"It's fast for me, though it's probably not to you." A pretty pink rushed up Kick's neck to her hairline. "Casual's new for me,

Thomas. Spending the night doesn't feel casual. I'm trying to embrace the idea, but what if I can't?" She raced through the gears on the freeway ramp.

"You want to wait?" His tone asked, but his heart stated it.

Kick moved into the fast lane and purred, "I... I think so. But I don't always trust my head. I'm afraid of sending mixed signals."

He chuckled at her answer. "There's no way you could. You express everything you think, both verbal and physical." Didn't she see he was the one wrapped up in contradictions, not her? He slowly kissed her knuckles and bit his tongue to keep from confessing everything.

24

RIVIERA PARADISE

THOMAS

*T*homas ran the hills of Château Longévité, Alaric Kraus's vineyard and the headquarters of the Felidae Society. Crisp autumn air cleared his head as he set one foot in front of the other. Rows of harvested grapevines were the country version of a grid of city blocks surrounding Lord University. Steep hills comprising the grounds were definite cousins to the Piedmont neighborhood.

Since he'd arrived in Bordeaux, Thomas had traded one set of stressors for another. The tension at dinner the first night was thick enough to cut with a steak knife.

He'd spent the previous day in the drawing room, giving his presentation and fielding questions from his colleagues. Each team had mission parameters dependent upon the others, therefore the Felidae met regularly. Despite the space's opulent size, Thomas struggled to breathe freely by evening. The room had developed a thick, musty essence.

Thomas welcomed this morning's fresh air and solitude. His body had left Raleigh, but his thoughts stayed with the chestnut curls, porcelain skin, and sparkling hazel eyes back there. He'd expected pressure to produce would put her out of his mind. Smug, competitive comments from Nigel, the head of the Oxford team, didn't do the job either. Braggadocious reports on the man's progress with telomerase did nothing to poke through Thomas's indifference.

Thomas didn't seek glory the way Nigel did. Thomas only wanted to be sure his unique life had made a difference before he let it go. Last spring, he'd craved results like they were water. He'd been certain his theories were the ones to follow, where he'd find the genetic secrets of the Felidae members. He and Nigel worked the same questions from different angles, hoping it helped them get answers faster. Certain it would change the world, solve most, if not all illnesses, he wanted to help. He wasn't sure what had happened.

Lately his passion for research had lessened. He was desperate to help Toni back in Virginia. However, he wasn't so sure about anything or anyone else. He wondered if Presley hadn't been on the right track for the wrong reasons. Maybe they should study the genes of the Felidae against random people. Maybe he was making it harder to find answers.

Thomas almost ran into a crew setting up mechanical harvesters in the last fields with fruit as his head swam with his new idea. The crisp aroma of white grapes riding on a breeze hit his nose before he heard the commanding voices. He pivoted, taking a two-track lane up to the top of the hill. Alone again, he rested on a boulder. Many stones of varying sizes lay under an ancient tree. They'd been there for decades and were used to repair garden walls and such. He had helped the grounds crew with this kind of work plenty of times.

Hard work wouldn't bring the peace he sought though. He'd woken from a restless sleep with a tight throat like he was suffocating. Staying in Banger's family's airy corner suite overlooking the river didn't help.

Growing up at the base of a Virginia mountain, Thomas learned to find solace in his favorite vista near his family's land. High above the frenzy of life, he could reset. He let his eyes soften and did just that on top of the rock.

The heads of tall grasses gone to seed tickled his ankle resting on the edge of the boulder. Before he knew it, he transported himself to a familiar, inner place he hadn't been to in ages. His breath slowed, clearing tension from his body. He found serenity in the nothingness. Light winds continued traveling through the river valley, surrounding him like a blanket, tickling too-long hairs on his neck, welcoming him back with faint scents of vegetable canning, meat smoking, and leaves burning. He didn't know how long he'd stayed on the rock. He let go of the stress pressing on him, let go of concern for his family, said goodbye to Presley and her potential. He let loose the sharp ache in his chest whenever he thought of her family's pain—a pain he knew too well.

In the quiet, there were no microscopes to use or theories to prove, no algorithms to run, no blood to study. There was only an accord with nature and an occasional bird call with a suspiciously Midwestern, sexy chuckle. Kick found him, even in this space, but he welcomed it. His lips curved up at the sound.

Thomas opened his eyes and saw a bluish light, similar to the waters of the French Riviera, running along his skin. This, too, he welcomed like a long-lost friend. It hadn't happened to him since Uncle Theo had died.

He knew some Felidae manifested unique physical abilities. It was part of how he adjusted his appearance when needed. He hated calling them "powers" as some members did. He'd heard others had developed an aura, usually when emotions were at their highest. He'd never mentioned his capacity to do so to *Grand-père* or anyone else since it had stopped long before he met the Felidae. Thomas had figured he'd lost it. Until this moment, he'd viewed the experience like it reflected inner feelings. He'd never considered it could bring peace. He wondered if it could do more.

"THANK YOU," THOMAS SAID TO ALARIC, "FOR LETTING ME TAKE the morning off. The break helped." He'd struggled for half a minute with the perceived lack of support for the other teams. Well, until he asked himself what would Banger do? Five minutes later, he was out the door.

Thomas and Alaric met for lunch in the old man's office, dining away from the rest of the conference attendees. His mentor took a special interest in Thomas and the North American team while Alaric's partner, Eleanor, had charge of the European members. She worked closely with Thomas's counterpart, Nigel, and the others at Oxford.

"*De rien.* You appear… invigorated," he answered with a sentimental concern. Alaric had taken Thomas under his wing when Banger brought him into the fold. Therefore the term *Grand-père* held a dual meaning. Most used it out of respect. For Thomas, it was personal.

Sitting behind a regal desk in a dark-paneled office with towering windows, Alaric looked out of place at first. He wore a collarless linen shirt, a homespun wool vest, and worn jeans, preferring simpler fabrics and style. Steady energy defied his silver hair and beard, though it reflected in his amber eyes. Bronzed skin gave evidence of his work in the vineyard. He had recently spent long days toiling to bring in the harvest, only leaving the last few fields to the grounds crew when the Felidae members arrived.

Photos going back more than a century stood in front of books lining three walls. The wood in the room was rich, cared-for, and original. The flooring was wide-planked and as worn as the Aubusson rugs sitting atop it.

"The morning was… enlightening. *Merci encore.*"

"*Ce n'est pas la mer à boire.*" Alaric waved his wrist, indicating his favor was no big deal despite the dirty looks Thomas had received from more senior members as he headed out for his run. The old man took a sip of seltzer water and lime before saying, "Tell me about your Toni. *Est-ce qu'elle va mieux?*"

Thomas nodded. "She's doing better, yes." *Grand-père* raised his brows, waiting for Thomas to expand his brief answer. He chuckled at the old man who missed nothing. "I'm not hiding anything. Promise. Joe has Toni meditating twice a day and goes with her to the memory-care facility when she visits Ken. Still, it's her transition. Neither Joe nor I"—Thomas tipped his head toward Alaric—"nor can y'all for that matter, do it for her."

"*Oui,*" his mentor agreed.

"For my research? Toni's shown quantifiable changes in telomere length. As I mentioned during the presentation, we've found a new DNA variance," Thomas continued. "I'm anxious to see what comes of it." He rubbed his chin, still thinking about his revelation during the run. "I want to dive deeper into studying her mitochondria when I get back. It would be helpful if there were someone else to study—someone in a similar stage to Toni. Y'all don't know of anyone, do you?"

Alaric scoffed in his Gallic way. "Only you had the foresight to keep track of extended family. The rest of us were too eager to hide from them."

"It was easier to hide back then too. It's damned-near impossible to keep tabs on everyone now." Thomas settled back in the chair. He had asked the question, knowing it wouldn't go anywhere. He hoped by saying it, someone else would go digging. He would quietly spread the idea around with other members.

He resumed sharing about the lab, remembering Banger's direction about not mentioning the blackmail. "Losing Presley was a devastating setback, but I'm pressing on. Her replacement made a huge mistake the night before I left." Thomas chuckled, remembering the embarrassment on Bethany's face. Her face was green when he arrived, making him worry she was about to vomit from fear. He almost canceled the trip, but Banger was the only member he knew who could consider a summons to be optional. "She'll never forget her blunder and won't repeat it at least."

"I don't like you doing this work around the unworthy. Too much is at stake."

Did Alaric know about Presley's letter? "I didn't have the credentials to set up a proper lab when I first started. My people all sign DNAs when they start working for me." Thomas pinched the bridge of his nose, readying himself to confront his greatest annoyance. "Moreover, my associates aren't unworthy, as you put it. Plenty of people outside the Felidae are important and worthy to me."

Alaric scoffed at the comment. "You'll understand one day."

Thomas shook his head. He understood their prejudices, but he'd never accept them as his own.

Grand-père glanced at his door, seemingly to verify he'd closed it. "The thing is, dear boy, it's vital that we are the ones who find the answers. We must beat the Oxford team. *Now.*"

Thomas leaned forward in his chair, his elbows on his knees. "Aren't we all working toward the same goal? Finding out who or how we are? Along with changing the course of disease resistance in greater humanity?"

Alaric's gaze sliced to the door again, then back to his protégé. His normally warm expression chilled. "I'm not so sure. Update me personally from now on. Don't use the computer portal. I'll pass pertinent information to the rest of the members."

For as long as Thomas had been with the Society, he'd never known it to have factions. There were teams in the Western Hemisphere and sister societies around the world, but they worked together. This sounded like discord. The secrecy conflicted with his understanding of research culture. "What am I to say if another team contacts me for a consult?"

The icy glare warmed with a hint of admiration. "You double-speak like a master." The old man broke into a gravelly laugh. "As long as you don't use it on me. But I'll know if you do. I always find out."

Thomas swallowed hard and bit the side of his tongue. The château and the Felidae had been a refuge for him since they'd found him wandering the Mediterranean—a veteran with PTSD. Until this visit, he couldn't imagine holding anything back.

The sound of Alaric's voice pulled Thomas back to the room. "Tell your Toni I'm thinking of her. As soon as you have valid proof of her transition, I'll come for a visit. We're excited at the prospect of a rare female."

"She's not yet old enough to make it official."

Alaric stopped Thomas with a raised hand. "As technology advances, so should our policies. N'est-ce pas? Quantifiable proof she's one of us could override an age requirement for me. We didn't wait for Raphael after all." Alaric only used Banger's given name. He was one of three people allowed to do so.

"He was different," Thomas said. "Banger's parents were already Felidae when they made him their ridiculous experiment."

In this one instance, Alaric and Thomas disagreed. The old man had given his blessing to more or less "breed" the rare Felidae woman way back when. It had been an epic disaster, breaking Banger's mother and shining a light on his father's monstrous side. No one ever attempted it again.

Even though Alaric considered it water under the bridge, it irritated Thomas that he had never apologized to Banger for his role in his friend's disastrous upbringing.

Thomas leaned forward to stand, but Alaric stopped him by clearing his throat. "There's more."

He sank back, feeling like a kid. "What can I do?"

With his fingers steepled, elbows on the centuries-old country desk, *Grand-père* began tapping out a scale pattern. Thomas's eyes fixated on the fingers, watching their rhythm grow faster and started when his mentor spoke. "Using your original name again... I worry about what it implies."

Thomas opened his mouth to answer but shut it when the old man raised a hand. "I know melancholy when I see it. You're lonely, no? You might not believe it, but I remember the feeling. Trust my wisdom and cultivate more interests."

"I have work, the gym, music, renovating the farmhouse. I'm also thinking about moving my horse down. I visited my neighbor's stable right before leaving."

Alaric nodded politely. "What about a bit of romance?" He flashed his eyebrows. "Your arrangement with the Vivienne woman was good for you, no?" He resumed the tapping. "I thought the new assignment would recharge you, but you haven't been the same since her."

Thomas's jaw dropped open. "Y'all knew about Viv?"

A corner of the old man's mouth lifted into a mischievous smirk. "I had eyes on her. We told you we'd vet our new members for security reasons." His head gently tilted side to side. "It was obvious you kept your vow to us, so it continued. It's admirable how well you have separated your lives. You could arrange that again."

Thomas shook his head, incredulous. He should've known. What did Alaric mean by *let it continue?*

Kick was nothing like Vivienne though. Thomas and Viv were madame and client for years before he moved her to New York

234 | KALLYN JONES

from Paris. Afterward, they still lived apart, spending time together but always keeping separate homes and agendas.

Kick was the anti-Vivienne. Involvement with her demanded a complete buy-in. There was his struggle. Hell, she gave everything to random customers. To a partner? She'd devote her soul. It would be beautiful. And he'd take it.

Thomas shrugged, unsure of what to say or do. "Life's different now, so are my needs."

Alaric's fingers stilled. He raised his hands in surrender. "All I ask is for you to find a way out of this mood. I don't worry about any... attachments you find. When the project's complete, I'll still need you. It'll only be the beginning."

Perhaps his mentor had a point, except... "You know you're asking two opposing things, right? It's nearly impossible to keep this tight schedule and maintain a social life. Hell, I had to stop coaching classes at the gym and rarely substitute anymore."

Alaric gave Thomas a distinctly French shrug. "You've handled more pressure with grace." He leveled Thomas with a piercing blue stare. "Maybe it's time to—"

A knock on the heavy door interrupted them. "Good afternoon, gentlemen." Eleanor Guillaume's voice carried from the other side. "May Chloe clear your plates?"

"*Oui*. Come in."

The elegant mistress of Château Longévité entered the room, wearing a concerned smile. She gestured for the maid to clear the desk, waiting with her hand across the back of Thomas's chair. Though she focused her daily efforts on the European team, she gave affection for each member without favoritism.

Thomas tipped his head to flash her a soft smile. She wore her tawny hair in a blunt bob and dressed as if she belonged in a sixty's movie with a Henry Mancini score. At first glance, she appeared maybe thirty, but her true age showed in her eyes and the way she carried herself. No one maintained the posture Ellie possessed—like a woman born to rule.

"The afternoon session begins in thirty minutes if you gentlemen are planning to join us."

He turned to Alaric, who nodded once, regal in his own casual way. Thomas pivoted back. "We'll be there *Grand-mère*. Thank you for the reminder."

Ellie brushed her fingers on his shoulders. "I know how you two lose time when you lock yourselves in here." She clucked her tongue and continued, "I miss the days when you could come and go as you please, Thomas... when you were Michael. Alas, you have a job now..." She took a step toward the door and turned back. "The clothes are new, no?"

Thomas shrugged, looking down at the jeans and button-down shirt Kick had helped him pick out.

"Everyone's casual these days—even the French." She shivered as if the thought equated Hades finally freezing over. "A wise choice, though I'll miss your formality. You were one of the few left to dress like a real man." She brushed her fingertips through the sides of his hair, the way a mother or aunt might. "I miss the gray sprinkles too."

Thomas made a note to himself to bring his old things the next time he visited. He hadn't planned what he'd placed in the suitcase. Outside of wanting to be professional at work, he didn't think about it much at all. His hands had practically reached for the new clothes on their own when he was packing. But if it made Ellie a little happier, he could remember for next time.

In the weeks since their afternoon shopping, T-shirts and a few other items had shown up in his mailbox with notes from Kick saying the item had been on clearance so he wouldn't fuss. That she thought of him made him warm to each piece.

"Thank you, Ellie," he said. "Your taste is impeccable, and your approval means a lot."

As she left the room, Thomas's cell phone buzzed with a text. He hoped it wasn't the lab with another mishap. He swiped the device awake and frowned.

Banger: 911. Call. Don't text.

Too many possibilities could be behind those ominous words.

"You frown. Is something wrong?" Alaric asked.

"An emergency from Banger. I'll return it up in the suite."

"I ASSUME YOU FOUND SOMETHING," THOMAS SAID TO BANGER over their secured chat.

"Two things, actually. I'm certain there's a mole, but I haven't found him, her, or them yet. So, watch your back, brother."

Thomas stretched his neck. "Wow, you and *Grand-père* are on the same page."

"Not sure I'd trust him right now either, though it's doubtful he's a mole."

"If I can't trust Alaric, I may as well get out, don't you think?"

"Would that we could," Banger answered. "The Felidae is more like the Hotel California, brother. No one leaves."

Joe had left though. Thomas pinched the bridge of his nose, wishing the merry-go-round would stop. "You said there was a second problem."

"Right. How do I say this?" Banger only worked with the best equipment, so the resolution on his face was crystal clear when his face darkened. "There's reason to believe your assistant was murdered."

Thomas's head dropped with exhaustion before his gaze returned to the screen. "How? Why?"

"The accident wasn't your standard hit-and-run. Think about it, Thomas. There were only two people in her research file, and you didn't kill her."

Incredulous, Thomas laughed. "You think Nigel did though? Damn, man, I'm the better candidate. Besides, her ultimatum had implications for all of us. If she *had* come after me, you know you'd have taken her out."

"True," Banger agreed, his tone icy and factual.

"Fine." Thomas sighed. "I'll keep my ears open and my mouth shut." Desperate to change the subject, he added, "What about Kick's ordering box? Did the camera pick up anything?"

"It did. We found a partial tattoo on one of the perps. None of her staff recognized it, but we're checking local artists. She also agreed to adding another camera back there." Banger's tone grew irritated. "She won't let me run the system at her house though. You need to talk with her."

Confused, Thomas asked, "Did something else happen? I'm kinda removed from y'all right now."

Banger shook his head. "It's the violence of the attack on her squawk box. The smear campaign continues too. This is beginning to look personal, and she's acting like a petulant child. My people could keep her in a ring of safety, but she won't let us."

"You make it sound like you want to trap her in."

Banger's eyes narrowed. "Not you too."

Thomas ran a hand along his jaw, thinking. He didn't want to admit Banger might be scaring him. "All right, are there other options? What if I can't get through either?"

"I'm working on it, but hate going rogue on a client, you know? Listen, I'm not asking you to fly your ass back here. Extra cameras probably won't pick up anything. But I can't do my job if I can't be sure."

"I'll talk to her, Bang."

"Make her agree."

Thoughts of research dissipated as he hung up with Banger and dialed the woman holding center stage in his thoughts again.

The call went to voice mail three times.

Dammit, they kept missing each other.

CONTROL

KICK

*A*t first, Uncle Hugh didn't see me standing in the doorway to his office. Or he acted like he didn't notice.

"You rang?" I asked in a failed deep, rumbly voice.

Without looking up, Hugh answered, "If Lurch had looked like you, I would watch *Addams Family* reruns." He gestured to my father's chair. Their desks had been on opposite walls. "Pull it over here."

I did as commanded and sat.

Still shuffling papers, Uncle Hugh dropped a bomb. "I want to make you an offer, Kick."

"One I can't refuse?" I asked, this time in a slightly better *Godfather* imitation.

He finally looked up. "You're full of jokes today."

I slumped in the chair. "I'm really in a bad mood and trying not to spread it around."

"Oh, well then, you better spill before I ask my question." Hugh rolled his hand as I sat in stubborn silence.

"Fine," I started, "it's Thomas. He's been a jerk ever since he left for Europe. I swear, a sense of foreboding had washed over me when I dropped him off at the airport. He's practically incommunicado when he promised he wouldn't be. Since I've heard all this before..."

"It brings up old issues."

I nodded. "Yup. Ones I swore I'd never allow again too. But enough about me."

Thomas had canceled our weekend plans for another emergency trip, this one to his home in Virginia, adding a week onto the timeline. He flew there straight from France. I understood responsibilities, especially when family needed you. I'd also spent too much time in the relationship limbo that came with a traveling man. It grew old quickly and only worked when there was a commitment to stay in touch. We hadn't though. It contributed to why I'd watched my patience slide through my fingers. One moment I'd wonder if there was a future for Thomas and me. In the next moment, I'd scold myself for thinking ahead when we were being casual, whatever that meant. Each day that passed made me doubt more.

"You two are an item then? I thought I saw sparks during the poker game."

I casually lifted a shoulder. "We're supposed to be *special* friends, I guess. Taking it slow. But this feels more like out of sight, out of mind."

Hugh clicked his tongue while shaking his head. "Young people... What the hell is a *special* friend anyway? In my day, when you knew, *you knew*. I asked Maggie to marry me after two weeks."

"Marry?" I almost yelled, certain I made a sour face.

"You don't want to marry again?"

I swiped my hand through the air. "*Hell* no. It doesn't mean I'm okay with living in limbo though." I also didn't want to dwell on my hurt. Most of my disappointment was in myself for the vulnerability that resulted in my bad mood. The last time we'd managed a solid minute of conversation, his voice was ice-cold, so I made an excuse and let him go. It grated. He knew I'd had enough of begging people to care, only to watch them drop me like a hot potato. He'd been the one to ask me to drop *my* walls? Let him in?

To add to the annoyance, Thomas and Banger had ganged up on me to have Angel Security install cameras with motion-activated mics at my house. My café participated in a beta group, testing the newest system, but Banger didn't have it in a residence and claimed it would be a favor to him as much as safety for me. The business was one thing, but hell if I'd agree to imprisonment at home.

I leaned on the front of Hugh's desk. "Can we skip my problems and jump to why you called?"

He inhaled a deep sigh, seemed to brace himself, and dropped a bomb. "I want to expand into cannabis…" My jaw dropping must have given away my shock. "Hear me out." Hugh cut me off.

I sat back and nodded, giving him the floor.

"Good. My contacts on the tobacco board are open to trying out a model where cannabis is sold in a smoke shop." He chuckled. "Most of the first round of licenses went to what they call the young hippie types. They think shops like mine will make it look more respectable. So I've been reading up on it."

Holy hell, I bet the cronies on the oversight board never even spoke to one of those "hippie kids." I'd been to a few dispensaries looking for pain relief. They had great intentions but tended to lack knowledge. I held up a finger and waited for permission to speak. "One, there's a lot—I mean a boatload—to learn about the product. People don't just smoke it anymore. Then there are the strains—"

"Like I said, I've been researching. I would hire someone to manage it." He leaned down like he had a secret. "Sylvie, next door, is letting her lease go in the spring."

"So you'd expand."

"Yes, it would be two stores in one."

I couldn't help thinking of the old video stores with the X-rated stuff in a back room. I laughed at the idea. Hugh's brow furrowed.

"Hell, I thought you planned to tell me you're selling. Are you sure you don't want to retire?" I asked.

"That's a big part of it. I'd feel better stepping back with bigger profit margins. It's night and day compared to what I do now. I'll be able to be an owner in name only."

That was practically his situation now, but I didn't want to sass. I said, "Well, if you and Maggie feel good about it, I say go for it. You'll have my support."

Hugh removed his hat, brushed it off, and set it behind him, signaling he wasn't through. "I want more than your support, Katie. I want your partnership."

"Wha-what? Why would I—" Did he not see my busy, crazy life?

"By the time we'd have our grand opening next fall, Liam will be gone to school."

"So I'll have enough time to run two stores? I love you, but are you nuts?"

He coughed and scratched his head. Sweat glistened on his forehead, and I finally saw Hugh's fear. He'd had my dad to lean on for this venture before. Now he was going it alone. I could relate.

Hugh sheepishly continued, "I see you as a consultant. Help

me hire the right person to set it up. Some retail-oriented dispensaries have classes that help cancer patients and others with chronic pain or illnesses. You know, like yours. I thought you could lead one of those if you'd like. Or at least steer me in the right direction to find someone." He wiped his brow. "Mostly, I need your signature. Despite their prejudices, my general assembly contact told me there's a preference for women and minorities getting the new licenses. He liked the idea of giving it to a proven businesswoman attached to a smoke shop with a good reputation."

It encouraged me that Hugh hadn't brought up the rumors about the coffeehouse or me. It let me know the nonsense hadn't spread beyond Oakville.

I lifted the hair off my neck. "I wish Dad were here to talk to." From what Hugh just said, they both would still want my help.

"Me too, Katie. Me too."

I gestured toward the folder in front of him. "Is this your proposal?"

"It's a copy of everything I've gathered so far."

"Hand it over. I'll take a look."

I settled in at my dad's old desk, reading Hugh's notes. His ask still had me in shock. I couldn't believe he'd want to take on such a project. Then I looked at his numbers and wished he hadn't already gone home. They seemed too good to be true. I highlighted them and made an entry on my calendar to call him in the morning.

I also tried Thomas's phone again. It went straight to voice mail. I left a quick message and braced myself for another rejection. My thoughts drifted to the past and lingered there, wishing life had been different. My phone buzzing a text snapped me out of the unhealthy daydream.

Liz: Are you free to talk to someone?

With a sigh, I resigned myself to dealing with the day. A new business opportunity could wait. So could my issues with Thomas. Maybe we were better off as friends. At least we'd only kissed.

Me: Coming.

Jonn Graham stood across the counter from Liz, in a situation reminding me of the one I'd found between him and my daughter. Did this kid never learn? "Do you like sushi?" he asked Liz. "I know the new bartender at the place up the road. I could pick you up later."

"What's going on, Liz?" I asked before she could answer Jonn. I didn't want her on his radar for rejecting him.

He turned to me and folded his hands at his chest. "Hey, Mrs. Mack. I didn't know you were here."

I nodded slowly. "I help Hugh out sometimes."

"Wow, you are Wonder Woman." He was unusually chipper.

"What can I do for you?" I didn't think he wanted cigars, but Liz could've sold him some anyway.

"I heard the old man here is hiring—" he began.

"I tried to tell him—" Liz interrupted before I held up my hands to stop them both.

"First, Hugh Reynolds owns this store. That's why it's called Mick and Hugh's. Calling him 'the old man' doesn't make a good impression, Jonn."

I stepped next to Liz and noted she had completed her inventory assignment. I gave the tablet back. "Why don't you finish up while I speak with Mr. Graham?" Despite his pleasant demeanor, I remembered his burst of temper the last time I turned him down. I wanted to put distance between Liz and us.

She did a double take to me. "Um, sure." Then she slowly made her way to the opposite wall.

I set my hands on the counter. "Jonn—"

He leaned in, his hands matching mine. "When we talked before, I may have had some bad bud. I apologize."

"Okay, but—"

"I'm serious, Mrs. Mack." He dipped his chin and looked through his lashes like my kids did when they were little. "You were right about the barista position, but I could do this. There's potential here, and I could help bring in a young vibe. I'd like to get real-world experience while I go to business school, then open my own store."

Shit. The kid made a good point. But Hugh didn't have the energy to mentor a kid like Jonn. He needed experienced help. Hugh really needed another manager, someone more like my father.

He leaned back on the counter. "What do you say? Can I fill out an application?" Before I could answer, Jonn added, "You told me before about going to school and finding my calling."

I nodded. "Yes, I did but—"

"You were right. *This* is my calling." Jonn moved his arm around the store.

I'll bet.

He continued, "It turns out I love business." He shifted and grinned. "I have my dad's talent for sales."

No kidding.

"I also hate construction. All those picky housewives..." The boy violently shivered for effect. "If I show serious interest in another venture, Dad will get off my ass—I mean case. Sorry."

I could understand him there. I might have loved dancing as a girl but not enough to do it professionally. The times Bobby and I butted heads after I gave it up made me shake too.

I stepped back and folded my arms, studying Jonn. This polite, humble version of him put me off. I'd never seen this side before. His cocky side still showed, but dare I say he possessed a delightful demeanor?

"Opportunities are also about timing. Mick & Hugh's needs people with experience. Maybe after you have some time in school." If he showed promise, minds could change. If we went ahead with the expansion, we'd have openings in a year.

Graham's eyes narrowed to slits, and he swiped a display off the counter before yelling, "So that's it? You won't even tell him?"

Ah, there was the asshole we all knew and avoided. My hands went up at the crash. "Whoa!" I caught Liz's eyes and tipped my head, telling her to move back to the counter. I wanted her near the emergency button in case Jonn wouldn't leave.

"That's not what I was saying," I started. Did it matter? Of course I'd let Hugh know about this, but Jonn's outburst changed everything.

The music switched right then to Janet Jackson's "Control." The words hit me like a sledgehammer to the gut. Since my dad died— hell, we could take it back to when I'd begun getting sick—the thing I'd fought the most for was control. Control of my body, of my world. The song gave me the push I needed to not back down.

"Mr. Reynolds receives notes on everything that happens when he's gone. It doesn't mean he'll have a different answer." My arm swept toward the door. "Now please—"

Graham's jaw flexed as his face turned red. "You McKennas are a couple of self-righteous bitches, aren't you? Dad and I wanted to help you. Make your bad publicity go away."

My temper was already on a short leash. I didn't want to lose it, but his words stopped me. "Excuse me?"

"My father is friends with the newspaper editor, plus he can put in a good word with the Chamber of Commerce."

I didn't know the kid knew the word *commerce*. I didn't understand what the Chamber of Commerce had to do with any of this. Nor did I see how the Grahams could make the sickening gossip go away.

Jonn snapped his fingers. "Poof. Everyone will love you again."

Sure, business was down and some of it had to do with the slander, but I had plans to deal with it. I had my own connections and figured it wouldn't be long until the spotlight turned somewhere else. I was more concerned about who was harassing Rachel.

I turned back to Jonn. "We've said our peace. It's time for you to leave. If you won't, I'll have Liz call the police."

"For what?" he spat out. "Tripping and accidentally knocking over a rack of cutters?"

He stepped at me, pushing me toward the walk-in humidor. My hands came up to block another advance, but they merely whooshed in a circle. Graham had vanished from my personal space, literally lifted into the air. By Thomas.

SEND ME ON MY WAY

KICK

"I'm not finished," Jonn Graham yelled.

"The hell you aren't," Thomas snarled. He took the kid by his collar and frog-marched him toward the door, leaving me equal parts stunned, infuriated, and turned on. My confusion returned.

Dylan arrived too, standing in the doorway; his eyes took a beat to settle on each of us. "What the fuck's going on?" He walked up to Graham, chest out and towering over him with as much menace as he could muster.

Thomas answered, "He's leaving."

Graham simultaneously said, "You'll see what happens when my father hears about this. Soon there will be two failing businesses."

Dylan opened the door, and Thomas pushed Jonn out with another growl of "You're done with the McKennas. If I hear you've been in the café or here, you'll deal with me."

Graham yelled from the sidewalk for anyone in earshot to hear. "Self-righteous assholes! Everybody knows you're sick." He pointed at Dylan. "You hardly work anymore. Mrs. Mack sells drugs to kids to keep the doors open 'cause no one's coming in. Everybody knows it. You need our help or you might as well close."

I jolted at his words. Did the community believe we were on the verge of going under? Right as I thought I was making incremental progress with my mountain of stress, it slid back down, stress boulders piling up around me.

The kid must have known about his father's offer. It shouldn't have surprised me, but it rankled having him use it against me.

Thomas's hand came to my back, rubbing gently to release the tension, making it worse. He wrapped his arm around my shoulders and pulled me into his chest, kissing my temple. "Think nothing of it, darlin'. The asshat's trying to save face."

Still absorbing Graham's accusations, I followed Thomas back into the shop, my eyes connecting with his smile but not responding. I'd gone numb. Part of me wanted to throw myself at Thomas and welcome him back. Thanks to his radio silence, it shocked me to see him.

Once inside, Thomas gathered me into his arms. "I missed you," he whispered to my ear.

As I stood against his body, the numbness melted into heat but not the heat of lust. My hands slid from Thomas's waist to the front of his chest, zapping my palms as if electrocuted. I pushed him back, and my eyes saw red. I wrapped his tie around my hand, not noticing he'd worn one of his sexy suits again.

Everything was annoying now. I pulled him into my office, keeping my cool long enough to say to Liz and Dylan, "Excuse us."

The word *control* came back to me as I kicked the door shut. Thomas's darkened eyes beamed at me, filled with lust and ready for action. To make matters worse, his sexy grin fanned my irritated flame. I'd give him action but not the kind he expected.

He wanted me to lean on him? To ask him for help. To be *more*. Then left me hanging. That said way more than his sweet little heart-to-heart had. It was time I took back control.

"How. Dare. You," I growled.

Thomas stepped back, hands in the air, confusion replacing desire. "What'd I do?"

I paced the room to pull my thoughts together. My emotions stood up and declared themselves, but the words came in spurts. "You... I had the situation handled, Thomas. You... you hadn't called or emailed. Hell, you barely texted."

"You haven't been easy to get ahold of either, lady."

I walked into a corner and pivoted while Thomas watched, his feet planted, arms folded across his chest. "One day. One day I had an issue and made you wait." I argued my case.

"You've been too tired to speak. Or a kid or an employee interrupted."

I ignored his last defense and kept on. "I've been supportive and made sure I wasn't whiny. It's what you told me to do. So I asked nothing of you and stood on my own two feet."

"Who told you to ask for nothing?"

"Your unavailability shouted it loud, pal. Then you galloped in here like some white knight and tossed out the bad boy dragon. I'm not a damsel in distress. I won't hide in the shadow of a brave champion anymore. I can handle myself."

"Didn't look like it to me," Thomas bit back.

"Liz was ready with the emergency button. I'd already warned Jonn. He was just getting in a last word before he left."

"He pushed you!"

I stopped pacing, spun, and pointed at him. "You have a hero complex."

"And you don't?"

"No."

"Think about it, Kick." Thomas pulled his phone from his inside pocket and swiped the screen, probably checking the time.

"Am I keeping you from something?"

He muttered, "I have a meeting."

"Then why are you here?" I mirrored his stance, facing off with him.

"I got back this morning and couldn't wait to see you. I figured fifteen minutes beat nothing. Was hoping we could make plans for tomorrow. Guess I was wrong."

I didn't want him distracting my righteous anger. I pointed toward the front. "I can fight my own battles."

"Never said otherwise. What did the asshole want anyway?"

"He came in here acting humble and friendly and asked for a job. I guess he figured he'd pull one over on the 'old guy'," I answered.

Thomas took two steps toward me. "He was ready to hurt you, Kick. Hurt. You. What if he'd taken you out and turned on Hugh's girl? Huh? I had the means to make it end easily."

It didn't matter that he'd landed on my worst fear about the incident. Or maybe it mattered more that he'd read my mind.

"You don't get to play helpful hero when it's convenient for you, Thomas. Either you're someone's *something more* or you're not. Right now it doesn't even feel like you're much of a friend."

"You know I have responsibilities."

I looked up, exasperated with the word. "To hell with both our responsibilities."

He threw his hands in the air and turned toward the door. "This is ridiculous. I have to meet my boss. Next time, I'll remember to let the little bastard kick your ass."

"If that's what you take from this, fine." So my insecurities had come true. "It's a good thing we didn't go any further. Obviously, we're not right for more."

His eyes narrowed as his chin tipped. "Obviously."

Thomas took a step, stopped, and looked over his shoulder. His eyes had gone to ice, the way they were when we'd first met. I wanted to cry witnessing their return but was too angry to apologize. The fact he could so quickly go back there with me told me more than any words. It was one thing if we decided we belonged back in the friend zone, but even my friends gave me time and respect.

Thomas beelined for the parking lot, a blaze of fury trailing behind him. And why not? Didn't they all leave eventually? It didn't matter. I was so over begging people to be my friend. It was one of the benefits of age.

I entered the front of the store, shaken, sad, and fed up. Dylan and Liz stared at me. For the first time since he'd entered the drama, I studied my son. His hair was messy and tending toward fuzzy, his mouth turned down, and telltale dark circles rimmed his eyes. Something had been bothering him before he arrived.

"Let's call the day, Liz. You finished your inventory. I'll pencil you out for your scheduled hours. Hugh will understand." I remembered Graham's sleazy little come-on to her. "Dylan, let's go get some sushi." At least the jackass had one thing right.

I'VE BEEN LOVING YOU TOO LONG

KICK

*T*he speakers in Dylan's BMW came to life in the middle of Eminem's "Lose Yourself."

Oh, this song. For a moment I forgot about everything else that had happened and revisited my longing for the past. I'd even take the parts that had annoyed me so much.

The song also let me know where Dylan's head had been before everything at Mick & Hugh's went down. I avoided songs like this for a reason. The pain could be intolerable. The fact I'd been hiding from the same headspace hit hard. The past—the guilt—kept poking me for months, trying to get me to deal with it. *Holy hell.*

"You okay?" he asked as he navigated our parking lot.

"No," I snapped, chest heaving, seeking a proper breath. Pounding beats fueled my angst with the past more than it did my anger with Thomas or Jonn Graham. I stared out the passenger window as the gas stations and strip malls rolled by. I saw none of it. I watched for a moment farther down Time's road, when I wasn't so alone.

"So… this song," I said to distract myself.

"Yeah." Dylan let out a sad breath. I hated how burdened he sounded. His life was only in second gear. He had miles to go before he was fully living his dream.

"You introduced Dad to Eminem."

"Yeah." The word shook with emotion. I turned my head to see why.

We pulled into a parking spot, and Dylan cut the engine before returning my gaze. The sadness in his baby-blue eyes sent my problems packing. "As much as he enjoyed teaching you fatherly stuff, he loved it when you brought something to him. Jaysus, lad, he adored you." My body shook as I reached out and squeezed my son's hand. "I don't know what's wrong, but there's nothing you can do to ruin how proud we are of you. Both of us."

Dylan lifted his head, his eyes tearing.

"Hey," I started but ran out of words. I patted his cheek. "You sure you want to go inside?"

He blew out a slow breath. "I need a distraction."

You and me both. "Okay. I'll order a carafe of sake. One of those small cups shouldn't undo my progress. You can have the rest. Then you'll tell me everything."

The owner of Sugoi Sushi had a child with multiple food allergies, so he was known in the autoimmune community for accommodating customers like me. We greeted the hostess and found stools at the bar. I was on a first-name basis with the staff, but a new bartender approached. His nametag read COLE. He greeted us with a tip of the head and said, "What can I get you two?"

Dylan spoke first. "A carafe of sake." He turned to me. "Hot, right?"

I nodded and added, "And two glasses of water with lemon. We know what we'd like to order too."

"Sure. Go ahead."

"I'll have a Tokyo roll—with coconut aminos instead of soy sauce—and the seven-piece nigiri with salmon on a blue plate."

"That's for allergies, right?"

"It is."

Cole winked. I wanted to snap at him to cut the flirty shit but knew it was my lousy mood talking. "Sure. For you, sir?"

"I'll have the shrimp teppanyaki and whatever she leaves on her plate."

The bartender chuckled. "Sounds good. Be right back with your sake." He left us to enter our order.

"New guy's a flirt," Dylan said.

"Eh." I shrugged. "It gets the tips. If he knows what's good for him, he'll knock it off though. Men are on my shit list today. I'm only tolerating you because you'll always be my baby."

His eyes grew wide with surprise. "Is this about what went down at the store?"

I bit my lip to stop an emotion overload and nodded. The real reason for my anger with Thomas coming into focus. "And other things."

"On behalf of my gender, what the hell did we do to you?"

But I couldn't tell him when I didn't have the words. The revelation in the car was still too new. I couldn't admit to my deepest angst about moving on, that I didn't think it possible. That I didn't deserve it. So I deflected. "Tell me what's going on with you."

"Here you go, guys." Cole set down the carafe and cups. "You're pretty cute together."

Before his words registered, Dylan chuckled. "What a moron." He blew on his cup and whispered, "I think the bartender thinks we're... on a date, Mom."

JaysusMaryandJoseph.

I closed my eyes and shivered. "Because why wouldn't I date a boy twenty-three years younger than me?"

Dylan's laugh grew. Well, he got his distraction. When he calmed, he said, "I've heard plenty of people tell you you look younger than you are. I look older than my age, especially with the beard. It's not so big of a gap then."

Big enough. I shivered at the thought. Then I shoved his shoulder and ended up moving myself instead. The kid was still built for a football field, like his old man. "It's not funny," I squeaked, creeped out. "Just when I thought today couldn't get any worse."

He looked up and caught my frown. "Aw, come on. It's funny as shit." Dylan's laugh eased into a snigger before settling.

"At least your mood has improved. If it comes at my expense, so be it." An empty cup stared back at me, tempting me to pour another. Remembering the number of doctor appointments still left on my calendar, I pushed it to the side.

I sipped on the water and Dylan threw his arm around my shoulder. "Anyway, we used to have mother-son dates regularly. What's wrong with doing it now?"

"Nothing, lad." I snuck a pointed finger at Cole. "Not what he meant though, is it?"

"True." Dylan poured himself another glass. "Either way, this is the first *date* I've been on in ages."

His comment didn't sit well with me. School packed both Dylan's and Suzy's schedules, but it sounded like they might be taking their relationship for granted.

We welcomed the break created from the arrival of our meals.

We ate while listening to Otis Redding's "I've Been Loving You Too Long." Lost in the melody and bleak lyrics, I sang along, letting the music say what my heart refused—that I was stuck.

As the song progressed, Dylan's pace slowed until he was picking at his plate. Nothing came between Dylan and food.

I set my chopsticks on the plate, looked around to ensure no one eavesdropped, and said, "Time to talk. What's going on?"

He rubbed his temple. "It's Suzy." He set his fork down but kept his gaze forward. "We fought all weekend." He ran his hand through his hair. It was getting long. "Truth is, all we do is fight. I don't know what I'm doing wrong."

"Then why did you ask me about money for an engagement ring?"

I almost got a laugh out of him. Almost. "I hoped it would make her happy. You know..." He shrugged. "Maybe if she sees I'm all in, she'll chill."

I could only think of one worse reason to get engaged but held my tongue. I couldn't hold in the wince. "Can you give me examples of what happened?" I folded my hands in my lap to keep them from shaking. A sense of dread had descended upon me.

"You know how we always have breakfast together because our schedules keep us out late?" I nodded, so he continued, "I usually make it, to... you know, spoil her some. Lately she claims I don't like her cooking. So I didn't make breakfast today, and she called me neglectful.

"Everything I do is selfish, according to Suze. She yells at Dummy and me for being smelly, and we've no clue why. She thinks the condo smells disgusting too."

"Medical school must be terribly stressful," I offered, my mind on alert.

"It's only going to get harder. Suzy hasn't started rotation yet. She wants us to leave her alone though. Dummy and I were roommates before she moved in. We aren't going anywhere."

His soulful eyes turned on me. "I wish she'd just say she wants out."

"Did you ask her if she does?"

He gripped his raven hair. "Yes."

"And?"

"She burst into tears and locked me out of our room."

"Jaysus." I dropped my head into my hand, resting my elbow on the bar.

"What?" He turned to face me, like a worshipper seeking answers from his oracle.

I counted off on my fingers. "Let's see if I have this straight—sensitivity to smells, extreme irritability. Is she fatigued?"

Dylan blew a breath and nodded.

"Any other possible medical issues? Like a virus? Pain?"

"Suze says she aches everywhere but doesn't want me to touch her." He took a sip of water. "Oh, she threw up a couple of times last week. Think she has the flu?"

Unfortunately, I didn't. "It's possible." I bit my lip, not wanting to ask. "Has she had a period recently?"

"How would I know? She's on the pill."

I shoved his shoulder. "Because you're supposed to be a responsible partner, knothead. Has there been any"—I circle my hand—"lady trash in the basket lately?" Being his only parent, this wasn't our first foray into the uneasy topic of Dylan's sex life. It didn't get easier.

Dylan whispered, his eyes wide, "I don't remember."

My head bobbed as I thought. "Well, lad, I could be wrong, but it's possible—*possible*—your girl's expecting. It's quick enough to find out. If she is, Suzy might be confused, pissed, and who knows what all at the same time."

He lifted his chin quickly, finally catching on we were discussing a possible baby. He poured more sake and downed it in one. "Shit, Mom."

"Ask her, Dyl. But do it gently. And listen." I took hold of his face again to make a point. "Don't get ahead of yourself and pick out names either. It'll only make matters worse."

"Are you sure?" His voice cracked like he was thirteen. It took all my strength to not squeeze him and say it would get better.

"No. But I remember when a brutal bout with mono turned into something else." The bartender walked by and did a double take.

Dylan lowered his voice. "You mean your autoimmune disease? You think—"

"No, son. I mean you. I'd thrown up so much with the illness, it didn't occur to me to get a pregnancy test. You didn't come along at a convenient time either."

"Why?" he asked with a shocked expression.

"Don't confuse inconvenience with being unwanted. That said, you were a surprise. Your dad had just landed a starting position. My job was all long hours and high stress at the ad agency. We had recently bought a fancy-ass house because we thought it was expected of us. Shit, I was younger than you."

"I miss him," Dylan blurted at the mention of his father, breaking my heart.

Rubbing his arm, the grief I'd felt in the car came back, catching my tongue.

"You never talk about him," he breathed out in frustration. "It's like he was never a part of our family."

My head hung. When moving on became excruciating, it was easier to pretend I'd always been single. It was also easier to make him the bad guy than deal with reality. "Oh, sweetheart." I dabbed at a threatening tear, thinking about Dylan's pain. "Guess you're right. Sometimes it was the only way I could get through a day. I think it became a habit. I'll do better, okay?" I took a drink of water to keep from crying in public.

"It'd be nice to talk about him."

"I made you think I don't want to?"

He nodded. My eyes squeezed shut at Dylan's honesty. In my

efforts to dodge the pain, I'd hurt my kid. "Do you share your grief with anyone? Suzy?"

"Snow and I do, mostly. Lee, too, sometimes. But he also likes to shove it down like you. I think he gets mad about how much he's missed. Since it's his senior year, it's a touchy subject." Dylan dropped his head. "I know what the counselors said. It's just... If I'd hadn't been such a dick—"

"No, lad." Tears long dried for my misery dropped for my son's pain. I scanned the bar again. As usual, the few people around paid us no attention. "Get this through your head... It. Wasn't. Your. Fault. No part of it was. Do you understand? You think I'd rather mourn you? No way I'd get over it."

"So you've gotten over Dad?"

No. Hell no. It's why the guilt kept kicking me when things warmed up with Thomas. I bit my lip, unable to say it aloud.

He gave me a pathetic attempt at a smile. "Snow, Lee, and I think you should date again, but maybe we're wrong. I don't know if I could ever get over it if it were me." Dylan's gaze returned to his plate and stared, as if he'd forgotten about it. He took a small bite. "We don't like the idea of leaving you."

I dipped a piece of sushi in my sauce and took a bite. It went down like sandpaper. That idea was fast approaching. "There are worse things than being alone."

Dylan furrowed his brow. "You're with Thomas though. Doesn't it mean you've moved on?"

A cynical laugh bubbled from my chest. How did one move on from a marriage that didn't end? Our journey together did, but not the marriage. Not for me. "Thomas was a mistake. Today proved it."

An expression looking a lot like a disappointed parent flashed across Dylan's face. "Over a little fight? Are you sure?"

Thomas and I started out with a fight. Maybe it was a clue. I took a pull of water and slid my plate Dylan's way. I nodded my response. I couldn't move forward when the past would always be unfinished. I could make a good life as a single woman. I'd figure it out.

"What if someone's trying to tell you to get back out there?"

I laughed at the suggestion. "I'm tired of trying to decipher what the universe wants for me. Every time I think I've figured it out, the universe"—I used the air quotes—"changes the rules."

"What about meditating? My friend—"

I touched his bicep to stop him. "Thank you, Dyl. I'm trying it, but it's not a magic pill." Argh that word! It was the secular equivalent of *Have you prayed about it?*

As I watched Dylan finish both our plates, my gratitude lifted to the universe for a kid who took a hint. I didn't want to talk about the future or the past anymore.

The bartender placed our bill where Dylan's plate had been, and my patience died.

I grabbed the ticket. "I'll pay for dinner with *my son*, thank you." A blush raced up Cole's neck. I pushed. "Don't assume. When a man assumes, it makes him an ass."

He took the bill and my card and disappeared. I watched for Cole to return, my face too hot for the minor offense.

Dylan leaned into me. "Are you still angry? Why don't you head to the car? I'll sign for you and apologize."

"Apologize for what?"

"Come on, Mom." He lowered his voice. "Cole may have been misguided, but he wasn't mean." He tipped his head, waiting for his words to sink in. I was the ass in the situation.

He added, "Go on, cool off."

SEPARATE WAYS (WORLDS APART)

KICK

*A*t home, Macushla greeted me by performing a pee-pee dance around my legs. Her doggie door had jammed, making her hold it in longer than she was used to. Fresh air appealed to my addled mind, so I joined her in the backyard. Dylan's situation mixed in with my troubles, competing for my attention like a tennis match of misery. Something told me his problems with Suzy were unfixable. Heaven help them if a child really was involved. I hoped I was wrong. I would've done anything for decent advice on what to advise him. After eight years of learning how to stand on my own, some days I'd still give anything to have my champion back.

My mother's favorite criticism—if I hadn't been whining about pain, I'd have kept my old life—buzzed in my head like reverb from a broken subwoofer. Then another one, also critical but voiced by many people, asked when I would move on.

Thomas and I had chemistry. It sparked whenever he entered a room. Plus he'd become a refuge. That would be the hardest part to let go, but I'd deal with it. The initial excitement to see him today irritated me because it felt so right. The guilt piled on higher, making me feel unfaithful. I'd rather lose Thomas than keep the unbearable guilt.

Another voice, sounding like Deana's, asked me if what Thomas had done earlier was so terrible. Wouldn't my friends have jumped in if they'd interrupted Jonn Graham and me? Hell yeah, but we'd have shown him the door together.

Fed up, I spun on the backyard patio to release the pressure, deciding some music would lift my mood and help me forget. Macushla did her zoomies around the yard while I opened up the house app on my phone. It allowed me to control the sound system and choose the outdoor speakers.

Desperate to silence the critics in my head, I paid no attention to which playlist turned on. Pink's "U + Ur Hand" perfectly fit my mood and I placed the phone in my pocket, giving myself over to the song. I spun, stomped, and pointed into the chilly night, singing about the men who drove me to madness. It was a karaoke performance to the universe, and I poured myself out, begging it to quit screwing with me.

Macushla joined in, wiggling her butt as she danced around my feet. Her blurry tail fed off my energy. Prince's "Let's Go Crazy" came on next, encouraging me to hang in there. Then I recognized the first bar of Gwen Stefani's "Hollaback Girl," squealing as the rebuke of the men in my life crescendoed. I finally laughed when Koosh did something looking like a doggy twerk, enjoying the release, wondering when I'd last laughed. Then she broke out into uncontrolled barking.

I looked down and glared my disapproval. "Shh! Spoilsport. We'll have to go in before someone calls the Po-Po."

Sufficiently tired from pouring out my pent-up frustration, I fell onto the garden bench when the opening bars to another song from the past came on. I patted the seat next to me for Koosh to jump up. Petting her helped my breathing return to normal as I watched her settle, placing her muzzle on my thigh. I told her my problems while singing along to Duran Duran's "Come Undone."

As Simon sang, I wondered who was there for *me*.

The question stung my heart the most. I'd had the perfect life until it tore me apart. We'd worked our asses off to make our life work, and it didn't matter.

My dirty secret? The one I admitted to no one? I envied my friends who divorced. Even those with messy ones. They didn't know how it was a privilege to fall out of love. Was I doomed to a one-sided fairy tale gone pitiful? Now *I* had to be the safe place to fall. The kids didn't have two parents to rely on anymore. So I couldn't afford to come undone. Instead, I waited.

The song peaked as ancient tears awoke and drenched my face. When it ended, I bent over Koosh, who licked me in an effort to soothe. Sobbing, I looked up at the sky. "Why'd you leave me, Shane?"

Crisp air touched the wetness, chilling my cheeks. My dog jumped from my lap and trotted to the sliding door to the master bedroom, staring in, her tail resuming a vigorous swish. I pushed the tears away, facing my future aloneness. "We done, sweet girl? Let's see if we can sleep."

I missed the glow as I slid the door open, stepped inside, and double-checked the lock. I moved toward the bed and stopped short. My heart leaped at the slightly transparent man sitting on the end of the bed.

264 | KALLYN JONES

Am I sleepwalking now? This wasn't the shadowed mystery with silver wisps in his hair from recent dreams. I'd known everything about this man and his body as well as I knew my own.

My man. The only one I thought I'd ever want.

He lifted his head and stared at me, becoming solid. Eyes the blue of the Caribbean Sea smiled as they perused me from head to toe. The room spun, and I stumbled, ending up on my knees in front of him.

"Shane?"

"Hi, Katie." The left side of his mouth raised, revealing that libido-stirring dimple, the one that thousands of young women drooled over twenty years ago. I'd been the only one for whom it came to life.

I scrambled back to my feet, retreating to a shadowed corner, my hands shaking at my lips. "H-how?"

Shane shrugged and clasped his hands, resting them on his knees. "From what I can tell, you brought me here."

When he first left, we'd met in my dreams many times. He provided the strength to get through the next day. He let me know he still loved and supported me. Sometimes I'd feel a light caress or sense a kiss on my lips. But it had been years since our last meeting. I figured my subconscious couldn't bear the pain of waking up without him anymore and abandoned it.

Macushla curled into Shane's side, no apprehension in her demeanor at all. "Hey little Koosh. Wow, have you changed." He thoroughly petted her from ears to tail until it became automatic.

"I don't understand."

Shane lifted his gaze and found my watery one. "Koosh isn't the only one who's changed. You have too. There's more out there than we realize, love."

His powerful voice soothed like the sound of waves on the shore. Shane had made me feel protected and secure. His heart was as big as his body. His wide-receiver frame towered over me by nearly a foot. He'd played football for Michigan State University when we met. He continued to play ball with friends after two knee injuries forced his retirement from a successful NFL career.

Ever the receiver, he'd said he'd always catch me. It was true. Until someone took him out.

"I've missed you, Katie." The words dripped with the same pain I felt.

I ran to Shane, falling to my knees, gripping him. My heart filled with warmth and electricity. Home again. Anyone who's known love knows home isn't a building. Home was Shane McKenna.

I gasped. "You're real? You're back?" It made no sense, but what did?

"Shhh." Shane stood, pulling me up with him, enfolding me in his big, protective body. It was different from what I remembered —cool to the touch. I didn't care. Life without my husband was too hard to sweat the minor details.

Shane's big thumbs lifted my jaw so my lips could meet his in a gentle kiss, purer than our first had been. Our tears mixed, became one as they slid down my face and neck.

With his right hand, Shane wiped away our tears. "Don't cry," he soothed. "Only smiles tonight." He dipped his head and smirked. "Let's just be. No questions. No explanations."

"I st-still don't un...der...stand." My heart pounded so fast I was afraid it would explode. I adjusted my breathing to calm myself and abide by his words.

"No one defines how or why we love. We just do."

"Sing for me," I begged. "Please sing our song." For me, Shane's tenor tone was the final confirmation of his return. Few knew Shane's passion was singing. Football had paid the bills and impressed the family, but he expressed himself with song.

Shane looked over his shoulder, tossed aside the decorative pillows, and sat against the headboard of our bed built for a king.

He had me sit in his lap. "Everything here is the same," he said, looking around.

"I couldn't bring myself to change it." *I couldn't say goodbye.*

He wrapped an arm around my shoulder, kissed my nose, then he sang "Lovesong," by the Cure.

I closed my eyes, listening. It was a shock to hear it so real, so near, not a distant memory or old video. I pressed a kiss to his still perfect chest and listened.

I never realized how the song described those last eight years, loving each other from afar. This was my truth, why I stayed single. The song ended with me raw and reeling. The guilt overwhelmed me. "Shane, I'm so sorry. I've been—" I meant to confess about Thomas and how my heart had wandered, but Shane cut me off.

His eyes pinned me with a look of disappointment. "I get it, Katie. It hurts, but I get what you did."

"I didn't mean to kiss Thomas at first. It was just nice to have a male friend again. Then I guess I was lonely."

Shane shook his head while pressing his lips. "That's not what I meant. Do you still not get it?" He skootched over, and I got a better look at him, vibrating with emotions as he studied the ceiling. "You won't let go, and you pretend I never existed at the same time." The disappointment cut through me like a sword. "You're holding us both back, Katie. And you're hurting the family."

My dinner with Dylan came back to me, twisting my heart. The weight of the eight years fell on me, and my voice cracked. "Somewhere in my mind, I knew it hurt you." I studied Shane's face, looking for understanding. I continued through the hitches. "But they needed strength, not a broken mess. I wasn't anywhere near remission back then." I tucked a messy curl behind my ear, turned fully to him, and continued, "You died in my arms, Shane. How was I supposed to move on? I still freeze when I hear sirens and get furious at drivers who text."

He squeezed my knee, as I found the compassion I needed on his face. "You know I didn't want to go, right?" The dog rested her chin on Shane's thigh when his voice caught. "It was supposed to be a quick grocery store run. I didn't see the SUV, but when I think about how I'd asked you or Dylan to do the errand, I'm glad the woman broadsided me."

"I'm not," I cried, jumping off the bed and pacing. "Anyone with half a brain could see you were better suited to be a single parent." My outburst turned into a whisper. "I've screwed up so much. What if I've messed up the kids? Dylan... he's—"

Shane reached for me, but I couldn't settle. My heart and mind still raced. I found my respite in those deep blue eyes with their thick black lashes. That is, until they blurred from my own watery gaze. I didn't know if I could take what he'd say next.

"I've always been proud you were the mother of my children. I still am." He spoke with his head down, more to the dog, while he continued. "I used to work hard to give you confidence. I know some of that was your family, and some of it was your illness. But you're formidable now." His gaze met mine again, this time filled with lust. "Your body's stronger, but so is your mettle. Remember the depression you struggled with when you got sick and no one listened? My God, the day you confessed you were suicidal, it terrified me to my core."

"I didn't want to be an autoimmune warrior. I've barely survived it."

"No, Katie, you've thrived," Shane said with an awe I'd never seen or heard from him regarding me. There was a sadness in his voice too. He wiggled his fingers, pleading with me to return to him, this time for his comfort, not mine.

I obliged, settling on the edge of the bed. "I'll give it up. The shops, the house... everything. Anything. Please, just stay." Taking his hand and placing it over my heart, I continued, "There's a hole here I can't fill no matter what I do. Like I keep adding dirt to it and fall in anyway. With you here, I can be whole again. *We* can be whole."

He shook his head. "What's done is done. The one we became when we married is still in you, as it is in me. You… you absorbed me, which is why you feel different. You *are* different now." Shane sighed and continued in a hushed tone. "That's the reason your heart opened to someone else, Katie. Don't torture yourself over it."

"I won't let you go." With my future on the line, I made as clear a case as I could. "I've tried. Don't you guilt me into being with someone else. I'll tell you what I told him—I don't need completing. If you won't stay, I'll wait until we can be together again, wherever you've gone. I'll run the café, but I'll be killing time, waiting to be with you."

Shane kept shaking his head. "You don't understand."

"She ripped you away in an instant," I yelled, surprising myself. I bit my lip and whispered, "The love remains though."

"I know." He took my hand, turning it to kiss my palm. "It always will, and that's how it should be."

More tears fell as I stared into his face. He hadn't aged at all. But he probably wouldn't.

"You need to know I'm moving on." Shane stood and came around to my side of the bed, kneeling before me. "Don't stop living so long before you die. Don't piss me off." He added the last with a smirk. "You deserve happiness. Fight for it."

"Stop." A tiny voice, so different from mine, pleaded.

Sadness darkened Shane's expression. "It's because of you that we have tonight. Do you understand? You're becoming more."

"Not at all." I scoffed. "You're what's missing. So stay."

"You have everything I could give you." Shane moved to sit next to me and pulled me into his side. "You'll take it with you no matter what you do. So hear this, Katie. I *want* to go. And I want you to be happy."

"Where are you going?"

He let out a sad chuckle, running a finger against my wet cheek. "You wouldn't understand it if I told you. I think you'll see eventually. That's how different you are. Do you hear me?" He pushed the hair out of my eyes, tucking it behind an ear. "It doesn't mean I don't love you even if I still want you to love again."

I heard Shane, though I tried not to. I dug my fingers into his dark waves in case this was my last chance and kissed him thoroughly. His lips weren't the warm silk I remembered. His body didn't give off the perpetual heat it used to. Shane might look exactly the same, but he wasn't my husband anymore either.

His words were finally sinking in. "How long can you stay?"

The dimple I adored showed up one more time. "You need to use the bathroom."

"Among other things," I said, biting my lip. I couldn't wait to get into my pajamas, but I'd wear my torturous bra forever if it kept Shane around.

He smacked my thigh, chuckling. "Go on. I'll be here." To prove his point, he lifted the covers and settled in. The dog circled three times and dropped down by his feet. The way she used to.

Five minutes later, Shane kissed my shoulder as I spooned against his front. "I've missed this spot," he whispered.

I forbade myself from thinking about the goodbye, choosing to bask in gratitude for our night. Against my will, I fell asleep in Shane's arms, my head tucked under his chin. As time passed, I'd remember hearing him say, "I'll always love you, Katie."

A COOL BREEZE TICKLED MY NECK FROM LOOSE CURLS FALLING OUT of my ponytail. My gaze dropped to the warm sand under my feet. Salty air filled my nose. I looked up, confronted by waves from the Atlantic, caressing the shore. The tide was moving out.

Why didn't I hear it? The wind was silent too.

I turned around and stood before a beautiful beach house. It was the summer house on Emerald Isle Shane and I had planned to build come to life. I smiled at the memory of him picking the town because the name reminded him of Ireland. We were consulting with an architect before his accident.

The house sat on a spectacular bank with full views of the water. Tight plantings of Crepe Myrtles kept neighboring homes from seeing inside, making window treatments unnecessary. Shouldn't it have hurricane shutters?

A porch wrapped around the two sides of the house I could see. I remembered how the plans called for it on all sides. We both had adored porch life.

Before.

Beach grass grew so tall and thick I couldn't see where the access emptied onto the shore. I stalked the area, looking for a path to the house. Hell, any path. Before me lay nothing but large clumps of grass and sand.

The wind picked up, shuffling sand, making the dune shift. Grains of sand hit my face like glass. I slid down a foot but remained standing. I panicked at not being able to reach the house.

French doors on the top floor balcony opened. Shane stepped out and went to the railing. His wavy black hair blew gently with the wind, easier than it was beating my curls. Wearing only linen pants, he took my breath away. He stared at me while his arms braced on the railing. Despite the distance between us, I made out his brilliant blue eyes. They matched the color of the sky he stood under. I expected him to compel me forward, but his expression held a resolved sadness instead. It shifted to peaceful, and I knew.

The house was his, not mine.

I cried out but made no noise. He didn't try to speak, yet his eyes said what I probably wouldn't have heard.

A low sound finally reached my ears. It was a complete

surprise. Our grandfathers conversed on the front porch, though no one sat in the chairs. As far as I knew, the two men hadn't met.

Our fathers had formed the original family bonds while working on the General Motors assembly line. We became friends at Michigan State when my dad asked me to tutor Shane in French. His grandfather was long dead by then. I only knew his voice from recordings. Shane's timbre was similar. And they shared the gift of singing.

My Grand-da Allen had spoiled me rotten. He was the rare family member who focused on my strengths growing up. He supported me instead of reprimanding my flaws. I'd clung to every generous, teasing encouragement as if it were a lifeline.

I looked through the picture windows to see if anyone stood inside. Instinctively, I knew it held the things Shane loved. Pictures of the kids, our parents, and his uncle Billy, rested on a mantel. A football-themed office occupied the northwest corner. His favorite dishes filled the refrigerator and freezer—the food I made before dietary restrictions became a thing. I touched my mouth to capture a giggle, and a sob escaped. Shane tilted his head and gave me a sad smile. It was the same sadness permeating mine. I finally understood what Shane had tried to explain. A blurry image of the love of my first life turned and silently padded into the house. It was time for us both to find something new. The gifted assurance he was at peace meant the world.

I turned away from the sight, walking up the beach, knowing I, too, was a new person. I didn't die that Labor Day afternoon, but I'd fundamentally changed in my core, my sinews, my soul.

At six o'clock, the alarm went off to Journey's "Separate Ways (Worlds Apart)." An icy chill had descended on my bedroom, making me desperate to share body heat. But there was only mine. I ached from the fresh scab over my heart and realized it could finally heal. Without glancing around the room, I knew Shane had left.

The singer's perfect angst reminded me how much I used to

long to turn back time and trade places with my husband. It had never been possible to switch or follow him, back then or presently. It was his message in the middle of the night. We both had to go our separate ways. I came fully awake as the song wrapped to the anguished cries of the singer accepting the truth and saying goodbye. Finally, for me... the goads I'd kicked against for the past eight years had won. I cried tears of submission, then acceptance for hours.

I couldn't rise to make Liam's breakfast or see him off to school, something I only did when extremely sick. The reality I'd fought so hard, for so long, had gutted me. Shane and I were finished.

Yet the survivor's guilt, the guilt for trying to move on, for changing—all of it dissipated. It was time to start the new Kick.

29

THIEVES IN THE TEMPLE

KICK

"What in the Sam Hill's wrong with you?" Deana admonished, planting her hands on her hips in a power pose in my doorway. Thanks to Banger's security upgrades, I couldn't sneak into my office via the back door anymore.

I stopped typing midstroke, eyes wide. "Deana Douglas, did you pseudo swear?"

She scolded me through her teeth to keep our conversation private. "Don't play cute. I might think you've lost your mind. Check that, I already do."

"Excuse me?" My tongue worried my cheek, afraid of where her admonishment would go. The past few days had drained me, but Dee was in the dark about most of it. I'd spent the morning after Shane, wringing out the tears. Unlike before, these were good tears as I allowed myself to recall wonderful memories. Then the sun came out, both literally and emotionally. Getting to say goodbye turned out to be a gift. With a weight lifted, I surveyed my bedroom, the shrine to our past. The gigantic bed, massive en suite furniture, and worn-out comforter had to go. They never fit me.

I had padded into the kitchen with my phone in hand and called Charlie Rodriguez, my friend and carpenter. She had brought my designs at the café to fruition.

After a quick exchange of pleasantries, I said, "Ready to redo my master. How soon can you get me on the schedule?"

"Why the rush?" she asked.

I yelled into the phone, not giving her time to find a quiet spot at her job sight. "It's time."

Background noise buzzed and hammered for a beat before she answered, "No kidding. Tell me what you want." Charlie's cut-to-the-chase personality had been exactly what I needed.

I gave her a brief description of my vision for a room completely mine.

She blew out a loud breath. "Wow. Cool. And you're in luck. I had a cancelation that put a crew on the bench this morning. They'll be glad to work. Can you clear out the room by tomorrow?"

"Absolutely." The goal wasn't to erase Shane from my life. I knew more than ever it was impossible. It was time to build a respite where I could fully move forward. "Oh, and I want a legitimate meditation area, maybe a nook."

"Sure. Let's talk it through in the morning."

"Fantastic. Thanks, Charlie. This is going to help."

"I know. I've tried to tell you."

I'd canceled my appointments and spent the next two days clearing out my bedroom and working with Charlie's people. It was great to use all my muscles again.

Deana snapped her fingers in my face. "Are you listening?" *Not really.* I looked up with a guilty pout. She continued, "The professor stopped in here looking for you with his sad face. I told him to give you a little time to cool off, but this is silly, Kick. It's not like you to hide."

Little did she know. I was a pro. I'd been hiding more or less for eight years. Deana did have a point though.

She continued, "Put on your big-girl panties and fix this."

I lifted my hair off my neck, my office suddenly hotter than Hades in the bad way. "You sure he was looking for me?"

She looked at the floor and shook her head. "He scanned every corner of the dining room like he had x-ray vision and I also caught him side-eyeing my monitor. Then he asked, and I quote, 'Is Kick working today?' Yes, shug, he asked for you."

"I figured I ran him off."

She clucked her tongue. "You and Thomas have circled each other since the day he walked in here. Who cares if you weren't on the hunt? You should've been. It doesn't take a psychology degree to figure out why you went off on him the other day too."

She stepped inside and sat in a chair. "It's time, Kick. I wish I'd met Shane. The stories about him remind me of Gordon. I'll be the first to admit those men are as rare as a lightning strike, but he's gone. The professor isn't like those other fan boys trying to get up in your Kool-Aid. He *knows* your flavor. You know how precious it is to find it twice?" She tapped her fingers on the armrests, waiting on my reply.

"Circling each other, huh? Like dogs about to fight?"

"Or mate." She smirked before pursing her sassy mouth. "You light up when he's around. You stop wearing the Widow McKenna mantle and let yourself be you again."

I set my elbows on my desk, collapsed my chin into my hands, and took a couple of deep breaths before blowing her away. "You're right. Oh, put your eyes back in your head. You know you're right. But we were just friends."

I swear, Deana rolled her eyes three times. "Keep telling yourself that. Both of you are h-o-t for each other."

Really? Now I had a fresh fear. "But... if you're talking about a *future*, future... don't you think Thomas deserves someone who can have babies and grow old with him? I can't have more kids even if I wanted to, which I don't. What if I'm a distraction until he wakes up to what he really wants?"

Her face softened, often a sign she was going in for the kill. "Don't make decisions for him. Thomas is a grown man who knows what he's getting, right?"

For all the TMI I'd shared, my hysterectomy hadn't come up. Then again, I wasn't sure if it mattered. "It's probably best to stay friends and no more."

She dismissed me with a *pfft* and continued. "He knows you're about to be an empty nester. Shoot, Liam's so busy you're basically one now. Doesn't take a genius to figure it won't be long until the word *Grandma* becomes a part of your vocabulary either."

"Bite your tongue," I grunted, grateful Deana didn't know about Dylan's situation. Her baby addiction would swing into overdrive. I rubbed my temples. "There's more, and it's embarrassing, Dee." After letting go of my grief for Shane, I'd been wondering if I should exorcise the ghost of my dream soldier too.

"Let's hear it," she said on an exhale, murmuring, "Should've made myself a latte. You require more caffeine."

"I've had a dream for a while." *JaysusMaryandJoseph.* Was I going to admit this?

"About Thomas?"

I shook my head. "No. The guy in it is fuzzy. He has long hair, tied back, with silver temples. A dark beard. Darkish eyes, I think."

Deana's brown eyes pierced my gaze with a skeptical one of her own. "Never call the police with this vague description."

I steeled my spine to overcome the embarrassment washing through me as I told her the rest. "The dreams have increased in frequency lately. They feel so..." I waved my hands in front of me, searching for words.

"You think he's real?"

"Well, wouldn't you?" I squeaked. "You talk about signs from God."

"Yes. Signs can be wrong. And shug, you've read this one *way* wrong. I promise you."

"You think so?"

"Unless..."

"What?"

"What about the Professor? Could he be the dream man?"

"No," I said. "Though it's misty in my visions—"

"As they are." She rolled her eyes again.

"One thing I know, the guy is older than Thomas. Like I said, his temples are a sexy silver."

"Newsflash, Kick. No one ages younger. For all we know, Thomas already colors away the gray."

I shrugged, confused. Having experienced an intense dream the night before, it lingered in my thoughts. Still, it could be another coping mechanism to get me through loneliness, like the denial I'd learned to live with regarding widowhood.

"It's just... Remember when I'd told you about the vision I had of Shane's funeral years before it happened? Then I'd had several nightmares about my dad having a heart attack?"

"Those are normal fears people have about family. I've had similar nightmares before."

I stood and walked toward the clerestory window, reaching my hand up to the dust motes in the sunrays, watching them float around my fingers. "They came to pass exactly as I saw them."

Deana rocked her hand and cut to the chase. "You didn't

know they were visions until after they'd happened. Kick, I'm telling you, keep your heart and your eyes open to what—and who—is here *now*. Let the visions sort themselves out in their own time."

"Okay. Thanks for not laughing."

She stood and initiated a hug. "I don't want to make fun of a message from the Lord. Just don't get caught up in it, aight? It's already clouded your judgment about someone who's right here."

"I guess." Ready to shake off the events of the past hour, I followed her out to the dining room. "Maybe we can stop circling, as you eloquently put it."

"Thank you." Deana turned and patted my arm. "Take a leap and put yourself out there."

A leap. Such a frivolous word when the butterflies in my stomach seemed more suited to jumping out of an airplane.

I stopped in the hallway, pulled out my phone, and sent a text.

Me: You have time to talk today? About our fight? I'd like to apologize, but there's more too.

Thomas: Sure. When?

FALLING FOR YOU

KICK

*M*y anxiety was too amped to meet Thomas in the Perked Cup's dining room in front of all and sundry. As the clock ticked closer to his planned arrival, I escaped to my office again. I'd looked at his response at least a dozen times, trying to interpret whether it was good or bad. My knee wouldn't stop bouncing.

So much stress was ridiculous. Neither of us had enough skin in our game to be this jazzed. Yet viewing our fight through a different lens made me see our whole friendship differently. With the guilt removed—it never should've been there to begin with—

I couldn't stop the sense my future hung on the next hour. I focused on the adage of hoping for the best and steeling myself for the worst. I closed my eyes and let my breath even out, falling into a trance.

Thomas broke it with a subtle knock on the doorframe and a clearing of his throat. His hands were in his pockets, his expression unreadable, like the words in his text.

A green-blue light hovered around my fingertips, tucked under my desk. Shaking them helped make it go away and bring my head into the present. "Hey."

"Hey yourself."

Macushla had been curled up in her bed, napping ever since Carmen had brought her over earlier. The drywall crew had arrived at my house and unnerved her with their banging. She padded over to Thomas, greeting him with a nudge to a pocketed hand. He slid it out, rubbing her ears.

"Mind if we take Koosh for a walk? She and I have been cooped up back here."

He nodded, still giving me nothing regarding his thoughts. I feared I might scream, ruining any chance to get this right. I wanted to pin him down and immediately find out where we stood but didn't want to make a scene.

Macushla scurried, her nose to the ground, as we traveled the greenway behind my shopping center. She caught an animal's scent as she zigzagged through the grass. Then she skidded to a stop and filled her nostrils with another scent. I took my own cleansing breath. *Remember we're friends first.* The thought spurred me to speak.

"I don't exactly know how to begin this."

He stared into the waning light. It finally dawned on me what I had seen in his eyes from the beginning. I thought his stoic expression held ambivalence, but I knew—not sure how, but I knew then—it was regret. I wished I knew why. If he'd let me, I would suss it out.

"We've never spoken of my kids' father. And I think you may have the impression he…" My heart pounded. My voice shook. *Spit it out, Kick.* "He was killed eight years ago—broadsided in a car accident in front of our sub."

"I know."

There was a shocker. Most people who knew about me from a Google search announced it as soon as they found out, exclaiming it as if I didn't know my late husband was famous in certain circles.

"Google?"

Thomas nodded. "Some things didn't add up the other day. There were other times too, like the things that Jim guy said when he hit on you. I figured it was time for a search."

I let out a long breath. "So, you already know everything."

Thomas turned to me, his breath puffing a little on his exhale. We were finally in for a frosty night. "I read the articles, but we both know they're never the complete story."

My words tightened in my throat. I still didn't want to talk about the details.

He dipped his chin to catch my gaze. "Y'all up for filling me in?"

My head bobbed absently as I lost myself in time. "Eight years ago—Labor Day—it was a harmless barbecue. Just the five of us since I was in the middle of a flare. We didn't notice we were out of hamburger buns until the patties were on the grill. Stupid, I know. *I know.*" I nearly cried at the words I'd exclaimed in my head a million times.

Thomas gestured to a bench a few feet away. "Sit."

Aside from a creek running along the greenway path, Southern pines surrounded the seat. The water provided enough humidity to pull essential oils into the air from nearby vegetation. I inhaled the pine oils mixed with wild dill, letting it open my chest and my heart. The bright, healing scents gave me enough of a boost to get through the hardest part.

"I asked Dylan to run to the store, but he didn't want to leave a computer game. Shane reluctantly grabbed the keys and took Dyl's little car since it was parked behind Shane's. To be honest, I think Shane wanted a few minutes of peace from me. My health grated on both our nerves that day. We'd fought about who should run the errand." I watched water swirl around a branch in the creek running alongside the path.

My voice hitched as I continued. "I stood on the patio, tending the grill when I heard a crash. I don't know how exactly, but in my gut, I knew it was Shane. Probably because I'd had dreams about it. Anyway, I jumped in my van and... the car was a mangled mess. He was so broken. He... Thomas, he died in my arms." My voice gave out on the last five words.

I waited, watching the creek waters swirl, my fingers blanching from gripping the edge of the bench. And I kept waiting. Knowing your deepest pain lives just to the side of every memory, whether awake or asleep, is one thing. Telling your truth is exhausting. Loneliness became a bottomless pit as I readied myself to fall back in.

The tension pulsing off Thomas equaled mine, like I could touch it. I knew my story disgusted him. My iniquities were too much, and we finished before we began. I braced for the words.

Thomas's inhale was a loud rattle before he turned to me. The mask finally dropped as he pulled me into his arms. "Come here."

I spoke into his shoulder. "Did you read about the bitch who was texting when she hit Shane? Local and national papers covered her trial. Former NFL heroes get coverage."

"Yes, they do." He pulled back to see my face. "Why didn't you tell me? Remember what you said in Target about the makeup mirror? You basically lectured me on facing my truth." He gentled his voice. "Was there a problem in the marriage? Some articles implied—"

"Trashy mags insinuate things about girls hanging around players, but no." I laughed before I broke. "The media knew him

as Touchdown, but his teammates called him Reverend Touchdown because they said he lived like a monk on the road. The
problem was... in the end, none of it mattered. We had a deep
love and a wonderful family, and we still didn't last."

It came back to me like a flash flood. The explosive noise of
the crash. Fear. Saying goodbye. The police holding me back
when I tried to rip the driver apart with my hands. Sirens. Guilt.
Fecking hell, the guilt.

Tears unleashed, filling my lashes, and Thomas crushed me
into his chest. "Shh, baby." He nuzzled his nose into my temple
while I collapsed into him, letting it all go. If he'd take the pain,
I'd let someone else share it for a while. My soul ached from the
weight and lifted with the experience. His strong body took my
pain and my shame, telling me, at the least, we were still friends.

I scoffed at another memory. "My parents made it clear I
should keep myself tight. But I grew tired of my solitary grief. I
tried to wish him away, but it didn't work. So a scenario opened
in my mind where Shane left us, and I hated him for it. I
convinced myself the fury would make me stop grieving. The
grand delusion kept me moving. For better or worse. For the
kids." I took a shaky breath and continued, my chin bobbing.
"You should be upset for Shane though. He didn't deserve a
dishonored memory. I still felt like I cheated on him anyway."

"With me," he said, not asked, blowing out a long breath.
"Your reluctance with me. Your heart hadn't let go. This makes
sense."

Macushla pulled at her leash, nearly yanking me off the
bench. She craved forward motion too. "*Chhtt!*" I corrected.
Thomas grabbed the loop and fastened a tie-out to a slat.

"I'm not angry," he said. "Confused is a better word. It's out of
character from the woman I've come to know."

I chuckled into his neck. "Self-delusion is highly underrated,
sweetheart. I admit it freely."

"It didn't work though. You held on to him."

"I did. I'm sorry." I absorbed what Thomas gave, slowly figuring out he didn't judge. "Folks weasled up to Shane to be near someone famous. Imagine what they'd do to his widow. Deana, Jake, and my kids are excellent guard dogs, though Daddy was best. From day one, he'd spot a superfan with rotten motives and run him off."

"Like that Jim guy."

"Yup, except he's harmless."

"What do they want?"

"Some men think I'll give them money for their attention." I shivered and added, "This may sound weird, but there were men who wanted a chance to say they'd banged an NFL wife. And I used to think only girl groupies were so nasty." I blew out a long sigh. "It's taken years to be my own woman."

Thomas released a low growl, and I let out a surprised laugh. I clicked my tongue, and Macushla jumped into my lap, lending more support.

Thomas swung his arm around my shoulders and squeezed. "I understand some of the things you're saying."

"Really? How so?" I looked up to his gaze and caught sight of the North Star in my periphery.

"Well." He bent to pet the dog before continuing. "I'm a widower."

I straightened, tucking a curl behind my ear. Despite my talk of visions, I hadn't seen this possibility. "Wow."

"I don't speak about it much either. But it's easier here. No one in North Carolina knows besides Banger."

"You haven't said anything at work?"

"There's no point. I'd rather honor my wife by letting her be. It was hell at first."

"Yeah." I sighed, feeling the camaraderie.

"One of the worst things I've been through."

"I hear you. But you're good now?" He was so young. I wasn't sure I believed he'd healed. Maybe he was delusional too.

"I am."

"What was her name?" I asked as if the names of our late spouses would tighten our bond.

Thomas's voice thickened when he answered, "Alicia."

I looked away for a moment as I absorbed its significance. "What happened to her?" My heart broke for him, and I had to know.

He stood, pulling me up as Koosh jumped down, jerking hard on the leash. Thomas gently unhooked her from the bench and took the lead. "Let's leave it for another day." He put his arm around me again. "This talk is for you and us."

Seriously? After I'd vomited my secret all over him, he held back. For all the support and forgiveness he'd shown me, it hurt not to be allowed to reciprocate. I thwacked him in the ribs. "Typical male."

"What?"

"You're good to go when discussing my crap but lock it down regarding your feelings."

He chuckled and squeezed me. "My stuff can wait. I don't want to get off track with what's most important now."

"Which is?"

"Two things." My brows peaked, questioning as Thomas grew serious. "First, are you sure you've moved on now?"

I smiled into the dark path, proud of my new self. "Yes."

Thomas blew out a breath. "There's a relief." My gaze snapped to his. "The second thing is… well, us."

"We still have an us?"

"I hope so. I'd hate to think we couldn't make it past one fight."

"Right."

He nodded in the direction we'd come. "Should we head back?"

"Is it bad I don't want to?"

"No. I like having you to myself." We approached a ledge built into an underpass, and he stopped, settling me next to him. The sound of the water next to us and tires thumping overhead echoed off the underside of the bridge. It kept our conversation private. A couple jogged past, but we ignored them.

THOMAS RUBBED HIS BOTTOM LIP BETWEEN HIS THUMB AND forefinger. "Let me make sure I understand." We'd spent several minutes rehashing our sides of our fight. "You felt ignored while I was away. You kept yourself together and handled business... as you do." He squeezed my shoulder at the last words. "Then I showed up unexpected, took over, and made you feel incompetent by throwing Graham out of the store without asking if y'all wanted my help. You know I was afraid he'd hurt you, right? I won't stand by and let someone do that. Ever."

"I would've been grateful for your help if you'd asked me. It's about—"

"Respect?"

I blew out a breath. "Yes."

"Tell me Graham hasn't been back since I threw him out."

"He hasn't," I said. "I was about to ban him myself." Enough was enough.

Thomas ran his hand through his hand. "I'm sorry, darlin'. I wish I would've asked before giving him the boot."

I bit my lip, remembering. "It was hot."

He barked a laugh, startling Macushla. "I knew I saw something in your eyes."

"Yeah." I blew at a curl the breeze teased. Cool air didn't keep my cheeks from warming. I let my head hang low as I continued, "Listen, I understand it's important to stay focused when you're traveling. It can bring you home faster too. I was disappointed by how hard it was to reach you but only because it sounded... intense. Shane's travel schedule was intense. It kept up after he retired and started his own company. Anyway, I figured you would fill in what you could when you returned. I mean, I have no real claims to your time or your thoughts—"

Thomas bent his knees to meet my eyes. "What if you had a claim?"

I chuckled before responding, "I've been back and forth on this question."

"Yeah?" He made a noise of affirmation. "What did you decide?"

"At first I thought it wasn't worth the trouble," I answered with a scoff. "But I cooled off."

"And now?"

I stared straight into his eyes and said, "I'd like you to have a claim on my time. Hell, you already fill half my thoughts."

"Only half?" He smirked, and we both laughed.

"Got me there."

My grin faded, thinking about the ways we could go wrong. "The thing is… I'd rather friendship than nothing, Thomas. If it's what's best for us, I'll be fine."

"What if you could be better than fine, Kick?"

It would be amazing. I was afraid to hope too. "I wasn't looking for a relationship," I muttered.

"Neither was I." He shifted his body to face me. "We're an inconvenience, but it could be worth it."

Thomas stepped away from the ledge, pulling me with him. Then he leaned against the wall, bringing my body up against his. His lips met mine in an invasive kiss, telling me we'd interrupted each other's lives with equal audacity.

I challenged his kiss with a harder one, my mouth opening to his. The kiss became a duel—him punishing me for stubborn independence, me punishing him for cold indifference, both of us annoyed with the poor timing.

Yet we rejoiced in the possibility of more. We wanted each other, and the want alone could be enough to go to the next step.

My toes and fingertips pleasantly buzzed, and I didn't care. I could've gone up in flames and taken us both.

I slid from Thomas's hold, elated. Not feeling one speck of guilt. Light from a streetlamp above wrapped under the overpass, catching Thomas's eyes in a striking silver. The cool bulbs bounced blue highlights off his raven hair, just this side of shaggy. A contrast to his usually crisp appearance, I took it as a visual confirmation of how hard his trip had been.

"*Jaysus*, you're handsome," I said, running my fingers through the hairs at his neck.

"Is this a new revelation?" he said teasingly, brushing his nose along mine.

Heat crept up my chest as I laughed. "No. But there's a difference between noticing the outside and what's in here." I placed my hand over his heart. "Without this, you were hot, smart, and a bit odd."

Thomas's chest rumbled against mine, sending electricity to my warming core. "I had the same impression of you."

"I'm not odd," I protested, indignant.

"Have you heard yourself order a meal?"

"It's not on purpose."

"I know." He kissed my nose. "It's adorable."

He reached down and grabbed my ass with both hands, pulling me against his erection. My body's response was instinctive. I ground against him and whimpered.

"Don't tell me you're not hot either. With an ass like this, I could walk behind you for the rest of my life and never complain." He growled, and I laughed, remembering I'd thought the same of him.

Thomas's words made me feel something I hadn't in way too long… sexy. Brazen. If this is a glimpse of what we could be, it would be everything.

He began peppering my neck with kisses while I wondered

what all this truly meant. In the middle of a kiss, he said, "I can hear you thinking."

"Does this mean we're..." My mind sorted through the possible labels. Each one came up unsatisfactory. Even Facebook's "in a relationship" sounded too clinical. Hell, we'd been in a relationship since we became friends. This was different, even from a few weeks ago.

Thomas's eyes creased to seductive slits as he slowly formed a smile. "Important?" He leaned in and whispered, "Maybe even essential?" His eyes flashed in mock alarm as if confessing a deep secret. "We're evolving, Kick."

"I like this," I answered, breathless.

"There she is." Thomas tilted his head, staring into my eyes. He ran his hands through my hair, brushing it off my face and catching his finger on a coil near my temple. I let it go. We'd talk about how to handle curly hair later. It was a sign. If he hadn't meant so much to me, the assumption he could mess with them would have irritated me.

"Who?" I asked.

"Kathleen. The woman who doesn't require a badass nickname to be strong. The woman who knows she's enough."

A tear fell down my cheek, realizing this was how Thomas saw me. In my mind, strength was necessary armor, not a trait. "I might like this woman," I confessed.

"She's amazing."

Wrapped up in each other, I treasured the warmth we created until a sharp breeze broke the spell, working its way between us. At the same time, a man ran by, catching Macushla's attention. She'd been curled up at my feet, having given up on us moving. She barked at the runner as if she'd asked him to rescue her from boredom.

We moved off the wall and turned back toward the Perked Cup, Thomas keeping an arm around me. "Let's get y'all back."

Crisp air filled my nose. The moldy-leaf-decay smell of early fall in the South was dissipating thanks to the incoming hard freeze. I shivered and tucked in closer to Thomas. The man practically emitted heat like a furnace.

"Your jean jacket is too thin," he said.

Words fled my mouth again as I confessed, "I'm afraid I don't remember how to do this and I'll screw it up."

"You know," Thomas began, scratching at his chin, "when you're trying something new, there's a good chance you'll have to do something you haven't done before."

"Are you patronizing me?"

His arm moved up my shoulder and draped my neck. He pulled me in for a quick kiss to my temple. My heart soared. "Only a little because I know your history. I'm in unfamiliar territory too, but we can figure it out."

We continued along the greenway, staying in a cloud nine bubble as I blitzed Thomas with questions about research and family. Wanting to know everything about him, eager for each answer.

He put his face in my hair, then whispered, "It's been a long day. Can we just walk?"

"Sorry," I said. "Some people get crabby when they're cold and tired. I talk."

"So you're exhausted all the time?" He laughed.

"Hey! You're lucky you're hot. Not to mention you have me buzzy and stuff."

Thomas stopped short, pulling me back and accidentally yanking Koosh. "Sorry, girl," he said, then turned to me. "Buzzy?"

After staring at me for several beats, waiting for an answer, I gave in. "Oh please. Like you don't know you can kiss me senseless, Mr. Magic Lips."

He laughed and resumed our course. His chest out, with a low, throaty voice, he said, "This is going to be fun."

"Buckle up, buttercup. I'm no picnic," I grumbled.

"Then, it's a good thing I'm a genius at solving puzzles. Sit back and relax, Kick. You have me now."

Thrilled and uneasy with his statement, I defaulted to what I normally did when panicked. I changed the subject. "Are you free for dinner?"

31

THANK YOU

THOMAS

"This butterfly art is gorgeous," Thomas said while helping Kick slide out of her denim jacket. The mix of jewel tones in a Celtic design intrigued him and looked custom.

"I commissioned it from a local artist." She lowered her lashes and twisted her lips. A slight blush spread from her neckline. "It matches a tattoo I had done in the wrong place."

Thomas arched an eyebrow, surprised. He hoped like hell he'd get to see it soon.

"The tattoo came first." Kick gestured to her lower back. "I intended to put it on my shoulder but chickened out, afraid of

Bobby's reaction." She raised her hands. "I know I'm grown. As you also know, I'm still working on giving up my fucks when it comes to her. Anyway, when I met the painter at an art festival, I asked her about commissions."

"It means something, yeah?"

Kick nodded and turned toward the kitchen area, speaking as they walked. "It's my Celtic zodiac animal. It's also the icon used most for thyroid disease since the organ looks like a butterfly. It fit my headspace at the time."

Kick reached Macushla's dish and fed her, the dog automatically sitting at attention while she waited for dinner. A sense of pride swelled in Thomas as he witnessed the discipline and trust Kick had built with her dog.

"You mean the metamorphosis imagery," he guessed.

"Call it cliché, but yeah. It still fits." Kick turned to the sink and washed her hands. A streetlamp to the left allowed anyone at the picture window to see passersby. She waved to a neighbor on the sidewalk.

"Be right back," he said, turning toward the guest bathroom, his mind mulling the butterfly imagery and Kick's life. He'd never thought of butterflies as a talisman. He liked the idea and decided to read up on it. He'd check on his Celtic sign too, for "shits and giggles," as his new assistant, Bethany, would say.

When he returned to the kitchen, Kick faced away from Thomas as she worked at the stove, her hair up in a high ponytail. The long line of her neck called to him, and he stepped up, placing his arms around her waist, peppering her neck with kisses. First they came soft and quick, then lingering and open-mouthed.

She tipped her head back, giving him more access. "Mmm. This is nice."

Something was different about Kick. When he'd entered her office earlier, she'd had the weight of the world on her shoulders. Now that they'd cleared the air, she acted freer, looser. He smiled against her skin. Her skittishness had made some sense after the Google search. Knowing the whole truth presently, Thomas felt like a king. Kick came alive in his arms. This was what he'd missed with all those disposable women. He didn't know if it was a dream come true or a horrible idea. More importantly, he didn't care.

His hands traveled under the hem of her Perked Cup T-shirt until they skimmed under her breasts. Thomas took his time exploring, kneading them, delighting in their weight in his hand. He grew more thrilled with the way Kick's spine flexed and pressed against him as he played.

"You like?" he breathed into her ear.

"Hell yeah. I've missed this."

Thomas laughed into her shoulder. "I haven't even begun. Give it time." Movement out the window caught his eye, and he asked, "Should I stop?"

Kick turned the heat down and spun around. "Not unless you're starving. Why?"

He shrugged. "Anyone can see us in here. And you're—"

She cupped his jaw and kissed his chin, her tongue briefly teasing his cleft. Thomas chuckled in response but stayed firm in his desire to protect her. "What did you say earlier? We're important? The neighbors might as well figure it out now."

Thomas didn't want to reflect on her words too long, or he'd admit she'd already become essential. He wanted more, and he wanted it now, like a spoiled child. However, he'd also learned the value in waiting.

Kick tapped his shoulder. "Let's plate up. Dinner's ready."

They ate at the kitchen island, listening to Sarah Vaughan. Halfway through "You'd Be So Nice to Come Home To," Kick's brows drew together. She stopped eating. Her fork seemed frozen, hovering inches above the plate.

"Something wrong?"

Kick settled her fork on the plate and sighed. "Before we go further... I should tell you something."

Thomas set his fork down and turned toward her. "I'm listening."

"*ICan'tHaveMoreKids*," she blurted in a breath, reminding him of the way Liam often spoke. "You should know."

He blanched, not because he'd thought they might have any, but because the prospect never crossed his mind. He'd assumed she was done, medically or otherwise.

"Also, I wouldn't want any more if I could," she continued, slower this time. "Pregnancy made my autoimmune condition worse, and motherhood—though worth it—didn't help my body at all. I'll never stop being a mom, but I'm ready to finish raising children. Anyway, I had a hysterectomy, so even if I did, it would be moot."

"Why are you telling me this?" When he allowed himself glimpses beyond the present, Thomas saw only his work, his hobbies, and recently, Kick. He suspected where she was leading though.

"You're in your prime, Thomas. You should have full disclosure, especially after you told me about already losing a wife."

"Thank you, but I don't want children either. I like your kids... but I also like how they're housebroken, in more ways than one. Well, almost for Liam." He smiled at his joke but didn't get it returned.

"What if you—"

"Dumped you for a hot coed? Is this where you're going?"

"Don't act like it's never happened. The odds aren't good for women in relationships with our dynamics."

Thomas wrapped an arm around Kick's shoulder. What could he say when he was sure every fool who'd entered such an arrangement probably also swore the same words he wanted to promise her? But they weren't him. None of them shared his secret.

"Is this why you've been hesitant with me?"

"Partially."

"There's more?"

She adjusted her ponytail and turned to face Thomas. She muttered, "I'm done with secrets."

Thomas cringed and covered with a nod.

"When I was a teen, I caught my mother with a much younger man at her dance studio."

"The reason you quit." He didn't realize he'd thought out loud until Kick jolted.

She lowered her head. "Yes. It led to a shitstorm I couldn't have imagined. If I could do it over, I would've kept my mouth shut."

"Who did you tell?" Thomas was afraid he knew the answer.

"My dad," she whispered, blinking her eyes. "He pulled it out of me two weeks later because I wouldn't stop acting out. I remember feeling like I was boiling inside. Being a kid, I didn't know parents did this to each other. If I'd kept myself together, Dad wouldn't have known. It broke him, Thomas. Then he had his own affair, to retaliate, I guess.

"To make matters worse, Bobby announced his affair at my graduation party and turned it into her personal martyrdom. She never let him forget it."

"And her affair?" Thomas asked indignantly. Nothing surprised him when it came to human behavior. He wished he could find a way to punish Kick's parents for dragging her into their mess, dead or alive.

"She blamed Dad for it too."

"I still don't understand why this made you hot and cold."

Kick pushed her plate away. Thomas hated seeing her struggle, wished he could give her his truth to make it easier, but his vow always came first.

"Bobby knows I blame her for everything that went down. I'm the only one who has, other than Shane. Hell, even Dad drank her pity punch. Apologies aren't in her DNA, you know. She responded to me with a certain... wrath. Anyway, if she can prove we're alike, her actions would be justified, and I would need to shut the hell up now and forevermore." Kick shivered like something terrifying had crawled on her. "If you haven't figured it out, I've made it my life's mission to be the Anti-Bobby."

"Even I can see you're nothing alike. Darlin', she's gaslighting you."

"I know." Kick waved off the words. She stood, paced around the island, then sat back down.

"Have you considered it might be healthier to cut her off?"

Thomas didn't know which was sadder, Kick's heavy sigh or her chin quiver. "In his last hour, Dad convinced himself she'd find happiness with him gone. He asked me to help her find it, and I agreed."

What a horrible burden to place on a daughter, he thought, but he knew well the desperate things a dying man would say to find comfort.

"Our circumstances aren't like your mother's and..."

"Juan," she gritted out.

Incredulous, he raised an eyebrow. Could there be a more stereotypical name?

"He did the Latin classes at the studio."

Bet he did. Disgusted, Thomas continued, "We're nothing like them."

Kick's eyes flashed with panic as he drew her into his chest. "I'm serious. Don't let your mother dictate who's important to you."

Thomas kissed her pretty, pouty mouth.

"You mean essential?"

"It would be nice, wouldn't it?"

She nodded. "Okay. If she brings it up, I'll tell her to shove off."

Thomas gave Kick a squeeze. "Thank you." He finished his

meal while she cleared her plate and loaded the dishwasher. He'd believed their schedules were their biggest hurdles, but this might end up harder than expected. He liked the possibility of putting Bobby in her place though.

She picked up Thomas's plate and asked, "Whiskey? I have a twenty-one-year Redbreast I bring out for celebrations."

"You're spoiling me." He smiled, anticipating the smooth drink. "Thank you."

She reached up on tiptoe and moved books around in a cabinet. Other liquor bottles waited patiently on a lower shelf. "Big cube?"

Thomas chuckled. She had designer ice cubes. Kick's attention to detail was turning out to be thorough in scope and intention. He'd see to it she knew he noticed. "Perfect."

She gave him a good pour, set it in front of Thomas, and replaced the cork top.

"Not going to join me?"

Kick patted her belly and scrunched her nose. *Adorable.* "Still on lockdown. The doctor doesn't want me drinking grain alcohol for at least six months either. We've had differing opinions on what the word 'distill' means, but I figured I'd capitulate this time. However, I'm not telling the family in Ireland." She laughed at the last sentence.

"Why not?"

"Uncle Billy... Shane's uncle and the McKenna patriarch. He teases me for not liking Jameson's. I only get a pass because I drink Redbreast and Bushmills. If he finds out about this, he'll take my Irish card away."

Kick filled her electric kettle and turned it on. She poured a small glass of what looked like pink iced tea from the refrigerator and brought a pillbox to the island. She sat on her stool and spilled the night's allotment, swallowing four at a time.

Thomas inhaled deeply, taking it in, still getting used to how much of her life was under constant supervision. "How are you feeling now? Is your program working?"

"I think so. Thanks for asking. The IVs are improving. I get an immediate boost—long enough to get home and crash. I have all-day energy the next day." Kick rolled her neck, the stretching making it pop. "It's better in small steps each day. I call it the autoimmune cha-cha. It's the kind of improvement I've learned to appreciate because it sticks."

Thomas chuckled at the phrase. "Autoimmune what?"

"Three steps forward, two steps back. It's still one step forward in progress." Kick shrugged. "The health journey isn't a straight upward climb. As long as there's improvement over time, you're hanging the moon."

Thomas thought it a fitting image of life in general.

Kick finished her medicine and put the pill organizer away as the kettle blew, ending with a cup of mint tea. She took Thomas by the hand and said, "Join me in the living room?"

They settled into the corner of her leather sectional and caught a few minutes of a sketch comedy. Pictures of the kids adorned the built-ins surrounding the fireplace. Pumpkins, witches, and other seasonal decor dotted the open shelves.

"Your Halloween tchotchkes are adorable, but I'm curious why you don't have any photos of your late husband," Thomas said.

Kick answered absently, "Everything's upstairs in the den. It's a veritable shrine to Shane up there." She looked up at Thomas. "It was too hard to keep the past in every corner, so I put it in one place."

He could relate. A miniature portrait of Alicia sat in his reading nook. It was the only surviving image he had, but he could imagine how oppressive it would be to keep a houseful. Alicia's presence still inhabited the rooms at his home in Virginia. He liked keeping her in designated spaces too.

Thomas looked down at Kick and gave her a soft smile. "I'd love to see it."

She finished her tea and sat up. "Sure. But before I take you up there, I have another question."

"Shoot..." He smiled, kissing her on the forehead. Like someone had opened a dam and he couldn't get enough. He didn't know where this emotional, mush-ball side of him was coming from.

"Halloween. Any chance you could help me with the party we throw in the afternoon? It's from three to five. It started for our high school regulars, though little kids have started coming, along with young adults who've graduated and stayed close. The neighboring shops join in now too."

"I can be free. I'd love to help. What would I do?"

"Pass out the candy as people enter." She flashed a cheesy grin. "And wear a matching costume."

His eyes narrowed in suspicion. "What kind of costume?" She'd lassoed him in like a sucker.

"I'm going as a fairy."

Thomas laughed and rubbed the pointy tip of her ear. "Of course you are. There's no way I'm showing my face in public in fairy tights. Sorry, not sorry."

"You don't have to wear tights. Liam's Renaissance Faire pants could work. And there's still time to pick up manly fairy wings."

"*There's* an oxymoron." She faked a pout, but he wasn't falling for it. He raised an eyebrow to challenge. Kick may have to turn in her Irish card, but he'd damn sure keep hold of his man card.

"Fine." She sighed. "What do you have to wear?"

"I have a Bela Lugosi as *Dracula* shirt."

"Sounds scary."

"I could... smile? Without bloody teeth."

"I don't know. You have resting grump face, and mothers will yell at me from the middle of the store if their kids cry."

"For Christ's sake. I'll think of something. Speaking of RGF, I should get Banger to stop by. It'll be *my* entertainment for the afternoon. And good for him to be nice to little kids."

"Are you sure? He scared me when I met him. He sports more of an RAF?"

"Uh… angry?"

"Asshole."

Thomas barked a laugh at Kick's accurate description. Still, he planned to mention it to Banger. He found himself surprised to admit he looked forward to the afternoon. He had shrunk his world too much over the years. Thomas rarely spent any time talking to young children.

They were halfway up the stairs when Kick asked, "Do you follow football at all?"

Thomas shook his head. "I'm more of a UFC, boxing, or martial arts kinda guy."

"I thought so, considering you had to Google me to find my connection to Shane."

Thomas reached the top step and took in the loft. A hallway to the left led to doors he assumed were bedrooms. A full bathroom lay straight ahead. A big sitting space composed the open area to his right. Another U-shaped sectional anchored the room with a large-screen TV on the opposite wall.

"Whoa." Thomas crossed to the shelves surrounding the television. Shane's photos, trophies, and other awards filled one side while the children's accolades covered the other. He was in many of these photos too. In one, Shane lifted a young Dylan, larger than the other kids in the picture. He beamed in a photo next to a smiling Rachel with a tennis racquet and first-place ribbon. He spent time with each relic, taking in the essence of life as a McKenna, overwhelmed by what they'd lost. No, whom. No, both.

It gave him a sense of why Kick worked so hard when he got the impression she didn't have to, why she didn't move the family to an easier living situation when she'd practically described the house as being haunted. He knew hauntings could comfort as much as cause upset.

Kick stood in front of a photo of a tiny Liam raising a football in an end zone, his gleeful face offset by everyone else in the frame. Some people grabbed their heads, brows furled. Others were bent over, laughing. A sad smile filled her face as she traced Liam with a forefinger. "He was so excited to get the ball; he never heard us yelling he was running in the wrong direction. The score went to the other team. Lee cried until Shane promised he'd still take him out for ice cream. He figured the boy deserved a celebration since he had caught a boomer of a pass and ran three-quarters of the field... against his own teammates." She shook with laughter by the time she finished.

Thomas wrapped an arm around Kick and kissed her temple. "It pleases me to know y'all were loved."

"Thanks," Kick whispered. "I'm glad my secret's out." She stood on her toes and placed a soft kiss on Thomas's lips. "When you're comfortable, you can tell me yours."

He bit his lip and stepped back. "I told you about my late wife."

Kick shook her head, moving closer, drawing his forehead to hers. She whispered, "I promise not to press, but there's more. I might figure it out though." She tapped the side of her head. "It's like a sixth sense I can't help. Secrets have a way of revealing themselves to me."

"Oh really?" Thomas lifted an eyebrow and smirked. He hoped Kick didn't honestly believe she had magical powers.

"Better believe it," Liam scoffed, standing at the top of the stairs. They both jumped at his words. "If I were you, I'd spill now. She's figured out every secret the three of us kids tried to hide. Fam's a McKenna legend. The Irish cousins say she's part Fae."

Kick looked between the men, a deep blush trailing down past her collar, her head shaking.

32

LOVELY DAY

KICK

I stood outside Thomas's office, my hand shaking, hovering in midair. It shook from hunger mixed with hopelessness. Setbacks are normal, but my doctor hammered me on stress, which only added more. It was wrong to come here after my disastrous follow-up appointment.

I practically ran to Thomas's office, eager to get away from everything wrong in my life. I'd fixed my issues over Shane and enjoyed my time with Thomas, though I still had a ton of work to do. Instincts led me to his office because I was needy, discouraged, and weak—all the consequences I hated about being autoimmune. I decided too late that he shouldn't have to deal with me dumping this on him.

"The glass in the door may be striated, Kick, but I can tell it's you," Thomas called from the other side, a smile in his tone. "Your hair gives you a specific silhouette. Door's open, darlin'."

I stepped inside, my fake-it-till-I-make-it smile plastered on. "You busy?" My gaze swept the office. Stacks of folders occupied every available surface, even a love seat. "You are. I'll leave you alone." I hoped Thomas would take them out. It was a mistake to stop in. The *old* Kick ran to her rescuers. Where'd the lessons of the past eight years go? My biggest takeaways had been that happiness is fleeting and only I can control my joy.

He tipped his head, studying me. "What's wrong, baby?"

This is wrong. I should've gone to University Gardens and meditated. I waved my hand to indicate everything was fine.

"If you wait a few minutes, I'll go with you to the Gardens." He took another step and kissed my temple. "But it's never a mistake to come to see me."

Shit. I'd voiced my thoughts. My shoulders slumped on an exhale.

He gestured to two library chairs, lowering me into the second one and taking the first for himself. "Doctor's appointment didn't go well?"

"How did you know I saw Dr. Chaddha?"

"Wouldn't you be at the Perked Cup otherwise?"

"Touché."

Thomas pulled my hand into his lap, stroking the top with his thumb. I tipped my head back when my vision blurred. "Yeah, it's the appointment. Mixed with stuff going on at the café."

"You mean the shiner Liam sported the other night?"

I nodded. Once my son finished cluing Thomas into my "voodoo-secret detection skills"—his words—I spotted his black eye and cut cheek, then proceeded to "lose my shit"—also Lee's words. I maintained it was justified. Thomas calmed us both and drew out the story of the fight in the coffeehouse. He kept me from marching up to there in a panic too. Instead, I called Jake, hearing his side, getting assurances they limited the damage to a broken leg on a chair. It happened when a boy said filthy things about Rachel. According to Jake, the kid riled Liam on purpose.

"It doesn't help our reputation in the community... There was another opinion piece on the neighborhood website yesterday."

"What did the doctor say?"

"She nailed me to the wall. Diet, medicine, and extras like supplemental IVs or massages can't make up for staying stressed." The frightful state of Thomas's office increased my unease. "I'm sorry to bother you when it's obvious you're swamped. I shouldn't be dumping this on you. I'll go... meditate."

"Hang on." Thomas squeezed my hand, the connection a sweet hum. It worked its way across my limbs and to my core, pushing back negative emotions. "Are you referring to this mess? An ancient file cabinet broke yesterday. The new one's out for delivery." He pulled me into his lap, bringing me into a tight hold, allowing the stress to take a short hike. "I'm thrilled you came to me. You weren't weak to stop by. It takes strength to show vulnerability. Plus strength is *facing* rough news, not ignoring it." He tipped up my chin with a gentle finger and pressed a kiss to my hopeful lips. "It's damn inspiring. I've had my share of setbacks lately. They make me want to punch the wall sometimes. You remind me setbacks are part of the fight too."

I soaked up his encouragement, appreciating what he offered. Fearing it too. It would be easy to lean on Thomas, but I was afraid to cross the line into becoming a burden. The little nagging voice in my mind kept taunting me, telling me this was too good to be true. My setback was proof I would never deserve another chance at happiness. The menacing voice had quieted with early progress, but it currently shouted at me with each additional problem.

And why was this the first I'd heard of Thomas's setbacks? Openness couldn't be a one-way street.

"How about lunch and a walk in the garden?"

Could he use the break as much as I could? I lifted my chin and studied his face, handsome as ever. But there were shadows under his eyes. Yeah, maybe we could lift each other up. The possibility of helping Thomas with his troubles made mine dissipate. "Sounds perfect," I answered.

Thomas helped me stand and moved to a coatrack in the corner. A quick knock caught our attention, and a gorgeous honey-blond coed stepped inside.

"Oh, sorry to interrupt, Professor. Thought you might be ready for my wicked hex key skills."

A corner of Thomas's mouth ticked up. "Sorry, Beth. The cabinet hasn't arrived yet." He turned to me. "Kick, I'd like you to meet my new lead assistant, Bethany. Beth, my… Kick."

I chuckled at the awkward introduction while extending my hand. "Nice to meet you, Bethany."

"Beth is fine." She shook my hand, her eyes a pretty peridot, bright with curiosity.

"You could've texted," Thomas said.

"True. I also thought you should see this." Beth pulled a folder from her backpack and handed it to him.

Thomas's forehead drew into tight trenches as he perused the sheets inside the folder. "This is the latest data?"

Beth's face also darkened as she nodded.

"Dammit all."

"I don't know how the original sample is doing so well when these others have telomere issues," Beth said.

My eyes flashed at the word *telomere*. I'd read about them and was expecting a report on my own soon.

"How do you feel about setting up for the next step, Beth?" Thomas asked.

I barely caught her panicked expression. My mind was busy watching them together—a ridiculously handsome, young professor with a devoted ingenue at his side. How was he *not* seduced by the scenario? I didn't doubt Thomas. He showed complete respect for their instructor-student boundaries. But I looked at Beth and saw my flaws—the autoimmunity, infertility, gray roots, extra weight, half my life already finished. I was the Anti-Bethany.

"Can you give us a minute?" Thomas asked.

I turned for the door, and his hand around mine prevented me from going any farther. "Thank you, Beth." She stepped through the door, closing it behind her.

Here I'd thought Thomas had been dismissing me.

His eyes perused my face before he pushed a curl behind my ear. He looked pained as he said, "I have to get to the lab. I'm sorry."

I tried to reassure him with a small smile and head tip. "Sure. I should've gone to the park anyway."

Thomas's thumbs stroked my neck. "I'm glad you didn't. Come by or call me anytime." The twinkle in his eyes matched the brightness of the sun streaming in his south-facing window. But it couldn't extinguish the festering darkness in me. "I wish I could join you."

"No worries, handsome. I understand."

He kissed my temple. "I know you do. Thank you."

"Will you still be able to do the Halloween party tomorrow?"

"Wouldn't miss it."

"Figure out your costume yet?"

A sexy grin filled his face. "You'll see."

Great. I batted my lashes. "It'll help my stress if you tell me."

He tapped my nose. "Not like meditating will." Thomas

lowered his mouth to mine in a soft, slow kiss. "I hope our visit helped. You sure made my day."

I stood in the hallway, watching the two walk in the opposite direction as my car. I couldn't help but think I was watching Thomas's true future or something like it.

I was such a lousy waste of his time.

33

HOLDING BACK THE YEARS

THOMAS

*A*nother dead end. Thomas slammed his hand in the desktop. It was late, but he couldn't go home. Not until he figured out the block. His finger hovered over Alaric's number. He'd spent the past twelve hours working on a setback he couldn't fix, but he couldn't place the call. Not yet.

Desire boiled in the pit of his stomach. It started the first time his lips met Kick's and grew with each encounter. Did he want out of the Felidae? Or would he settle for more autonomy? The choice wasn't clear yet, so he waited. He'd mastered waiting by necessity. If Thomas could snap his fingers, he'd get his break, proving the genetic origins of the Felidae members and others like them, and he'd hand the next phase off to someone else. Hell, he'd give it to Nigel even if Alaric protested. They might not be best buddies, but they were allies in the work. Right?

Thomas let his mind wander to the morning with Kick. It might be easier to keep her off the Felidae's radar if he returned to real estate. He'd been a developer before going to school. If he talked to his business manager, he could slip back into the game.

He'd grown fond of Liam too. Both Kick's boys, really. He didn't know Rachel well since she was staying in Raleigh. Banger hadn't tracked down the source of the girl's online harassment yet. Still, Thomas wanted to know her better too.

He enjoyed encouraging an anxious Liam the other night, already upset from defending his sister's honor. The boy had been anxious over physics. ADHD made it hard for Liam to focus, but he was whip-smart. Thomas knew the frustration of trying to work when your mind was elsewhere.

He hoped her kids would give him and Kick their approval before things went further. Wait, was he honestly contemplating a serious commitment? He thought back through their last two meetings and texts. They were growing close fast. Perhaps too fast. But damn if his every cell didn't respond to Kick when she was near.

Thomas ran his hands through his hair, grabbing at the roots. How had his calm, collected demeanor wandered off? He hated not being able to see a clear path. Now it was obscured, both personally and professionally.

THOMAS SPOTTED BANGER FROM THE PARKING LOT OF THE twenty-four-hour diner, the only customer sitting alone in a booth. Other couples and groups sat around tables on the other side of the space. Knowing Banger, he'd probably paid the waitress to keep the section empty.

Thomas joined him, a chin tip from each for a greeting. He wordlessly perused the menu, noting how nothing fit in Kick's diet. The waitress stepped up, coffeepot in hand, and took their orders. Thomas made sure he chose as few carbs as possible. He needed energy to get through another long day.

Banger's eyes followed their waitress back to the kitchen before breaking his gaze and addressing Thomas. "Why did you drag me out of my house in the wee hours?"

Thomas muttered, "You were awake."

"Not the point."

He gripped the back of his neck, swiveling it from side to side in a futile attempt at a stretch. He filled his friend in on the issues at the lab. Thomas hoped Banger's logical brain could help him look at the problem from a different angle.

"Not to be Captain Obvious, but you freak out when you're on the verge of something big. Since I'm not in a hand-holding mood, I'll say congratulations. I knew you could do it."

Thomas took a sip of weak, tepid black coffee and slumped. "Fuck off."

The overly bright lights gave Banger's pale skin an unfortunate, ghostly appearance. He lifted his hands in surrender. "It's not about wanting to help. If you had a hardware or software issue, I'd be right there even if it went against the university's protocols. Based on my understanding of what you do, it sounds like you're on track. Have you considered calling Nigel?" Banger's nose flared at the name. For as long as he'd known the man, they'd shared an animosity.

"Considered? Yes. But Alaric and Ellie are trying to pit us against each other for a reason they won't share. It makes no sense."

"Not to you."

"Something going on I should know?" Thomas asked. "There were more closed-door meetings than usual back in Bordeaux."

Banger shook his head. "Don't know, brother. But with each

day that passes, I'm convinced there's a bonafide traitor in the Felidae."

"Christ, I never thought about it like that."

Banger casually lifted a shoulder. "Make sure your lab stays secure twenty-four seven. Let me do my thing. I want to know ASAP if anything seems off."

Thomas agreed as the food arrived. They ate in silence, Thomas scarfing down his eggs and sausage, leaving the toast and jam.

Banger set his coffee cup down abruptly. "What else is going on? You're holding so much tension you're making my TMJ ache. Have you banged Kick yet?"

Thomas dropped his fork and scowled. "Come on, man."

"I'm serious. What's taking so long? You look like a man who wants to blow out his carburetor. Get it over with and let her go." Banger took a bite of pancake and circled the air with his fork. "Or make another Vivienne arrangement."

Thomas shook his head. "It's not so simple. I traveled more back then. A similar arrangement wouldn't work when I'm in town most of the time." He didn't want to add *he* was different too. Thomas didn't want the distance, physical or otherwise, again.

"Sure it could. Tell her you're available on weekends and leave it at that."

Thomas tried to school his reaction to the idea souring his stomach. Between the kids, the people at the Perked Cup, and Mick & Hugh's, he'd been accepted into the fold by everyone. He liked them all. This wasn't only about Kick.

"Oh hell." Banger dropped his fork. "Bad idea, brother. Stay the fucking course." He pointed at Thomas. "Still don't know why you won't stick with the pretty little bics. Consider yourself like a stud dog. If the animal doesn't blow a few times a year, he gets unreasonable—even violent. He gets some? He calms the fuck back down. We're the same way. A disposable woman is the perfect solution. A few weeks of bump and grind, we're happy, they're happy. We move on."

"You know..." Fatigue made Thomas irritable. "With you, everything's disposable."

"You wound me," Banger said, dramatically touching his heart. "And you, my friend, hold on to everything. How long have you had your car? *Jings Crivvens*, get a new one already."

Thomas's bubbling emotions made him get real. He exhaled an exasperated breath. "Don't you tire of living outside real society? I thought the Felidae would help me finally belong, except I don't live on the vineyard full time."

Banger scoffed. "Who wants to?"

"Exactly. We're still on the outside, man."

"I like to think of it as moving between two worlds. I get to choose." Banger shoved a chunk of pancake in his mouth, speaking around it. "It's about perspective." He chewed and swallowed.

Thomas looked at Banger's plate again—four plates, actually. Lord, when would their breakfast end? This had been a mistake.

"I've thought about it, and everything *is* disposable. As soon as it's not useful, it has to go."

The words made Thomas want to hurl. But he grew tired of talking. He craved the connection he'd already cultivated with Kick. Something deep down told him sleeping together would grow their spark, not quench it.

Banger let out a long sigh. "You're worse than I thought. You still making music? My piano fills the lonely spaces late at night. I was working on Ravel when you texted."

Thomas arched a brow. "You already play his stuff better than the man ever dreamed of it. Anyway, I'm moving Eddie down here soon. Not that my horse will fix this."

Banger muttered while stabbing a sausage, "Don't know, brother. He's a good horse."

Thomas held in a laugh. "Eddie's coming because I'd like a

piece of home nearby. I also don't want him thinking I've abandoned him." Thomas hoped to share Ed with Kick too.

Banger shook his head, then slapped the table. "I know what's going on. I recognize it now. This is a midlife crisis. I had a major one about a year before we met. Hell, I'm surprised you haven't had one already." He drank the last of his coffee in time for the waitress to refresh the cup. He sent a flirty wink her way before continuing, "I fell hard for a dark-haired feisty miss for a minute." Banger snuck a wistful glance out the window. Darkness wrestled with the dawn, leaving the sky a tortured gray. The emotion was universal then.

They turned back to each other. "We had a rare connection. Then reality slapped me in the face. I couldn't grow old with her. So I left. I'll admit ghosting was hella easy then." He made a wiping motion with his hands. "It was better for her. Then I banged my way from Europe to Australia. Ended up surfing in Polynesia for months. Tourism was taking off, and the ladies were more than happy to have a lesson and a screw from 'an exotic ginger'." Banger waggled his eyebrows.

"Bet they were," Thomas said. He could see it too—Banger's usually buzzed blond hair long, his face constantly sunburned. The women would've eaten it up.

"As I said, man, I can't just leave. I have a contract with the university." Thomas drank from his warmed-up cup. "I could stop going to the café, but we still might run into each other." He didn't want to admit a future with Kick excited him, but it was the picture forming in his mind. He didn't care about growing old with her. He'd do what he must. Thomas wasn't sure how far they could take it. He just knew he hadn't felt this good in forever.

Then his phone rang. Thomas checked the caller and said, "It's Alaric. You mind?"

"Go right ahead." Banger pretended to zip his lips shut.

"*Oui Grand-père.* Thank you for returning my call."

"Certainly. Do you have news?" Alaric asked.

"It's not good. The general population samples keep failing. Toni doesn't want me to use her family's DNA, and I won't break her trust."

"I thought I impressed upon you how urgent progress is now," Alaric snapped. The man cleared his throat and changed his tone. "I'm a patient man. I have to be. But now isn't the time for caution. It's time to push."

"Isn't trust more important for the long game? We can't have Toni running away... or worse. She's more than potential Felidae. She's family."

"*We* are your priority and your family. I can't have you conflicted, my boy."

Thomas remembered his induction ceremony. The vows were easy since Joe took them at the same time. The pull of loyalty began when Joey left the group, calling it all bullshit. Thomas had never parsed out exactly what had ticked him off. Joe refused to say. Maybe he'd ask again the next time he went home.

"I haven't forgotten my vow."

Banger rolled his eyes and looked up at the ceiling.

"Focus is everything," Alaric urged.

"Understood." Thomas's hand shook as he set the phone down.

"I can get the DNA sample for you," Banger offered.

Thomas's hand found the back of his neck again. "I might take y'all up on it," he answered, distracted.

From the moment he'd made his vow, the Felidae came first. Why did it sound like Alaric had spoken about more than family ties with his warning? More than once, Thomas thought Alaric had the gift of sight.

Perhaps Banger was right. The timing for him and Kick wasn't right. He shouldn't let himself get caught up in their newness. He should back off.

34
THRILLER

KICK

$\mathcal{O}$ur Halloween party began earlier than expected when moms of preschoolers stopped in for lunch after class. My crew didn't mind since the candy bowls were ready. We had color-coded buckets to make it easier for kids with allergies. The regular bucket was refilled twice before the high schoolers arrived. If the pace kept up, the day would've been our most successful by far.

Jake and Deana ganged up on me, insisting I ditch the fairy wings since they kept knocking into the staff. I'd barely missed poking out Deana's eye twice. Thus my fairy costume became an elf's.

I didn't mind. I was flying high on the joy of my second-favorite holiday, my bedroom remodel was due to finish soon, and I'd made peace with my doctor's earlier admonishment. I'd even meditated and worked out first thing in the morning.

"You look oddly happy," Bobby commented from her perch at the counter.

"It's Halloween," I answered. "The sun's shining. Pumpkin spice fills the air." It wouldn't be long before I could add decaf coffee back into my regimen. I marked it on my calendar. "It's a good day, Mother." *Wow, Bobby's presence didn't bother me.* I shifted my shoulders, searching for tension. Nope. My spine was set but not tight. Hell, I was on a roll.

"It *is* a good day." She'd handed out candy when I sent Crystal to get more from the grocery store. Plus she didn't stage-whisper mean things about the children or their mothers. "Are you enjoying your time with that younger man?"

"Uh, I am." She didn't need to know about our fight or making up. She also didn't know about Dr. Chaddha's comments and most definitely wouldn't hear about my insecurities over seeing Thomas with a more suitable woman. Bobby and I worked best when we took the British approach to conversation and kept it to the weather.

"Well, good." Bobby nodded into her cup. "He looks like the kind of man who can help you lose your extra weight."

I paused midwipe during my counter-cleaning ritual. On a great day like the present, it was easy enough to let the comment roll off, so I said nothing and kept to my work until the wood sparkled.

"You know," she added with a defensive tone, "he's fit. I bet he'll be fun to work out with." My non-comments often startled her more than arguing back did.

"He is fun to walk with, but the good doctor didn't clear me for anything harder than lifting small dumbbells and bodyweight exercises."

"Which explains the tummy," Bobby said.

Jake handed off an order, shaking his head.

"I suppose it's better than when you had no curves at all. Poor thing." She backpedaled. "When your doctor lets you run again, you'll return to a proper size."

I knew Bobby only saw her flaws when she looked in a mirror. So I chose to view her words as positive and moved on to serve a customer. In some ways, I preferred her clueless warnings to the outright jealousy she'd shown when I'd lost the hundred pounds.

As high schoolers sauntered in dressed in costumes, Deana still passed out candy. She always left by three so she could pick up her grandchildren at the bus stop. With a smile on my face, hiding my concern, I approached her. "Not to scare you, Dee, but shouldn't you scoot now?"

I held my hands open to take the bowl from her, enabling a quick escape. A grin washed over her before she responded. It turned out she wasn't freaked about being late. "I forgot to tell you... my Maceo took the afternoon off and went to the school parties. He's bringing Genesis's kids home too. I want to stick around and see which big kids dressed up."

"Aw. Mace is such a wonderful dad." Looking out the window for approaching teens, I added, "Hope my kids turn out like yours."

Deana's smooth laugh rumbled from her chest. "If they don't, I'll discipline them myself."

"Hey, do you have any photos ready to hang in here? If we get some up now, you could schedule holiday sessions next month." Deana had recently set up an indoor studio in her house. I hoped she'd take the leap and turn her side hustle into a full-fledged venture. I'd miss her face around the café, but she had talent and had proven her business savvy as my manager.

"There's a handful left to frame. I'll bring them on Monday."

"Perfect."

"Is Cyndi stopping by?" Deana laughed. "She sure knows how to put together a costume."

I moved my chin from left to right. "Cyn's booked, and she's doing the grown-up party thing tonight," I added.

Dee opened yet another bag of candy, restocking the buckets. She looked over her shoulder at Bobby and turned back to me, talking low near my ear. "You and the professor aight now?"

"We're good," I started, checking over my shoulder as well. "I'm taking everything one day at a time. Enjoying each moment." Something stopped me from opening up completely about my concerns. I wasn't sure how to take the insecure feelings from yesterday. Were they related to my emotions from the doctor's appointment, or did they happen congruently? Or maybe I didn't want the words released into the same air Bobby occupied, fearing they'd magically find a way to her ears. It was Halloween after all.

Liam's arrival interrupted us. He came by straight after school, wearing his brother's old practice football gear with zombie makeup added.

"Hey, weeman." I circled my face with my forefinger. "Please tone down the makeup before more littles show up. Don't want to scare anyone."

"Fine, fam," he grumbled. "Yo Grams," he said to Bobby.

She returned it with a "Hello, pumpkin. Have you grown?"

Liam and I both did a double take her way. We weren't used to her saying anything close to complimentary toward my youngest. She'd decided Liam would be my scapegoat child from day one. From what my brother Bert told me, she did the same with his youngest. He had two boys and no girl. Bert's saving grace came from living in the Detroit area. Our mother only visited them twice a year unless they traveled down. Thankfully, she planned to be there in December. I'd thought spending the first Christmas without Dad with her favorite child would ease any pain the holiday might bring.

"You look just like Dylan," Bobby said.

Liam lifted the practice jersey by the collar. "It's his old football gear."

"Ah. I see," she said, taking a sip of coffee. "Can you refresh me?"

"I'll get it," I said and reminded Liam to clean up.

Lee came back from the bathroom, looking more dirty than scary, and walked straight to me. "When am I going to get my parking space in the garage back? The morning frost is getting thick on my car. It's not *my* stuff filling my spot either."

I cringed, watching Deana and Jake eye me suspiciously. "You're right, sweetheart. You can have my space until the furniture gets moved. We'll be ready for it in a day or two."

"Thank you." He sighed.

Deana arched her eyebrow, wordlessly demanding an explanation.

I laughed before saying, "You know about the remodel, right?"

She looked to Jake, who shrugged. "How could we not?"

"Well, I bought a smaller bedroom suite. Hugh and Maggie are downsizing and had a mint-condition Stickley set. It's a queen sleigh bed and perfect for me. Some guys from the crew moved it a couple of nights ago for side money. Since the room's not yet ready, it waits in the garage."

"I see. Were you planning on saying anything?"

"Dee, I see you so little lately we spend most of our time catching up on business. You can come see it when everything is done." The corner of my mouth lifted, happy with my self-defense.

Bobby tsked and shook her head. "You had a perfect set before. I don't know why you had to get a used one. From the *Reynoldses* too."

"It suits me, Mother. Did you hear me say it's mint? I've loved that style forever. Plus they practically gave it to me when a dealer would've paid them beaucoup bucks. Besides, the old one's in storage for Dylan."

"Oh," she said, seeming appeased by the notion it waited for her favorite grandchild. She didn't understand my son was on the verge of success greater than anything his father or I had dreamed of at his age. Since she didn't understand computer science—hell, I barely did—I let it go too.

We spent a half hour busting through a busy line. It was like old times except for the two people missing—my dad and Rachel.

Deana was wrapping up her shift when she looked out the window and said, "Thank heavens he's here. I was hoping I'd get to see his costume."

I sidled up to her. "Who are you...?" I spotted Thomas walking away from his Camaro. "Oh. Wow." I shook my head, laughing at his costume. Silly, but scorching hot too.

You could hear Thomas's spurs ting against the floor as he entered the Perked Cup. They wrapped a pair of well-worn cowboy boots, followed by perfectly broken-in jeans, an empty, albeit worn, gun holster (thank goodness), a sheepskin vest, poncho, western hat, and a cigar nub. He swaggered better than Eastwood himself and looked like he could be comfortable roaming a desert. On a horse. Hunting bad guys.

My face turned red as my knees weakened, and my underwear dampened from the sight. A grin split my face as he neared. I didn't even care if Bobby picked up on my vulnerability. The man looked too scrumptious for words. I wished my bedroom were finished so I could convince him to spend the night and play cowboy and... elf something. *Whoa, where'd that come from?* Okay, I wouldn't, really. Not until I knew Liam was comfortable with him, but *Jaysus*, I wanted to.

Thomas was my icing on a fantastic cake of a day. He stepped up to me and placed a kiss to my cheek, keeping the cigar nub in place. "Hey beautiful."

"Hey yourself." I tipped the hat, still grinning. He'd let his stubble grow since yesterday. "Don't you think you're a little dark for Blondie?"

"Look again, darlin'. He isn't exactly a sunny surfer boy."

"Good point. It's an awesome costume, actually." I stood on my toes, kissed his cheek back, and whispered, "Sexy too."

Thomas's eyes flashed with amusement and lust. "Think so?"

"I do."

Thomas bent and whispered, "Enough for a feel-up in the office?"

My knees weakened more from the offer. "How about after the party?"

He pretended to pout before his mouth curled up on one side. "Can't wait." He touched my shoulder. "What happened to the wings?"

I jutted my chin toward Jake and Deana, who was saying her goodbyes and waving out the door. "I bumped into them too much." I spread my Celtic embroidered tunic out at the hem. "I'm an elf now."

He touched the tip of my ear and grinned back at me. "An elf suits you better."

Bobby choked on her coffee, taking a few coughs to resettle. My pointy ears were another of her embarrassments.

"When's this party happening?" Thomas asked.

"It should start in earnest in about thirty minutes. You want a coffee before it picks up?"

"Sure."

"One of the famous pumpkin spice lattes?" Liam asked from the order area.

Thomas scrunched his face, his nose getting an adorable crease I'd never noticed before. "Christ no, kid. An Americano is fine."

"Well said, my dude."

"Was he testing me?" Thomas asked me.

I shrugged. "You never know with him." I tapped Thomas's chin. "You should lose the stogie, pal."

"It's not lit," he argued. I answered with a sigh and squint. "Mothers yelling in the middle of the dining room?"

"Among other things." I held out my hand for it.

His face scrunched in disgust. "No, darlin'. I'll take care of it. Go see to your customers."

Thomas went to the bathroom, came back minus a cigar, then talked Bobby into handing out the allergy candies. It was the lightest bucket. There were plenty of us behind the counter to handle the crowd once it kicked in. Parents of the elementary school kids brought them by after school for heavy snacks and early trick-or-treating before heading home.

The inside became standing room only, causing customers to hang around on the patio too. The afternoon was perfect for alfresco partying but made it impossible for us to keep track of everyone. The café filled with Hogwarts students of all ages and houses, gruesome monsters, pretty princesses, and superheroes from the year's blockbusters.

I was in my element, as was the rest of the crew. We even danced a few steps to Michael Jackson's "Thriller" and other Halloween songs while waiting on customers, enjoying the buzz of the crowd.

I rang up an order for a mother in desperate need of a large pumpkin spice latte, with a juice and cookie for her kindergarten-aged Batman. An earsplitting series of bangs filled the dining room, erupting near the windows. The sound deafened like rapid-fire gunshots.

ONCE IN A LIFETIME

KICK

*J*ake flung himself over the counter with a fluid jump before I registered what had happened. The bangs, the screams, and the stampede all blended together. I looked down at little Batman, his face filled with shock and terror, tears already streaming down his cheeks. I grabbed him, his mother, and two nearby teens, brought them behind the counter, and made them stay down.

Someone cried out, "It's a mass shooter!"

Another voice shrieked as if hurt. The space filled with smoke and a sulfur smell. Liam grabbed a fire extinguisher and sprayed a smoking object on the floor.

Panic filled me. "Liam!"

"It's out," he called back over his shoulder.

I pulled the first aid kit from under the counter and shoved it at our new girl. "Crystal, take this and help Lee."

People held their phones above their heads, filming. Thomas had his phone raised, and I stepped to him, fury boiling over and skewing my judgment. My anger toward the person who'd done this channeled into a rage at him for adding to what I feared would become a media frenzy.

Charging forward, I yelled, "No!" and slapped the cell from his hand. Despite the unrelenting noise, his phone seemed to clang as it hit the floor, shattering the screen. The sting to my fingers came next as the reality of what I'd done set in. We both stared at each other for a beat, equally shocked by my response.

"What the hell?" he growled, his jaw flexed, nostrils flared.

"Some motherfucking asshole set off firecrackers to create a panic. And it worked. If your video gets on tonight's news, it could shut me down."

"Come on, Kick." Thomas oozed disappointment. "I was calling 911, then Banger. If the alarm hasn't gone off at the Angel office, they need to know. They should be looking at the feed right now."

My chin quivered when his words set in. I'd let my temper override logic again. "I'm so sorry."

Little Batman had been peeking over the counter, his eyes wide. He'd watched our interaction and heard me swear. "Sorry about the yelling and naughty words, sweetheart. I'm really, really upset." His mother's eyes sent evil daggers my way. *Jaysus, I had to rein in my temper.* I patted little Batman's hoodie ears before his mother batted my hand away. "It was only a mean prank. No one shot anybody. The scared people are saying things they don't understand."

"Don't you touch him," the woman snapped. My guilt grew for my part in the spread of panic.

"I want to go home, Mommy," he whimpered. "I hate Ha-wo-ween."

Lovely. I turned my attention to the mother. "Take the back hallway to the rear door." I told her the code to open it and looked at the teens hovering by her. "Take the girls too."

Giving little Batman's mom a job helped her settle. She moved the kids out efficiently.

Liam called 911 while Thomas and Crystal triaged a few teens who'd been near the attack—now a smoking, shredded backpack under the front windows. Both panes suffered spider cracking, and one had a small hole burst in front of the bag. Teens on the patio were helping another with cuts in her leg.

"Send an ambulance to the Perked Cup, please. We have three burn victims and others with cuts as far as I can tell," Liam said. He wasn't the only one calling in our attack either.

I turned away to gather ice and clean rags.

Quickly what looked like the entire fleet of Oakville PD cruisers skidded to a stop in front of the café, in full tactical gear. Half remained outside, taking charge of the crowd. The other half came inside with weapons drawn. More screaming ensued.

Scanning the room, I made sure everyone kept their hands up. The collective terror on my customers' faces made my knees buckle in despair. I murmured under my breath, "We can't go down like this. We can't."

Gaping at Thomas, a defiant tear dropped down my cheek. Not only was my festive day ruined, my business might be too.

I yelled to the officers, "It was firecrackers, not a gun."

The lead one looked in the direction I'd jutted my chin and turned back. "Still need y'all's hands up, ma'am. Anyone see who did it?"

"I think my barista went after him."

Everyone around me kept our hands raised until the police

decided the scene was secured. Liam, Thomas, and Crystal were allowed to continue assisting the wounded until the EMTs showed. I shuffled around the space, giving reassurance to shocked kids as best as I could. I hated that they had to have their party ruined by someone. *Oh hell. What if this was related to the harassment?*

During the entire calamity, Bobby sat on her stool, watching it go down. When my eyes finally landed on her disapproving expression, I couldn't help but laugh from relief. I counted my family members. Staff too. They were safe. It appeared the burns, though painful, were second degree.

I wanted to puke from the sulfur smell still in the air as I made my way to my mother. "You okay?"

She pointed to her cup. "Someone knocked over my cappuccino." I burst into an inappropriate belly-laugh, grateful she hadn't tried to leave during the stampede and hurt her weak knee. Jayz, they could've crushed her.

"I'll get you a new one."

One officer cleared his throat. "Detective Ross is almost here, Mrs. McKenna. He wants you available for questions when he arrives." He turned to my mother. "He'll want to talk to you too, ma'am."

"Not until I get a cappuccino," Bobby sassed. At her age, she expected respect from law enforcement but didn't hold any for them. I raised my hand to intercede when the officer opened his mouth to argue.

"May I make her a quick cup? Please. I can make one for you too, Officer..." I checked his name tag. "Taylor."

He let out a long sigh and frowned. "Make her the drink, but no one else. If you haven't noticed, you're done for the day... at the least."

Oh, I'd noticed, but I said nothing. I sent him a grateful grin and dutifully made my mother a Bobbi-ccino, also known as a latte.

Right then, Jake and Dylan approached the crowd outside, man-handling Jonn Graham, of all people. He wore a Dumbledore beard minus the robe, wig, and hat.

"Get your goddamn hands off me," he yelled, twisting and pulling to get away.

With the crowd quieted and sitting on the ground, I watched officers speak to the trio. Jonn spit in one's face and tried to donkey kick anyone near him.

Someone inside shouted, "There's the guy!" An officer inside moved to the boy to get his statement.

In a matter of minutes, they cuffed Jonn and hauled him away, but not before they bumped his head against the doorframe. I knew his father would make the department pay for that one.

Dylan cautiously stepped through the crowd and embraced me. "I'm glad you guys are okay," he said.

"We're not, lad." I gasped. "We're so not okay. How did you know?"

"Was working in the window and saw the asswipe sprinting, shedding his costume as he ran. Then the screams and chaos. Instincts kicked in and I took off. Caught up to him in the woods behind us and tackled the fucker. Jake reached us then and showed me how to secure him and keep him from getting away." He gave me another hug. "Don't worry, Mom. The cops have him now."

Thomas appeared at my shoulder. I turned in to his arms, my breath hitching, holding in a sob. "I'm so sorry," I said into his chest.

"Shhh." He comforted me. Over my head, he asked Dylan, "Can you get us water?"

"Sure."

"We're not supposed to se-ser-serve anymore," I said.

Thomas tipped his chin down to me. "It's bottled water. It'll clear your head for the detective. Mine too. In fact…" Thomas caught Liam's attention and crooked his fingers so he'd come to us. He asked me, "Why don't the boys see to handing out water to those still here? It'll help everyone settle, especially your sons."

"What's wrong with my boys?" My head peeked around Thomas's shoulder, panicked they may be hurt.

He cupped my chin up to hold my attention. "You're rattled. So they're rattled."

"Oh." I sank into a chair, and Thomas took the one next to me, setting his arm around my shoulder.

Detective Nick Ross arrived and eased into the chair across from me. I couldn't believe it was my fifth statement to him this fall. Since he'd been the lead in Shane's case, we were sort of friends. "Detective." I exhaled on a shaky breath.

"We must stop meeting like this, Kick." He sounded both concerned and annoyed. I wasn't sure which emotion applied to me.

"You know, as much as I like to spoil you and your fabulous colleagues, I hate talking to you too. Professionally speaking, I mean. No offense."

He chuckled, pulling a tablet out of his jacket to begin our interview.

"What am I going to do, Detective?"

He lifted his gaze to mine. "You'll let us do our jobs. We have a suspect, the backpack, and remnants from the firecrackers. At least you have cameras now," he said. "Tell me everything you remember."

My mind swirled with faces, some laughing, some crying. I couldn't reconcile the cheerful beginning of the day from the smoky, panic-stricken end of it. I turned to Thomas. "Maybe you should go first."

Thomas pressed a gentle kiss to my temple. "You can do this. You're the only one who was here the whole day. Start with what you remember last. Before all hell broke loose."

The vision of Thomas in his spaghetti Western costume,

strutting across the parking lot, flashed through my mind, making me smile. "I remember you."

"Good." Nick nodded approval. "Go from there. Don't forget, we have a suspect in custody. The kid's been making trouble around town for a while. Give me as clear a picture as you can, and it'll go a long way."

He helped me with memory-jarring questions: if anything unusual happened—*it was a party*—if anyone new stopped in recently—*the place was packed and most wore costumes*. Plus I'd been in and out this fall for appointments. I didn't know for sure if there were new customers or new delivery drivers for that matter.

Thomas did a great job giving a clear and concise account of what he remembered. For the first time, I envied his nearly robotic, calm disposition. His statement added a lot to mine. Still, the evidence against Jonn Graham was circumstantial. I was grateful he resisted arrest.

One by one, witnesses told their stories and left. Dylan drove Bobby home with her car while Jake and Liam followed in Jake's truck. Then they went to the hardware store and picked up supplies to board up the front windows. I sent the rest of the crew home and cleaned the equipment. We were shutting down for a few days. The OPD took off as soon as they could. They asked the morning crew to come down to the station to make sure they fleshed out the details from the day. I couldn't help feeling like I'd ruined everyone's day.

I wanted to think we'd made it out lucky. There wasn't a shooter. The windows didn't crash down on the crowd outside. The newspaper articles would report some ankle and wrist sprains, cuts, and abrasions, along with the few burns, but everyone survived.

Except scared little eyes haunted me every time I closed mine or even blinked.

INTEGRITY BLUES

THOMAS

*T*homas was helping board up the Perked Cup's windows when Banger arrived.

"Took y'all long enough," he grunted, holding a corner while Jake drilled a screw into the opposite side. Thomas couldn't shake the feeling someone watched them. He believed he could keep Kick and her family safe, but Banger possessed an almost mystical sense regarding danger. For the first time that evening, Thomas took a deep breath.

"My team and I went over the feeds. Made other arrangements too."

"Yeah? Like what?"

"Let's talk inside," Banger directed. When his tone had this edge, bad news usually followed. Except Thomas didn't care. News couldn't get much worse, and he wanted answers now. Watching the whole thing go down, seeing what it did to Kick, rattled him too. Hell, he wanted to wring the neck of anyone involved in this, especially Jonn Graham.

Plywood at the large span of windows darkened the usually bright and cheery interior of the café. If it hadn't been for the row of windows over the prep counter, it would have resembled a cave. The café felt dark and sad anyway.

Kick didn't turn around when they entered. She vigorously scrubbed the espresso machines, her hands a bright red. Thomas approached, clearing his throat, and she jumped, the rag and brush in her hands flying in opposite directions.

He caught the panic in Kick's eyes and raised his hands. "It's me darlin'." Thomas tipped his chin to the table where Banger set up. "Bang's here. He wants to talk."

Kick scrambled to pick up her supplies, placing them on the counter. She kept turning her head away from him, biting her lip, then worrying her cheek with her tongue. For all the shit she'd put up with since they'd met, she'd never been this out of sorts. He hated it.

Then again, Thomas kept finding himself pumping his fists at his thighs to keep his hands from shaking. He wanted to stay calm and do better for Kick, though part of him wished he'd put Graham in the hospital when he'd had the chance. His lawyers would've taken care of any charges.

He grabbed her by the shoulders and dipped his head to catch her gaze. "Y'all right?"

A sarcastic "Just dandy" left her lips before she winced. "Sorry."

Thomas pulled her in for a hug. "No. It was a dumb question.

I know you're upset. I want to say it'll be fine tomorrow, but I can't. We are working on it though."

Kick stroked his back, returning comfort. "Helping me clean is huge."

Banger cleared his throat, waving them over. "Can we start?"

Kick answered, "I'd like the fellas to hear this if you don't mind."

"Suit yourself," Banger answered.

"I'll get them," Thomas offered. The guys were already packing up outside. They set the toolboxes on the now empty floor space by the front door, then gathered around Banger.

As he typed on his laptop, he asked, "Have any of you seen the footage yet?"

They all shook their heads.

"I can't. Not yet," Kick answered.

"And the rest of us have been busy with the cops and clean-up," Jake added.

Banger glared at Thomas and Jake, tapping the screen as he turned it around for everyone to see. "This should've come first. Especially for you two."

Thomas's back bristled, thinking of how it would've looked to abandon Kick and her family to run to the back, but Banger was right. He'd been letting too much slip lately. He had to get back to directing his life instead of letting life happen to him.

Banger played the video of the outside cameras. The spiderweb shatter made the crowd jolt even if the window hadn't disintegrated. So did the explosive sounds of firecrackers. Everyone on the patio suddenly ducked in the footage. Kick gasped and jumped, watching.

Thomas pulled her to his side and rubbed her arm.

She kept an intense gaze fixed on Banger and the screen.

"Here's our suspect." Banger followed the running form with his finger. "There goes Dylan." Jake was out the door a second later.

"He's good at avoiding cameras." Banger cued up the interior feed, and Kick raised her hands. "Can I have a day? One day... before I see it? Just tell me what you know, Banger."

He stopped the video. "Fine. It was brilliant on his part to do this on Halloween." Kick's shoulders fell at his words, and Thomas glared. Banger showed indifference, keeping himself about the business and getting shit done. It was why Thomas pressed him into helping Kick initially. "The wizard getup helped our suspect keep his face away from cameras."

"Then how do we know it really was Jonn?" Liam asked. "The guy's an ass, but he's also a wuss. Maybe the noise scared him."

Jake cleared his throat. "Dumbledore never ordered. I figured he was waiting on friends. Then the explosions came from the area where he stood."

Banger continued, tracing the running trajectory with a pen tip. "He didn't run toward the smoke shop even though the closest exit is near there. Makes me think he knows about the new cameras. Good thing you talked Hugh into using my team too."

"Why today?" Kick squeaked before her face pursed with indignance. "Hurting *me* is one thing, but the café was crawling with kids. The little ones..." Her voice broke. "Their eyes. I know what it's like to have a real-life horror show on a loop in your mind, and I'm a grown woman. If the windows had waterfalled on the kids outside..." Her voice hitched, and Thomas's vision went red. "Don't get me wrong, I'm thrilled the injuries were few and minor. But we altered those lives today..." Kick beat her breast, and another defiant tear let loose despite her tight jaw. "In my place. *My*. *Place*. If this is Jonn, I'll kill him."

Jake, Dylan, and Liam shifted in their seats, reminding Thomas of hungry predators. Everybody tensed, poised to beat the shit out of the boy at the word.

"If you don't mind..." Banger opened up some still shots. "The cameras caught two details." The first one showed a partial tattoo on the lower part of a bicep. It was a still from when the boys turned Graham over to the police.

Thomas said, "This looks similar to the tattoo you showed me before."

"It does."

"You mean the tattoo from my vandalized squawk box?" Kick asked.

"But this isn't the same man." Banger cut in.

They were a group of some kind then. Christ, he hoped this wasn't a gang.

"The other guy was shorter, stockier." Banger clicked on the second still. It showed the suspect's ear as he left the café. He had turned his head, leaving a clear shot of a stud earring, though not a run-of-the-mill diamond. This was a sapphire stud.

"Well, fuck me sideways. There it is." Dylan shoved open hands toward the screen, shaking with violent anger.

"Holy shit. We got him," Liam said, his face scrunched in fury.

Thomas looked around the group. "Fill me in please."

Kick' head fell on a deep sigh. "The boys are right. Jonn Graham wears his mother's sapphire stud as a memorial to her." She pointed to the screen. "But why not remove it when we know this?"

"The guy's a moron, Mom," Liam explained.

"He wore a disguise. The hat fell off as he left, remember? Plus he's cocky. I bet he got off on the idea of doing this right under our noses. His calling card in plain sight, so to speak," Jake added.

Kick slammed her hand on the table. "But why? What does he want?"

"He's pissed about being thrown out of the store?" Dylan guessed.

Kick's jaw sliced to the side. "The drive-through tattoo thing suggests he's been up to something for a while."

Banger stopped her speculating with raised hands. "Let my team work on it. Graham's in custody. OPD's already going over the evidence. These tattoos are my primary concern right now because Kick's right. The tattoo connection suggests he's done more."

Thomas made sure his friend caught his disapproving glare. Banger often took freelance work outside the confines of the law. It left him to conclude the police were optional. But law enforcement was already involved. Thomas wanted to make sure Kick's family kept the police on their side.

Banger stared back a beat before reluctantly adding, "I'll pass the information to the cops too."

Thomas mouthed, "Thank you," and let his friend finish.

"In the meantime, we need to make changes. Will any of you be working tomorrow?"

Kick nodded. "I'm meeting with the insurance rep, the window repair company, and who knows what else."

Banger continued, "Then I'm posting a security guard here." He raised his hands when Kick opened her mouth to speak. "For now. Until I can upgrade you again. Plus we're installing the *full* Angel System in your house." She opened her mouth again, but he cut her off. "Yes, it's necessary."

He closed the shot of the earring when she wouldn't take her eyes off it. "You're in shock. Trust me. You'll think clearer after some sleep."

Kick scoffed, "Like that'll happen."

Banger's visage changed. He stared at the five of them for a lifetime of seconds, his jaw pulsing. Then he leaned forward and vowed, "I promise to sort this out, Kick. If it's just a hateful kid, we'll still make sure he goes away." He tipped his chin to Thomas. "We'll both take care of you."

Kick sighed with relief. "Thank you."

Thomas wondered if she understood everything his friend

had done. Banger was taking the McKennas under his personal protection, and Banger McHenry's fealty didn't come easily. Thomas swallowed hard, remembering his friend's words about commitment at breakfast. Promises were vows to Banger, and he'd been clear-eyed serious when he'd said everything was disposable. Could he be changing his mind in this regard?

Banger went on. "You and your boys should take shooting lessons with Thomas. He's built a range on his property."

"What?" Kick screeched, her face pivoting to Thomas.

He knew where Banger was going with this and agreed.

Banger pointed at Dylan and Liam. "Look at them, Kick. Their tension and anger are palpable. You want to kick ass, don't you two?"

"Abso," Liam answered.

"Fuck yeah," Dylan said.

"You have a range?" Jake asked.

"Don't y'all have a place to keep your skills up?" Thomas asked back. He assumed a veteran like Jake would want to shoot with his buddies.

Jake lifted a shoulder before a slight blush formed. "It gets expensive after school bills."

Thomas raised a hand. He didn't want to add guilt over an employee's debts to Kick's list of burdens. He guessed she'd already paid her staff more than average. "Say no more. You're welcome to it. We'll set up a time for us to meet. Then I'll only have to explain the safety system I've set up with my neighbors once."

"Sounds good," the men said.

"Fuck me." Kick dropped her head into her hands. Thomas didn't know how much more she could take. She'd been such a source of sunshine earlier.

He rubbed circles between her shoulder blades, murmuring, "I swear it will be good soon."

Banger didn't seem to know when to shut it. "One last thing: I don't want you staying at your house tonight. I have a relationship with a hotel you can check into."

"What about the dog?" Liam asked.

"No. Come with me," Dylan offered. "Koosh knows my condo and does fine with the fenced patio."

"But Graham's in jail... and Liam's school—" Kick started.

"It's a teacher workday, remember, fam? The first quarter ended today."

Banger added, "Until your upgrades are made and I'm certain how many people are behind this, I don't feel comfortable about you and the kid staying at your house. What if it's being watched?"

"Well, hell." Kick dug her fingers into her hair. "But Dylan... after everything we talked about... you honestly think Suzy will agree to two extra McKennas and a dog? We'll fill up the living room."

He shrugged and sighed. "Your safety comes first."

Banger typed on his phone. "The crew will be at your house first thing tomorrow."

Thomas asked Dylan, "Do you have two guest rooms?"

"There's a futon in the office, and the living room sofa is big enough for a night."

Thomas said the words he'd been thinking. After his talk with Banger at breakfast, he thought they might send his friend over the edge. But hell if he cared anymore. Something had shifted in him when Jonn Graham dimmed the light in Kick's eyes. He turned to her. "Send Liam and the dog to Dylan's. You're staying with me."

Banger flattened his mouth in a tight line and sighed a sound of reluctant acceptance. No one else caught it. Thomas told himself he didn't care.

. . .

THOMAS SETTLED KICK ON THE SOFA IN HIS FAMILY ROOM. A FIRE warmed the room, and an old *Animaniacs* episode played on the television. She looked like she belonged. Thomas designed the room for his comfort—a place to unwind after a long day wracking his brain. Kick softened and brightened it with her presence. It didn't matter if she was strung out and still in shock. She'd relaxed too.

He'd set up one of the guest rooms and left her to change clothes when they arrived. When she descended the stairs in a sweater and lounge pants, her face washed and hair in a clip, he'd never seen anyone prettier. Kick's posture stood taller than it had walking up the stairs. She wasn't the bright star she'd been before the Halloween party, but she reminded him of the warm glow of light when dawn first broke, promising more. Jonn Graham had dimmed the light, but he couldn't extinguish it.

However, when Kick reached for her cup of mint tea, her fingers shook.

He beat her hand to the cup and passed it over. "Something wrong?" He bit his lip. Another dumb question. "I mean, is there anything else I can do?"

Kick's mouth rose in a shy smile. "No. Thank you." She moved the cup to her left hand, flexing the fingers on her right. "It's silly, but they tingle whenever I remember smacking your phone out of your hand. It's the ghost of remorse, I guess. I'm sorry."

Thomas took the hand in his and kissed her knuckles. "No more apologies. I'll get a new phone tomorrow."

"But my temper—"

"Shh." He set the teacup on the coffee table and pulled her to his side. "Everyone was upset."

"It's just… It's how my mother would've reacted. Hell, it's what any of the Sullivans—Bobby's family—would've done. They're a shoot-first-aim-second kinda bunch." She was quiet for a beat before she laughed. "I still can't believe Bobby sat through the whole thing without a scratch. It was so unlike her."

It took a moment before the tears fell.

Thomas wrapped his arms tighter. "Let it out." He lost himself in the dancing flames while she cried, the only noise occasional sniffs. He often sought clarity in a fire. They were incredibly wise.

Kick finally spoke in hushed tones. "Thanks for all you did today."

Thomas kissed her temple, still contemplating the flames. "What did I do?"

She took his face in her hands and turned him. "You stood by my side, but you didn't treat me like a delicate flower."

"How so?"

"Well, you knew I could give my statement to Detective Ross when I didn't think I had anything left. I wanted to run and hide under my desk. But you steadied me. When you said it, I believed it too."

Thomas had to catch his breath. "First, you're not frail. You're one of the strongest people I've ever met. They knocked you down, but look at you…" He squeezed her shoulders. "When you came down the stairs, you already stood tall again. No darlin', you're a *precious* flower, but not one too delicate for foul weather. You're a bloom that opens as soon as the clouds clear, stretching toward the sun."

She sniffled one last time. "You really think so?"

"I do."

The corner of her lips lifted. "You're right, I am. I'm grateful the damage was limited too." She tipped her head back and sighed. "It could've been much worse. There's a lot to be grateful for. But I'm not ready yet. I'll focus on it tomorrow."

"Sounds perfect, baby."

"Baby?" she challenged, mischief back in her eyes. "You've used the term before. Is it a thing now?"

"Have I?"

"Let me guess… it's an ironic dismissal of our age difference?"

Thomas smiled. "Sort of." The breadth of the joke stayed with him. For now. Maybe forever. It was the last hurdle he had to jump. Until he could put it behind him, his cards—and thoughts —stayed close to the vest.

To change the subject, he kissed Kick thoroughly. The heat generation in the room switched from the fireplace to them. Thomas moved to the corner of the sectional, bringing Kick half alongside him, half on top. His hands drifted down her back until they were cupping and kneading her perfect ass. She writhed on him, creating magnificent friction for his erection.

His lips worked their way across her jaw and down her neck. He was about to take a bite when Kick stilled. He sensed hesitation from her and mentally smacked himself in the head. Dammit all, she'd been through hell this day, and he was taking advantage.

He pulled away as they both said, "I'm sorry."

Thomas placed his fingers over Kick's mouth. "You don't owe me a damn thing tonight. You've had a hellish day. Literally. You're staying here for your safety and comfort." He took her hand and pressed a kiss to her palm. "The company's fantastic. But I'm one hundred percent honest when I say we will go upstairs to our separate rooms and it'll be fine."

She scrunched her nose. "So you don't want to…"

"Hell yes, I do." He swept a curl out of her eyes and tucked it behind an ear. "I want nothing more than to carry you up to my bed, strip you down, and have a proper introduction to the most perfect ass and prettiest tits I've ever seen." He grabbed her bottom again to make his point, his fingers lazily trailing up the seam of the yoga pants.

She acknowledged her desire with an honest-to-God whimper. He didn't know he could get harder. The switch in blood flow made him dizzy, or it was just Kick? Her voice was dark and grave when she asked, "Is… is that all you want to do?"

So his feisty lady liked kinky talk? Good Lord, she'd be the death of him—a sentence he'd gladly pay. "No…," he continued, his words a primal rumble. "First I'd pin your hands above your head and take you hard and fast as punishment for what you're doing to my safe life. I'd nip your body with my teeth because I don't know if I can keep my cool around you. Then I'd taste you. No, I'd *feast* on you."

Kick's breath caught in a gasp, her lust a squeak from her lips.

"You like that?" Thomas adjusted her body in his arms.

Wordlessly nodding, her eyes wide with possibilities. He couldn't lose his cool. Not now. *Not yet*. With every throb of desire, he felt like the world's biggest asshole.

He kept his lips against her cheek as he spoke. "I want you, baby, but I don't think tonight's the night. When you're here because of want, not protection, then I'll do those things and more. I'll show you what your body does to me."

A slow gulp descended Kick's throat. "You're not making it easy."

"Good. It sucks to be the voice of reason right now."

Kick sat up, catching her breath. She downed the rest of her tea and stood. "You're serious?"

"I am. The timing isn't right."

Her head bobbed slightly several times. "Sure. Okay." She wrapped her arms around her chest, retreating into her thick sweater. She pivoted around, stopping her gaze at each landmark on all four walls. "I love your house, Thomas."

"Thank you." He walked to the fireplace and turned it off, shut off the television, and led Kick back to her room. He stopped them in the hallway and kissed her on the forehead. "Go to sleep, darlin'. Forget about today. We'll talk in the morning. And we'll make plans."

"Well, good night." She reached up and pulled his mouth down to meet hers in a long, sweet kiss. It was nothing like what he wanted from her. But he damn well wouldn't be a selfish bastard.

Thunder rolled quietly in the distance as Thomas paced his large, empty room in the opposite wing of the second floor. He feared it would be another sleepless night, only this time it wasn't worry over loyalty or research keeping him up. A sexy, curly-haired woman down the hall had him bothered.

DANCING IN THE DARK

KICK

"**D**oor's open, Kick." Thomas's voice sounded like slow tires crunching gravel. My nerves amped up as I cautiously opened his door. A crash of thunder made me jump into the black void of his bedroom. The night-light in the hallway behind me kept my eyes from adjusting. Plus I'd fled the bedroom without my glasses, thinking only of my need. They didn't make much of a difference late at night anyway. A quick flash of lightning hinted at Thomas's form in the bed, staring at the ceiling.

"Need something?" Compared to his warmth in the family room, his distant voice sent a chill through me. Hope forced me to speak the truth.

"Yes." I stood in the doorway, my arms folded around my torso, shuffling my feet, not so much from the cold wood floors as from the wanting. My new self craved his attention. I'd paced through at least two songs on my playlist before the little voice sounding like Cyndi's convinced me to take a leap. I kept kicking myself for agreeing to let the mood fizzle earlier. I'd never been good at telling a man what I wanted. It was time to learn. "I can't sleep."

Thomas scoffed, "Join the club, darlin'."

The same Springsteen song playing in my room filled his dark space. "I was listening to 'Dancing in the Dark' too." It was part of the problem. I'd put on my lusty playlist and tried to take care of myself, only to end up making things worse. I was a live current drawn to the one who could help me find myself again.

"I know. After pairing with Angel System, it can play in any room."

"Right." Grateful for the dark, my face heated. Did he know why I had it on? He had to. If it were possible, it turned me on more.

"Why 'Well, You Know'?" Thomas asked. "It's an odd name for a playlist."

"It's an inside joke between my brother and me. When we were teens…" I steadied my racing heart with a cleansing breath. "My father didn't trust Bobby to say anything nice about sex… during our talk… about it."

"All right. And…" Thomas pushed. I hated his impatient tone.

Lightning flashed, and thunder followed soon after. It wouldn't be long until it was overhead.

"So… Dad took me out for a burger. He asked me if she'd said enough to me about, and I quote: '*Whale… ye new.*'" I imitated my father's lilt. "In our twenties, Bert and I realized Dad had used the same words with him. It's been our euphemism ever since."

A small chuckle floated to my ears. "Cute."

I turned and shut the door, blinding me outright. I took a determined step toward the sound of Thomas breathing.

Struggling to figure out his abrupt attitude change, I asked, "Are you thinking about work?"

A sarcastic scoff followed. "No."

My swallow hit my ears louder than the rain. "Then why are you brooding?"

Another thunder roll filled the silence. "Physics. The laws of attraction."

"So, you mean... me." I took another step. "I've been thinking about you too."

"Kick," he warned. "Don't do this. We admitted the timing isn't right."

"Why? Because today was horrible?" Lightning flashed again, followed two seconds later by a bang. Thomas's lump showed on the side closest to me. I glimpsed a sitting area near the window before everything returned to black. "What if that makes it the perfect time?"

"I won't take advantage. I want this to be... well, different." This time his tone changed from cold to disappointed.

"You were in the café too. Besides, it's not in you to take advantage."

Another strangled grumble laced with sarcasm.

I sighed, frustrated. "I can tell there are hard things bothering you, but you're also young, Thomas." How could I tell him to stop wasting time, like I had done, without sounding like a horny teenage boy just wanting to get some? I was afraid I'd already patronized him. I moved to sit on the edge of the bed but couldn't find it in two steps and didn't want to ruin the moment by falling.

I started over. "The past eight years have taught me to be strong on my own. Today I saw what it could be like to be strong with someone. Strong with you." I let my hands drop, and the robe opened. I wore a basic satin button-down nightshirt, nothing fancy or seductive. I'd packed fast in a hurry to get to safety.

"Stop." Right. Thomas's eyes were adjusted to his room. "My restraint's at its limit. Come closer, and I don't know..." The intensity in his voice communicated more than his words, shivered through me.

"Maybe I'd like to see you lose control," I confessed. My body ached for the things he'd suggested. The robe dropped off my shoulders, and I undid the top buttons. A deep intake of breath let me know Thomas could see me.

Lightning and thunder met directly over us, shaking the house and illuminating the room through another set of flashes. As if pushed by the storm, Thomas sprung at me, pulling me to him. His loud growl drowned out my surprised squeal and the remnants of thunder. Then I found myself straddling Thomas's abs, his deft fingers finishing the last of my buttons. His hands ran up the sleeves before pushing it off and into the night, leaving me exposed.

Gentle hands caressed my skin from my knees, up my thighs to my apex. A rumble of approval as nimble fingers explored the folds there, making me shake as they tested my clit. A quick press set me to rumbling myself, like the storm outside.

His hands stalled, and I feared he'd stop as he had downstairs. "Why are you fighting this?"

"The things I want to do with you..." His timbre turned to sadness. "This should be a celebration."

I shook more than my head. "After the day we survived, it is. Or are you scared?"

Thomas's hands met at my breasts and cradled them. My head

fell back, and we both moaned as his fingers rolled over my nipples. He was exploring, seeing where I ignited.

"I'm terrified." His fingers continued to play, feeding my need, distracting me from his answer. "All right. I'll take what you're giving, baby. I'll take it all."

The storm bellowed again, seeming to cheer us on. Thomas pulled me down to him, joining our mouths in a devouring kiss, releasing the day's emotions. Two people who had spent the day terrified found peace in the storm's violence. He opened my hair clip, throwing it into the abyss, and shook out my curls until they surrounded him. "I've wanted to do this for so long." My shivers almost broke our spell. I shifted my legs and Thomas hissed, "Damn, your feet are like icicles."

I giggled as he palmed my arch. I'd been too distracted to notice the cold. "They're always freezing."

Thomas lifted the quilt and arranged us so I was on my back while he lay alongside me, his fingertips making long sweeps of my body. I found the remedy for what my soul longed for under his covers, surrounded by his scent—sandalwood, citrus, him. I shifted until my hand touched his hard cock, barely contained in pajama bottoms.

He hissed in pleasure as I said, "I wouldn't mind an introduction either."

The bottoms disappeared, and we set to discovering each other in earnest. His hard abs thrilled my fingers as they traced each muscle. They traveled farther down until I squeezed his erection.

"I knew you'd be impressive."

I treasured the sound of Thomas's smile in the dark. "What do you mean?"

I peppered his pecs with quick kisses. "Everything else about you has impressed me. From your retro suits..." A flicker of licks around each nipple received rumbles of approval. "To the way you instinctively knew how to lead me in a dance..." More kisses across his abs. "To the way you've befriended my kids, my crew." I scooted down his body, taking note of the source of my praise. I ran my tongue from his base to tip and through the pre-cum weeping from his cockhead, licking my lips and humming my approval of Thomas's taste.

"Fuck," he gritted, pulling me back up the bed despite my protests.

"Let me take care of you tonight." He bit down on my breast, easing the sting with eager flicks of his tongue, then asked, "What do you want, baby?"

I pulled his ear toward my mouth. "I want you to fuck me, Thomas. Hard."

His sexy growl of agreement curled my toes, made my skin feel like my internal electricity might become real. There was power in my honest words. And in his approval.

Thomas granted my request, beginning with a devouring kiss, exploring my mouth with aggression. His intensity equal to the weather outside, my core matched it with thrusts against his erection. He showed his appreciation by grabbing my wrists. A flash of light caught his playful, spectacular smile. "You trust me?"

"You know I do."

He stretched both hands over my head and placed them under the bottom of the headboard. I remembered what he whispered in my ear downstairs, and my pussy throbbed with anticipation. "Don't let go until I say."

"I won't be able to touch you."

"Touch me later. Let me feast while you feel."

"Oh, okay," I gasped into our dark refuge. Without the light, I may as well have been blindfolded. My senses heightened by Thomas's direction. Each passing minute made my pulse pound like a drumbeat. It drowned out all sound until my moan from his magic tongue filled the room. I scissored my feet, begging for more.

"Uh-uh," he scolded. "Keep still."

"It's torture."

Thomas dropped his lips to my folds and spoke against me. "You make torture fun." He pinned each thigh with his hands and licked up one side, then the other. "Christ, you're soaked." He added a finger, then two, inside and went to work on my clit with his exquisite mouth and fingers, slowing as I neared the edge of reason. He relented with a laugh when I growled.

"You like this." He observed with quiet awe. "How you grip my fingers."

"Thomas… I want your cock. Or I'll let go and make you give it to me."

He laughed, reaching for the nightstand. The telltale crackle of foil drowned out the rain, heightening my anticipation. "Don't worry, Kick. I want to feel each squeeze of your pussy until you force me to come inside you."

I reached for the latex. "Let me?"

Thomas thrust himself through my hands as I rolled the condom on him, hard and soft, like silk covering steel.

Another crack of thunder exploded directly above the house. This one rattled more than windows and walls. I felt it in my bones.

"Y'all right?" Thomas checked in, stroking my lifted thighs. But I wasn't scared by the weather or by what we were doing. We were finally here. On the precipice of everything we'd chased for weeks. I took the storm above as the sign I'd once sought. The universe was cheering us on, shredding the baggage we carried, washing our slates clean.

We'd become our basic elements, electrical currents sharing our energy, restarting our hearts. Instead of answering, I chanted, "Fuck me, Thomas. Fuck me. Fuck me…"

He stood to the side of the bed and grabbed my ankle, spinning me, pulling me to the edge. "Like this?" Thomas lined himself up as I nodded, too lost with lust to speak.

He braced and thrust in, filling me until he was seated to his balls and froze again, hissing a sigh of relief. "Perfection. *Christ*, you feel good."

So did Thomas. It was more than a cure for a lustful want or forgetting a bad day. He fixed the ache in my soul. Thomas wasn't a replacement for what I'd lost. He uniquely filled the new me. A tear slid down to the mattress, rejoicing as a new peace set in.

He brought my hands over my head, taking my mouth as he filled my pussy. His emotion-filled moans were bringing me to the edge. "I choose you, Kathleen." Thomas's gritted declaration sounded angry, like he was rebuking the night.

"What?" I didn't understand. The fire of lust we'd lit grew again. I cried out, "More."

He bent and drew a nipple into his mouth, sucking and pumping and starting the countdown to my orgasmic launchpad. My body responded to the luscious sensations of his pulsing. I adjusted my angle to catch my clit on his inward slides, squeezing on the way out.

The bed slid with each powerful thrust. "How can I say no to you?"

He picked up the pace, surprising me with more to give, creating a delicious friction. I climbed to heaven and jumped off at the top of the steps into the bliss of letting go, chanting, "Yes, yes..."

"That's it, baby," he encouraged. "Beautiful angel."

I met his thrusts with equal fervor until Thomas lost himself with his own yell.

I arched my head back into the mattress, overwhelmed by the fervor of my climax. Aftershocks continued running through us, sparking more lust with the slightest shift. Our union was more than either of us dared hope.

After cleaning up, we lay together in bed with me wrapped around Thomas's side. "I feel so alive," I whispered, sliding my fingers through his chest hair.

"We're *definitely* doing that again… after I fortify the bed." He laughed at the same time kissing the top of my head.

After the buzz of ecstasy wore off, reality returned to my thoughts, and I said, "What did you mean you choose me?"

"Umm…" Thomas let his answer hang in the quiet.

It stung to have him still holding back after what we'd just done, but we couldn't discover all our secrets in one night. I snuggled deeper into Thomas, letting him know he could keep his answer to himself. *For now.*

My jaw cracked on a loud yawn. "Can I stay here with you?"

"You'd *better.*" Thomas turned me, spooning behind, pulling me right into him, murmuring. "All the things I could do to you. You're a sexual muse." He kissed the back of my neck. "I'm already addicted."

"Thank goodness." I sighed and confessed, "I was afraid your hesitancy earlier was from… disappointment with my body."

He let loose a low growl. "I'm such an idiot." He turned my chin and kissed me deeply. "I'm sorry, beautiful. Everything about you is amazing, including your body. But there's a shit ton to do tomorrow… I mean later today. Get some sleep."

One of his hands absently kneaded a breast while the other nestled between my thighs. The storm settled down, becoming a quiet rain cleansing the land and our hearts for the rest of the night. I dozed off with his lips against the back of my neck and didn't dream at all.

Thomas moved one of the sound protection muffs from my ear and said, "Nice job, darlin'."

"That's lit, fam!" Liam cheered.

"*Noice,* Mom." Dylan patted my shoulder.

"Very pretty, Mrs. Mack," Jake added.

"You certainly *irritated* the target." Banger said, rubbing his chin. I took it as high praise.

Giving in to my desperate need for progress, I threw my hands in the air and did a victory dance, after placing the gun back on the table, of course. I heard P!nk in my head and wiggled my booty for the sheer joy of it for the first time in days. It didn't matter how much work we still had to face or how many unanswered questions we waited on. The McKennas were okay, and I was enjoying having Thomas by my side even if he was often one of those unanswered entities. All new, important relationships had their mysteries in the beginning.

Everyone continued gushing about the well-placed shot pattern I'd made on the target with Thomas's .38 revolver. In my mind, it was beginner's luck. I admit to being shocked at holding a six-shooter at all. I thought today's badasses used semiautomatics. Thomas wanted the boys and me familiar with all his handguns since the police had found a revolver in an ankle holster on Jonn Graham when they patted him down.

When Thomas first brought it out, he told me criminals liked them because the casings stayed with the gun, meaning fingerprints on said casings also remained inside the gun. I didn't know what to make of a geneticist's knowledge of such a thing. I found myself staring at him a minute too long yet again wondering about his past.

Graham was still at the police station, the camera footage and identifying marks making it hard for his father's lawyer to keep the authorities at arm's length. Banger's people continued to work their magic, so we cleaned up the café and waited. And took firearm lessons.

It had been three days since my night with Thomas. My time since had been packed with fixing up the Perked Cup. Restoring its reputation would take longer. Thomas had also worked late at the lab each night. While I agreed with him about spending time with each of my kids before he slept over, the ensuing nights had been long and lonely.

Since Banger and Jake joined us, we had three marksmen for

three trainees. The boys had run through the paces with Banger and Jake while Thomas and I made lunch at the house. Thomas's agreement with his neighbors regarding the range involved making sure only one person fired at a time. He also raised an orange flag on a tall pole for visual confirmation the noise had Thomas's permission without them having to leave their property.

We'd walked the peaceful path from his garden to the range when it was my turn. I thought the boys would hear the word *food* and take off for the farmhouse, but everyone stuck around to watch me shoot.

I held the Sig Sauer the way Thomas showed me, stood in what I knew as mountain pose—a yoga term fitting the instructions he'd given me.

"Remember your breathing," he coached.

Breathe in, aim; breathe out, squeeze. It was empowering, really. Knowing I could shoot a gun, *several actually*, boosted my confidence. I emptied the clip and did the same thing with his Glock.

Dylan had the best patterns of the three McKenna newbies, but mine were a close second.

"Well done." Thomas kissed my cheek, mindful of our company. He stood behind me like a mental spotter, fortifying me while I went through the paces with each shot.

Thomas shut us down when a few dogs began uncontrolled barking. It turned out to be the longest he'd ever had the range active. The poor pups had had enough. We packed up the gear and decided to do our lessons individually from now on. We lowered the flag and walked back to the house for lunch.

Sitting at Thomas's table, around a platter of subs for the men, my gluten-free sandwich lay plated in front of me. My body relaxed for the first time since the night I'd slept over. Having to wear the mask of strength at work became a burden I welcomed. My staff needed Strong Kick. Hell, *I* needed her when I was there, sorting through the mess. In this setting, each man eased a little of the burden, giving me a chance to recharge.

I cut my sandwich in half. Thomas took advantage of me wiping my hands and grabbed my left one under the table, holding it in his lap while we ate. I already missed him something fierce. Though my bedroom suite was finished and Banger's team had completed their upgrades, I'd woken each morning from either a nightmare or a spicy dream about the handsome professor currently stroking my palm. My eyes flashed to his at the memory of a yummy thing he'd done with his tongue right before my alarm woke me in the morning.

Thomas arched an eyebrow, his eyes bright with amusement. I wondered if he'd been dreaming of me too and couldn't help my grin.

We sat around an oversized rustic table filling the dining room. I adored the contrast of regal and casual. Southern-exposure windows flooded the room with sunlight. An antique dry sink-turned-sideboard sat against a creamy wall. The color in the room came courtesy of a striking painting of a woman and a horse, hung above the sideboard. Vivid colors in the style of Marc Chagall electrified the room. My head had done a double take as I passed by the painting, my eye catching the signature. My degree had been in fine art, not art history, but it looked like the real deal to me.

"Holy shit," I'd muttered, forcing myself to stop thinking about the probable cost. I had a feeling this one sat at the high end for a real Chagall. It left me wondering again about this man who managed to carve some space for himself in my heart. What else would I find here? Or in his head? The rumination would wait though. There was a crew to feed, more plans. Discoveries could come later.

Banger ate in silence for a while before saying, "How is Angel-at-Home working so far?"

I blushed, wiping my mouth to hide my embarrassment about

having put him off. "Better than I thought it would. Thank you. I haven't minded having sound in limited areas. And the extra security helps me sleep." My eyes flashed to Thomas's, the heat of a scarlet tint spread across my cheeks.

"Good," Banger continued. "From now on, listen to me the first time."

"Yes, boss." I rolled my eyes.

"My team will be finished with the upgrade to your café by the end of the day too."

"Yippee," I fake-cheered. "Does this mean the security guards can go?"

"Well, now—" Thomas started.

"Kick." Banger dropped his sandwich on a sigh.

I held up my hands, certain I wasn't a petulant child. "The Perked Cup's reopening is tomorrow. I didn't think our reputation could be more smeared, but the neighborhood website found a way. People are posting en mass about how they won't come back. Don't you think big burly guys… nice as they are… lurking in the corners will scream, 'We're not safe'?" I refreshed my throat with a pull from my LaCroix. "Adding an array of monitors visible to the public was genius, Banger. I think it'll be a perfect deterrent."

Dylan lifted a shoulder. "Mom has a point."

"Thank you, lad."

Banger and Thomas stared at each other, sharing a silent conversation like they were siblings.

"Fine." Banger let his shoulders drop. "Make sure your staff is up to speed on the panic buttons… *and* they must install my panic app on the home screens on their phones."

My gaze moved to Jake. "Can you be in charge of this? It would mean coming in early to train Deana and Liz, but I could take your shift."

"Kick," Thomas warned. He had the disappointed professor look down pat. *And it worked.* By saying my name, he reminded me I was overscheduling. Plus we'd managed to set up a lunch date.

Jake bailed me out. "How are you feeling, Mrs. Mack?" Jake was the only non-McKenna at the table who'd been with me before my health setback. He'd witnessed the descent without the personal attachment of a son fearing something was wrong with his mom.

I chewed my sandwich bite, using it as an excuse to self-check and answer honestly. We'd experienced unbelievable stress in the past week, but I hoped I'd become better at letting it roll through me. Since my flare, I'd learned stress's negative effects could be attributed more to the attitude of the person in question. If I believed stress would hurt me, it did. I'd made sure to meditate every day and got my movement in by helping set up my new room.

I rolled my shoulders. "Feeling well, all things considered. Thank you, Jake."

"I wouldn't mind working a double if I could take an extra day at Thanksgiving."

I ran the preliminary schedule through my head. "It should work. Thank you."

"Appreciate it, man," Thomas added.

I grinned wide and caught Thomas's eyes, twinkling silver this time. I felt fantastic. The McKennas were down but on their way back. Again. Thomas had told me the lab was making progress too. And I held tight to our promises of more.

The boys made the table laugh with their banter and tales of Dylan taking Liam and Macushla home to Dyl's girlfriend, Suzy, and roommate, Dummy.

The last drops of my LaCroix traveled down my throat when the doorbell rang.

A curious expression crossed Thomas's face as he rose to answer it. He disappeared into the entry, his smooth voice rising and nearly cracking when he greeted the visitor.

"Tess? Hello. What a surprise!"

Thomas returned, leading a stunning young woman with the kind of tan I'd never achieve. As she looked around the room, her eyes landed on Banger. It shocked me when she said in a sharp, albeit breathy tone, "Hello Raphael."

Banger dropped his head into his hands. "Fuck. Me."

To Be Continued...

WONDERING WHAT TO DO NOW?

You can make a difference in an author's career by leaving a review.
Seriously. Writing a few words with your retailer of choice and/or at Goodreads.com can help readers like you find their next favorite book.

Want more of Kick and Thomas? Hang in there. The next part of the their story is coming soon. You can pre-order Kick Back at your favorite retailer.

If you can't wait, **sign up for Kallyn's newsletter**. In addition to staying on top of all the Southern Oaks series news, you'll receive a bonus scene called, *Like to Get to Know You Well*! It takes place in the middle of chapter thirty-seven, the morning after our couple's big night together. There are no plot questions answered. It's not a scene that must be read to understand the story. It's simply Kick and Thomas spending a few hours getting to know each other better.

FOLLOW KALLYN

To stay on top of all things Kallyn, ~~stalk~~ follow her on:
Website: kallynjones.com
Facebook: KallynJonesAuthor
Instagram: KallynJonesWriteNow
Twitter: JonesKallyn
Blog: kallyjones.com/blog

Did you notice the Chapter Titles are Song Titles too?
Songs are a big part of the Southern Oaks Series, so there's
definitely a public playlist! Click the link to listen or enter the
playlist title in the Spotify search bar.
Spotify: Tunes for Kick Start

ANOTHER AUTHOR'S NOTE

Dearest reader,

You probably noticed that there are speculative elements in this series. The science aspects will be explained as the series continues.

I do want to note that at the time *Kick Start* went to press cannabis was not legal in North Carolina. That's where the "this is a work of fiction" disclaimer at the front of the book comes in. Please don't plan a road trip to Raleigh to visit a dispensary. Odds are, you'll drive through numerous other states where it is legal anyway. Fingers crossed there will be more than CBD shops here soon.

Because of this, I was able to imagine which tack the politicians in the NC General Assembly might take in regards to a federal legalization law. In real life, I have no idea if this is the way a comprehensive law would play out. It is based on the unique ways this state approaches the sale of tobacco and alcohol.

XO, KKJ

ACKNOWLEDGMENTS

- To my editors extraordinaire Jenny, Lisa, and D.A. There aren't enough words to thank you for turning a feral manuscript into something readable.
- To the vibrant writing community in the North Carolina Triangle area. You have inspired and supported me more than you know. Extra hugs go to Laura, Annie, Jennifer, Renae, Sheon, Jamie, Patti, Jeanne, Stuart, Jo-Ann, Crista, Jake, Nancy, and Beth. Your advice and support are immeasurable. Writer friends are a treasure.
- To my friends and family who have been so supportive during this long, tiring journey. Thank you for always believing I could do it. A thousand thank-yous for never asking if the book was done yet.
- To my beloved, adopted hometown. I'm so grateful to live in a "foodie" town that takes allergy issues seriously. I've yet to meet a person who eats like I do by choice. Thank you also for those glorious blue skies, long springs and autumns, and blessedly short winters. My joints are eternally grateful to be out of the cold.

- To the medical providers who let me write in fifty-minute sprints in their waiting rooms while they brought my son back to health. It was a miracle to experience each small step out of his hell and into a new normal.
- Finally, to my beloved, Wayne and our boys. It's incredibly hard to live with a sick spouse/parent, let alone a creative one. I'm ever grateful to you for your enthusiasm and support for this new venture. Love you forever.

ABOUT THE AUTHOR

Kallyn Jones spent years as a freelance artist and graphic designer before returning to her roots as an author. She writes about sexy, down-to-earth characters and the crazy families they make along the way. She delights in finding heroes and heroines in unusual places. She believes the happily-ever-afters that are fought for the hardest are also the sweetest.

An autoimmune warrior for most of her life, she's also a mom to an autoimmune kid. She champions those who often find themselves flat on their backs, for days or weeks at time, through no fault of their own. *The Southern Oaks* series is dedicated to them.

Kallyn lives in her adopted hometown of Raleigh, North Carolina, with her own hero, their three sons, and a dog. In her spare time, she enjoys trail walking, digital painting, and testing out new, "healthy" recipes. She's proud to say her fellas usually like these experimental dishes. Usually.

facebook.com/kallynjonesauthor
twitter.com/JonesKallyn
instagram.com/KallynJonesWriteNow
pinterest.com/kallynjonesauthor

Made in the USA
Monee, IL
03 November 2021

81335542R00218